THE BISHOP'S JAEGERS

BOOKS BY THORNE SMITH

The Bishop's Jaegers. Topper Takes a Trip. Turnabout.
The Night Life of the Gods. The Stray Lamb. Topper.
Did She Fall? Dream's End. Biltmore Oswald.
Out O' Luck. Haunts and By-Paths

THE BISHOP'S JAEGERS

By THORNE SMITH

Illustrated by ROESE

THE SUN DIAL PRESS

GARDEN CITY, NEW YORK

PRINTED AT THE *Country Life Press*, GARDEN CITY, N. Y., U. S. A.

FOR

FRANK C. REILLY

FROM

THE FOUR STRAY LAMBS IN FRANCE*

**The lambs being June, Marion, Celia,*
and the author himself, no less.

CONTENTS

PROLOGUE

Dealing in Drawers

BEFORE HOISTING THEM OVER HIS STURDY, ECCLESIASTICAL shanks the Bishop contemplated his drawers with nonsectarian satisfaction. It was not the Bishop's wont thus to dally with his drawers. Far from it. As a rule the Bishop paid scant heed either to his own drawers or to those of his parishoners. He took it for granted they wore them.

And although, during the course of a long and active career devoted to good works, the Bishop had been responsible for despoiling the dusky limbs of innumerable South Sea aristocrats with drawers of surpassing unloveliness, he did not look back on his success in terms of drawers alone. Not at all.

To Bishop Waller drawers were merely the first move in a long, grim contest with the devil, a contest in which long, grim drawers served as the shock troops of righteousness. They were an important but unattractive gesture in the general direction of God—a grotesque but essential step in a complicated ritual of spiritual costuming.

Perhaps it was partly owing to the fact that none of the Bishop's so called savage converts had ever turned to him and remarked in tones of mild complaint, "This Adam chap of yours never wore a pair of drawers in his life. Why should I?" that the good Bishop had so far failed to give due consideration to the rights of the vast anti-drawers-wearing element still shamelessly thriving on this and probably other terrestrial globes. For Bishop Waller was above all things a fair man. It simply never occurred to him that a fellow creature could commune either with himself or his Maker with any degree of equanimity unless a great deal of his person was securely done into drawers.

For women the Bishop's program was a little more elaborate. Women were quite different. It was difficult to decide which half of their bodies needed to be covered first and most. Both halves were dangerous, both to be greatly deplored. Either one of them made virtually impossible a constructive consideration of a life beyond. Repeatedly he had been pained to discover that in the presence of unconverted island girls, men were quite content to risk the somewhat nebulous joys of the life beyond for the assured ones closer at hand.

Therefore it was the Bishop's conviction that all women should be all covered at all times. It was safer—far, far wiser. Men found out about such things quickly enough as it was without having them dangled before their eyes. For this reason religion for men began with drawers and for women with shirt and drawers—preferably with the addition of a voluminous Mother Hubbard.

This morning there was a special reason for the Bishop's rapt contemplation of his drawers—new, judiciously selected, upstanding garments. And if they could not be called things of beauty, these brave long jaegers of the Bishop's, they did without question represent the highest expression of the drawers-maker's craftsmanship. Not that the Bishop's jaegers were in any sense crafty. No franker or more uncompromising drawers could have been devised to protect the modesty of man. Once they had been decorously adjusted, they made absolutely no weak concession to the curiously roving eye.

As Bishop Waller, forgetting for the moment his rather shocking condition, held his jaegers extended before him at arm's length, he presented a picture of innocently happy concentration. He was gratified by the chaste austerity of these drawers. They were the ideal drawers for a bishop. There was no monkey business about them. They pretended to be nothing more than what they were—simply and definitely drawers—long ones. Once a man had sought refuge behind or within their rugged embrace there was little likelihood that any woman no matter how optimistic would ask him to emerge from his unattractive concealment. The exterior view was far too depressing—too utterly discouraging to light dalliance and abandon. They had a numbing effect on the mind, those jaegers of the Bishop's. They reared themselves like a mighty tower of righteousness in a world of makeshift and evasive garments. No one could imagine their wearer leaping sportively in pursuit of a wanton nymph. The very beasts of the fields would have staggered off in horror to their lairs.

As he proceeded to plunge his vast nakedness into the even vaster reaches of his jaegers, the exact structure of the Bishop's thoughts is, of course, not known. However, it is safe to assume that as he stood appreciatively before his mirror conscientiously adjusting them to the last strategically plotted button—a formality seldom if ever observed by the average run of laymen—Bishop Waller was saying to himself:

"I might have my faults as a bishop, but no one can say a word against my drawers. Not a bishop in all these United States can produce a finer pair than these."

So much for the Bishop for the time being, now that he has at last got himself into his drawers and girded his loins with righteousness if not with romance.

2

The drawers of Josephine Duval were a different matter entirely. Accurately speaking, they were hardly drawers at all. They were more like a passing thought or an idle moment. Compared with the splendid new jaegers of the Bishop's—if one's chances of salvation will not be eternally damned by such a sacrilege—Jo's drawers were as nothing. Not even a flash in the pan.

One is occasionally perplexed by the great quantity of different-looking dogs one meets in the course of a day or a week. One is given pause by the fact that such totally unrelated objects in appearance should be even loosely classified under the covering name of dog. Yet in spite of this, one seldom or rarely ever stops to consider how many different-looking drawers there are in the world either gracing or disgracing the limbs of humanity. Perhaps this is due to the fact that one gets more opportunity to look at dogs than at drawers, which is, no doubt, just as well for everybody concerned. However, the fact still remains that drawers can be so bewilderingly different and yet come under the general classification or family name of drawers.

Between the Bishop's drawers and Jo's drawers lay all the difference in the world—different aims and aspirations, a different philosophy of life—a gulf, in fact, which could never be bridged except under the most incredible circumstances with which there is no occasion here to deal. No good end can be served by further prolonging this rather questionable comparison.

Looking logically at Jo's drawers—an attitude exceedingly difficult to maintain when they were inhabited as only Jo could inhabit them—one could see no proper reason for their being in existence at all. To say that they were the direct antitheses of the medieval *ceinture de chasteté* is to state the case mildly. Not that this brief consideration of the young lady's even briefer garments is to be regarded as a plea for the return of the chastity belt. On the contrary. There are too many locks already in this world. As a matter of record the efficacy of the chastity belt has never been clearly established. Love has ever had the last laugh on the locksmith. Furthermore, the belief is now held by several eminent students of the question that the employment of the chastity belt was directly responsible for the rapid rise of a class of gentlemen extremely annoying to absent husbands because of their nimble and industrious fingers. As time passed and experience was passed along with it, respectable husbands found that not only were their women no longer secure but also neither were their treasure boxes and safe deposit vaults. This situation was just too bad. During foreign wars and crusades the activities of these notoriously home-loving pick-locks became so widespread, in fact so much in demand, that medieval locksmiths grew quite inured to the sound of ironical laughter.

But if conditions were loose in those days, they are running wild today. The time when women selected their nether garments logically has long since passed into oblivion. It is the regrettable tendency of the times for women to regard this item of their apparel not in the light of logic but rather in that of allurement. And men are just low enough to regard this change with approval. Even the name itself has fallen into disrepute, as if it suggested some humorous connotation. Whereas men with the utmost indifference still struggle along quite cheerfully with the old-fashioned and time-honored name of drawers—drawers plain and unvarnished—women have far outstripped them. Theirs must be known now by such frivolous and leading appellations as panties, scanties, briefs, fleshies, woolies, step-ins, dansettes, speedies, and other similar evocative terms. Bloomers, which at one time were considered no end daring, are today rarely if ever encountered in actual circulation, and then only after the most patient and exhaustive research for which the majority of men are constitutionally disqualified unless very carefully watched.

However, although these new underthings give rise to all sorts of nonsense, it must be admitted they are nice.

Jo's were, at any rate.

This morning, at about the same time the excellent Bishop was contemplating his equally excellent jaegers, Miss Josephine Duval, whose paternal grandmother still sipped her wine in France, rolled a body of the most disconcerting loveliness out of its bed. It was Jo's own body, and she sat with it in lazy companionship on the bed's edge while she permitted several tremendous yawns to escape her recklessly red and rebellious lips. After this she stretched, and the effect was devastating. For a moment even the world must have paused in its revolutions. As the girl's small and not unbecoming feet sought with all their ten useless toes a pair of mules that were a sheer waste of time, her cool white arm automatically reached out and the hand on the end of it affixed itself to one of the garments under discussion. Whether they were briefs, scanties, or step-ins is an open question, but for the sake of this history they might just as well be called step-ins. Bending a dark red head of tousled hair over her trophy, she allowed her brown eyes to consider it none too favorably.

They were far from being the step-ins of her choice. However, many a girl would have thought herself fortunate to have been caught in a gale in such a pair. In a nutshell, which would nearly have accommodated them, they were good, middle-class businesslike-looking step-ins without a great deal of foolishness about them, yet sufficiently attractive to do justice to their subject. Josephine's French blood cried for fairer step-ins, while her French sense of thrift assured her that for a hard-working secretary who spent most of her time sitting they were altogether adequate.

"If I didn't have to work so darned hard and scrimp so much," yawned Jo to herself, "I'd buy me some bang-up underthings, wouldn't I just. Regular knockouts. Black and very, very bad."

With a supple flexing of her body which should have been prohibited by an act of Congress, she shook off her nightgown and snapped on her step-ins. The movement combined the speed of a fireman with the deftness of a contortionist. Catching a glimpse of herself in the mirror, she regarded her step-ins critically.

"Good enough for day-in-and-day-out service," she decided, "but hardly suitable for occasions should they ever arise."

To what occasions Jo was alluding, it would be better to leave to individual preference. Jo had her own clearly defined ideas about almost everything. For the most part they were uniformly unedifying. However, they enjoyed the advantage of having been dragged out into the open, where they operated in a state of healthy activity to say the least.

"Pay day today," she gloated as she continued with her dressing. "A beggarly sum at that—a mere pittance. I'll spend it all on underthings as soon as the office closes, see if I don't. Even though a girl should be good, she doesn't have to feel that way. Funny thing, I always feel at my best when I'm feeling thoroughly depraved. There's no use of a girl trying to tell herself anything different, either. Women are born that way."

Accordingly her thoughts veered to Mr. Peter Duane Van Dyck, who at that moment was very busy doing things about his own drawers, as were thousands of other New Yorkers of high and low degree.

Peter Van Dyck was of high. He scarcely realized the fact, and whenever it was forced upon him by his relatives he showed a decided lack of appreciation. His respect for the traditions of his ancestors, those early Dutch settlers, had been interred with their bones. He was Josephine's employer —her boss. She was his secretary, and it would not have required much enterprise on his part to make her even more. As it was, he admired the young lady for her efficiency, but was alarmed by her bold eyes, which to his way of thinking, had a suspiciously bad look about them. They were not good for the coffee business, whose destiny he guided along well-established lines.

"He's an old stick," Jo decided as she tightened up her stockings so that they gleamed on her well-turned legs. "Doesn't seem to know I have these. Not an eye in his stupid head. I'll make him know, doggone it."

And Jo deftly curbed her abundance within the delicate web of a brazen brassière.

3

To Peter Duane Van Dyck drawers presented no difficulty. He never considered them at all. They were merely a part of the scheme of things. He disregarded drawers. Automatically he changed them. Not every day, like other nice men of his station, but whenever the idea occurred to him. Sometimes he lost his drawers; that is, misplaced them, forgot where he had seen them last.

This morning he was in this quandary. With exasperated diligence he searched for his drawers, completely blind to the fact that he had lazily left them crumpled in his trousers upon retiring the previous night. It was not a Van Dyck trait, this leaving of his drawers in his trousers. It was a habit characteristic of Peter—one of his little labor-saving devices which would have been revolting to the long line of Van Dycks from which he had sprung without any great show of agility.

Abandoning all hope of ever seeing his drawers again, Peter put on a new pair and dragged on his trousers after them. The fact that the old pair remained untidily wedged in his trousers caused him no discomfort at the moment. He ascribed the slight fullness on the right side—a tendency to bind, as it were—to some inexplicable caprice of his shirt tail. He would deal with his shirt tail later if in the meantime it did not adjust itself of its own accord. Shirt tails usually did in the course of a day, he had found. He hoped this one would, because he hated to trouble himself with such matters. It would have been wiser had he done so.

He did things to his sandy-colored hair, decided after a quick scrutiny of his vaguely blue eyes that they had a peculiarly harassed appearance, wiped some dried soap off his right ear, and left the room wearing two pairs of drawers and carrying one towel. On the Van Dyck landing he became conscious of the towel still clutched in his hand. Draping it over the bare expanse of a statue of an Aphrodite seemingly seized with qualms or cramps in a near-by niche, Peter Van Dyck permitted his five feet ten inches of body to find its way downstairs unassisted by any mental effort.

He entertained hopes of filling it with coffee and lots of breakfast. Peter was thirty-four. Also, he was hungry.

4

An hour or so later it was Miss Yolanda Bates Wilmont's turn to deal with her drawers. Rightly speaking, Yolanda Bates Wilmont seldom if ever dealt with her drawers in person. She had a maid to deal with them for her. And to continue rightly speaking, what the maid dealt with could not by the wildest stretch of the coarsest imagination be called drawers. They were creations—fragile poems done in gossamer and lace—real lace. In fact everything was real about them except the woman they adorned. She was too good to be true, but she did not realize this. She considered herself a young lady of the highest principles and the most unassailable morals. With the exception of herself and a few chosen members of her social standing she heartily disapproved of any unnecessary display of feminine blandishments. With herself it was quite different. Yolanda Bates Wilmont sincerely believed that she knew as no other woman exactly what she was doing, that she was by the divine right of birth the arbiter of good taste and refinement, that she had limbs whereas the general run of girls merely had legs and far too much of them.

As she gazed at herself in the long pier mirror this morning, she was thinking quite unconsciously that it was a fortunate thing indeed so few girls could afford to wear such lovely step-ins as hers. The average woman could not be trusted in so expensively chic underthings. No telling what one of those lower-class girls might do if she suddenly found herself in possession of such a pair. Certainly she would not keep them to herself. No. The cheap, feminine display complex would get the better of what little scruples she had, if any. The modern girl was permitted to show too much of herself as it was. Take the beaches and the buses and the dance halls—disgusting. Such liberties should be enjoyed only by members of exclusive house parties and by girls who knew how to be careless without being common—girls whose reputation needed no protection. The same held for drinking and all the other amenities of life. Her one regret was that when she should marry Peter Van Dyck, as had been ordained from the beginning of time, she could not have her baby in a different and hitherto unattempted manner. In a fleece-lined capsule, for instance, or a handsomely tailored cowl. The usual way was far too popular.

After the maid had done every possible thing for her except think and breathe, Yolanda allowed herself to be helped into a ravishing negligee. This was negligent to the point of aggressive indecency, but was perfectly all right on Yolanda because she was so utterly different from other women, although, from the various samples of herself she so generously displayed, the untutored eye would have gained the impression that she was made very much in accordance with the usual specifications.

Also the eye—even the untutored one—would have gained

the impression that these specifications had been most skillfully carried out. Yolanda was a good-looking girl, well built, attractively colored, and perfectly finished. There were deep blue eyes, fine golden hair, vivid lips, and a healthy outer layer of pink and white satin-smooth skin.

Yet beneath the outer layer Yolanda was exactly like every other woman who had ever entertained the illusion that she was different from all of her sisters. Nor would Yolanda's highly refined reactions have been especially cordial had anyone taken the trouble to supply her with this gratuitous piece of information.

No one ever did.

5

In quite another quarter of the city Aspirin Liz heaved her generous bulk out of bed and wearily dragged a pair of tent-like bloomers over enough body to make two of Yolanda's.

Grunting comfortably as she reached for the kettle sequestered in a dark closet, she proceeded to make herself some coffee. Also she found time to take a couple of aspirins, for which she was well named. These little duties being performed, and a shirt and flowered dressing gown added to her toilette, she collapsed in a chair and gloomily considered a hole that had but recently appeared in her bloomers. True, they were old bloomers, but still that hole had no right to be where it was. And it was not the first time either.

As Aspirin Liz regarded this new evidence of the bloomers' unworthiness her heart was filled with bitterness and indignation against the low-lives who had made the bloomers as well as the dirty dogs who had tricked her into buying them.

"Never put enough reinforcement into the damn things," she grumbled to herself, little realizing that hers was a figure that demanded more in the line of reinforcement than either the looms or sewing machines could profitably afford to supply. "Always busting out in a fresh spot like one of those all-fired Holland dykes."

Idly her mind drifted back through the years until she saw again a small boy thrusting some part of his body through a hole in a dyke. Just what part of his body it was remained a little vague to Aspirin Liz, but she was reasonably sure it was either an arm or a leg or a foot. It might even have been a finger to begin with, and later on an arm. She knew the little boy had not stuck his head through the hole, because her own common sense, of which she had a lot, convinced her that no little boy could have been as big a damn fool as all that.

She had always liked that story as a child. Game little beggar, that boy. As she had progressed through life, she had kept her eyes peeled for such a youth but had never come across one, although she had met many who had played games, and not very nice games at that. Even then they had cheated.

There was hardly anything Aspirin Liz did not know about men, and even less to their credit. They drank and cursed and treated women like hell and left the place all messed up. The more work you did for a man, the more things he could think up for you to do. If God had only made men more like animals, more like dogs, for instance, without any too much brains, things would be a great deal easier for women. But unfortunately men had brains, mean, bad-acting brains that kept interfering with the business of living. Women could handle their bodies all right, but the devil himself could not deal with a man's brains.

Aspirin Liz picked up last night's newspaper and broodingly considered a salaciously illustrated underwear advertisement.

"Wouldn't have lasted a minute in my day," she told herself as she studied the delicate lines of a pair of step-ins. "Yanked 'em clean off you, they would. Nowadays everything's so fancy. Didn't need all that nonsense when I was a girl. God knows nothing could have been more discouraging than those long, dangling, iron-clad, rock-girt flannels I grew up in, yet everybody seemed to do pretty well in spite of 'em. Drawers were drawers in those days. And when you took 'em off you knew you had 'em off. No two ways about it. Now take these makeshift bloomers. . . ."

It does not really matter where Aspirin Liz took her makeshift bloomers. She was always taking them somewhere. This morning, as on every morning, she had a bit of a headache. Perhaps a spot of gin would help. She took one. If it did not help her head it did at least make her solitary existence a little more endurable. Another cup of coffee and a fag. Liz yawned and stretched her heavy frame.

Once she had been an artist's model and very much in demand, very much in the front of things. Now . . . oh, hell, a woman couldn't keep her figure always. Use it while you have it and then forget it. So said Liz.

But she could never quite forget the figure of her heyday, for what it had once been was still hanging in several New York galleries she occasionally visited when all other comforts failed.

"Got to find a needle and thread," muttered Aspirin Liz, "and do something about these bloomers before the whole damn dyke pours through. Game little nipper, that kid was. Must have been his leg."

6

When Little Arthur exhumed himself from a disorderly pile of bedclothing and stood up, one of New York's most astute pickpockets was once more on his feet. But unlike Mr. Peter Duane Van Dyck, Little Arthur did not have to look for his drawers. He already had them on. Little Arthur had slept in his drawers, as was his invariable rule.

Gentlemen devoted to Little Arthur's profession frequently find it the wisest policy to sleep that way. Even a pick-pocket has some qualms about making a surreptitious exit when clad only in nothing. The criminal classes are notoriously more modest, more observant of the little niceties of convention than those who remain smuggly within the boundaries of the law. Little Arthur would have willingly faced arrest and long detention rather than to have presented an unadorned rear view to a callously jeering group of pursuing Irish minions of the law.

Yet even though Little Arthur habitually slept in his drawers, he was not altogether unmindful of them. This morning as he moved round his room he was thinking in a dim way about the state and efficacy of the miserably shabby garments he was wearing. They were unpicturesque, to say the least. Little Arthur felt they did not do him justice. The things he had on had never been intended to do any man justice. However, they were amusing, assuming one recovered from the shock of seeing them in action.

Nevertheless those drawers meant everything to their wearer. That is literally the truth. Yet, truthfully speaking, they were not drawers at all. They were a complete costume, a sort of overall arrangement that concealed the facts about Little Arthur from his scraggy neck to his pipe-stem ankles. A visitor from Mars would have found it difficult to believe that the body within was human.

However, the parts of Little Arthur that one was permitted to see were not entirely unprepossessing. He had a brisk little face, hardly any hair to speak of, and a devouringly alert pair of mild blue eyes. Frequently Little Arthur took those eyes to the movies, where they wept copiously over the sad parts and sparkled with pleasure when virtue triumphed and won its own reward.

Little Arthur's thoughts were now toying with the subject

of drawers. He was discontented with his present ones. He felt that he deserved a new deal.

"Can't very well snatch a pair of drawers off a customer's legs," he regretfully observed to himself. "Funny thing, that. Easier to steal a man's purse than his drawers."

Second-story men were lucky. They could steal all the drawers they needed—more drawers, in fact, than a man could reasonably use, although second-story work probably was exceedingly trying on drawers. Take a pickpocket now. A pickpocket was by the very nature of his calling entirely cut off from drawers as a source of loot. Oh, well, a dip should not expect to have everything. He was better off as he was. Climbing had always made him dizzy even as a boy. A man should stick to the job he was best fitted for instead of drifting from pillar to post. Never establish yourself that way. Little Arthur felt grieved over the fate of rolling stones. If he had a good day today, Little Arthur promised his legs a new pair of drawers.

With this promise in mind the weird-looking little man retrieved a last night's edition of the morning's paper from the floor and ran a professional eye over the list of public events.

CHAPTER ONE

An Embarrassing Situation

VAN DYCK COFFEE HAD BEEN RESPONSIBLE FOR KEEPING more generations of New Yorkers awake than had the product of any other importer in lower Manhattan. In the early days of the company's activities the Van Dycks had endeavored to popularize the beverage among various tribes of the less homicidally inclined Indians. However, finding that these original Americans seemed to prefer gin almost as avidly as Americans do today, the cannily hospitable old Dutchmen promptly broke out the square bottles and prospered greatly thereby.

With this phase of the business the current generation of Van Dycks habitually dealt with commendable vagueness. Inasmuch as the Van Dycks had been fairly respectable even before they took up the New World in a big way, it never occurred to their descendants that their present exalted state was established on the hang-overs of a great multitude of red men.

Peter Van Dyck knew far less about coffee than had any of his predecessors. He was somewhat less backward where gin was concerned. Peter found it difficult to break himself of the habit of regarding coffee in the light of a personal indulgence rather than as a commercial asset. Some mornings it tasted better than others. That was about the extent of Peter's knowledge. This morning, he decided, it did not taste so good.

As he left his house in the West Seventies he was wondering vaguely why his eyes had such a harassed expression and his coffee such a comfortless flavor. The season of the year was propitious—late spring with summer lounging among the buds. Business not too bad when compared with that of his competitors. As a matter of fact the morning paper had announced the untimely end of one of his closest rivals, yet even this gratifying occurrence failed to lend zest to Peter's day. Something was radically wrong with him.

Then, suddenly, a thought rose bleakly from his subconscious mind and flopped down heavily on his conscious one, where it lay like a dead weight. This afternoon his Aunt Sophie, his statuesque and painfully modern Aunt Sophie who presided over his household, was giving a cocktail party for Yolanda Bates Wilmont. And at this party the cat which had long since been out of the bag was obligingly going to crawl back into it again to permit itself to be officially released. After today he, Peter, would no longer be a freelance in the courts of light dalliance. He would be irrevocably engaged to Yolanda with all her beauty and wealth and firmly rooted convictions. This knowledge somehow failed even more lamentably than had the sudden departure of his business rival to add zest to Peter's day. Yes, there was no doubt about it. Something was radically wrong with him. His responsive faculties seemed to have become strangely atrophied by the thought of life and Yolanda Wilmont.

For a few brief moments Peter's troubled blue eyes dwelt on the lines of a well-formed girl sitting opposite him in the downtown subway express. Little suspecting the highly improper trend of his thoughts, Peter felt that he would like to lie down quietly somewhere with that girl and talk the situation over. He felt the need of a female confessor as well as entertainer. There had been too few women in his life. With a sense of panic he began to realize this as the imminence of his official betrothal confronted him. Quickly he averted his eyes. The girl was chewing gum. This girl, in spite of her lines, was definitely out of the picture. Well, was not life exactly like that? At its most alluring moments it suddenly began to chew gum in one's face. Revolting, Peter shrank slightly and returned to his paper.

It was not until he had reached the seclusion of his private office that the extra pair of drawers he was unconsciously wearing began to manifest themselves. Even then he was not aware of the exact nature of his difficulties. He experienced merely a sense of unwonted fullness—a growing sensation of insecurity. Suddenly, however, as the drawers gathered headway his alarm and discomfort became acute. In his anxiety forgetting that his office though private was not quite impenetrable, Peter allowed his trousers to descend several inches, the better to deal with the perplexing situation.

Miss Josephine Duval, armed with the morning mail, entered the room quietly and closed the door behind her. For a moment she allowed her cool but curious gaze to dwell on the orange and black stripes decorating all that could be seen of the southern exposure of Mr. Peter Van Dyck's shorts.

"Looks like summer awnings," she observed more to herself than to her employer. "And to think I never suspected!"

With a low moan of distress Peter's body went into a huddle as only a body can when plunged into such a situation.

"Haven't you got sense enough to get out?" he demanded, twisting a strained but indignant face over his shoulder.

"I have the sense, but not the power," Miss Duval retorted calmly. "Your condition has robbed me of that."

"For God's sake," the man almost chattered, "hurry! Suppose someone should come in and find you here?"

"I'm all right," said Miss Duval. "It's you who would give rise to comment."

Something was slipping farther and farther down the right leg of Peter's trousers, slipping stealthily but relentlessly to the floor. And the trouble was that Peter, not suspecting the presence of a stowaway, visualized the worst. What a fearful picture he must be presenting from the rear, yet the front view would not improve matters any. How could such a demeaning thing happen to a man in this day and age?

"Won't you please go away?" he asked in an agitated voice. "What would people think?"

"Well," replied Jo with dispassionate deliberation, "from the trouble you seem to be having with your trousers, people might get the impression you'd asked me in here to watch you do tricks with your shorts."

"What's that!" exclaimed Peter, more upset by the girl's attitude than by her words. "Oh, you're fired. There's no doubt about that. This time you're through for good."

"Do you realize that I could play you a decidedly dirty trick?" Jo inquired lightly.

"What do you mean?" asked Peter, his fingers furtively fumbling with various buttons.

"If I should scream now——" began Jo, but was interrupted by Peter's heartfelt, "Oh, my God!"

"If I should begin to shout and rush about," she continued, as if savoring the idea, "there's not a jury in the world that wouldn't convict you of at least breach of promise."

"Swear to God I never knew there was such a woman in the world," Peter Van Dyck replied in an emotional voice as if appealing to some unseen audience. "If you'll only go away and let me finish what I'm doing you'll not be fired."

"How about all this mail?" she demanded.

"Am I in a condition to go into that now?"

"I should say not," said the girl. "You don't know how awful you are."

"Then don't trouble to tell me. I can very well imagine."

"Before I go," Josephine continued, placing the letters on the desk, "would you mind explaining what was in your mind when you got yourself into this terrible condition?"

"I don't know," Peter answered. "And I fail to see how it's any of your business."

"Well, it's a sight a young lady doesn't see every day of her life," replied Jo. "Especially in an office building and at this time of day."

"I don't make a practice of it," Peter retorted, with an attempt at dignity.

"I wouldn't," Miss Duval assured him. "There's an unpleasant suggestion of senility about it. And by the way, if you're looking for an extra pair of drawers you'll find them sticking out of the right leg of your trousers. Although why you want two pairs I can't for the life of me understand. The ones you have on are giddy enough."

As the door closed quietly on his tormentor, Peter Van Dyck reached down and, seizing the offending drawers, hurled them furiously in the general direction of the waste basket, upon the edge of which they sprawled unbecomingly.

"Damn my absent mind," he muttered, "and damn that woman's impudence. What a decidedly unpleasant occurrence! She actually seemed to enjoy it. These modern girls . . ."

A few minutes later Jo briskly followed her perfunctory knock into the room and found her employer wearily seated at his desk. He was gloomily scanning a letter.

"Oh," exclaimed Miss Duval amicably. "Quite an improvement. All tucked in, I see."

Before Peter had time to think up a fitting retort, William, the office handy man, entered the room and cast about for something on which to exercise his talents. Spying the drawers dangling over the waste-paper basket, he held them aloft admiringly.

"Fine pair o' drawers, these," he observed in a conversational tone of voice. "A real fancy pair. Begging your pardon, sir, but are they yours, Mr. Peter?"

Mr. Peter preferred not to notice William's polite inquiry. Jo saw fit to bring it to his attention.

"William wants to know," she said in level tones as she seated herself in a chair with her dictation pad open on her knee, "William is anxious to find out if those—if that florid object belongs to you."

"Tell him they don't," Peter mumbled unhappily.

"It would be more manly if you spoke of such things yourself," the girl replied. "However—he says they're not his, William."

"Well, I'd like to know how they got here, then," William continued stubbornly. "All spread out like that. They must be his."

If William had not emptied many a waste-paper basket for Peter's departed father, the man would have been fired on the spot. As it was, a friendship of many years now stood in serious danger of an open break.

"Is there any reason why you should doubt my word about those drawers?" Peter asked the man coldly. "Someone might have left them here as a sample."

At this William shook the drawers playfully and chuckled his incredulity.

"Not these, Mr. Peter," he declared. "We're in the coffee business."

"Well, even coffee merchants are supposed to have some self-respect," replied Peter.

"Not the coffee merchant who wore these," asserted William with a wise shake of his head. "Couldn't keep much self-respect in them things. They'd suit my Alf to a tee. He'd go crazy about them drawers with their funny little pink dots."

"I'll damn well go crazy myself if you don't get them out of my sight," Peter assured his handy man.

"Yes, William," put in Jo Duval. "Why not take them through the office and inquire of the gentlemen if they have lost a pair? We might be able to find a home for them that way."

"No need to do that," said Peter hurriedly. "Take 'em home to Alf with my compliments. Do anything with them you like so long as you let me hear no more upon the subject. I'm completely exhausted by drawers."

"Thanks, Mr. Peter," the grateful man replied, giving the garment a possessive flirt as he made his way to the door. "As neat a little pair o' drawers as I ever laid eye on. All full of funny pink spots, they are."

"William is getting old," observed Peter Van Dyck, to break the pause following the man's departure. "I'll have to lay him off with a pension one of these days."

"Wouldn't mind a little bit of that sort of thing myself," replied Jo, carelessly crossing her legs and fixing her employer with a level gaze. "Why don't you pension yourself off, for a change? You're not interested in business."

"What makes you say a thing like that?"

"Well, obviously a man who has such playful ideas in drawers can hardly be expected to keep his mind on work."

"Is that so!" grumbled Peter. "You've been with this company altogether too long. Take a couple of letters."

Jo indulged in a short but ironical laugh.

"What's wrong now?" he asked suspiciously.

"I was only thinking that while you're dictating letters to me," she replied easily, "William is probably exhibiting your disinherited drawers to the entire office force."

"Take a couple of letters nevertheless," said Peter Van Dyck, with characteristically Dutch stubbornness. "Just because an old fool chooses to make a public display of a private affair, I can't leave the coffee business flat."

"What a man!" remarked Jo in a low, admiring voice.

Once more he regarded her suspiciously.

"How long have you been with us?" he asked.

"Much longer than I expected to remain in a purely professional capacity," she told him.

"I very much doubt if you could remain long purely in any capacity," said Peter, feeling a little set up by his unexpected burst of repartee.

"Some girls might take that amiss," said Jo, "but I consider it a compliment. I didn't think you knew."

"Knew what?"

"My attitude—my moral outlook."

"Oh, I don't know that," he said hastily. "And I don't want to find out. You take too many liberties as it is. If you hadn't been here already when I took over the reins, I'd have fired you on sight."

"And driven the business into a ditch," Jo replied complacently. "You haven't the foggiest idea where anything is—not even the most personal of things such as your——"

"Don't let's go into that again," he interrupted.

"I have no desire to," she assured him.

But Peter Van Dyck was destined to take up the matter of drawers once more before it was definitely dropped. There was a scrambling noise outside the door, a nervous scraping on the glass partition, then the door flew open and Freddie, the small but aggressive office boy, excitedly waving the erstwhile drawers of his employer, hurried into the room with William close at his heels.

"Beg your pardon, sir," said Freddie, waving the spotted garment in the indignant William's face, "but ain't these drawers yours? He says they're his. I saw you with my own eyes—you had 'em on one day when you were in the——"

"Stop! Stop!" cried Peter Van Dyck in a stricken voice. "And please close the door."

"Here's a go," murmured Jo Duval. "Those drawers seem to have a mind of their own."

Peter Van Dyck looked hatefully at her, then drummed distractedly on his desk. Once his glance strayed in the direction of the drawers. With an effort he averted his fascinated eyes. Finally he spoke. His voice was low and cultured. In it was a note of despair.

"Freddie," he said, "those drawers are the property of William. They are his without let or hindrance—his irrevocably. Do you understand that, Freddie? Then hand those drawers back to William who I hope to God will put them in his pocket and take them home to Alf. If he doesn't I'm going to fire you all, and that includes you." His eyes burned with bitterness as he studied the expression of bland enjoyment on his secretary's face. His voice gathered volume. "And as for you, Freddie, if you kept your eyes more on your business and less on other people's drawers you might grow up to be a coffee broker yourself some day." He paused to consider his words. Somehow this rebuke of Freddie seemed to lack in strength what it gained in dignity. Once more his eyes were attracted to the drawers; then his dignity and self-control departed. He rose, spluttering. "William," he thundered, "if you don't take those miserable drawers away I'll drag yours off your baggy-looking legs."

"No need to get personal," Jo reminded the aroused man.

"What!" cried Peter. "I'd like to drag yours off, too."

"Thanks," she answered. "Hadn't you better ask the gentlemen to withdraw first?"

"Oh!" said Peter as if stung to the quick. "Oh, my God!" He sank back in his chair and held his forehead in his hands. "That will be all about drawers for this morning," he said at last. "Please leave the room quietly with—with them. Don't bring them back."

When Freddie and William and the drawers had departed, silence reigned in the room. Peter looked wearily out of the window. He was considering whether it would not be simpler to hurl himself through it. The door opened and William thrust in an apologetic head.

"Sorry, Mr. Peter," he said. "I kept telling young Freddie that just because he happened to see you yanking 'em up once it didn't mean you were going to wear 'em all the time. He hasn't gumption enough to know that a gentleman changes his——"

"Can't you explain to William?" Peter interrupted, turning appealingly to Josephine. "He doesn't seem to understand."

"William," said the girl quietly, "Mr. Van Dyck is too upset to hear any more about his drawers today."

"Ever," put in Peter.

"Yes, William," Jo continued. "Don't ever talk to Mr. Peter about his drawers again. Talk about something else—his socks, for instance."

Peter winced. His eyes were filled with disgust.

"Thank you, miss," said William. "I'll try to remember. You said his socks, didn't you?"

"Yes," replied Jo. "His socks, although from his expression he doesn't seem so fond of those either."

"The door—the door!" grated Peter. "Close it on your horrid face, William."

The door was closed.

"Did you want to dictate a couple of letters?" Jo asked imperturbably.

"Yes," replied Peter. "Take a couple of letters." For some time he sat in gloomy concentration, then abandoned the effort. "Oh, hell," he said, "I can't think of one letter, much less two."

"I'll answer them for you," Jo assured him soothingly. "You need a long rest." She looked him over appraisingly. "Wonder how Alf's going to look in those——"

A strangling sound from Peter cut short her sentence.

"Go!" he whispered, pointing to the door with a trembling finger. "Get out! I don't give a damn how Alf looks."

"You should consult a doctor," she told him as she prepared to leave the room. "There's something preying on your mind. Do you drug, perhaps?"

"Do I what?" demanded Peter.

"Do you drug?" she answered simply.

"No," he replied confronting her, "but I can still drag, and that's what I'll damn well do to you if you don't get out of here."

With a glance of deep commiseration Josephine gracefully left the room. The provocative fragrance of her perfume lingered in the air. Peter Van Dyck wondered why he did not discharge the girl. Little did he realize that her perfume was one of the reasons.

CHAPTER TWO

On a Park Bench

SEVERAL HOURS AFTER THESE UNDIGNIFIED HAPPENINGS Peter Van Dyck emerged from a restaurant in which he had been lone-wolfing, being able to think of no language fit for decent conversation. In the crowd outside the door Josephine Duval caught sight of his slim and dejected-looking shoulders. Without a moment's hesitation the young lady abandoned her window-shopping and blithely set off to dog the footsteps of her employer. Having snatched a glimpse of the girl out of the tail of his eye, Peter immediately divined her intention. This stalking procedure had occurred more than once. Accordingly he quickened his pace. Emphatically he assured himself he had seen quite enough of his secretary for one day. She was a creature totally lacking in either pride or pity. Several times he glanced back to ascertain if his dodging tactics had succeeded in eluding pursuit. Each time he was disappointed. Josephine was still there—grimly there. A most annoying situation. Disgraceful. Why was she making no effort to cut down the distance? Was it torture? Peter was seized by a nervous impulse to take to his heels and run. However, he checked himself, feeling convinced that Jo would have no compunction in doing likewise. She might even find it amusing to shout his name through the streets. Hang it all, what did the girl want with him, anyway? The street was littered with unattached men. Why did she not confine her attentions to one or more of them? He was an engaged man. Within a few short hours he would be a doubly engaged man. Officially hooked if not spliced. Vaguely he wondered whether he was endeavoring to elude Josephine or the thought of that engagement. He crossed over to Battery Park and sat down on a bench close to the waterfront. The fragrance of Jo's perfume still lingered in his nostrils. Presently it grew stronger. He stirred restlessly. She was there.

"You'll be late at the office," he announced, without turning his head.

"I'll say I was out with you," said a small voice beside him.

"And I'll say you deliberately followed me through the streets of New York," he told her.

"Would you like the office to know that?" asked Jo.

"No. I would not."

"Then why not be friendly?"

"I'm quite friendly enough for a person who wants to commit murder. In fact I'm damned patient. Don't let's talk; then people won't suspect we know each other."

"Why won't they suspect?"

"They'd never think that a person like me would talk to a girl like you."

Jo considered this insult judicially while swinging her small feet.

"Oh, I don't know," she said at last. "You don't look so awful."

"What?" exclaimed the man indignantly. "You entirely misunderstood my meaning."

"Peter." In a very small voice.

"Yes." Grudgingly. "Mr. Van Dyck to you."

"Your father called you Peter."

"Well, you're not my father."

"But I helped to bring you up in the business. It's been three years now."

"Seems longer."

"Does it? Well, it hasn't been long enough to make a coffee man of you."

"Is that so?"

"Yes, that's so. You're a hell of a coffee man."

Peter looked pained.

"It doesn't speak well for your teaching," he said.

"You never give me a tumble. Don't even call me Jo. Everybody else in the office calls me Jo."

"What do I call you?"

"You don't call me anything. It's 'Please take a letter,' or 'How do you feel today?' or 'Sorry to keep you late.' Never any name. To you I'm a nameless woman. Might just as well be a—a—little bastard for all you care."

This time Peter was profoundly shocked. He actually

looked at the girl beside him. His eyes held a mixture of alarm and disapproval.

"Don't use bad language," he said.

"Why not use bad language?" she retorted. "You flaunt your drawers in my face."

"Is that quite fair?" he asked her. "You stormed into my private office. Didn't stop to knock. And there I was. That's all there is to it."

Jo laughed tragically.

"So that's all there is to it," she flung back with a mean sneer. "I suppose you think I'm going to be satisfied with that—a mere matter of drawers."

When Peter looked at her this time, alarm had utterly routed disapproval.

"My God!" he managed to get out. "What do you mean about not being satisfied with that?"

"Exactly what I said," she replied. "I want to see all. Everything! It's whole hog or nothing—that's how I am."

Peter felt his reason slipping. He could not believe his ears.

"Well," he said at last, "all I can say is that it's not a very nice way to be. It must be your French blood."

"I don't care whose blood it is," she replied stubbornly. "I want to see all."

"Let me get this straight," said Peter. "Do you mean all of me?"

Josephine looked him over from head to foot. Peter felt a little undressed. Then suddenly she began to laugh.

"You'd look awfully funny," she said at last, as if actually seeing him that way. "What a fright! Imagine!"

"Don't trouble yourself," said Peter acidulously. "I'm not exactly deformed, you know."

Jo stopped laughing and regarded him through moist eyes.

"I don't believe it," she said. "You're hiding something from me."

"Do you expect me to walk about my office naked?" he asked.

"After this morning I don't know what to expect."

Peter Van Dyck shrugged his shoulders helplessly.

"I'd prefer not to continue this conversation," he remarked coldly. "No good can come of it."

"Very well," replied Jo. "Let's sit like a couple of bumps on a log."

"You may sit as you jolly well please," replied Peter. "However, I don't see why you are sitting here at all."

"Why don't you push me off?"

"Nothing would please me more, but I'm too much of a gentleman."

"You mean, you're afraid," she taunted.

"Please be quiet."

"I suppose you're afraid Mr. Morgan or some other international banker might come along and see us talking together?"

"I am," replied Peter.

"Well, listen to me, Mr. Peter Duane Van Dyck. If one of those old bozos got an eyeful of me he'd give you money instead of lending it to you."

"You seem to fancy yourself."

"I know my own value, and that's more than you do," she retorted. "I've a good mind to sell my body to an international banker."

"I wish to God you'd sell it to an international vivisectionist and have done with it," Peter asserted brutally.

"Why?" she inquired. "Does my body bother you?"

"Not at all. It means nothing to me."

"You mean you can take it or leave it—just as you please?"

"Will you kindly keep quiet? I've a lot of things to think about. If I could take it and leave it somewhere else I'd feel much better."

Several minutes of silence passed. Josephine's gaze was idly sweeping the harbor. Presently she spoke.

"Peter," she said.

"Yes," replied Peter. "What is it now?"

"Do you see that liner?"

"Can't help seeing that liner. It's blocking up the whole harbor."

Jo snaked her supple young body close up beside her employer.

"Would you like to be on that liner, Peter?" she asked him.

"Listen," protested Peter. "Are you trying to sit on my knees? We're huddled up together on this bench like a couple of lost waifs. It's not a cold day."

"Sorry, Peter. Wasn't looking where I was going. But you haven't answered my question. Would you like to be on that liner?"

Peter considered the girl briefly; then his gaze returned to the outbound ship now stepping delicately on her way to open water. The bay glinted with sunlight, and its blue was very blue indeed. Like a virgin murmuring indiscreetly in her dreams, the soft air spoke of summer, of summer and secret places remote from the haunts of man. There was a note of promise too in the voice of the old gentleman who owned the long telescope gleaming on its tripod.

"Visit the harbor and its institutions without budging your feet an inch! The Statue of Liberty and Governor's Island—all points of interest like as if you was there in the flesh."

Moodily Peter watched a customer tentatively approach a self-conscious eye to the telescope and begin his visit to the harbor. Peter followed the movements of the man with some anxiety. He wondered what point of interest the fellow was visiting now. Was he seeing anything at all or just pretending to, as most people did when involved with the end of a telescope? Peter had peered through a telescope once. There had been certain things on the moon—mountains, craters, or warts, for all he had been able to discover. He had lied about that moon. Said he had seen everything. Dwelt on the wonder of it all. Inwardly he had suffered from a sneaking sense of guilt and frustration. This visitor to the harbor was doubtless experiencing similar difficulties. That dusty mop of a dog curled up under the instrument knew perfectly well that the visitor was seeing nothing—less than nothing. They never did. For a moment the dog leered cynically at Peter, then transferred his gaze to a sparrow. He would dearly love to chew on some of that sparrow.

Now the liner was spreading her wake along the channel. Soon she would find the sea. What the hell was wrong with him, anyway? Mooning here on a park bench with an impudent chit of an office girl for a companion. Maybe it was spring fever. Then maybe it wasn't. Maybe it was the thought of that cocktail party. He rather more than suspected it was. After the party he was scheduled to take Yolanda to some stuffy house party in New Jersey over the week-end. Not much comfort in that. Peter objected to house parties. Bridge, booze, and boredom. Gay laughter as false as hell. Feeble wisecracks and smart talk—the smug assurance of one's daily bread whether school kept or not. Golf links, motorcars, tennis courts, and swimming pools—all the paraphernalia of good, clean sport. Healthy bodies and tanned hides. Thoughts and manners cast in the same mold, case-hardened with the same prejudices and polished with the same culture. And here this poor devil, having paid his ten cents, stood all spraddled out vainly endeavoring to snatch a moment's enjoyment from the end of a telescope. The subtle invitation of Jo's perfume once more assaulted his nerves.

Peter liked that perfume, and the fact that he suspected he also liked its owner a little more than was seemly made him deliberately hostile.

"You haven't answered my question," she said.

"What question?" asked Peter uneasily.

"About that liner. How would you like to be on her?"

"I'd like it," said Peter surprisingly.

"You mean us?" put in Jo. "Just you and I . . . outward bound . . . springtime in France . . . windows on the sea—think of it, Peter. Just you and I. Married, perhaps, or almost the same thing."

Peter gasped at the immoral conclusion to this lyrical outburst.

"I'd jump off the ship," he said.

"Oh, no, you wouldn't," the girl replied with every show of confidence. "If I had you alone for five minutes you'd jump in only one direction, and I'm too much of a lady to mention that."

"Are you just naturally plain bad through and through?" Peter asked her. He was really interested to know.

"I'm what you've made me," she answered humbly.

"What!" exclaimed Peter. "I haven't done a thing to you."

"I know. That's just the trouble. That's why I'm bad. Don't you realize a body has to be bad before it can plop down and be good?"

"I don't care to discuss bodies. Much rather swim after that ship."

"Why don't you? I hope you drown." Then with a sudden change in her voice, "What's on your mind, Peter? You haven't been so gay lately."

Her brown eyes studied the features of the man with their suggestion of gauntness. For a moment they rested on his expressive lips, broken by a faintly ironical twist. She moistened hers, then peered inquiringly into his eyes, unremarkable mild blue eyes, rather gentle and easily tired yet strangely capable of conveying a world of hidden meanings. He was not a good-looking man, yet Jo had always found him attractive. Especially his eyes, in which in spite of their apparent weariness he seemed to live most of his life. He was a kind of old young man to Jo, an old young man who had never been really young and who never would grow really old. He belonged to an old unclassified type—no three-dimensional hero, Peter, yet very definitely himself. At present his eyes were haunted with all sorts of unexpressed difficulties.

"What's on your mind?" she repeated.

"Nothing definite," said Peter, allowing his gaze to rest on the girl with a little less disapproval. "You know. One of these cocktail teas—stupid things."

Jo did not know. She was deeply interested, as are all daughters of Eve, in social functions in which they are not included.

"Today?" she asked.

"After office," said Peter. "My aunt's doing it for Yolanda Wilmont. We get engaged at it—officially engaged and all that."

"All what?" she inquired suspiciously.

"Oh, just all that."

"I hope you don't mean what I'm thinking," said Jo.

"At my lowest moments," he replied, "I never could mean what you're thinking."

"Thanks," murmured Jo. "What's she like? Of course, I've seen her pictures in the scandal sheets. They've given me many a good laugh."

"You're just envious," retorted Peter, hardly spirited enough to be stung to a defense of his fiancée.

"I might possibly be envious about all that," she admitted, "but certainly not about being engaged to you."

"Neither am I," replied Peter cryptically.

The girl cast him a swift look—a look of sparrow-like

intelligence. She was snatching at crumbs of comfort now, yet at the same time finding room to feel a little bit sorry for Peter.

"So that's why you'd like to swim after that ship," she observed in a thoughtful voice.

"After any ship," said Peter.

"I understand," she answered.

"No, you don't," replied Peter, suddenly getting up from the bench. "As a matter of fact I'm very happy. I'm a decidedly lucky man."

"Of course you are, Peter," she assured him.

This time he cast her a swift look.

"An exceptionally lucky man," he reiterated with quite unnecessary emphasis. "Getting far more than I deserve, in fact."

"Now you're talking," said Jo. "Much more than you deserve, and you're pretty bad."

"What do you mean by that?"

"I don't mean anything, Peter. I'm agreeing with you."

"Well, don't," he snapped. "I dislike the way you do it. Anyway, it's time to get back to the office. Can't remember ever spending a more trying luncheon hour."

"Would you believe it?" said Josephine. "It's been much longer than that. Time passes so quickly for a young girl when she meets an interesting, middle-aged party."

"Middle-aged hell. How old are you?"

"Swear to God I'm twenty-four, mister."

"Well, I'm only ten years older."

"Just the right age, although you do look a wee bit faded."

"The right age for what?" Peter was unwise enough to want to know.

"For fatherhood," she told him, looking glowingly up into his face.

Some hidden strain of old Dutch modesty forced Peter to lower his lids.

"Come," he said. "We're going back to the office."

But before they left, their eyes sought the liner nosing far down the Narrows. Jo gave a little sigh, the wistful ghost of a great big wish. In Peter's eyes the harassed look had deepened. It was verging on the desperate now.

CHAPTER THREE

Revelation of the Legs

THE DAY WAS DRAGGING ON, AND BY NOW THAT LINER must be far out at sea. Peter sat thinking about it. In his thoughts were mingled fleeting visions of Yolanda Wilmont and Josephine Duval. What was it all about, all this uneasy speculation, this sensation of approaching loss and separation? Separation from what, from whom? Obviously, he must be in love with Yolanda Wilmont—had been in love with her for years. That was all settled, one of the established facts of his life. She was beautiful, she was cultured, and she seemed to find nothing especially wrong with him. Of course, she had never allowed either herself nor him to become in any sense intimate on the strength of this engagement of theirs. She was not at all like that. Just the opposite of this Duval woman. That was something to be thankful for—but was it? Peter wondered. On the other hand he seriously doubted if one man could last long with an oversexed creature like Josephine without calling in outside assistance, which did not make for a happy married life. Josephine was impossible. He failed to know why he was thinking about her at all. What business had that brazen vixen preening herself in his thoughts? She was merely his private secretary, an efficient one but forward. She, too, had become a fixture in his life. His father had found her amusing, but then, the elder Van Dyck had been a loose liver after office hours. He had found any good-looking wench amusing. Peter was not like that. He had never had the chance. As he sat there thinking, he found himself rather envying his father's disregard of convention. Closer than had any other Van Dyck immortalized in the family record, the old gentleman had approached the open ground of disreputability. He had been keenly alert to every female leg in the office, and he had personally seen to it that every leg in the office was first-rate. Yet everyone had been fond of old Peter Van Dyck, including his son. Young Peter had been too greatly occupied fearing the consequences of his father's ambitious but questionable experiments to embark on any of his own. Many a father has lost his morals in saving those of a son, although it is highly problematical that the elder Van Dyck had this idea in mind as he tidily tottered among his vices. His interest in Jo Duval, however, had been restrained to one of fatherly admiration mixed with a little fear and respect, emotions few women had ever inspired in him.

Peter's thoughts were interrupted by the entrance of Josephine Duval. Without so much as favoring him with a glance, she marched up to his desk, smacked down on it an intra-office memorandum, then turned and retraced her steps. At the door she paused and fixed him with a pair of glittering eyes. Peter quailed before their malevolence. In the way she closed the door behind her there was a suggstion of a challenge.

Why was this creature so disturbing? Peter wondered. At times, when it so pleased her mood, she acted exactly as if she were in a play. It wasn't natural. Imagine! This stalking into a man's office, then stalking out again with never a word. And what a look she had left behind—what a downright sinister look! What had she meant by that?

With the least interest in the world in intra-office routine Peter picked up the memorandum and glanced at it. Quite suddenly his bored expression changed to one of consternation. He read:

To PETER VAN DYCK, *President:*

The moment you consummate your marriage with Yolanda Wilmont (what a name!) I want my resignation to take effect. However, until that moment it's still anybody's game, catch-as-catch-can, and you're It.

Respectfully yours,

JOSEPHINE DUVAL.

P. S.

A carbon of this memorandum will be found in my files under "Unfinished Business."

As if it were scorching his fingers, Peter hastily destroyed the compromising slip of paper. This was going too far. He rang for his secretary.

"Haven't you got any better sense than to start in playing childish games with me?" he demanded.

"The games I intend to play with you will be far from childish," she assured him.

Peter began to think this over, then decided it would be better to leave it alone.

"Sit down," he said in a reasonable voice, "and let's try to get things straight."

Josephine flopped down and recklessly tossed one silken leg over the other.

"In the first place," began Peter, "why have you selected today of all days to deport yourself in an especially hellish manner?"

"I'm like this every day, only some days I let go," she told him.

Peter considered this for a moment.

"Do you mean you're like this with everybody," he inquired, "or just with me?"

"Just with you," she confided. "If I was like this with everybody I'd have a much nicer time."

"You don't mean nicer," said Peter. "You mean better, perhaps."

"It's too fine a distinction for me to understand," she replied. "But it's the truth just the same. I let go only with you."

"Why with me, may I ask? Do you regard me in the light of a small office boy—a person to tease?"

"Hardly," she said. "I regard you as a weak but adult male."

"Apparently," replied Peter. "But would you mind not letting go with me, or try letting go with someone else, for a change?"

She looked at him thoughtfully.

"I'd rather not," she said.

"So would I," replied Peter, not realizing what he was saying.

"You mean you'd care if I let go with someone else?" she asked.

"Certainly not," replied Peter. "I don't care if you let go with Mahatma Gandhi, with all due respect to that gentleman."

"It wouldn't be hard to let go with that one," Jo observed. "He has so very little to let go of."

"That's neither here nor there," said Peter impatiently. "You'll have to stop letting go with me or I'll let go with you."

"I'd like that," replied the girl quite seriously.

"I mean, I'll have to let you go." he corrected himself.

"You haven't even got me yet," she answered.

"And I don't even want you," said Peter.

"How do you know?" she demanded. "You don't know anything about me. You don't know I live in New Jersey, that I support a drunken uncle, that I'm an orphan on both sides and sleep on the left. You don't know that I love salted almonds and that I don't earn enough money here to keep myself in nice underthings. You wear pure silk drawers. Don't tell me—I saw them with my own two eyes. What sort of drawers do you think I wear? Answer me that. What sort of drawers do you think I wear? Pure silk? Bah!"

"I'm sure I don't care to know that," Peter interrupted. "And please don't keep repeating the question."

"No," she sneered, "you don't care to know. You're too much of a coward. Well, if you must know, I'll tell you. They're artificial silk—not all silk like yours—but the lace on 'em is real."

"Must I know all these things?" asked Peter weakly.

"Certainly you must," she snapped. "You're dealing in human souls."

"I had hoped to deal in coffee," he replied with a show of bitterness, "but you don't give me time to sell a bean."

"I wouldn't be found dead in those things you have on," she continued. "Mine are better for less money."

"No doubt," Peter said coldly. "But did it ever occur to you that I have no desire to be found dead in yours?"

"Of course you wouldn't," she flung back. "Not dead."

Here she laughed significantly—suggestively, in fact. Peter Van Dyck was most unpleasantly impressed by the insinuating look that followed. Helplessly he turned his eyes to the window.

"I fail to see where all this is leading to," he said at length. "Hadn't you better take a couple of letters?"

"All right," she retorted. "Give me a couple of letters. It's better than getting nothing. But while we're on the subject, there's another thing you don't know."

"I'm off the subject. Most definitely off it."

"Well, you've got to know this," she continued. "One of the last things your father asked me to do was to make a man of you."

"If you followed his ideas on that subject," said Peter, "you'd make a wreck of me instead of a man, I'm afraid."

"You're certainly not the man he was," she admitted with uncomplimentary readiness, "but I'm going to do my best with the little there is."

"That's very gracious of you, I'm sure. But let me get this straight. Do you intend to make a man of me or a wreck?"

"I'm going to wreck you," said the girl, "and enjoy myself doing it."

"A nice young girl!" murmured Peter Van Dyck. "An admirable character all round!"

"And while you're talking of nice young girls," said Jo, "you might as well know your father wasn't any too fond of that nice young girl of yours with the name of a fairy princess. And as for an admirable character—pish! I'd rather have a swell shape."

"Couldn't you strive to develop both?"

"I'm fully developed as it is," she asserted. "If anything, a little too much so in places, but you'd never know that."

"I have no desire to be further enlightened," Peter hastened to assure her.

"You have no ambition," said Jo.

"How about a couple of letters?" he asked.

"All right. How about 'em? I'd almost given those letters up."

"And will you take the carbon of that memorandum out of your files?" he asked her.

"If you don't hurry up with those letters," Jo replied, "I'll take it out of the files and tack it on the bulletin board."

This threat so upset Peter that he in turn upset a box of paper clips. As he bent over to pick them up, he came face to face with Josephine Duval's knee. Some artists claim that the knee of a woman is not an object of beauty. No such claim could be made against Josephine Duval's knee. If an artist lived who, upon seeing Josephine's knee, did not want to do something more than paint it, he was not worthy of his brush. And the wonder of it was that Josephine had two knees. Peter Van Dyck was gazing at them both. It was an experience he never forgot—a revelation. For the first time in his life he realized that a woman's knees and legs were capable of expressing personality. And with this realization came the explanation of his distaste for the cocktail party and what it represented. In the course of his life he had seen a lot of Yolanda's legs, but never once during the period of this long association with them had he been moved by a desire to do anything other than look at them, and not so strongly moved at that. As Peter sat half crouching in his chair, it came to him, with a sense of having been cheated, that Yolanda's legs had never meant anything more to him than something to separate her body from the ground, something to move her about on from place to place. They might as well have been a pair of stilts or a couple of wheels. In spite of their gracious proportions they were totally lacking in personality. They exercised no fascination, no irresistible appeal. They were cold but beautiful legs. Josephine's legs were different. The more Peter looked at them the more he wanted to see of them. He frankly admitted this. Not only were they beautiful but also extremely interesting—breath-taking legs, legs seen once in a lifetime. He wondered what had been wrong with him not to have noticed them before. Why had he made this startling discovery at this late date, virtually at the very moment when he was going to become officially engaged to an altogether different pair of legs—to legs he would have to live with for the remainder of his days?

Josephine's voice cut in on his meditations.

"Have you decided to conduct your business in that weird position?" she asked. "Or have you been seized suddenly by a cramp?"

"I'm not going to be like this long," he answered, "nor am I subject to cramps. I am merely thinking."

"Then I think you're overdoing it," said the girl. "First thing you know you'll be having a rush of blood to the head."

"I have one already," replied Peter in an odd voice.

Slowly he straightened up, then sank back in his chair. Almost immediately he fell into a brown study, and although he was looking directly at Josephine his gaze seemed to pass through and far beyond her. The girl eyed him curiously. What had come over this man? Little did she suspect that what she had so often wanted to happen actually had happened without her knowledge or contrivance.

In the presence of this startling revelation Peter Van Dyck sat bemused. For the first time in his life he concentrated his mental forces on legs. How, he wondered, had a leg, a mere leg, the power to move a man so profoundly—to revolutionize his entire outlook on such matters? All legs were more or less alike, he argued, so much skin and so much bone. Take his own legs, for example. He had never derived any pleasure or satisfaction in contemplating their hungry contours, if they had any contours to contemplate. He supposed they had, yet he was not in any way moved when he cast his eyes on them unless it was by a feeling of distaste. As a matter of fact, he preferred not to look at his legs at all. He rather avoided them. Yet wherein were they so different from those of Josephine Duval? They were composed of the same elements, served the same purpose, and reacted to the same external influences—heat, cold, kicks, and bites. Certainly mosquitoes did not differentiate between legs. About Jo's legs there was something impudent and piquant, a devil-may-care attitude. She had, morally speaking, a wicked pair of legs.

"Take a couple of letters," he began in a dull, preoccupied voice.

"That would be amusing for a change," said Jo sweetly.

"Almost anything would be amusing for a change," he agreed. "Get on with it. This is to Mr. Benjamin Clarke. You have his address. Dear Ben." Peter's eyes strayed downward. "Dear Ben," he resumed.

"Dear Ben twice?" asked Jo.

"Once or twice," replied Peter. "It doesn't matter. He knows who he is. Dear Ben: Referring to our recent conversation about knees and legs——"

"Pardon me," smoothly interrupted the girl. "Did I understand you to say knees and legs?"

"Means and ways," corrected Peter.

"Were you and Ben discussing means and ways to knees and legs?" she asked him. "You've got me all mixed up."

"That doesn't matter either," said Peter. "I never discuss such subjects. You should know that."

"It would do you a world of good," she assured him.

"Please keep such advice to yourself."

It was at this moment that Jo became aware of the direction of her employer's intent gaze.

"Are you, by any chance, looking at my legs?" she inquired in a pleased voice.

"Yes," he answered. "One can scarcely look at anything else."

"You mean they're so attractive?"

"No. I mean they're literally all over the place."

"If I'm not being too bold," said the girl, "would you mind giving me a rough idea of what you think of them?"

"I don't think of them," he answered coldly. "I look at them the same as I would look at a chair or a desk or—or—the Pyramids."

"Go on," she said in a dangerous voice. "Why bring up the Pyramids?"

"I am trying to explain to you the impersonal attitude I take to your legs."

Jo sprang from her chair. Her face was flaming, and from her eyes fire flashed through two angry tears.

"And I'd like to explain to you," she said in a low voice, "the personal attitude I take to your words. You may criticize my typing as much as you please, but I won't allow you to say a word against my legs. Your Yolanda may be able to afford better stockings, but taking her leg for leg she's a hunchback compared to me."

"Aren't you getting your anatomy a trifle scrambled?" asked Peter in a collected voice.

"I'd damn well like to scramble yours all over the map," she retorted. "Hitting below the belt."

"Quite," replied Peter, coolly measuring her figure with his eyes. "I should say about twelve inches or more."

"I'm going to get out of this room," she declared, "and never come back into it again. If you want to hurl insults at me and talk in a low, lewd manner you'll have to do it outside where everyone can hear what a lecherous creature you are."

"On your way to your desk," he called after her pleasantly, "will you be so good as to ask Miss Bryant to stop in?"

"Sure," she flung over her shoulder. "I suppose you'll compare hers to Pikes Peak or the Empire State."

"I'll have to consider them first," said Peter.

The sound the door made when it closed had in it the quality of a curse.

CHAPTER FOUR

Riding to a Fall

BETTY BRYANT WAS NOT A BAD-LOOKING GIRL. PETER realized this when, a few minutes after Jo's impassioned exit, the young girl entered his office and stood waiting expectantly before his desk. Since the demoralizing revelation of his secretary's knees and legs Peter had begun to feel that he was looking at women through an entirely new and improved pair of eyes. Now, when it was almost too late to take advantage of his clearer vision, he was beginning to regret the opportunities he had missed in the past as well as those he would have to forgo in the future. The situation was nothing less than tragic. Life owed him many unclaimed women. The reprehensible blood of the elder Van Dyck throbbed rebelliously in his veins.

"Miss Bryant," he said, protecting sections of his features behind a letter, "I wish you would toss on your hat and buy half a dozen pair of stockings at one of the smarter shops in the district. Would you mind?"

Miss Bryant certainly would not mind. She would be glad to go to even greater lengths for Mr. Peter Van Dyck. She would, however, have been interested to know what clearly impure motives lay behind this unexpected request. From the little she could see of Peter's features she was convinced they did not belong to a thoroughly honest face.

"Have you any particular shade in mind, sir?" she asked him.

"Shade in mind?" repeated Peter. "Er—oh, yes, of course. Naturally." He laughed for no reason. "Flesh," he announced, coloring slightly. "I mean all shades. You know. All the fashionable shades. Youthful. They're for my Aunt Sophie. She has rather silly ideas—ambitions, one might say."

"Oh," said Miss Bryant. "So they're for your aunt."

"Yes," retorted Peter. "I said they were for my aunt. Why? Is it funny?"

"No. Oh, no. Not at all. I was wondering what size stocking your Aunt Sophie wears, that's all."

"Any size I give her," replied Peter, striving to maintain a casual note in his voice. "I should say about the same size as that Josephine Duval or any other girl her size."

"I think I understand," said Miss Bryant thoughtfully.

"I was very much afraid you would," remarked Peter as he handed the young lady several crisp notes. "And while you're about it, treat your own legs to a pair on the house," he added. "Fine feathers make fine birds, you know. Ha, ha! Capital!"

With her employer's false laughter ringing in her ears, Miss Bryant departed, wondering why she had never suspected him before of being mentally unsteady. These old families got that way in spots. Too bad.

When she had successfully fulfilled her mission and delivered the stockings to Peter, he summoned his secretary. Although she had flatly announced her intention of never entering his office again, Josephine Duval appeared almost immediately.

"What improper suggestions have you been making to that Bryant thing?" she demanded. "She's gone light in the head all of a sudden."

"I know nothing about that," said Peter. "She struck me as being an uncommonly sensible and willing young lady."

"Willing, no doubt," snapped Josephine, and laughed disagreeably.

"I particularly dislike the sound of that laugh," said Peter, "as well as the coarse implications behind it. Here are half a dozen pairs of stockings—pure silk stockings—all silk stockings, in fact. Yank a couple of them over your legs and let's hear no more on the subject. This has been a fruitless day, and it's not going to get any better."

Josephine took the extended package and tore off its wrappings. For a moment there was silence in the office as she examined the contents with an experienced and rapidly calculating eye. Presently she turned and looked darkly at Peter Van Dyck.

"And for this," she said, "I suppose you expect to own me body and soul."

"I'm not interested in your soul," Peter informed her curtly.

"Oh," said Josephine, momentarily nonplussed. "All right. It's a bargain. We'll let it go at a body."

"I have no idea what you are planning on letting go," Peter replied uneasily, "but I strongly advise you to hold everything. And please get it into your head that I have no desire to own either your body or your soul."

"How about a little loan?" Josephine suggested.

"Will you now go away and stop talking wildly," said Peter. "After all, I am your employer. You're supposed to be working here, you know, and not paying me little visits throughout the day."

Josephine looked at him furiously.

"You're going to own my body," she said between her teeth, "if I have to ruin yours in the struggle."

"An edifying picture," Peter dryly observed. "However, I shall keep on the alert."

"If they weren't pure silk I'd cut these stockings to ribbons."

"Glad you like them," said Peter mildly. "If I were you, I wouldn't carry them about with me in the office. People might talk."

"I'll stick 'em down here," she declared, thrusting the six pairs of stockings down the front of her dress, where they produced an interesting, not to say scandalous effect.

"If you go out there in that condition," observed Peter, "people will do more than talk. They'll swoon in your face. Even I, in full possession of all the facts, cannot suppress a pang of uneasiness."

"You're responsible for my condition," she flung back.

"Granted," replied Peter reasonably. "But I'm not responsible for what others might erroneously conclude was your condition."

"Anyway, here I go," said Josephine. "We have a secret between us now."

"It looks as if we have a great deal more than that," Peter replied.

"Nobody will notice anything if I go like this," the girl explained, placing her hands across her stomach.

"Oh, no," agreed Peter. "They'll merely think I kicked you in a moment of playfulness, that's all. Please hurry. It upsets me to look at you the way you are."

At the door Jo turned and glanced back at him.

"You can't tell me," she said, "you didn't have something else in your mind when you gave me these."

The door closed behind her, and Peter leaned back in his chair. He was wondering himself exactly what he had in his mind in regard to Jo Duval. Time passed while Peter sat thus steadily accomplishing nothing. He had contributed very little to the success of the Van Dyck coffee business that day. Presently he stirred and reached for his watch. After thoughtfully considering the time of day it announced, he compared it with the clock on his desk.

To make assurance doubly sure, he rose and, opening the door, glanced at the office clock. As he closed the door he got the impression that Betty Bryant was studying him with new interest. Perhaps there were others, he unhappily decided. Crossing the room to the window, he stood looking down on the narrow street. People were already turning their released expressions homeward. They were looking forward to a few hours of personal living, a few hours of individual freedom. Five p. m. was for them a daily declaration of temporary independence. Not so for him. He had to go home presently and let that damn cat out of the bag. He would much rather wring its neck. Was he not voluntarily thrusting his own neck into a noose for life? It was still not too late. Why not take a ferryboat to Staten Island and live among the trees somewhere? Why not cross a bridge and lose himself in a swarm of unfamiliar streets? Why not scuttle through a tube and seek oblivion in a waterfront speakeasy? There were any number of things he could do. As he stood there by the window, he became uneasily aware of the fog drifting through the street. Figures of men and women were cutting through it, zigzagging past one another, going north, going south, ducking down the side streets. Boys were whistling. Boys always were. Why? Why were they always whistling? From two rivers came the haunting voices of ships—tugs, liners, ferryboats, yachts going up to pleasant moorings. Foggy as hell somewhere. What sort of mooring was he going up to? An anchorage for life. Maybe something would happen. Lots of things could happen in a fog. He turned from the window, walked slowly to the hatrack, and collected his hat and stick. As he bade his office staff good-night, he felt he was saying good-bye. Josephine Duval had already gone.

The subway crowd was familiar, but not friendly. It was composed of individuals, each having tenaciously held ideas about his or her place on the platform. They knew where they wanted to go and how they wanted to go there, and nothing was going to stop them or change them or soften them. Looking slightly pained, Peter Van Dyck, with a delicate but nevertheless protesting arc in his back, allowed himself to be catapulted into a train in which he stood tightly wedged, suffering from a loss of both dignity and breath. He decided he was lucky to lose no more than that in such a frenzied stampede.

"If you don't stop doing that to me," said a woman's voice somewhere in the neighborhood of his chest, "I'll slap you in the face."

Peter's first reaction was to glance nervously about him to ascertain if the entire car had overheard the woman's intentions. Then he spoke in a low, reassuring voice in which was a note of appeal.

"I'm not doing it," he whispered.

"Don't tell me that," said the woman. "Can't I feel? There you go, doing it again. You're getting a lot for a nickel ride, mister."

"My God," thought Peter, striving unsuccessfully to remove himself from the woman, "what a thing for her to say!" Crouching over, he muttered to the top of a small hat, "Madam, I can't help it. I'm——"

"Do you mean you've lost control of yourself?" the woman's voice cut in.

"No," he protested. "I can't think of what I'm doing."

"I don't like to think of what you are doing," the woman continued. "Lay off, that's all. Do you want me to scream for help?"

Straining his neck down and to the side, Peter succeeded in getting a glimpse of his accuser. It was as he had been suspecting for the past few moments. She was there—Jo. Peter did not know whether to be relieved by this or alarmed.

"Don't go on like that," he pleaded.

"Don't you go on like that," she told nim. "Should be ashamed of yourself. Of all the things to do."

"But what in God's name am I doing?" he asked in desperation.

"To explain what you're doing would be even more embarrassing than to submit to it," she told him with elaborate dignity.

"It can't be as bad as all that," he said.

"I'd hate it to get any worse," she replied, "at least with so much public about, I would."

"It is too close for decency," agreed Peter.

"You seem to find it so," she retorted. "Suppose they knew at the office?"

"Knew what?"

"Never mind about what. You know perfectly well. I hate that sort of thing—that type of man."

"So do I," replied Peter earnestly. "The very idea is revolting to me."

"Then obviously, you don't believe in letting your left hand know what your right hand is doing," she retorted.

"Both of my hands are busy," he declared.

"Don't I know that?" said Jo. "I'd call them frantic. Only married couples should be allowed to travel in the subway during rush hours."

"What did you do with the stockings?" he asked her, hoping to change the subject.

"You couldn't get closer to them unless you put them on," she assured him.

"Then they're still in the same place?"

"Either there or hanging on my backbone."

"How ghastly!"

"It's your fault if they are," she replied. "Do you still intend to go through that mock engagement announcement?"

"Why not?" demanded Peter.

"Shouldn't think you'd have the nerve after this ride."

"Don't be silly."

"I'm not being silly when I tell you," she replied quite seriously, "that I doubt very much if you get yourself engaged today."

Peter glanced quickly down into her upturned face. In her eyes he read an expression of grim determination. For some reason her portentous threat or warning did not strike the disagreeable note one might have expected. Peter received it almost with a feeling of relief. In fact, he found in her words a fragile straw of salvation. If it would have served to delay the formal betrothal announcement, Peter would have welcomed a localized earthquake. So far as his engagement to Yolanda was concerned, he found himself strictly neutral. He was on the fence. It was not as if he wanted to call the engagement off definitely and forever. Peter simply did not know. Why had they not gone through with it several years ago, instead of waiting until the idea had grown stale? No. Yolanda had wanted to travel on the Continent unattached.

She had wanted to develop her art. She had wanted to enjoy her position as a much sought after débutante. She was one of those young ladies who wanted Life with a capital L, yet who would not know what to do with it should it come to her. She had wanted ever so many things and she had got all of them. And in the background she had also wanted Peter, Peter in a waiting capacity safely packed in ice. She was such a glittering, assured sort of person, so certain to be right, so well versed in all the social amenities. She would be quite a comfort when people called, as they inevitably would call, in droves—dumb, well-dressed, well-nourished, chatty little droves of really nice people. Peter wondered unhappily in his increasing morbidness what they were going to do with all the people who called. Where were they going to put them? How deal with them? The years ahead presented themselves to Peter as pillars in an endless hall lined with nice people who shook hands and chatted delightfully about non-essentials.

And all the while he was puzzling over these things, Jo was looking up into his troubled, rather sensitive face from beneath the heavy lashes of her amused but devoted eyes.

"Hang it all," he said at last, "why do you like me, anyway? I should think you'd fall for a truck driver or a professional wrestler or a strong man, or for one of those great big silent chaps who make the maximum amount of empire on the minimum amount of words. The movies are full of them. Look at me—I'm virtually a physical and mental wreck. Might just as well be an idiot. I catch cold almost always, my nose gets red in the winter and even worse in the summer—frost and sunburn vie for honors—I probably snore enormously and, as you know for yourself, I don't even know how many pairs of drawers I'm wearing half the time, whereas during the other half I daresay I'm not wearing any drawers at all. I'm quite impossible any way you look at it."

"I realize all that," she said, "but I bet you know a lot of dirty stories, and I fairly wallow in those."

Peter groaned spiritually. This creature was beyond belief—literally incredible. And to think that he had been in the same office with her for three whole years, and before that his father had been subjected to the same demoralizing influence. Perhaps that accounted for the old gentleman's perennial bloomings.

"Furthermore," the girl's voice continued, "professional wrestlers and strong men and those silent birds you mentioned are notoriously moral. They hold deep-rooted convictions and have exceedingly piggish ways. Now you—you're quite another proposition. Without realizing it you are so morally flexible that you must have been born corrupted. I'd much rather live amid physical ruins than stagnate amid moral perfection."

"Your sentiments and opinions do us both credit, I'm sure," observed Peter Van Dyck. "What sort of life are you planning for me to live with you—one of pillage, rape, and arson?"

"Pillage and arson, perhaps," she said briefly. "The other will not be necessary."

"Aren't you getting off soon?" asked Peter.

"Yes," she replied as the train lurched into Times Square. "Right here. Good-bye, for the moment, and don't be surprised at anything that happens. Remember, I'm on your side."

Peter's gaze followed her through the door of the train and out onto the platform. As she looked back at him Josephine decided she had never seen a more lost and miserable expression in any man's eyes. Being of a primitive nature, she still had room for pity. Her scheme for helping this man and at the same time helping herself crystallized there in her mind as Peter's train drew out. Tossing her shopping expedition to the winds, she boarded the next up-town express.

On her way to 72nd Street she revolved many desperate remedies in her mind. At the same time she found occasion to congratulate herself for having come to a decision while still in the subway, for thus she had saved the price of another fare. Jo was passionate about everything—even thrift.

CHAPTER FIVE

Little Arthur in Quest of Drawers

LITTLE ARTHUR'S AGGRIEVED MEDITATIONS ON THE GREATER advantages enjoyed by second-story men in providing themselves with the drawers of others had led him far afield. As a result of these meditations he had momentarily yielded to the temptation to stray adventurously a little outside the professional limits of his calling. Having established the fact that Central Park was virtually barren of loot of the smaller species, he found himself this afternoon wandering watchfully through the streets of the West 70's, his disarmingly mild blue eyes constantly on the alert for a convenient house to second-story. Once he had selected a suitable subject for his nefarious project, he had certain ideas of his own in regard to carrying it to a successful conclusion.

After tentatively weighing the pros and cons of an areaway that impressed his sensitive nature with its unmistakable air of good breeding, Little Arthur proceeded down it until it eventually terminated in Martha, one of the trimmest of the Van Dyck maids. The kitchen being unchaperoned at the moment, Little Arthur with his usual subtleness prevailed upon Martha to invite him in for a cup of tea. He achieved this by convincing the guileless maid that in him she was beholding not merely one of the offshoots but absolutely the very flower itself of depression.

Presently, seated at the kitchen table and made confidential by a cup of tea, the two of them were bending their heads prettily over the tepidly glowing allurements of a spurious ruby ring.

"Wouldn't be a bit surprised," Little Arthur admitted softly, "if that gem hadn't belonged in its time to one of them far-Indian potentates."

"No!" exclaimed young Martha. "You don't mean ter say? One of them redskins like?"

"How should I know," put in Little Arthur, "not ever rightly having seen the color of this here potentate's skin? May have been red. May have been brown. May have been as white as the back of me hand."

The back of Little Arthur's hand somewhat spoiled the effect of this ill-chosen comparison.

"That far-Indian potentate wouldn't have been so white,

at that," remarked the maid, Martha, prompted no doubt by that nasty streak which lies ever close to the surface in all members of her sex.

Little Arthur delicately removed his hand from the critical examination of the girl's frankly skeptical eyes.

"It's the hand of an honest man, at any rate," said he with a note of bitterness.

"Mean ter say this old potentate's hands weren't strictly honest?" Martha's large gray eyes grew larger and a little frightened.

"I keep telling you I never met this here far-Indian potentate," Little Arthur protested, amazed by the hopeless irrelevance of the feminine mind. "But you know how them potentates are."

"No," the girl admitted quite frankly. "I don't know much about potentates. How are they, now?"

"Well," replied Little Arthur, heartily wishing he had never brought up the subject, "you can't quite say how they are. They sort of take things when they fancy 'em—like women and gold and jewels."

"Maybe this jewel belonged to one of this potentate's women," said Martha in an awed voice. "Think of it! This jewel being on the hand of one of his favorite slaves. Guess she didn't need to wear much more than that."

Little Arthur embodied his disapproval of the trend of the girl's remarks in a slightly offended cough.

"I hope," he replied, "that the lady who wore that ring was a step above a harem hussy."

"What's a harem really like, mister?" Martha asked him wistfully. "I've often wanted ter know."

A gentle pink was finding its way into Little Arthur's ears. The conversation was becoming increasingly more difficult to maintain. Once more he endeavored to signify his disapproval through the medium of an especially refined cough.

"Shouldn't think you'd want to fill your head with a lot of truck like that," he observed with some severity.

"But I do, mister," pleaded the maid. "Go on and tell me. The movies make 'em fine."

Fearing lest refusal might endanger the outcome of his enterprise, Little Arthur compromised with his scruples as have many an artist before him. He made a brave attempt.

"Well," he began, "a harem, properly speaking, is sort of like a nursery only for grown-ups, yer understand. It's a place where you sort of have fun in and lark about."

"I knew you had fun," admitted Martha innocently, "but I'd never heard about that nursery part before. Sounds kinda dull."

From beneath eyebrows arched in pain, Little Arthur distastefully regarded the girl.

"It's like that," he said shortly. "Dull. Now about this here jewel. I——"

"Always thought I'd like to join one of them harem places," Martha interrupted dreamily. "Dancing all day and resting on piles of pillers . . . eating fruit and drinking wine and telling great big naked slaves to get a move on with them fans. Flies tickle something fierce when you ain't dressed for 'em."

Little Arthur's eyes were almost bulging from his head.

"Just a minute," he put in hastily to prevent further disgraceful admissions on the part of his alarming companion. "Let's get back to this here potentate's jewel."

He had no intention of allowing the situation to develop any further along its present lines. He had insinuated himself into the good graces of this girl with a definite object in view. He had staked his professional reputation to procure what he firmly believed to be the most personal article of a gentleman's attire. It was far beyond the scope of his operations to jeopardize the integrity of his own in so doing. To victimize the maid was one thing. To become her victim was quite another. He would leave that sort of conduct to his betters.

"All right, mister," said the girl. "What about that jewel?"

"Now you're talking," replied the little man, allowing a note of approval to rob his voice of its former austerity. "I'll let this jewel go for less than nothing because of the tea and all."

"And how much is that in money?" the girl inquired nervously.

"About two dollars," he confided. "And I should be shot for doing it."

Not for a moment suspecting how thoroughly the artful little man deserved to be shot, Martha rose from the table.

"All right, mister," she announced. "I'll run upstairs and get my purse."

"Where's that?" he demanded.

"Servants' quarters," she told him. "Top floor."

This suited Arthur's plans to perfection.

"Don't be long," he warned her as she turned to the service stairway.

The moment the sound of her tripping feet had died away in the upper regions of the house, Little Arthur deposited the ring on the table and silently hastened up the stairs. Attaining the second floor with a thrill of elation, he crept up to the nearest door and listened. Then, like a half-starved shadow, he faded noislessly into the room. It was a large, pleasant room—a man's room, he was quick to note—and heavy portières were hanging from the windows. Crossing swiftly to one of these, he looked out to ascertain the easiest means of exit. There was no easiest means of exit. It was a sheer drop to the street from every window. At that moment he heard the knob of the door turning. Little Arthur could not recall ever having listened to a more unwanted sound. Ducking round a table laden with bottles and a siphon, he secreted his small person with the deftness of desperation behind one of the portières. To have been released from his present predicament, not only would he have willingly sacrificed his prospects of ever obtaining the drawers of others but also tossed his own into the bargain as a gesture of good will.

Peter Van Dyck, ruffled by the world in general and the subway in particular, slowly entered the room. Little Arthur, catching a furtive glimpse of his expression, decided that here indeed was a man who would regard none too favorably any slight familiarity from a member of the criminal class. Why had he, Little Arthur, not been satisfied with the drawers that had served him so long and well? Why had he allowed shallow frivolity to cloud and confound his discretion? All the drawers in all the world were not worth the anxiety he was experiencing there behind that curtain.

Suddenly the small, unhappy man caught his breath. Good God! What next? The owner of the room was actually undressing. Could he be going to bed at this hour? What a glutton for sleep! But some men were like that, only they seldom stopped to undress. It was shoes and all with them. Suppose this chap took it into his head to sit up and read? He himself was given to that small relaxation after a difficult day. He might be forced to remain concealed until he fainted from sheer exhaustion. Little Arthur was becoming panic-stricken.

While this scene was working up to its inevitable climax, Josephine Duval was resolutely ascending the front stoop of the Van Dyck residence. Just what she intended to do when she got inside, she had not the slightest idea. However, Jo was one of the world's most successful opportunists. Something would be sure to turn up. Something always did. But what turned up at first was not any too reassuring. This was no less a personage than Sanders, the Van Dyck butler.

"Would you mind telling your mistress," said Jo, neatly

slipping past the great man, "that there's a lady calling on her who is in an interesting condition?"

Now this form of announcing herself, especially in view of the fact that it was entirely misleading if not worse, might strike some as being particularly ill-advised. However, Jo found herself in the position of one suddenly called upon to speak when there is absolutely nothing to say, and so she very wisely decided that it really did not matter much what she said so long as she said something—anything. Furthermore it cannot be denied that her opening speech was not without an element of surprise. Even the impeccable Sanders found the information difficult to take in his stately stride.

"Thank you, madam," he replied, his suavity jarred a note off key. "Has my mistress any special reason to be interested in your interesting condition, may I ask?"

"No," snapped Jo, "but her nephew has. And while we're on the subject you might as well know that I'm not a madam yet. I'm still a miss, if in name only. And you'd better carry on with a click. My condition grows more interesting by leaps and bounds. Soon it may become engrossing."

Sanders had encountered many extraordinary young women in the course of a long and inactive career but never one quite so buoyantly extraordinary as Josephine. She impressed the astonished butler as being actually exuberant over a situation which any properly constituted girl would have considered, if not desperate, at least disturbing.

"I quite understand, miss," he replied soothingly. "If you'll pardon me a moment I'll withdraw to consult——"

"And if I'm not here when you get back," Jo broke in, "you can look for my body in the nearest river—which one is that?"

"The Hudson, miss," said Sanders hopefully. "About three blocks over to your left as you go out."

"You're almost too eagerly explicit," Josephine observed as the butler turned a dignified back and departed.

As soon as he had gone, Josephine looked quickly about her. From a room opening off the hall about ten feet away came the hum of conversation. Also the sound of clinking glasses. The cocktail-tea party was already getting under way. Josephine was greatly interested. She yearned to see everything—how these people lived and what they intended to do to Peter, who by now had become in her illogical mind irrevocably her man. Regardless of the laws of decency and self-respect, she must prevent this engagement. The door to what appeared to be a clothes closet presented itself as the most obvious means to this end. As she slipped into this closet and closed the door behind her, she was still assuring herself that something would turn up to delay the formal announcement of Peter's betrothal to that snake-hipped Yolanda Wilmont. The closet was fairly commodious, but without light. Innumerable unseen coats were hanging on all sides of the girl—fur coats, storm coats, top coats, motor robes, and dusters. Thinking how grandly the rich lived, she disappeared behind the coats and temporarily withdrew from active participation in the destiny of the Van Dycks.

Abovestairs, in his room, Peter was wondering if the shower bath he fully intended to take was going to improve matters any. Did condemned men take showers before they faced the firing squad or marched to the chair? The only condemned man he knew anything about was himself, and what little he knew about him was hardly interesting enough to be told. However, things might be worse. He was not actually getting married today. There was always poison as a last resort. He wondered whether he should take it himself or give it to Yolanda.

And while these speculations were passing through Peter's mind, equally perplexing ones were engaging the mind of Sanders as he stood in the hall below and looked round for signs of the vanished Jo. Presently he shrugged his shoulders as if to dismiss the incident. Evidently the young lady had decided in favor of the river. Under the circumstances that was probably the most tactful arrangement for all concerned. In spite of her bold manner the young woman must have had some sense of the fitness of things. Had he said the river was three or four blocks over? He did not quite recall. Too many things to think about. By now she should be quite definitely drowned if she had not changed her mind. She had seemed like a determined character, if a little callous. There were other things to be done. Cocktails to serve. Sanders moved away, leaving the hall deserted.

Several times while undressing, Peter had approached dangerously close to the curtain behind which Little Arthur stood concealed. Altogether too close for the peace of mind of that small pickpocket. Now that his uninvited host was completely naked, there was the possibility he might be prompted by modesty to draw the curtains entirely. That was what Little Arthur would have done had he been in the same condition. Maybe the rich were different. Maybe they did not care. If he could only create some diversion, thought the man behind the curtain, some little distraction sufficient to occupy the other's attention long enough to enable one to get out of that fateful room.

What could he do? Peter had turned and was looking intently at the portière. Had he noticed anything, any slight, betraying movement? Little Arthur broke out into a gentle weat. Those eyes—those probing eyes. As soon as Peter looked away, the pickpocket's arm slid from behind the portière and withdrew with the siphon. Little Arthur had not the vaguest idea what he intended to do with the bottle, but at least it was better than having nothing at all, better than facing with bare hands an infuriated and naked property owner. Once more Peter's eyes strayed toward the portières. Why did he look at that one portière always instead of some other? Surely he suspected something. Yes. He did suspect something. He actually knew something. Once more he was approaching the portière. He was halfway across the room, and naked as a primitive man. Little Arthur was as much unnerved by what he saw as by what he feared. His grip tightened on the object in his hand. Two thirds across the room Peter stopped and, turning his bare back, reached down and meditatively scratched his leg as men will. This was a trick, Little Arthur decided. No man, unless fired by some sinister determination, would permit himself to appear in such an unfavorable light. Furthermore, the rich, if they took advantage of their opportunities, should have no occasion thus to scratch themselves. Little Arthur was not to be deceived. This was a trick. If Peter Van Dyck had been hoping to rattle the small criminal, he had virtually succeeded. To witness these preparations was even worse than facing the attack itself.

It was at this moment that Little Arthur was seized by a mad impulse, an uncontrollable desire to squirt the contents of the siphon on the exposed back of the busily scratching man. It was an impulse not difficult to understand. Virtually everyone is visited by it at least once in the course of his life. Some persons never outgrow it. To them a siphon and a naked back mean only one thing—immediate contact. At the moment Little Arthur had not sufficient mental stamina to resist any impulse. He raised the siphon, drew an accurate bead on the exposed surface, then pressed the lever. The liquid missile splashed smartly against Peter Van Dyck's back and broke into little cascades along the ridges of his spine. The effect was instantaneous. Peter snapped erect and looked wildly about him. Astonishment, shock, and indignation fought for ascendancy in his eyes. But his gaze encountered nothing enlightening. For a moment he feared for his reason. Was it possible that in his spiritual turmoil he had imagined himself under the shower? The water trickling down his flanks annoyed but reassured him. Then anger mounted within his breast. A Van Dyck would stand for no nonsense, especially a nude Van Dyck. The perpetrator of this outrage against his privacy and person must be concealed somewhere within the room. Probably behind one of those portières. Almost slithering with excitement, Peter warily advanced upon one of the hangings. That he had selected the wrong one did not rob his activities of interest. Little Arthur was interested and also a bit relieved. As a matter of fact he was even faintly amused. The idea of a naked man stalking an empty portière had its lighter side.

As Peter, quivering with purpose, sprang upon his portière, Little Arthur, quivering with no less purpose, sprang from behind his and sprinted to the door. Reaching this before Peter had time to turn, the flying pickpocket dashed out into the hall and slammed the door behind him. The sound of the door brought Peter back to action. Passionately cursing the portière, he sped across the room and threw open the door. The intruder was gone, obviously having succeeded in putting the front flight of stairs between himself and pursuit. This time Peter was right. Little Arthur, tossing discretion to the winds, had nipped down the first flight of stairs that offered itself to his frantic feet. For a brief moment Peter hesitated in the doorway, then, adding decency to discretion, he tossed them both to the winds and took up the chase.

On the landing he ran into Martha.

"Gord, Mr. Peter!" she gasped. "Whacha doing?"

"Running," said Peter briefly. He had no time for explanations.

"I should say," murmured the maid after his bare back. "Running wild like Adam hisself."

CHAPTER SIX

The Loquacious Closet

PETER'S DESCENT INTO THE FRONT HALL FORTUNATELY went unnoticed. More guests had arrived, and more guests were due to arrive. It was this latter possibility that brought Peter to a full and blinding realization of his position. For the first time he saw himself as indubitably he would appear in the eyes of others. He saw himself not as an innocent man seeking justice, but simply as a stark naked coffee importer, dazzlingly greeting his guests at the doors of his ancestral home. The picture was somewhat too vivid for his nerves. He delivered the soul of his craven attacker into the arms of divine retribution and flung himself into the clothes closet a split second before Sanders appeared to answer the summons of the doorbell.

Reaching out in the darkness, Peter's hand groped horrifyingly over a face. Now this is a decidedly disagreeable experience, perhaps one of the most disagreeable in the world. It is especially so when one is under the impression that there are no faces about. Even married people, after long years of propinquity, are frequently revolted when in the still hours of the night they inadvertently extend a hand and find themselves fumbling drowsily with the face of a mate. The same holds true even of one's mistress. One receives quite an unpleasant shock. With other parts of the body it is not so bad, but with the face, yes. It was certainly so with Peter. Had it not been for his nakedness, he would have emitted scream upon scream. Little Arthur, too, was far from well.

"Who are you?" demanded Peter, his voice hoarse with consternation.

"I'm Little Arthur," chattered a voice in the darkness. "You know, mister, the guy you was chasing."

If it had not been for the fact that every instinct in Peter's being cried out against further association with any part of Little Arthur, the man would have been strangled there and then in the blackness of the closet.

"Sorry I squirted the water on you, mister," the little dip began in mollifying accents.

"It doesn't matter really," said Peter with false politeness. "I was going to take a shower anyway. May I ask, though, what you were doing in my room?"

"I'm a burglar," replied Little Arthur, too depressed to be other than truthful. "But I wasn't looking for anything valuable. Only a pair of drawers."

"If only I had a pair myself!" muttered Peter. "And to think that just this morning I had more drawers than I needed—more than I could comfortably wear. What are you doing in here, Little Arthur?"

"The same thing as you, sir. Keeping out of the public eye."

A moment's silence, then Peter's voice, nervously: "You seem to be in front of me, and yet I distinctly feel you breathing heavily on my back. How do you manage that?"

"I'm not doing it, mister," said Little Arthur. "I ain't got strength enough left to do any breathing at all."

"No?" replied Peter, turning. "That's funny. Oh, my God! I'm surrounded."

He had thrust one of his fingers into Josephine's mouth, and she had instinctively bitten it for lack of anything better to do.

"Remove your finger from my mouth this instant," she gabbled furiously.

Peter's hand was quicker than the eye.

"What are you doing in here with Little Arthur?" he demanded, nursing his damaged finger.

"I hadn't thought of doing anything with Little Arthur," Jo retorted. "Don't even know what to do with myself much less with anyone else. He must have come in here after me."

"The dirty little crook!" said Peter. "I'll strangle him with these two bare hands right here in cold blood."

Little Arthur closed his eyes, yet still saw two bare hands floating through the darkness.

"Go on and do it," urged Josephine. "There are too many of us in this closet already."

"I don't want to be in here alone with you," Peter told her. "And the dead body of a criminal, perhaps."

"It won't make any difference so long as the body is good and dead," Jo explained.

"Oh, what a terrible woman!" Little Arthur chattered from his corner. "Where did she come from?"

"Don't know why you followed her in the first place," said Peter.

"I won't ever again," vowed the little man. "Didn't even know she was here."

"He's a nasty little liar," whispered Josephine. "He deliberately came in after me."

"Don't you believe her, mister," Little Arthur pleaded. "She's trying to turn you against me just as we were getting along, like. I know her game."

"Shut up, you rat!" the girl flung at him. "I'll claw your wicked tongue out."

"Don't let her at me, please, mister," Little Arthur put in. "She wants to get us both in trouble."

"We are in trouble," Peter reminded him. "Terrible trouble. Suppose someone should come barging into this closet?"

"I'll swear I was lured in," said Jo.

"On what pretext?" Peter demanded.

"A fur coat," she answered readily.

"Wouldn't speak well for your morals," he snapped.

"Nor any better for yours," she replied. "But if you don't like that, I'll say that the two of you dragged me in."

"Wouldn't put it past her, mister," warned Little Arthur. "She's a bad one, she is. Glad I can't see her."

"You horrid little crook!" shrilled Jo. "Where do you get off?"

"I'll have to ask you both to shut up," said Peter. "You'll be having the whole damn house in."

"Oh, dear," murmured Jo. "Here I am cooped up in a closet with a naked man and a thief. I don't know which way to turn."

"Well, don't turn this way," said Peter. "And how do

you know I'm naked? Oh, for God's own sake, is that your hand? I've been thinking it was mine all the time. I'm so upset. No wonder you know how I am."

In the darkness Jo laughed evilly.

"I saw your impassioned entrance," she gloated.

"If you don't keep your hands off, you'll see my impassioned exit," he retorted.

"All women seem ter be loose," muttered Little Arthur moodily, his thoughts reverting to Martha and the harem. "Weren't like that when I was a boy."

"You're no bigger than a nipper now," retorted Jo.

"Perhaps not," said the pickpocket, "but I got more sense. Why don't you keep your bold hands off the gentleman? He don't understand your common ways."

"I'll make them unmistakable," said the girl.

"What are we going ter do, mister?" Little Arthur asked hopelessly. "There ain't no good in her."

"Why don't you do something?" demanded Peter. "You got me into this."

"No, I didn't," the pickpocket protested. "I was trying to get away and you insisted on following me."

"Naturally," replied Peter.

"Must have wanted me mighty bad," observed Little Arthur, "to have followed me in your condition."

"I wanted to kill you," admitted Peter, "and I'm not at all sure I won't."

"Don't think about it any more," said Little Arthur soothingly.

"My, you're thin," said Jo in a surprised voice.

"Take your hand from my ribs," Peter commanded. "Haven't you any shame?"

"No," answered Jo promptly. "Not since you started in. This morning in the office you try to take off your drawers. On the way home you practically assault me in the subway. And now to cap the damn climax you follow me nakedly into a dark closet. How do you expect a girl to have any shame left when you act like that?"

"Is that right, lady?" asked Little Arthur, thinking that indeed he had got himself into bad company. "Did he do all them things, taking off his drawers and all?"

"Sure, I'm right," said Jo. "It was just his drawers this morning. That seemed to satisfy him. Now it's all or nothing. Don't know what he'll think of doing next."

"Hope he stops thinking altogether if he's going ter carry on like that," said Little Arthur, making no attempt to disguise his disappointment in Peter.

"Someone will have to do some inspired brainwork to think us out of this place," Peter announced to his unseen companions.

"Does your spine begin there?" Josephine suddenly asked in an interested voice.

"No," replied Peter passionately. "That's where it ends."

"Oh," said the girl rather hurriedly. "I'm sorry."

"Then why don't you keep your hands to yourself?" demanded Peter.

"Thank Gord it's dark in here," murmured Little Arthur. "I wouldn't know where to look if it wasn't."

"Throw the little beggar out on his ear," urged Jo.

"Think I'll get out myself, naked as I am," declared Peter. "It's better than staying in here and being explored like a map."

For some minutes Sanders had been evincing an unusual interest in the closet. Aunt Sophie, sailing from the drawing room with a group of guests at her elbows, chief among whom was Yolanda, actually saw the man with his ear almost if not quite pressed to the door.

"What on earth are you doing there, Sanders?" she inquired fussily. "You look as if you had seen a ghost."

Sanders nodded his sleek head wisely.

"I believe I'm hearing them, madam," he vouchsafed in

a low voice. "This closet suddenly seems to be endowed with the gift of speech."

"Nonsense!" the splendid lady tossed out. "You're running down, Sanders. Closets don't talk."

"This one does," Sanders assured her. "It carries on a three-cornered conversation in as many different voices, madam. One sounds strangely like a woman's."

"What?" exclaimed Aunt Sophie. "A woman in that closet? That is queer."

"Perhaps Sanders had better look," Yolanda Wilmont suggested. "Sneak thieves, you know."

"Sneak thieves are not given to holding animated conversations in closets," objected Mr. Prescott Gates who, because of his remote connection with a law firm, felt that his knowledge of sneak thieves was more extensive than the others.

"We're not acquainted with the habits of sneak thieves," Yolanda contributed coldly. "However, I do believe that closet should be investigated. There are several valuable furs inside."

"By all means," agreed Miss Sophie Van Dyck. "Open the door immediately, Sanders."

But the door, when Sanders endeavored to carry out this order, seemed inclined to argue the point. For several moments it quivered elastically like a thing of life and purpose in the hands of the butler; then, with a groan of utter despair which sounded hollowly in the hall, it flew partly open. Sanders recoiled as if from the pit of hell itself. Instantly the door closed of its own volition with a bang of remonstrance. Inarticulate sounds issued from the closet, sounds of whining protest.

"What on earth is it, Sanders?" Aunt Sophie demanded in a strained voice. "Sounds like an animal."

"Must I say, Miss Van Dyck?" asked Sanders in a cornered voice.

"Certainly you must," she retorted. "What would Mr. Peter think if he came home and found his closet full of strangers? He dislikes things like that."

Wondering in a dazed sort of way what things could be even remotely like the things he had momentarily glimpsed, Sanders looked speculatively at the door.

"Hurry, Sanders, What's inside?" Yolanda Wilmont asked insistently.

"Well, madam," said Sanders reluctantly, "there seems to be more in there than valuable furs at the moment. Looked like quite a gathering to me."

"Tell them to come out this instant," Miss Van Dyck commanded.

"I'd hardly suggest that, madam," said Sanders in a shocked voice.

"Here, Sanders," put in Prescott Gates. "I'll handle this situation. I'll jolly well make them come out, whoever they are."

"I strongly advise against it, sir," said Sanders. "Not with the ladies present, if I may say so."

"What on earth, Sanders?" exclaimed a young and rather swagger looking maiden whose eyes gave the impression of having seen about all there was to be seen in life. "Just for that I'll never leave until that closet has given up its dead."

"Why not tell us, Sanders," remarked a stout lady in cascades of lace, "exactly what you saw, and then let us decide?"

"Yes," agreed Aunt Sophie. "We're growing decidedly impatient with all this beating about the bush. Speak up, man!"

"Well," began the butler in a voice of academic detachment, "you see, there seems to be an entirely naked gentleman in that closet——"

"Impossible!" exclaimed Miss Van Dyck.

"I very much wish it were, madam," Sanders continued piously. "But that's not all. This gentleman has either been undressed by a lady or, having undressed himself, is about to undress her."

"Need you be so graphic?" inquired Yolanda.

"The picture was remarkably vivid," explained the butler.

"I wonder where they think they are?" Aunt Sophie wondered aloud.

"Certainly not at a private reception," observed the lacy lady, regarding the door with thoughtful eyes. "That is, not at a nice reception."

"What can they be doing in that closet?" Aunt Sophie continued, bemused.

"Practically anything by now," said the girl with the worldly eyes. "Especially if the gentleman has succeeded in carrying out his intentions."

"You mean in that closet?" Yolanda demanded incredulously.

"What's wrong with the closet?" demanded the other girl philosophically. "Many have managed with less."

"What a shocking situation!" murmured the lace-bedecked lady. "Shouldn't something be done? Can't you speak to them, Sanders—admonish them?"

"Certainly, madam," replied Sanders, his suavity regained. "How would you suggest wording it?"

"Why, tell them to stop, of course," Aunt Sophie snapped irritably.

"Stop what, madam," the butler inquired.

"You can be most exasperating at times for a man of your age, Sanders," Miss Van Dyck complained. "Tell them to stop whatever they're doing."

"But, madam," the butler patiently explained, "we're not sure just what they are doing. It would be pure speculation."

"Not so pure at that," put in the girl, "but it does seem logical, doesn't it, Sanders?"

"I must confess, Miss Sedgwick," said Sanders with becoming modesty, "I have never been in the same situation."

"No more have I," the girl retorted, "but I can use my imagination."

"I wish you wouldn't," Yolanda remarked frigidly.

Mr. Prescott Gates now felt called upon once more to display his greater knowledge of the seamy side of life.

"If they are professional sneak thieves," he advanced weightily, "I hardly think they'd endanger their chances by that sort of nonsense."

"What sort of nonsense?" Miss Sedgwick inquired with disarming innocence. "And what makes you call it nonsense?"

"Don't answer her, Prescott," said Yolanda.

"And all this time we're talking here," Aunt Sophie burst forth in a tragic voice, "God only knows what is going on inside that closet."

"Perhaps only God should know," replied the stout lady with the resignation of a true believer.

"I have an idea," Miss Sedgwick offered. "Perhaps a man and wife wandered into that closet and not being able to find their way out became so exhausted—you know, so discouraged about it all—they just decided to go to bed."

"Don't be childish, Madge Sedgwick," Aunt Sophie scolded.

"Well, at least, I've got 'em married," said the girl. "That's more than any of you have done."

"You said a 'gentleman,' Sanders," Aunt Sophie went on in a worried voice to the butler. "Are you sure he was a gentleman?"

"That's difficult to tell, madam," said Sanders. "He didn't have a stitch on."

"I can well understand that," Madge Sedgwick agreed sympathetically. "Without any clothes on there's not a scrap of difference between a sneak thief and a gentleman."

"I should think all naked men would look a little sneaky," the lady in lace unhelpfully contributed.

"There should be some distinction," Miss Van Dyck protested indignantly.

"Yes. It would be convenient on occasions to be able to tell at a glance," Madge Sedgwick remarked as if to herself.

"What did he look like, Sanders?" Yolanda Wilmont demanded. "Did you recognize his face?"

"I didn't see his face, Miss Yolanda," the butler explained.

"What did you see?" asked Madge with lively interest.

"His back, miss," said Sanders. "He turned it rather briskly, I thought."

"At least he had the instincts of a gentleman," remarked the stout lady.

"Oh, I don't know," Madge Sedgwick countered. "Even a sneak thief might have his little qualms."

"Did you recognize the woman?" Prescott Gates inquired.

"I got the impression I'd seen her before, sir," admitted the butler. "Looked very much like a young woman who was here a little earlier announcing she was in an interesting condition."

"Sanders, you keep the most extraordinary things to yourself," Aunt Sophie said with severity. "Do you mean to say you put this person in that closet to bear her child?"

"No, madam," Sanders smoothly replied. "I rather concluded she'd left to commit suicide. She was inquiring about the rivers. I gave her adequate directions."

"Maybe she came back to find out which was the deepest," Madge Sedgwick suggested.

"Heavens on earth!" exclaimed Aunt Sophie distractedly. "What are we going to do? Here we have a naked man in the closet and a woman going to have a baby or commit suicide or something even worse. Prescott, you're a man. Why don't you suggest something?"

"I'm going for a policeman," Mr. Gates replied with surprising decision as he hurried to the door.

"Should think a preacher or a doctor would do better

according to the circumstances," Madge flung after him, but Mr. Gates was already gone.

"That tears it," whispered Peter Van Dyck to his companions in the closet. "That unweaned ass has gone to get a cop."

"Gord!" breathed Little Arthur. "There ain't a pair of drawers made that's worth a pinch."

"Ah," came the voice of Josephine, "how about mine, Little Arthur?"

"Make her stop talking like that, mister," the small thief asked in an injured voice. "We're in a very bad spot."

"Don't tell me," said Peter. "I know it already, and I'm going to get out of my section at once."

"Don't mean ter say you're going out there in front of all them people the way you are?" the man inquired in an awed voice.

"Almost," Peter told him. "With the addition of this coat."

Fumbling in the darkness, he seized the first coat his hands encountered and squeezed himself into it. Fortunately for Peter's self-assurance he was unable to see how he looked. He was wearing a fur coat belonging to his Aunt Sophie. It was short but luckily full.

"Wait a second," said Josephine. "You're not going to leave me alone in here with that dip. I'm going to disguise myself, too."

"No fear," shot back Little Arthur. "I don't associate with the likes of you."

"Oh!" cried Josephine, enraged. "I'll strip him to the buff."

"What's that?" asked Arthur anxiously.

"I don't know," the girl replied, "but it must be awful."

"Will you two please stop bickering?" cut in Peter. "Or wait until I've gone."

"I'm ready," said Jo. "Go right ahead. I defy recognition."

"What have you got on?" Peter was interested enough to inquire.

"Goggles and a long duster," the girl said briefly.

"Let's change?" Peter suggested.

"Too late now," she told him. "We've got to hurry right along."

"Don't leave me here alone," Little Arthur pleaded.

"I'd like to leave you lifeless," Jo informed him.

"Almost wish you would," bleakly Arthur replied.

The policeman, followed importantly by Prescott Gates, arrived just in time to witness the emergence of Peter Van Dyck. What struck the officer as being especially remarkable about this odd affair was the length and bareness of Peter's legs. In real life Peter's legs were not really so bad. Though long and slim they were at least not distorted. They were just ordinary male legs, which are never much to get excited about. Now, however, protruding as they were from a woman's fur coat, they fairly screamed for attention. The officer's eyes responded. He could not recall ever having seen such peculiar-looking legs on either man or beast. In spite of this they seemed to carry their owner along busily enough as he made for the front staircase. Behind him trailed a strange object which at first glance did not appear to be entirely human. Josephine in goggles and duster hurried to the front door, where she was stopped by the officer, who told her, "Oh, no, you don't!" in what can only be described as a nasty voice. Little Arthur, apparently preferring arrest to being left alone with his thoughts, brought up a shrinking rear. Walking nervously on tiptoe, he started to follow Peter. Aunt Sophie's voice stopped him. Aunt Sophie's voice stopped everyone, in fact.

"Peter!" she cried. "Peter!"

"Yes, Aunt Sophie," Peter replied in a natural tone which contrasted strangely with his attire and which almost stupefied the policeman, who had expected something entirely different from such an object. "Yes, Aunt Sophie. Were you calling me?"

"Peter," continued the outraged lady, "what in the world have you been up to?"

"Nothing at all, Auntie," he assured her, growing more uncomfortably aware of a sea of upturned faces. "Merely getting ready, you know. Making little arrangements."

"Is that person following you?" Miss Van Dyck demanded, pointing a quivering finger at Little Arthur, shaking as unobtrusively as possible on the stairs.

Peter started visibly. He found himself extremely nervous. "What person?" he gasped; then, glancing back and encountering the mute appeal in the miserable little creature's eyes, his heart melted. "Oh, that person," he said hastily. "Yes. He's following me—how do you do, everybody." Here Peter thought it best to bow carelessly to those below him. "Yes, Aunt Sophie," he hurried on. "He's following me. I asked him to. He's helping me to get ready. My new valet. Do you like him?"

"Decidedly not!" exploded Aunt Sophie. "He has the face of a born criminal."

"Say," put in the policeman, "how many more of you are there in that closet?"

"What, officer?" said Peter. "How many more of me are there in that closet? No more at all. I'm the only one."

"Does your nephew happen to be nuts, lady?" the policeman asked Miss Van Dyck.

"No," Yolanda answered for the stunned woman, "but I fear he's suffering a little from overwork."

"Thank you, Yolanda," called Peter with a fearful smile. "But if you want to know, I'm suffering hideously from overexposure."

"The coat! The coat!" shouted Madge. "It's slipping, Peter. Look out!"

Peter snatched at the coat in the nick of time, then waved

lightly to the girl, who of all the group had not averted her eyes.

"Thanks, Madge," he called. "Wouldn't want that to happen."

"I wasn't anxious about it for myself," she replied. "I was thinking of your aunt and Yolanda."

"Thanks," Yolanda told her. "We are quite able to think for ourselves."

"Oh, very well," said Miss Sedgwick. "I don't care if he takes it off altogether and dances like a savage."

"No doubt," said the other sweetly.

"If it's all the same to you ladies," called Peter, "I'd prefer to keep it on. And I don't feel like dancing."

"My stockings! My stockings! They're gone!" burst suddenly from the object behind the goggles, making a frantic dash for the closet, only to be brought up in mid-flight at the end of the officer's arm.

"None of that," he said rudely. "You're staying here."

"Oh, am I?" Jo replied, dealing him a clever Gallic kick. "I want my stockings."

"Ah-ha," observed Madge Sedgwick, triumphantly. "Then he did undress her."

Probably because they assumed it to be a part of a policeman's duty, no one seemed to pay the slightest attention to the officer doubled up in anguish. That is, no one save Little Arthur, who, for the moment forgetting his own troubles in the presence of those of the law, was laughing weakly upon the stairs.

"Did it hurt much?" solicitously asked Peter, who from his Olympian heights had witnessed the incident.

"Hurt?" gasped the policeman, stung by the inadequacy of the word. "It's ruined I am to the grave."

"See what you've done to our police force," said Peter, looking down on Josephine clawing in the closet.

"Can't help that," she answered. "No low cop can come between me and my stockings."

"Oh, this *is* too disgraceful," Sophie Van Dyck informed all present. "Too disgraceful for words."

"Not disgraceful enough for my words," muttered Josephine. "Ah! Here they are—my stockings!"

As the girl rose with a wad of stockings in her hand, Sophie Van Dyck directed on her the full force of her attack.

"Young woman," she demanded, "did you tell my butler you were going to have a baby?"

"After being cooped up in that closet with your naked nephew," Jo replied indignantly as she stuffed the stockings back in their tender concealment, allowing one of them to dangle untidily down the front of the duster, "after being in there like that, I wouldn't be a bit surprised if I had a male quartet. Would you?"

Miss Van Dyck saw no good in being dragged into this discussion.

"May I ask if you have anything on beneath that duster?" she asked.

"What do you think?" replied Josephine. "What has he got on beneath that fur coat?"

As she pointed to the odd figure on the stairs, everyone looked up and decided it did not have much. Before the direct fire of so many calculating glances Peter shrank a little. By this time the injured officer had discovered he could stand erect.

"What are you laughing at?" he demanded reproachfully of Little Arthur.

"At them," said Little Arthur, pointing to the legs above him.

"What!" cried Peter, turning fiercely upon the pickpocket. "You lying little——"

"Don't say it, mister," Arthur pleaded. "I wasn't laughing at all."

"You'll be hysterical when I get you up before the boys," the assaulted policeman promised him.

"Aunt Sophie," Yolanda said in a low voice, "there can be no announcement today. This has spoiled everything."

"I agree with that," Aunt Sophie replied. "But just the same we'll carry on as if nothing had occurred. Take our dear guests back to the reception room."

"Hoorah!" cried Jo, tossing up her arms, the hands of which lay concealed well down in the sleeves of the duster. "You're saved, Peter. You're saved."

"Saved for what?" he asked her. "Another day?"

"For us, of course," she replied. "For me!"

"A living death," he answered.

"Gord spare you, sir, from that one," put in Little Arthur piously. "No matter what you've done."

The bell rang, and Sanders, as if arising from a long illness, admitted several guests. With startled eyes they regarded the group on the stairs, then transferred their gaze to the enigmatic figure lurking within the voluminous folds of the duster. It was peering at them like a strange bird from behind a pair of goggles.

"What's that?" asked a tall gentleman, his face growing pale beneath a fresh massage.

"Don't know," gasped a lady with him. "It's awful. And Peter Van Dyck is almost . . ." Her voice trailed away.

"It's charades, my dear" Aunt Sophie smoothly explained. "It's been such a lark, Yolanda, take them directly to the drawing room. Cocktails."

Yolanda did.

"Now, young lady," Aunt Sophie continued severely, "your conduct has been most disgraceful. I don't know what to do with you. Obviously you are a thief—perhaps even worse. You must leave this house at once, quietly and without further violence. You will, of course, leave our stolen articles behind."

"They're not so hot, anyway," said Jo.

"And they're not stolen," called Peter, momentarily feeling sorry for the small, defiant creature looking a little lonely in the great hall. "I'll explain everything, Auntie. You see, I'm sending those things over to one of my friends. He's going on a trip. Wanted to borrow them. Sent one of the maids—a fresh piece, I admit—but that's how she got here."

"But why is she wearing them in that ridiculous fashion?" Aunt Sophie persisted, her curiosity overcoming her eagerness to believe in any comfortable explanation.

"Oh, that," replied Peter, thinking quickly. "More convenient, you know. Doesn't have to carry them. Perhaps it even amuses her."

"Well, it doesn't amuse me," declared Aunt Sophie with conviction.

"Come, Little Arthur," said Peter. "Get me ready."

He paused and looked back at Jo, who had snatched off the goggles and was standing gazing up at him like a child about to be sent to bed; a child, Peter decided, who certainly should not be allowed to sleep alone.

"Good-bye, mister," she said. "And thanks for all the things you've done—even though you shouldn't have."

Jo made sure that Yolanda, emerging from the drawing room, overheard her parting remark.

"Hold on!" cried the officer. "Don't I make no pinch?"

"Pinch yourself, brother," said Jo. "You're sleeping on your feet."

The front door closed behind her.

CHAPTER SEVEN

Six Characters Embark in a Fog

WHEN PETER VAN DYCK CLOSED THE DOOR TO HIS ROOM his action was accompanied by such violence that Little Arthur, doglike at his heels, barely escaped bisection. Unlike a dog, however, the small, dishonest man emitted no yelp of protest. He merely stood looking at the door and thought of the policeman whose indignant voice still sounded discordantly in the hall below.

"Sanders," he heard Aunt Sophie saying, "take the officer to the kitchen and provide for him properly. Perhaps a bottle or so of that Canadian ale might help to relieve his pain."

Little Arthur's heart sank. Retreat was cut off in the rear. Ahead of him lay a decidedly delicate, not to say dangerous, interview. Squaring his thin shoulders, he raised a timid hand and knocked.

"Come in, you criminal!" a hoarse voice shouted. "Since when have you troubled to knock on doors?"

Automatically the shoulders resumed their former droop of nervous exhaustion as the criminal entered the room.

"Since when have you troubled to knock?" the voice repeated disagreeably. "Answer me that."

Arthur noticed with increasing dread that the owner of the voice was drinking whiskey straight in great gulps.

"Always knock, mister," he muttered. "Outa hours, that is."

"When not calling in a professional capacity," Peter added sarcastically.

"That would be silly," said Little Arthur on the defensive.

"You malignant germ!" replied Peter, his throat working horribly, Arthur thought, as whiskey splashed down its bobbing length. "You less than louse—worse than louse!"

"Mister," protested Little Arthur, for some strange reason feeling more hurt for the other's lack of refinement than for any reflection cast on either himself or his habits, "is that a nice way ter talk?"

"Perhaps not," said Peter after a moment's reflection. "There isn't any nice way to talk—not to you."

"But I'm only a pickpocket," the man modestly explained. "This was my first second-story."

Peter gulped down some more whiskey while considering this statement.

"How do you mean," he asked, "your first second-story? Are you trying to confuse me?"

"No, mister," said the little dip, "I'm giving it to you straight. This is the first time I ever done a second-story. I was only after some drawers—an old pair or so."

"You lie," Peter told him. "You know as well as I do you couldn't wear my drawers. They'd hang all over your little wizened legs."

"I ain't perticular," Little Arthur said stoutly. "Scrunch 'em on somehow, what with a pin or a string or an old nail, for that matter."

Peter thought this possibility over while absently redonning his recently shed raiment.

"You must be mad about drawers," he admitted at last, "and I don't care a damn if you are. Might be much worse. As a matter of fact, some nice, clean persons might even consider it creditable, Little Arthur, for a man to risk losing his shirt for the sake of a pair of drawers. But I, who don't care a snap of my fingers about either shirt or drawers, can't see it in that light."

"That's a powerful queer-looking pair you got on now," vouchsafed Little Arthur. "Orange stripes, no less! Can't say as I'd care a lot for them drawers myself."

"Critical, eh?" Peter remarked coldly. "Well, I'd like to know who sat you up in judgment on my drawers? You never had a pair of silk drawers on your mean little shanks in your life. Not real silk," he added, his thoughts reverting to Josephine Duval.

"No, mister," Little Arthur agreed. "I wear regular drawers—men's drawers. After taking a pike at them things,

I can see that all my trouble has been a sheer waste of time."

"Just for that," said Peter, with a whiskey glitter in his eye, "I'm going to make you wear a pair of my drawers, the funniest pair I've got, and believe me, I've got some funny ones. Much funnier than these," his voice trailed on as he rummaged busily in a bureau. "Ha! This pair's a humdinger. A regular scream. You'll go well in these. Wonder how I was ever so mad as to buy them myself. Red and purple grapes—bunches of 'em. A cute idea." He turned with the garment to confront the stricken eyes of the petty felon. "Down with those trousers," he grated. "Yank 'em off with a snap."

"But, mister," objected the shocked man, "I'd have to undress naked to put them things on. You see, I wear allovers like—long legs and all."

"Eh?" said Peter. "Oh, all right. That doesn't matter a bit. You can drag 'em up over your long ones. Make it snappy now."

"That wouldn't look right, mister." Arthur's voice was eloquent with reproach.

"You're going to wear these drawers," Peter told the pitiful object, "if I have to disjoint you to get 'em on. Hurry up, man. Don't make me lose my temper."

"If you make me put them dreadful drawers on," said the other, "I think I'll lose my mind."

"You'll lose more than that if you don't," Peter snapped, taking a step towards the man.

"Oh, Gord," whined the unfortunate creature, hastily removing his outer garments, "all this terror and disgrace just because I got a yen ter feel clean!"

"You don't look so hot, yourself," Peter assured him as he contemplated the homely lines of the battered union suit. "From the back you look simply shocking—worse than I ever thought a man could get."

Little Arthur spun round as if stung.

"Cut it out," he said in some confusion.

"Now yank these on right over them," commanded Peter. "Anything to blot out that awful sight. The back especially."

Little Arthur yanked them on, and Peter was vividly reminded of a medieval court chamberlain who had fallen upon evil days.

A knock sounded obsequiously on the door. Sanders entered on silent feet. Even his iron self-control was taxed to its utmost to restrain a slight outcry. All the human side of the butler cried out to inquire what inconceivable events were taking place in this room. However, his professional ethics forced him to present a passive face. In his eyes alone could be detected a faint gleam of revulsion. The expression in Little Arthur's eyes as he stood like a shamed maiden in a slave market, as well he might in his weird attire, defied all description. This was because Little Arthur, realizing the delicacy of his position, had bashfully lowered his gaze. Sanders cleared his throat behind a large fat hand.

"Beg pardon, Mr. Peter," he murmured. "Is this the new valet?"

"The very newest, Sanders," replied Peter. "I've been trying to get some conception of how I look in my own drawers. Never had the opportunity before. What do you think of them, Sanders?"

"Very nice, sir, I am sure," said Sanders, who prided himself on his esthetic reactions. "The background is a trifle dingy."

"Oh, that's all right," remarked Peter airily. "We can remove the background and have them washed."

"Burned," suggested Sanders.

"That ain't nice," broke in Little Arthur with a sob in his voice. "Call that there copper and let him take me away."

"I was instructed to inform you, Mr. Peter," went on the butler, disdainfully disregarding the little crook, "that Miss

Yolanda and your aunt await your presence below, sir. It is almost time to call the motor if you intend to cross by ferry."

"Why the ferry?" demanded Peter.

"Miss Yolanda finds the tube rather common, sir," said Sanders, and God only knew what the man was thinking. "She has decided objections to the ventilation."

Peter took another drink.

"Little Arthur," snapped Peter, suddenly brisk, "pack a suitcase for me—not for yourself, mind you, but for me."

"Me, mister!" protested the pickpocket. "Pack it like I am?"

"Certainly," replied Peter. "It will amuse me while I'm dressing. And listen to me, Sanders. Tell Miss Yolanda with my compliments that if she doesn't like the tubes she'll have to bear with the subway downtown. I won't drive or be driven in traffic on a night like this."

"I quite understand, Mr. Peter," said Sanders, and with a lingering glance at Little Arthur quietly withdrew.

"You oughten ter have let him see me like this," complained the little man in the large drawers. "It's more than flesh can bear."

"I think Sanders stood it admirably, taking you all in all," asserted Peter, "which is the only way to take you. Step lively with that packing."

Half an hour later Peter and Yolanda left the Van Dyck residence on foot for a week-end in New Jersey. Behind them came Little Arthur. He was bearing up as well as he could under the weight of two suitcases. Peter was a little drunk and Yolanda a little peeved. Peter's explanations of his conduct had been almost incoherent. He had expected her to take too many things for granted. Still, until the country had recovered somewhat from its protracted attack of melancholia she saw no advantage to herself in precipitating an open break with her fiancé, who was indubitably more than enough mad. As long as coffee remained in popular favor, she would put up with his eccentricities—humor them, in fact.

"The rest will do you good," she told him as they walked to the subway.

"I never find these house parties in the least way restful," replied Peter complainingly. "They wear me down a lot."

"I know, my dear," she said tolerantly, "but one must be seen. Especially persons in our position. Can't afford to stagnate, you know. Must carry on. In these bad times it is expected of us."

"You mean going to house parties, dinners, dances, and all?" incredulously Peter asked her.

"Obviously," she replied with the superior patience of a higher being.

"What good does that do?" the man wanted to know.

"Keeps society on an even keel. Offsets the influences of radicalism—communism," she assured him without batting an eye. "Shows the nation at large that the real people are not taking seriously all this talk about depression."

"Strikes me as being a bad excuse for doing even worse," observed Peter. "And as for stagnation, that's all you do at these house parties—stagnate. Not that I object to that, but I prefer to do it in my own home."

"You're such a child," said Yolanda, tapping him lightly on the arm.

Peter's reply to this was rotten but inaudible.

From the shadows of a building a small figure in a ridiculous duster watched Peter's progress with wicked but devoted eyes. When Little Arthur had lurched by with his burden, the figure discarded the duster and became an exceedingly well-built young woman. With a set face and a determined eye Josephine Duval proceeded to stalk her prey. She was bound for New Jersey herself. She might just as well kill two birds with one stone. And if she did not succeed in killing them, she could at least make them quite uncomfortable.

Josephine had a lovely body, but her mind was altogether bad. An ideal combination.

Ahead of her Little Arthur stumbled through the fog blowing in from the river. He was wishing he had the courage to drop the bags and run, realizing with a pang of regret that he could not make his escape with them.

That same evening Bishop Waller was gratified to discover that both God and his own inclinations coincided in calling him and his newly acquired jaegers to the state of New Jersey. Accordingly he decided to answer this call in person as well as in jaegers. Furthermore it was his ecclesiastical preference to approach this friendly state through the instrumentality of a ferryboat, which he earnestly hoped would be less crowded than the tubes.

"And Blakely," he told his man, at the same time striving to tune out of his voice an overtone of mundane pride, "be sure you put in an extra pair of those new jaegers—the spring-weight ones."

Blakely had hoped to be permitted to pack a pair of these new jaegers. He admired them tremendously. In fact, in his quiet humble heart of hearts he almost found the hardihood to wish that he too were a bishop so that he might be able to wear drawers similar to the man he served.

"They're an excellent pair, sir," he observed as he reverentially carried the new jaegers to the suitcase. "An excellent pair, if I may say so."

"Certainly, Blakely," beamed the Bishop. "By all means admire the drawers." He found himself greatly pleased. Crossing the room, he stood for a moment by his man and admired the drawers with him. "They are excellent in every, respect," he continued pontifically. "Honestly made and generously fashioned. I find them exceedingly comfortable."

"I'm sure you must, sir," agreed Blakely, his eyes involuntarily straying to the lower half of the Bishop as if endeavoring to visualize the ineffable comfort enjoyed by this man of God.

A few minutes later Bishop Waller departed. Stepping into a taxi, he instructed the driver to proceed with judicious perseverance to a downtown ferry slip. Then, with a clean conscience and a contented mind, he settled back in the cab and awaited future developments.

Bishop Waller had not long to wait. The future developed almost too soon.

At about this time Aspirin Liz, after a dust-mottled sort of day, felt herself deeply stirred by a craving for beer—beer and a little companionship over a table unspoiled by a cloth. She desired to relax for a while with the knowledge that a bar was within easy call, that she had merely to press her finger lazily on a bell to have her modest and essentially reasonable wishes filled to the brim, nay to overflowing.

In her youth, when she derived both pleasure and profit from her figure, she had sedulously aschewed beer. Now, when her once lovely body had become an expense without compensation, she indulged it affectionately for the sake of what it had been. She gave it beer up to and sometimes past the limits of its ample capacity. With grim satisfaction she plunged into it great sides of corned beef rising like rocks of Gibraltar from choppy seas of cabbage. She talked to middle-aged ladies of similar tastes, and discovered that, no matter how dissimilar their lives may have been, their interests in life were basically the same—a little rest, a little peace and quiet, food, drink, an audience, and a room of one's own where one could remove in comfort one's stays and shoes.

For Aspirin Liz the most satisfactory escape from the solitude of her four walls lay on the opposite bank of the Hudson. It was her custom occasionally to take a ferry headed for this bank and, arrived there, to seek out one of several waterfront cafés in which she was both known and admired for her true worth—a good, solid, level-headed woman with a sincere fondness for beer and a capacity to hold it.

After a day devoted to aspirin, the retired model felt she owed herself beer. And this is an excellent way to feel—one of the most satisfactory feelings extant. Many persons want beer, and almost as many drink beer, but it is given to few—and then very rarely—to be convinced that not only do they want beer but that they actually deserve beer, need it, in fact.

Therefore, it was with a feeling of rectitude almost approaching the self-sacrificial that Aspirin Liz prepared her face, adjusted her hat, shrugged her hips into proper working relations with her corset and, after looking both for and into her pocketbook, departed in the direction of the river.

Thus it came about that the same ferryboat was enabled to set at naught the various plans and prospects of a diversity of characters. Even more. It was given to this ferryboat to mingle the interests and alter the destinies of persons whose lives had hitherto developed along seldom-intersecting paths.

And as these several characters converged upon this ferryboat, the fog blew in their faces and blanketed their lungs. Figures swift with purpose lived jerkily for an instant in the eyes of others, then faded out. Trucks tunneled through wet fluff and dragged a hole behind them. Sound and light were muffled. Distance ceased to be. Each man carried with him the boundaries of his universe. Out there on the river a little hell of whistles dwelt in the heart of the fog.

The ferryboat drew out. Mist rolled down on its exit. A

sharp report and a spit of fire. Then fog where a figure had stood—a half-crouched shape peering in the direction of the ferryboat now unseen.

There were very few passengers who ascribed the report of the gun to a cause other than the back-firing of an automobile.

Little Arthur was not one of these.

CHAPTER EIGHT

A Shot in the Arm

IT REALLY DOES NOT MATTER WHO FIRED THE SHOT OR AT whom it was fired, save for the fact that it caused Little Arthur to fall promptly to the afterdeck of the outgoing ferryboat and to remain there, to all intents and purposes a dead pickpocket. And let it be added that no one was more convinced of this fact than was Little Arthur himself. To begin with, the day had proved too much for his delicately organized nervous structure. Add to this a frail body and two suitcases, and it immediately becomes evident that Little Arthur was in no condition to stand a great deal more of anything. In short, this pocket edition of petty larceny was through—a broken reed.

At the same moment that his newly acquired valet fell to the deck, Peter Van Dyck lurched a little as a stinging sensation manifested itself in his left upper arm. This he promptly dismissed in favor of peering down into the face of the stricken man. It was not much of a face to peer down into—in truth, it was a face he would much rather not have seen at all. From the unprepossessing expression Little Arthur turned to the world, it was obvious he had been mortally wounded.

But what creature in the world was so lacking in aspiration as to want to wound Little Arthur? At his most vigorous moments the small felon was only half alive. This did not mean that the man responsible for his death would be regarded by law as only half a murderer. Not at all. Peter in his heart swore that if he ever discovered who had fired the shot he, Peter Van Dyck, would make it his business to see that the wretch was regarded as being something more than a murderer. In the short time Little Arthur had been with him, Peter had formed a sort of watchful yet commiserating attachment for this unreliable visitant from the underworld. It was one of those inexplicable affections that defy all natural laws, because it was far from natural to be fond of Little Arthur. Most people found it impossible. But Peter was not like most people. He was a great deal worse than those who knew him suspected, and at the same time much better. They had been through a lot together in a few crowded hours, he and Little Arthur. They had suffered much. Side by side they had passed through humiliation and public disgrace.

With a sudden pang Peter thought of the drawers he had forced upon the now lifeless legs. Then came another thought—a worse one. What would the undertaker think about those drawers? Would the man be able to survive the shock? Would he be able to approach those drawers in a purely professional capacity or would he consider them in the light of a personal affront? No undertaker, no matter how case-hardened, would be able to regard them with indifference. No, those drawers presented a problem. Peter felt a little responsible. Life was funny—always letting one in for things.

While these thoughts were flashing through his mind, a small but keenly interested crowd had collected round Peter and the fallen man. Peter knelt down and began to examine him. There was no mark of a bullet wound. No sign of blood.

"Who pipped him, mister?" asked a man's hoarse voice.

"Who did what?" Peter inquired.

"Pipped," replied the voice. "You know—gave the little bloke an airing."

"If you mean who murdered this poor devil," said Peter, strongly objecting to the speaker's language, "I wouldn't be surprised if it were you. Gave him an airing! Is that any way to speak of a man shot down in cold blood?"

"Where's the cold blood?" another spectator morbidly wanted to know.

"There ain't a speck on him," announced still another spectator disappointedly. "Not a speck. And blood ain't cold to begin with, even a silly-looking geezer's like that."

Peter was moved to reply.

"Don't let's go into the temperature of his blood right now," he observed with what he hoped was withering sarcasm. "You'd look silly yourself if you were murdered, and I'd feel greatly pleased."

"No, mister," answered the other. "I'd look plain scared."

Dismissing this person as unimportant, Peter endeavored to turn Little Arthur over to ascertain if he had been shot from behind. Once more he felt a stinging sensation in his left arm.

"Yolanda," he called, for the first time remembering his fiancée. "Would you very much mind giving me a hand with Little Arthur? He's been shot."

"I wouldn't touch Little Arthur with a pair of tongs," Yolanda coldly replied from the outer fringe of the crowd. "I am waiting for you to take me to my seat."

"I'll help you," said a familiar voice, as Jo knelt down beside him. "Aren't you strong enough to turn the little blighter over yourself?"

Peter tried without success to conceal his relief when his worried blue eyes looked into the warmly brown ones of Josephine.

"I'm strong enough," he muttered. "Merely a little nervous."

"I get you, mister," the girl replied in a voice that denoted long years of close companionship. "Let's go."

"This isn't a sporting event," said Peter. "Don't be so snappy about it. You'll roll him off the boat."

Together they turned the still figure over. Peter was unable to find any sign of bullet marks. He had been cowardly enough to leave the trousers for Jo to examine. This did not appear to gag her in the least. Several heads were peering down interestedly over her shoulder.

"From the holes in them pants," said an awed voice, "it looks like he'd fairly been riddled with bullets."

"Must have been a machine gun that pinged him in the pants," another observer declared.

Peter also objected to the use of the term "ping." However, he refrained from protesting, realizing that these callous persons must have cut their teeth on lethal weapons and played tag with machine-gun bullets.

"If he was hit by a machine gun," said Jo in a brisk voice, "the bullets must have balked at his drawers. From the little I can see, I don't much blame them at all."

"Those are my drawers," objected Peter.

"What are your drawers doing on him, mister?" a deeply interested voice inquired.

Peter looked pained.

"Does it matter," he asked, "what my drawers are doing on this man? He's been mortally wounded. That's what matters now. Whether my drawers are off or on him makes absolutely no difference. In fact," he added with a touch of bitterness, "it doesn't very much matter if he's wearing any drawers at all."

"Well, a guy's got to wear some sort of drawers," retorted the rebuked spectator in an injured voice.

"Not the sort I see bits of," objected another.

Josephine's calm voice cut short Peter's reply to this fresh insult.

"Why do you let yourself become involved in these futile discussions?" she asked. "There might be some life left in the little crook yet."

They returned the body to its former position and looked at it with baffled eyes. Peter's left hand brushed against the pale face. Instinctively he drew his hand back. Little Arthur's face presented a red smear.

"Gord," a voice whispered, "the little feller's just beginning to bleed. How do you make that out?"

"Ain't bleedin' from no hole," said another member of the helpful gathering. "Must be bleedin' through his pores."

"How do you mean," a third voice inquired, "bleedin' through his paws? He ain't no dog."

"Didn't say he was a dog," the second voice snapped back. "Don't have to be a dog to bleed through your pores."

"But you got to be an animal," the other announced triumphantly. "I ain't as dumb as all that."

"I mean the pores of his skin," the second speaker replied somewhat wearily.

"Never knew skin had no paws," said his stubborn opponent.

"You keep thinking of dogs' paws," the second man replied almost pleadingly, "while all the time I'm talking about skin pores—tiny little holes."

"Well, why don't you say little holes," the persistent party demanded, "instead of using a lot of foreign language?"

"Would you believe it possible?" Peter asked Josephine in a low voice. "And in the presence of death, at that."

"The trouble with you," said the girl, "is that you let yourself get dragged in. You're just as dumb as they are. Help me——"

She stopped suddenly and looked at a dark stain on the left sleeve of Peter's coat; then her eyes sought his hand. Blood was dripping slowly from his knuckles. For a moment her hand flew to her mouth, stifling a little cry. Then she said quite calmly, trying to keep her feelings from flooding through:

"You've been shot in the arm, Mr. Van Dyck."

"Me?" inquired Peter. "That's odd. My arm does feel a bit funny now that I come to think of it."

"What I want to know," put in a fresh voice, a rough argumentative voice, "how can this guy bleed when the other feller's shot?"

"Perhaps the bullet went clean through the little feller," a spectator explained, "stopping on its way first to kill him, and then bunged into this other bloke."

"Knew it wasn't his paws," an all too familiar voice put

in. "He ain't shot at all. Them holes in his pants are just natural holes, worn out, like."

"Mean to tell me," another man demanded, "this big guy gets shot and the little one falls down for him? It ain't reasonable."

"I don't mean to tell you nothing," the first voice cried excitedly. "Wasn't talking to you anyway. Just making a harmless suggestion."

"You mean useless," sneered the other.

By this time it was Peter's turn to become indignant. He looked darkly upon the recumbent form of Little Arthur while Josephine did things to his arm.

"Then that dirty dog of a thief," he said as if to himself, "has been having a nice long rest while all the time I've been shot in the arm and feeling sorry as hell for him."

"If you will select your valets from the scum of the underworld," Josephine told him, looking closely at Little Arthur, "you must expect things like this to happen."

"Nobody could have expected this," said Peter.

"Say, mister," put in a voice admiringly, "you must be pretty used to bullets if you don't know when you're shot."

"Either that or he's just plain dumb," another passenger explained. "I'd damn well know if I was shot."

"I damn well wish you were," grated Peter; then, turning to the girl beside him: "I've a good mind to pull down his trousers and see if he hasn't been shot. Something's surely wrong with him."

"Go on," replied Jo. "Pull his trousers off for all I care."

Whatever the part of Little Arthur it was that remained alive must have been the modest part, for at the mention of his trousers his hands clutched them firmly and his eyes snapped open.

"None of that," he got out weakly but distinctly. "Them pants are up for good."

"Ain't you even shot, buddy?" a voice called out.

"How do I know?" Little Arthur answered. "I heard a shot and felt its breath."

The interrogator laughed ironically.

"I guess you're O. K.," he said. "To hear a shot is one thing, and to feel a shot's another. You just fainted from fright."

"Oh, yeah?" retorted the small man, sitting up with an indignant snap. "Well, this shot didn't sound like no lullaby to me. It didn't exactly croon in my ear, if yer get what I mean. You'd of fainted, too."

Little Arthur turned a pair of injured eyes on Peter, whom he regarded in the light of a patron and protector, but he found scant comfort in that quarter.

"If you've settled your discussion entirely to your own satisfaction, Little Arthur——" Peter began coldly.

"Oh, I don't mind the likes of him," the recovered crook assured Peter.

"That's good," continued Peter with false solicitude. "But as I was saying, do you think it would inconvenience you too much if you got yourself to hell off that deck and looked for those two bags?"

"Can't you hunt 'em up yourself while I'm getting my breath?" was the pickpocket's reasonable suggestion.

"Little Arthur," replied Peter, a feverish glitter burning in his eyes, "I'm afraid you don't quite understand the position. By rights I should be lying down where you are and you should be where I am. In other words, while you have been taking your ease on the flat of your back I've been slowly bleeding to death looking for your wound, you craven-spirited, low-down, grubby little snatch-purse. Is everything quite clear? Get up, damn your eyes."

Little Arthur rose hastily from the deck.

"Mean ter say you're shot, mister?" he asked nervously.

"Sure, I'm shot," growled Peter, "and have been shot ever since this ferryboat shoved off a couple of days ago."

"Then why are you standing up on your feet?" the small thief incredulously inquired.

"We all can't lie down on our backs," Peter told him with due bitterness. "You got there first. Find those suitcases and come inside. I'm getting weak."

Before they moved away, Josephine found an opportunity to add to the pickpocket's mental unrest.

"And if anything happens to Mr. Peter," she assured the small man, "anything serious, that is, you're going to spend the rest of your life flat on your back in jail, and I'm going to put you there."

"Gord, lady!" said Arthur. "Don't feel that way. I ain't done a thing."

"No," she replied coldly, leading Peter away. "And you look as if you never will, you dip."

Yolanda met them at the entrance of the women's section of the cabin.

"It's taking terribly long to get across," she complained; then coolly surveying Josephine: "You have met a friend, I see, Peter."

"Don't you remember me?" Jo asked her sweetly. "I was the young lady behind the goggles. Your fiancé was nude with me in the closet."

"Heavens!" exclaimed Yolanda. "I should think you'd be ashamed to admit it. Are you really going to have a baby?"

"Several, I hope, some day, but not today," said Jo. "You see, Miss Wilmont, your quondam fiancé has been wounded."

"Why do you say quondam?" asked Yolanda. "Mr. Van Dyck is still my fiancé."

"You mean—after all that went on in that closet?"

"Would one of you mind taking a look at this arm?" Peter edged in weakly.

"Just a minute," retorted Yolanda. "What did happen in that closet, now that this woman has brought up the subject? I insist on knowing."

"In detail?" Jo inquired.

"Don't be common," snapped Yolanda. "I demand a plain statement from Mr. Van Dyck."

"Well," said Josephine with a shrug of her charming shoulders, "we might as well confess, Peter." She turned to the waiting girl and extended her outspread hands in a helpless gesture. "The usual thing," she said. "You know—the usual thing."

"I think I do know," replied the other, "but I certainly did not know it was the usual thing. Is she speaking the truth, Peter?"

"Well, didn't you see for yourself?" Jo cried in exasperation. "He was as naked as a coot, wasn't he? What else but the usual thing?"

"It might be usual with you," said Yolanda, "but I didn't think it was with Mr. Van Dyck—especially in a closet. Is it, Peter?"

"Eh?" asked Peter. "What's that? Oh, no. Certainly not. Most unusual in a closet—almost unthinkable."

"There you are," said Josephine with finality. "He admits it. Says it's unusual, but only in a closet, mind you."

"I want to sit down," said Peter. "Aren't either one of you going to do a thing about this arm?"

"I'll look after you in a minute, Peter," Yolanda told him.

"No, you won't," said Josephine. "After all that has passed between us, that is my privilege."

"My dear young woman," replied Yolanda, "you have no official standing."

"I can hardly stand at all," said Peter. "I'm going to sit down before I fall down."

Finding a place on the long seat, he sank wearily down beside a stout, neatly arrayed woman with an anticipatory expression in her eyes. Although Peter did not know it at the moment, this woman was thinking entirely in terms of beer. So engrossed had she been in her thoughts, so spiritually steeped in beer, as it were, she had failed to notice how long it was taking for the ferryboat to nose its way across the fog-piled river. Beneath her breath the woman had been humming "California, Here I Come"—an old favorite with Aspirin Liz. Peter's near collapse on the bench beside her drew the thoughts of the bemused woman back to her present surroundings, which were not nearly so congenial as those of a waterfront café. She gave the wounded man a quick survey, then turned halfway round on the bench and faced him. Her eyes were fixed on the dark, moist stain on his sleeve. Liz promptly drew the logical inference. Here was a wounded gunman who with the invariable delicacy of his kind refrained from drawing attention to his little contretemps. From the appearance of this gunman, racketeer, gangster, or whatever his class or creed, Aspirin Liz concluded that his present contretemps was something more than a little. The man looked downright bad. Aspirin Liz, with the quick comradery of her training, was worried about him.

"In trouble?" she asked in a low voice.

Peter started nervously. Liz attributed the movement to guilt.

"Yes," he muttered. "Terrible trouble. Shot in the arm."

"Are you asking for a shot in the arm?" Liz asked him. "Or have you been shot in the arm?"

"Yes," said Peter. "I've been. Never take dope."

"Good," replied Liz. "That's one thing you've missed, anyway."

"What do you mean?" demanded Peter. "Did you take me for a dope fiend?"

"Never can tell," said Liz. "Ought to do something about that arm."

"What should I do about it?" asked Peter.

"Take it out of its coat sleeve and shirt, for one thing, then take a look at it."

"In front of all these people?"

"Why not? Never been in your shirtsleeves before?"

"Much less than that," said Peter, thinking back over the past few hours. "You might not believe me, madam, but I've been dashing about naked."

Liz's opinion of the man underwent a quick change.

"Oh, I see," she said. "That explains it. Then you're not a gangster?"

"Certainly not!" indignantly.

"Sort of shot in the line of nobody's business," said Liz. "In the pursuit of pleasure, so to speak. Are all husbands born with gats? Come on. Off with that coat."

"It wasn't that," complained Peter as she helped him to slip out of his coat. "Not what you mean at all."

Josephine and Yolanda, having succeeded in giving each other thoroughly bad tempers, presented themselves before Peter at this moment.

"What did I tell you?" demanded Jo, pointing a finger at Peter. "There he goes again. Getting undressed already, and I bet he hasn't known the woman five minutes."

"You viper!" said Peter. "You'd rather let me bleed to death than stop telling lies."

"I see you brought your trouble with you," observed Liz in level tones. "Those two your molls?"

"Not both of us," said Jo promptly, with a nod indicating Yolanda. "She is. I'm just his fancy lady."

"What am I?" Yolanda demanded.

"It doesn't matter," replied Aspirin Liz with an amused smile. "I don't care if you're a couple of nuns. This man's been wounded. You can wash your dirty linen later."

"Dirty linen!" put in Yolanda disdainfully. "Peter, am I to be insulted in your presence?"

"Yes," said Peter, disgusted. "You are. I'd like to do it myself."

"You have," replied Yolanda.

"And speaking about linen," Jo tossed in, "I know the color of his drawers." Peter groaned aloud at this. "That," continued the girl, "should be enough to convince you of the irregularity of our relations. They're not linen, his drawers. They're silk—all silk with orange stripes. Look for yourself, if you don't believe me."

"Is that true, Peter?" Yolanda demanded.

"Oh, I don't know," he answered distractedly, flinching beneath the investigating hands of Liz. "Maybe she does and maybe she doesn't. I forget myself. Why don't you drag my trousers off and get my damned drawers witnessed by a notary public?"

"Apparently," remarked Yolanda, "you don't care what woman undresses you so long as you get undressed."

"No," gritted Peter. "I like myself that way."

At this moment an impressive gentleman in clerical attire introduced himself to the contentious group.

"I was told a passenger had been shot," he began as if passengers were always being shot. "Can I be of any help?"

"Well," Jo replied, favoring the Bishop with a glowing smile, "he's not quite ready to be buried yet, but if this boat doesn't land somewhere soon you may have the pleasure of chucking him out at sea."

Bishop Waller permitted himself a faint smile, then stooped over and examined Peter's arm while Aspirin Liz looked at him with respect bred of the awareness of a slightly dappled past. Soon the two of them were working in complete accord to staunch the wound and bandage it, Liz acting in the capacity of water carrier to the man of God. When it came to procuring a bandage she promptly solved the difficulty with a coy look at the Bishop.

"I can see those two ladies don't wear them," she said

reprovingly, "but I do and always have and always will. Here goes."

Turning her back on the Bishop, who in justice to his exalted spirit was not at all interested, she did some considerable ripping. Her face flushed from exertion rather than from the inquiring scrutiny of several dozen passengers who sat patiently following her movements with the dull curiosity of the mentally vacant, she turned back to the Bishop and offered him a strip of cloth. This he accepted with a word of dignified commendation, then bound Peter's arm.

"Under the circumstances," he said when his task was finished, "this is about the best we can do, but the moment you get ashore, sir, I strongly advise you to see a physician to guard against infection. May I ask how the unfortunate accident occurred?"

"Merely one of the commoner risks of contemporary life in America," said Peter. "A stray shot, you know."

"Exactly," replied the Bishop. "Today one can hardly telephone without having the booth shot from around one."

He seated himself beside Peter with the air of a man both able and willing to watch the whole night through.

"Most people in telephone booths deserve to be shot," Josephine declared. "It's the only way you can get 'em to come out."

Bishop Waller received this bloodthirsty sentiment with unexpected approval. He had frequently felt that way himself about people in telephone booths, but had never gone so far as to put his feelings into words.

"Of course," he said judicially, "one's attitude may change considerably according to whether one is doing the telephoning or the shooting."

"That's so," replied Jo. "Hadn't thought of that."

The Bishop's smile embraced her.

"Of course, my dear," he said. "Such minor considerations escape us all at times."

Hardly had the Bishop rounded off his sentence as such gentlemen will and must, when the ferryboat fairly tore its heart out in a protesting blast against fate in the guise of fog. As the engines sent chills along its timbers the reversed propellers bit back into the hidden water. From dead ahead came the answering scream of a half-crazed whistle. Danger ten feet off. Passengers ran to look at it, faces pressed against the windows. Eyes too filled with the wonder of ignorance to know they should look frightened. Waiting . . . drifting smoothly . . . then a soft, silly bump, a mere touch in the fog.

"Well, your reverence," said Aspirin Liz, "there's one of those minor considerations we didn't quite escape."

"Bishop Waller, madam," the excellent man informed her calmly. "Episcopal bishop of the Eastern States. And should this present consideration prove a little less minor than we would like it, let us face it with the fortitude and courage of true Christians—civilized Christians, that is."

Even at this serious moment Bishop Waller insisted on stressing that nice distinction existing between civilized Christians and savage ones—those who always wore drawers and those who gleefully discarded them after the closing hymn.

A small figure between two suitcases was taking up a great deal of room as it staggered across the cabin towards Peter Van Dyck.

"Here's your bags, mister," gasped the pickpocket, supporting himself between them.

"Thank you, Little Arthur," said Peter. "But we have neither the time nor privacy to dress before sinking, I fear."

"Are we doing that?" the small man asked in an even smaller voice.

"You had best prepare yourself to meet your God either now or a little later," Bishop Waller told the pickpocket in a gentle voice.

"If you don't mind, your honor," Little Arthur chattered, "I'm going to pray to God to meet Him much later—with all due respect to Heaven and Himself."

"You'll never meet Him at all, you thing!" Josephine assured him.

"Peter, please do something," Yolanda burst out. "My nerves are on an edge."

"Don't worry," said Liz brightly. "They might be all wet, you know."

"Ugh!" gasped Little Arthur. "What are we going to do?"

Then a great voice drilling down through the fog told Little Arthur in no uncertain language exactly what to do.

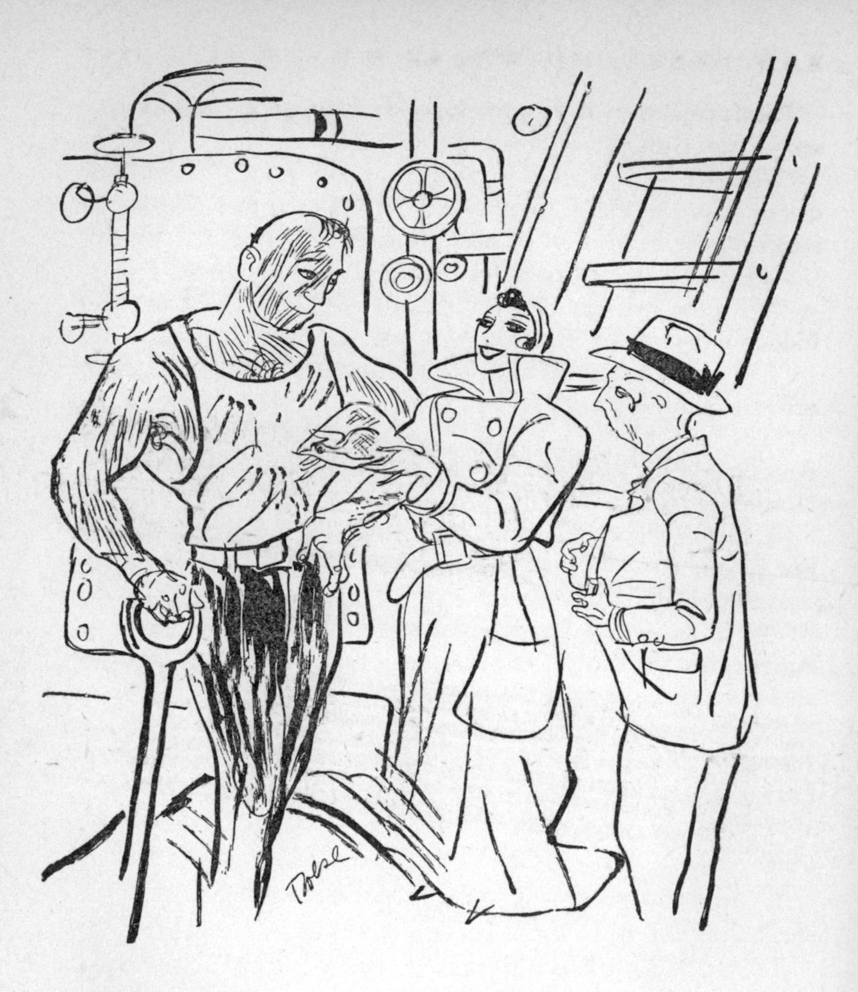

CHAPTER NINE

Bad Talk and Worse Weather

"GET THE HELL OUT OF HERE, YOU BOOBY!" BOOMED OUT the great voice, making an unpleasant evening even more unpleasant.

"Seafaring men have such unbridled tempers," mildly observed the Bishop.

"I'd hate to be called a booby even in a fog," Peter declared. "It's a word to which I strongly object. Seems to strike at the very roots of one's being."

Apparently the skipper felt the same way about it.

"Who the hell are you calling booby?" he cried from the hidden aloofness of his little pilot house.

"I'm calling you a booby," answered the other skipper across the milling fog.

"You're a booby yourself," retorted the defender of the ferryboat, seeing no reason to improve on the word. "A blundering booby at that."

"Call me a booby!" almost screamed the other voice. "I'd like to cut you in two. What do you mean running into an ocean liner, endangering the lives of my passengers?"

"What do you mean by picking on a ferryboat carrying American citizens?" demanded the local skipper, introducing an international flavor to the dispute.

"Your passengers don't count for a damn," he was informed. "They're dirty commuters. They aren't even human."

"Is that so? Well, so are yours. You're all boobies—the lot of you."

A clatter of protesting voices burst through the fog. One shrill, ironical voice made itself disagreeably articulate.

"You can drown commuters by the handful," announced this voice, "and the world would be better off—much better off."

This time the commuters' voices shattered the fog with indignant discord.

"Your passengers are a lot of pleasure-loving swine," screamed the skipper of the ferry, his voice rising above the disgraceful din.

"Will you keep that rabble quiet?" came the voice of the liner's skipper. "Can't hear a word you say."

"Keep your own immigrants quiet," retorted the small craft's skipper. "Why don't you fumigate 'em?"

The reception of this crude suggestion by the passengers of the liner was deafening. Obviously they were infuriated far beyond the bounds of good taste. The ferryboat jeered triumphantly, and the word "immigrants" found immediate favor, also such terms of endearment as wops, kikes, bolshies, anarchists, reds, and a few others that will not bear repetition. In the midst of this hubbub the voices of the two skippers could be distinguished passionately cursing the passengers they had so recently been defending. Gradually the voices died exhaustedly away so that the respective representatives of the opposing ships were enabled to continue insulting each other in comparative peace and quiet.

"An edifying way for ships to act," observed Peter, "when fogbound far at sea."

"If you don't take that waterlogged louse of yours away from my ship I'm going to run you down," the voice from the liner shouted. "I've got a peace delegation aboard."

"Sounds more like a mob from hell," the ferryboat replied.

Upon hearing this, the peace delegation apparently became so warlike it had to be roundly cursed back into silence. Aspirin Liz, with the light of battle in her eyes and closely supported by a quivering Josephine, made for the head of the ferry. The others followed the two women.

"Go to hell, you!" shouted Aspirin Liz as soon as she had taken up her station. "We've got a bishop of the Episcopal Church on our boat and if you don't believe that his name's Waller."

"My dear! My dear!" protested the Bishop. "Don't use my name in all this fog."

"What's wrong with your name?" snapped Jo, then

shrieked through her hands at the opposing ship. "His name is Waller—Bishop Waller. Never heard of Bishop Waller, you big stiff?"

"I'm doing the shouting, lady," the ferryboat's captain called down to Jo.

"Don't give a damn if he's the twelve apostles," the seafaring skipper blasphemously retorted. "Go tell him to waller in the waves. That's where he'll soon be and you, too, you Jersey broad."

"My God! He called me a broad!" cried Josephine, white with rage, then furiously to the fog, "Shut up, you lily."

"What!" screamed back the fog. "Me, a lily! I'd like to come down there and punch you on the nose."

"A most violent character," objected the Bishop; then, suddenly losing his ecclesiastical calm: "Take your vile craft out of the way, you zany, and let God-fearing people proceed in peace."

"Yes," yelled Aspirin Liz. "Get a move on. I want some beer."

"Who the hell cares about you and your beer?" the liner flung back coarsely. "All you'll get is salt water and lots of that, you dizzy Jersey broad."

"Lily! Lily!" sang out Jo. "Think up another name."

"Oh, my God," came the voice of the distracted skipper, and Peter in his mind's eye caught a glimpse of weather-beaten features distorted with impotent rage. "Oh, my God," came the strangled voice. "If I could only come down there and pull your nose."

"Oh, my dear, how vicious!" Josephine tossed back girlishly. "We're thumbing our noses at you, in case you can't see us."

"Make that woman stop," called the liner's captain, appealing directly to the commander of the ferryboat. "By rights she should be put in irons for calling me such names."

"Oh, you lily!" yodeled a chorus of voices through the

fog, a group of truck drivers seeming to be especially gifted at this form of derision.

"You're forgetting to sound your whistle, sir," the local skipper pleasantly reminded the other. "It ain't sounded for seven minutes. I'll report that little neglect of duty."

"I'm forgetting I'm a human being," the voice came back wildly from the liner. "I'm forgetting I'm an officer and a gentleman. I'm forgetting I've got a soul." The last word rose in a howl. "I'm mad. I'm going mad, I tell you," it resumed. "Going mad alone in the fog." A burst of maniacal laughter followed, then a snatch of demented song. "All alone on the telephone," quavered the voice of the liner's skipper. "Sleep, sailor, sleep all alone on the telephone—ha, ha, ha!" The climax was a volley of incoherent obscenities, which ceased suddenly as a new voice was heard, a quiet, reasonable, cultured voice.

"Sorry," this voice sang out, "but our skipper has just lost his reason or had a stroke or something. Do you happen to know where we are?"

"Too bad about your old man," answered the ferryboat captain. "Merely having a bit of a jaw-back. I swear to God I don't know where we can be."

"Might be off the old Rock herself for all I know," the other replied hopelessly. "Sounds like open water to me."

"Are you anchored?" asked the ferry captain.

"Been anchored for hours," he was told.

"Well, I haven't got any anchors," declared the skipper of the ferry.

"Wish you had one round your neck," a vulgar voice observed weightily, "an' that you was right with it forty fathoms deep."

"Pipe down, there!" cried the cultured voice. "I say, Captain, would you care to tie up 'longside of me?"

"No, thanks," replied the other. "I'll go smousing round for a bit yet. Might find something. Hope the old man gets well."

"And tell him for me," Little Arthur surprisingly shouted, "a ocean-going liner shouldn't have a weak-minded skipper."

"Shut up, you worm!" snapped Jo. "You would pull a wisecrack just when we were getting nice and friendly. Don't you realize you aren't good enough to insult even a body-snatcher?"

If the skipper of the liner had been incapacitated, his passengers still remained loyal. As the two ships parted company in the fog their insults fell thick and fast. The ferryboat did not remain silent. Foul words and frantic filled the air.

"If an angel should appear now," remarked the Bishop with a sigh of regret, "I very much fear he would mistake the earth for a region far below. These maddened voices in the fog sound like spirits in torment."

"How long have we been afloat?" Peter asked a little wearily.

"Nearly two and a half hours," replied the Bishop glancing at his watch.

"I'm hungry," complained Little Arthur.

"We're not interested," Jo retorted, then considered him with sudden interest. "Come here, Little Arthur," she said at last in a dangerously honeyed voice. "I want to have a friendly talk with you."

"Are you sure it's friendly?" he asked with justifiable suspicion. "I've had more than enough trouble for one day."

"There's not going to be any trouble," Josephine assured him. "You're going to like this."

For a few moments they conversed earnestly together; then, with a backward glance at the others, wandered innocently off in the direction of several trucks hunched in the gloom of the traffic alleys filled with fog and the fumes of gas. Peter and his companions returned to the relative comfort of the cabin. A trifle depressed after the excitement caused by the recent encounters, they sat down and confronted the faces of their fellow passengers. Those faces were a study in conflicting emotions. They furnished ample food for thought if one felt inclined to think under such exasperating conditions. Peter's brain was working dreamily on the borderland of sleep. His head felt hot and heavy. There was a throbbing pain in his arm.

So many interrupted lives, he mused. So many routines broken. Wives waiting all over New Jersey. Dinners getting cold. Children staying up for Daddy, then going to bed without him. Mothers glancing out of windows and running to front doors. Little speeches of greeting being rehearsed. Furious little speeches—perfect gems of sarcasm and sweet recrimination.

"No, dear. Little Junior couldn't wait up until dawn. Sorry, but if you must stop off at a speakeasy, you'll have to do without your son. Of course, it doesn't matter about me. I haven't counted in years. Do you find it close in here, dear? I'll open up all the windows so the neighbors can enjoy your breath, too. No. Don't try to get around me. Keep your horrid hands off. Save them for one of your flash stenographers. You seem to prefer their company to mine."

Peter's thoughts veered off at another tangent. He was convinced that the little chap with the pinched face across the way was making up a lie already. Years of experience had taught the man that his wife would never believe the truth. He must perjure his soul to keep peace in the family. He must tell a lie to give her the pleasure of catching him in it. If he told the truth and stuck to it, the lady would feel herself injured. She always felt injured. She was born with an ax to grind with life in general, and he had been feeling its blade for years until he was chipped away to his spiritless soul.

That quiet-looking fellow a few seats away seemed actually to be enjoying the situation. He was probably welcoming this fogbound interlude in his unadventurous days. Doubtless wished the ferryboat would never find its rightful slip. Peter felt that the man hated that ferry slip, had been hating it night after night, week after week, for many years. No wonder war was popular when life was unable to dig up anything better than a couple of ferry slips with uncongenial destinations at either end.

But there was a person eager to get home. Newly married, Peter placed him. Probably a baby on the way. No word from his wife for twelve whole hours. The poor devil was too nervous to sit down. Kept walking about and doing silly things with his hands. Aimless things—futile gestures. And all because some unremarkable girl in some equally unremarkable town in New Jersey was about to add her even more unremarkable contribution to an already overcrowded world. But none of it seemed unremarkable to this young fellow. Neither the town nor the girl nor the baby. Life for him was touched with wonder. For him there was a zest in things. Peter decided that if he had the chap in his office, he would give him a worth-while raise.

There was a pretty girl who had had about enough of fog horns for one night. Probably worked in some office near the river. Had been hearing them all day long. Some day she would probably contribute to the world's population. Funny thing, that. She would grow old and change and look different, and years from now another girl looking not unlike her would come there and sit in that same seat. And the whole thing would begin over again. Just like a picture with the same picture in it and the same one in that, only a little smaller, going on forever.

Peter wondered drowsily if he were growing a little delirious. Snatches of conversation kept getting mixed up in his mind. Why was he leading these people's lives for them, hearing the things they said, imagining their thoughts? The world was being eaten up by fog and driven mad by fog horns. A detective story would go well now. Somebody should be murdered. Somebody almost had been murdered. A few inches to the right with that bullet, and he would not have cared whether the boat made land or not. Where would he be now? Out there in the fog somewhere, lending his voice to the whistles?

That girl down the line—what was her trouble? Why that bitter expression? She was getting along in years now. Already that deadly look of efficiency, that expression of command, was stealing into her face. Perhaps she had passed up a date to spend the week-end somewhere with her boss. Maybe her last chance—her last chance to find out about a lot of things, to experience a lot of things. When she reached home tonight—if she ever did—two old people would be waiting there for her. A little worried always. Always a little fearful. Something might happen to this girl of theirs, this girl growing old like themselves, yet still almost as inexperienced as the day when she was born. Family loyalty and self-sacrifice could be carried too far. Always was. This girl would never add to the world's population, and she damn well should. Someone should seduce her—make a mother out of her, give her a break in life. Peter wouldn't want to do it, but then there was always someone.

Peter's brain was once more snatching conversations from the air—Hello, J. B. How's tricks? Reached your quota yet? He's a ten-thousand-dollar-a-year man. Must be a nice guy. Thought you always rode up with another party—tall, dark feller. Usually do. He's a fifteen-thousand-dollar-a-year man. Must be a wonderful guy. The little lady all right? Nervous—this depression. Have to send her to Lakewood. Mine, too. Got to pack her off. Women can't stand depression. Nobody can. Depression's bad for the country. That's what I say. See that guy over there? He's a five-thousand-dollar-a-year man. Must be a washout. Where does he get off to carry a cane? There's a pip—what a leg! Know her? Oh, you do—any good? I should tell you. Hoover's a gentleman, at any rate, not a goddam red. Get your ticket ready. Here comes Pete. Getting old, Pete. Been punching my ticket for the past seventeen years. Got a piece I want to read. Bedtime stories? Right. Tell 'em to the kiddies. Nothing like kiddies. She *has* got a swell leg.

The synthetic snatches faded away. Peter's head sank lower and lower. Aspirin Liz collected it and propped her well-padded shoulder against his cheek. Close to the surface of consciousness Peter slid along through the fog.

In the meantime Joe and Little Arthur were lurking round the trucks like wolves round a wagon train. They were inspecting the trucks with careless-seeming yet calculating eyes. Each truck was wondered about, each truck peeped into, poked and felt. Their hands were furtively caressing. Little Arthur's favorite truck gave promise of fancy groceries. He opened a knife in his pocket, looked quickly about him, then operated on the truck with the skill of a surgeon on a mere appendix. Jo's hands were darting into another truck. Jo believed in bread. She succeeded in snatching cake, also a thermos bottle, the personal property of the driver. Little did Joe care whose personal property it was. She had to provide for her own.

"This is the first time I ever stole a chicken," Little Arthur whispered, pointing to a bulge in his coat.

"Put it back!" said Jo. "Put it back. The damn thing will squawk all over the ferry."

"It ain't that kind of a chicken."

"Mean it's a dumb chicken?"

"No, it's a dead chicken."

"But raw?" asked Jo.

"Very," admitted the crook. "Cold and raw."

Jo thought rapidly but effectively.

"Come," she said at last. "There must be a fire in the engine room. We'll borrow a chunk of the ship's fire, but listen, Little Arthur, let me do the talking."

"Don't I know!" the little chap replied. "I'd never try to can your chatter."

"Follow me, little thief," said Jo almost tenderly.

A few minutes later some passengers were slightly interested in seeing two figures, crouched as if in pain, move swiftly to the small door of the engine room and neatly disappear behind it. Jo descended a short steep metal ladder, regretting the while the absence of an audience below. She felt sure that had the engineer been present he would have granted her every wish. Men were like that—foolish. A blackened face seated on a box rolled two white eyes at her from behind a stanchion.

"Hello!" said the face. "What's up?"

"Nothing much," replied Jo easily. "I'm the daughter of a ship's captain myself."

"I'm not a ship's captain, lady," the face replied, "much less his daughter."

"Don't be silly," said Jo. "I want to cook a chicken."

"Oh, yeah?" the face grinned back. "I'd like to run races. Is that the bird you want to cook?"

The face pointed at Little Arthur.

"No," said Jo. "Hell isn't hot enough for that one."

"It's too noisy here," the dip complained.

"What do you want to do?" asked Jo. "Sing?"

"No. It hurts my ears."

Jo turned away from Little Arthur and considered a small black door, through the edges of which gleamed a frame of fire.

"Might cook it in there," she remarked.

"To a cinder," grinned the man.

"Might fix something up."

"Sure, lady. What do you think this is, the Ritz?"

"Slip me that chicken," said Jo.

Arthur produced the chicken as a magician produces a rabbit and handed it to Jo, who in turn passed it to the man with the black face.

"Pretty slick chicken, that," allowed Jo.

When the man had finished his examination the chicken looked pretty black.

"It's a good chicken," he agreed, holding it out to Jo.

"I don't want it," she told him. "Put it on some fire."

"Listen, lady, are you nuts?" the man asked.

"Certainly not," the girl replied. "Why?"

"Nothing," said the man. "Only I was afraid you figured yourself home in your own kitchen and had mistaken me for your cook."

"You don't look a bit like my cook," said Jo. "You're much nicer."

"Come on, quit your kidding!" The man looked pleased.

"Can't you cram it into some fire?" asked Jo.

The man looked at her and grinned. Then he spat copiously. After that he got up.

"You're a funny sketch," he said at last. "This chicken all ready?"

"Don't know," replied Jo. "Let me look at it. No. You look at it."

The man thereupon elevated the chicken and sighted through it, one white eye professionally closed. It was not a nice scene to witness under the most favorable conditions, but in that engine room and done by a man with a black face it was almost more than Little Arthur could bear. He closed both his eyes.

"What do you see?" the girl asked breathlessly.

"Wish I could see land," said the man. "We seem to have lost that. Even the fog horns are getting scarcer, but I'll cook your chicken for you, lady."

"That's swell," said Jo. "You're a good egg, chief. I've a sick man up there. He's been shot."

"Heard about that guy," the chief replied as he moved searchingly about the confined area. "Sort of queer thing, that. And all the time there's some man sitting quietly on this boat who was intended to stop that bullet. It just shows.

You never can tell. Who'd ever thought I'd be cooking a chicken in a fog?"

"Ain't he even going ter wash it?" asked Little Arthur.

"What for?" asked Jo. "We'll burn the dirt off."

Little Arthur shrank even smaller.

"Always like my chickens washed," he muttered.

The black-faced man had found what he wanted. It was a pan—a large pan. This he filled with glowing coals upon which he placed another and smaller pan.

"Ask him to dust the ashes out," urged Little Arthur.

"Will you be quiet!" said Jo, who was by now greatly interested.

From a suspicious-looking can the chief poured some water into the smaller pan, plopped the chicken in it, then covered the whole affair with a galvanized washtub.

"Wouldn't want no better oven than that," he remarked, surveying his rude creation.

"Who wouldn't?" muttered Little Arthur.

"You're a genius," said Jo admiringly. "Have a hunk of cake."

She produced a box of cake from beneath the duster she had managed to retain and tore off the cover.

"Just a little," said the chief.

"Go on. Take a lot."

He accepted the cake and munched.

"Good cake," he observed. "I like cake. You know—good cake."

Little Arthur decided that here was a man who would be at home in any surroundings. He was the same as a dog or any other animal. His reactions were the simple ones of the brute. The girl was like him. Little Arthur, to show how much nicer he was than his companions, produced his knife and cut himself a slice of cake.

"Nice, ain't it?" said the chief, rolling his eyes at the little man. "Orange icing's good."

Little Arthur waited until his mouth was clear, then spoke with marked distinctness.

"Not bad for store cake," he replied. "It's sticking on your chin."

"What?" asked the black faced man.

"The crumbs," said Little Arthur.

The man once more laughed coarsely.

"If that's all," he got out. "Bah!"

"That's not all," replied Little Arthur meticulously. "There's bits of waste and coal dust and oil."

"I guess that chin can stand it," the man remarked, not even taking the trouble to wipe his chin.

"No doubt," agreed the pickpocket, "but I almost can't."

"What do you mean?" the other demanded truculently.

"Oh, nothing," said Little Arthur, "only there's a lady present and you ain't doing yourself justice with that chin. Looks like an ashcan, it does."

"Oh, all right," the chief grumbled, looking furtively at Josephine, now seated on the box by the chicken. "All right. Here goes."

He produced a wad of waste from his pocket and drew it across his chin.

"That makes your chin look better," said Arthur, "and the rest of your face worse."

"Don't mind him," Jo put in. "I like your face as it is. Let's take a look at the chicken."

With a steel rod the man raised the washtub. Three pairs of eyes were fastened on the chicken.

"Smells good," said the man. "She'll be done pretty soon now—sooner than in a regular oven."

She was. The chicken was done, or partly done, in a surprisingly short time. The man with the face refused.

"No, thank you, lady," he protested. "I put on the feed bag before we shoved off. Take her up to your young man with the compliments of the chef."

For some reason Jo blushed. She realized she was blushing, and that made her blush all the more. The girl was amazed. She had never thought of herself as having a young man. With her it had always been grabbing off a guy or being grabbed herself. She had never had a real, acknowledged young man for herself. Hers had been the easy-come, easy-go type. For a moment she caught a mental image of Peter's pale, bony face with its sardonically set mouth and mild blue eyes full of vagrant fancies. God knows what he actually thought of her. She had not tried to show herself in an any too favorable light. Making herself impudent and more than plenty tough. True, he wasn't quite a young man, but then she did not care much for that sort. There and then amid the smells and grime of the ship's clanking bowels she knew that Peter meant much to her and that she was going to make herself mean even more to Peter in spite of all the Yolanda Wilmonts in the world. But perhaps he was dead by now. She had forgotten about his wound.

"Thanks, chief," she said, holding out a hand to his. "Got to hurry. Grab that bird, Little Arthur, and come right along."

"Here," said the man with the black face, producing a thick cup, and tipping the gravy from the pan into it. "Here. Might as well take this along. It'll strengthen the young feller up."

"God bless your black face, chief," said the girl as she turned to the ladder. "You're white, clean white inside."

"I know that poem, too," cried the man, as if someone had touched a button somewhere concealed about him. "I can say it all by heart."

"Wish he hadn't said that," thought Josephine as she toiled up the ladder. "If Peter knows that poem I'll eat this chicken myself and throw the bones in his face.

CHAPTER TEN

Dinner Is Served

"LISTEN, PETER," SAID JO A FEW MINUTES LATER. "DO YOU know any poetry?"

Peter skidded back to consciousness with a wince. His arm was bad. Little flames of pain licking stiff flesh.

"What's that?" he asked, blinking at the girl. "Do I know any what?"

"Poetry," said Jo. "You know. Like Milton or Ogden Nash?"

"I can't quote a line written by either gentleman," Peter told her. "Did you wake me up with the weird hope that I'd say little pieces for you?"

"No," went on Jo, "but if you're sure you don't know any poetry and you swear never to learn any, I'll give you a cup of chicken soup and a chunk of the chicken from which it oozed."

"I don't know any poetry and I never will," said Peter in a disgusted voice. "I don't feel at all like poetry unless it's composed entirely of bad words."

"Good!" exclaimed Jo, then hesitated. It could not be true. "Sure you don't know anything about the mighty God that made you and you're white, clean white, inside?" she asked, watching his face anxiously.

"No," said Peter, "and I doubt very much if I am. Got a lot of different colors inside. So have you."

"Let's not go into that," Jo hastily put in. "Here take this soup and get that inside. Little Arthur, break out your magic knife and carve that ruddy chicken. I've got some cake and a small ration of coffee."

She produced the cake and thermos bottle. Little Arthur placed the chicken between Aspirin Liz and the Bishop, then attacked it with his invaluable knife. Peter sat drinking an exceedingly pungent liquid which was nearer to chicken grease than chicken soup. However, it was hot and had food value in it. The other passengers looked on with expressions ranging from greed and envy to revulsion bordering on nausea. The little group, through lack of even the most primitive implements, was forced to be rough in its dealings with the chicken. Even Bishop Waller went at his section with tooth and nail. Yolanda strove to be dainty about it and nearly lost her share as a consequence. Soon she was gnashing away as cheerfully as the rest of them.

"My dear," said Bishop Waller after his portion had disappeared into the pontifical belly, "my dear young lady, how did you manage the chicken, may I ask?"

"We stole him or her," Josephine replied. "Little Arthur and I."

The good Bishop thought this over with a slight frown on his fine face. At last his expression cleared, and he favored Jo with a smile.

"I am glad I asked that question after rather than before eating," he admitted with happy sophistry. "It was a delicious chicken in spite of the irregular circumstances surrounding its getting. But perhaps the less said the easier digested."

"Was it already cooked?" asked Aspirin Liz.

"No," replied Josephine. "Just dead. We cooked it down in the engine room. There's the sweetest man there with a dirty black face and grimy hands. He helped us cook it."

"Oh, dear!" murmured Yolanda, looking as if she had been poisoned. "A dirty black man!"

"Only his hands and face," Jo protested. "Don't know about the rest of his body. May have been as white as yours, if that's saying anything."

"It's saying too much," Yolanda retorted. "What did you cook it in?"

"A couple of old ashpans," Jo informed her.

"My word!" said Yolanda, looking at the others with round eyes. "Think what we have inside us besides chicken!"

"A lot of satisfaction," Peter put in, "where before there was nothing but craving. Good work, Jo! Our tame thief is a credit to his profession."

"May I ask," began the Bishop, "why you occasionally refer to this seemingly harmless little chap as being a thief and a criminal?"

"Because he is," Jo answered proudly. "A regular thief."

"Only a pickpocket, yer honor," Little Arthur protested. "Just pockets, yer know. Little pockets. Never much in 'em."

"But you take what little there is, don't you, Little Arthur?" Jo insisted.

"Nobody ever minds much," he answered.

"Nobody has much these days to mind," Aspirin Liz observed. "You'll have better and bigger pockets to pick before you die, Little Arthur."

"I'm thinking of giving it up," he declared. "Now that I've met a holy man—a real, live bishop, that is."

"Splendid, Little Arthur! Splendid!" cried the Bishop. "I'm gratified my presence has done some good. You might celebrate your career of regeneration by returning to me the watch you borrowed when Mr. Van Dyck asked for the time out there on deck. I've been wondering which of you had it."

"Honest," said Little Arthur, producing the watch from a side pocket, "that watch had just gone clean out of my mind."

"Very little can go clean out of your mind," Aspirin Liz assured him.

"Honest, now," the small crook repeated. "Honest. I mean it. The Bishop shouldn't take out a valuable watch like that in a lot of wet fog. It's fairly criminal, it is. He'll spoil it."

"It was most unwise, I'll admit, with you around," said the Bishop with a benevolent smile as he courteously accepted the watch. "However, all's well that ends well. We'll say no more about it."

"Thank you, yer honor," said Little Arthur gratefully.

"Your extensive acquaintance with judges, I imagine, has led you into error," the Bishop continued. "I do not judge men professionally, Little Arthur. Rather, I endeavor to save them. Privately, I have my own opinions which, I am sorry to say, are not high—far, far from high. I am not 'your honor.' If you insist on a title I might bear up beneath the weight of 'your reverence.' "

"Thank you, yer reverence," said Little Arthur. "Nice-sounding name, that—yer reverence. Never liked 'yer honor' much. Always meant worry and trouble and a lot of——"

"Lying," Jo helpfully supplied.

A large, rough-looking person wearing a strangely ingratiating smile had been standing for some minutes gazing down from his impressive height upon the remains of the chicken. It speaks well for Josephine Duval's character that she never suspected anyone of being really bad at heart save herself, and she rarely if ever thought much about that. A few other passengers had gathered unobtrusively round the outskirts of the large, rough-looking man.

"Young lady," he now inquired, addressing Jo in tones of respectful admiration, "that was a mighty slick trick you did with that chicken. How did you manage to work it, if I may be so bold?"

Flushed with triumph, Jo turned to one whom she fondly believed to be her latest conquest.

"You're right it was a slick trick," she told him. "When it comes to the survival of the fittest you can't afford to stand on ceremony."

"I should say not," the man replied, a little overenthusiastically. "What did you do, miss? Let me in on it."

"What did I do? Why, I helped myself, of course," she asserted. "And this little beggar helped me."

"I found it," Little Arthur proudly declared.

"Oh," said the man, beaming so energetically he looked as if he were going to explode. "So you found it. Now that is good." His voice dropped to a confidential whisper. "And where did you find it, miss?" he asked.

"That would be telling," Josephine hedged.

"Go on, miss," the great man almost whined. "Why not tell us? We're all hungry, too—like yourselves."

"I suspect the integrity of that large individual's motives," Bishop Waller murmured to Peter.

"There's an air about him," agreed Peter. "A faint suggestion of menace."

Jo looked undecidedly at the man for a moment, then her impressionable French heart melted. Besides, it would cost her nothing. Furthermore, she decided, when a man as big as this one got hungry all over he was a danger to his fellow men until glutted with food.

"Well, I'll tell you," she began. "There's a boob of a truckman aboard this ferry——"

A spasm of terrific emotion passed over the great man's face.

"Yes, miss," he broke in, his voice trembling with what Jo fully believed to be eagerness. "You said a boob of a truckman. Hear that, everybody. Ha, ha! A boob of a truckman! That's good! Oh, that's very good!"

Pleased by the reception of her words, Josephine endeavored to better them.

"Yes," she continued, "a regular boob of a truckman. Must be a poor fish——"

"Ha!" cried the great man. "A poor fish, eh? So he's a poor fish no less than a boob?"

Jo nodded quite seriously.

"Yes," she said. "Do you know what he did, the saphead?"

"What did he do, lady?" the man whispered, as if he were having trouble with his throat. "Tell us what the sap-head did."

"Why, he left his truck unguarded," replied Jo. "That's what the sap-head did—just strolled off and left his truck flat."

"And what did you do?" asked the great man.

"My dear," broke in Bishop Waller, "I strongly advise against any further exchange of confidences."

But the Bishop's cautious admonition came too late. Jo was in full cry.

"What did we do?" replied the girl. "Why, naturally, we helped ourselves. Little Arthur there yanked out his knife, cut a hole through the canvas covering, and reached out a chicken just as easy as taking a rabbit from a hat. And the funny part of it is the half-wit who's driving the truck isn't any the wiser yet. When he discovers that hole I'd like to take a look at his face."

An amazing transformation had taken place in the great man's features. They were congealed now in an expression of superhuman malevolence in which a smile of tremendous bitterness cracked about his bared teeth. Outside of the movies Jo had never seen such a face, such an evil, sadistic mask. The man was wheezing as if someone had kicked him in the stomach.

"You'd like to see his face?" he gasped; then, squatting with surprising agility, he flung out: "Then take a good look at it. This is his face, see—the boob's face, the face of the poor fish—the—the—the—" his voice broke in a sob of rage—"the face of the sap-head. Take a good look at it."

But Jo had looked at the man's face once, and it was the last thing in the world she wanted to do again. It was nothing to see, that face. As a matter of fact it was too much to see. The girl closed her eyes, but that awful face still hung suspended in her memory. Then the face moved and brought its baleful influence directly to bear on Little Arthur, who recoiled in mortal terror. Still squatting and with hands extended, their fingers suggestively working, the owner of the face drew near to Little Arthur. In a surprisingly short space of time he was dangling in mid-air and then approaching both his mortal as well as rear end at a high rate of speed. With an effect of complete finality the small man made a large noise as he hit the deck and remained very much there.

Then, as if what had already occurred had not been sufficiently surprising, an even more surprising element literally mingled itself with the situation. Before the great face had time to pick up Little Arthur and do some more things with him, Bishop Waller, with a roar of righteous indignation, launched himself in defense of his so recently acquired convert. It was a magnificent and inspiring spectacle. It became even more stupendous when the bared ecclesiastical head established resounding contact with the ungodly abdomen of the truckman and sent him crashing to the planks. Outside, the fog horn told the fog what the ferryboat thought of it, waves splashed against the sides, and ghostly voices drifted past, but within the cozy cabin the truckman lay stunned while Josephine and Aspirin Liz took up positions and stood waiting for the kill.

In the meantime the highly edified passengers, feeling sure the truckman would never survive to drive his truck to its destination, made a general movement in its direction. One can gain no true conception of the rugged determination of commuters, of their resource and clever teamwork, until one has witnessed them in concerted action. Respectable husbands and fathers—not to mention business executives, clerks, and stenographers—literally swarmed all over the truck. Men accustomed to the feel of golf clubs now swung chickens aloft with equal dexterity. The backbone of the nation was looking for its grub and finding it in lavish quantities. Presently other trucks were attacked by fresh detachments of commuters unable to find standing room on the original one. Everyone seemed to have entered into the spirit of the occasion. Everyone was alert and eager, ready to do his or her bit. Outcries of gratification could be heard as new discoveries were made. In vain did the drivers of the trucks protest. They were borne down and walked over by the sheer weight of numbers.

It was upon this scene of pillage and confusion that the

originator of the outbreak opened his shocked and amazed eyes. With dawning comprehension he saw several figures, each provided with one of his chickens, dart through the small door leading to the engine room. It was enough to drive the past from his memory. The present was all-important. With a wild cry he sprang to his feet and staggered to the defense of his truck which, by the time he reached it, contained little to defend.

Bishop Waller with a sigh of relief sank back on the seat and received the congratulations of the party. Loudest among these were those of Little Arthur, now partially recovered from his cataclysmic contact with the deck.

"I don't know what has come over me," the good Bishop observed rather sadly. "It must be this fog. First I lend my voice to an already sufficiently undignified and acrimonious dispute with an unseen ship, then calmly enter this cabin and assault one of our fellow creatures after having devoured his property. I have forsaken God, I fear."

"But what that monster was doing to me was something fearful, yer reverence," Little Arthur advanced consolingly. "You arrived in the nick of time. I was nearly jarred out, I was."

"Granted," responded the Bishop, "I had some slight provocation, but Little Arthur, for all of that, it would gall me immeasurably to lose my chance of salvation through saving your wicked life, as invaluable as it may be to you."

Not knowing which end of this observation to accept, Little Arthur maintained a discreet silence.

In the meantime the situation was developing in the engine room. The man with the black face was telephoning passionately to the captain.

"Yes, sir," he was telling him. "They're stealing all my fire, every blessed damn coal."

"What do they want with your fire?" the captain wanted to know. "It ain't as cold as all that."

"They're trying to cook some chickens," the black face roared.

"Where did they find the chickens?" came back the skipper's voice.

"How should I know that?" screamed the engineer. "And does it really matter? Maybe they flew aboard."

"Did you say chickens?" asked the skipper. "Sure they're not seagulls?"

"Think I don't know the difference between a seagull and a chicken?" the other end of the wire inquired none too pleasantly.

"Not saying you don't," said the captain. "But a seagull and a chicken might look a lot alike when they're skinned or unfrocked or whatever they are when all their feathers are off."

"They look altogether different," said the engineer with cold dignity. "And the word is 'plucked' in case you want to use it sometime."

"How do they intend to cook these chickens?" asked the captain, a note of real interest creeping into his voice.

"Fricassee," howled the engineer, his black face becoming swollen with anger.

"Not a bad way," said the skipper thoughtfully. "Very fond of chicken fricassee. You know, Charlie,"—and here his voice took on a persuasive note—"you see, Charlie, I've been thinking. We've been a long time without food. The way things stand I don't know where the hell we are and where the hell we're going, and as long as that fire ain't doing us any good we might as well be using it for something. What do you say, Charlie?"

For a few moments Charlie was unfit to say anything.

"I say," he managed to get out at last, "that my engine room ain't no damned galley for a flock of commuters with their goddam chickens. That's what I say."

"But listen, Charlie," said the skipper, trying to reason with the man, "fricasseed chicken's mighty nice eating when it's properly done."

"Should we be worrying about fricasseed chicken," demanded Charlie, "when it looks like the fishes will be gnawing on our bones?"

"Might as well gnaw on the chickens' bones first," came the philosophic voice of the skipper. "Gnaw and let gnaw, say I. How about it, Charlie?"

For reply the telephone broke into an incoherent babble. The skipper hung up the receiver, called a weary-looking deckhand, and went below to deal in person with the situation.

It was a strange scene indeed that greeted the skipper's gaze. Had it been not quite so small, the engine room or stokehold of the ship would have called to mind a prairie dotted by the fires of early American settlers engaged in cooking their rude evening meal. Perhaps it was because the place was entirely treeless that the captain gained this impression. One glance was sufficient to convince him it would be difficult to find a more unusual situation on any ferryboat anywhere. Commuters, squatting in all positions, were holding chickens or various parts of chickens above piles of glowing coals. So frequently were such figures encountered that the captain found it difficult to walk without stepping on one of his passengers. The room was pervaded with an appetizing aroma of sizzling fowl. It was enough to make his eyes as well as his mouth water. In a corner of the compartment the engineer was standing with a newspaper raised between himself and his uninvited guests. After his conversation with his superior offcer he had apparently lost all interest in what was going on in his engine room.

"Hello, Charlie," said the skipper smoothly. "Catching up with the news, I see."

"Why not?" replied Charlie over the rim of his paper. "You seem to care more about chicken than running this here ship. I'm interested in racing, myself. Picking tomorrow's winners."

"Well," observed the skipper, "from the way it looks now you'll have to cable in your selection from mid-Atlantic. I don't even smell land about, but I do smell chicken." He smiled engagingly down upon his passengers. "You've taken things into your own hands, I see," he continued in a not unfriendly voice. "Well, I'll tell you what we'll do. If you provide us with a brace of chickens, we'll let you continue cooking yours."

Several chickens were immediately produced and offered for the inspection of the skipper. Selecting two promising specimens of looted fowl, he turned to the newspaper.

"Charlie," he began, "what do you know about cooking chickens? Here are two beautiful birds."

"Everything," replied Charlie surprisingly. "Slip me those chickens and I'll show these home-loving train-snatchers how to cook. I don't care what happens to this engine room any more."

He rigged up his odd-looking oven and put the chickens through their paces. As he watched the expressions of envy on the faces of the pioneers gathered round him, his annoyance died away and he felt himself a little consoled.

"Can't you cram just one more in that contraption?" a voice asked wistfully. "My fingers are better done than my chicken."

Good-naturedly the black-faced man complied with the request. Sometime later when the skipper emerged from the stokehold on his way to the pilot house he was gnawing on a chicken leg and carrying various carefully selected parts in his other hand. The driver of the assaulted truck followed the happy man's progress with gloomy, misanthropic eyes.

"Gord," he muttered, "what a trip this turned out to be. Even the captain himself is no better than a thief."

Quiet water and moonlight and a world lost in fog. Hardly anyone awake now. A few shadows by the rail. Sleep had overcome the commuters, their stomachs no longer empty. Back in the cabin they, the commuters, were draped and crumpled about in fantastic shapes as if a spell had been laid upon the ferry, it's passengers turned to inanimate objects, inanimate save for the noises they made in their sleep. These are never attractive.

Moonbeams strained through fog—an eerie effect. It was like living inside a huge halo, its edges washed by black infinity. The ferry glided smoothly on, ever maintaining its position in the center of a white circle. It was as if New York had been packed in cotton and magically removed. There was no New York, no Jersey shore, no open bay slashed by the prows of ships. Only fog horns sounded remotely in the darkness, and the occasional warning clang of a bell.

"Sounds like a cow out there in the fog," said Peter to the girl leaning on the rail beside him. "A lonely cow with a bell on grazing among the waves."

"The old girl will get all foggy inside," said Josephine poetically. "Maybe we're scaling a Swiss Alp and are coming to a pasture."

"Wouldn't mind that in the least," said Peter.

"But wouldn't I be a drawback?" she asked. "A sort of depraved lady fly reclining brazenly in the ointment?"

Peter looked down into the face upturned to his. Full lips a little moist, and shadows round the eyes. Somehow she contrived to make herself every inch a woman. And she made every inch felt.

"You're more like a wicked spider," he told her thoughtfully. "A dangerously attractive spideress."

He heard her laugh softly and did not dislike the sound.

"I cling to the words 'attractive,' 'wicked,' and 'dangerous,'" she said. "They are more than I usually get from you. How about going inside and lying down?"

"A dangerous spideress would make a suggestion like that," he observed.

"I mean on opposite sides of the ship," she assured him. "Under the circumstances your interpretation would be madness."

"Then I say, no go," he said. "My head feels too giddy to park itself anywhere at present, and this damn arm keeps on throbbing. I like it out here with you."

"Mean that?"

"Yes, strange as that may seem."

"I don't think it's so strange. After all, I'm sort of nice."

"Can't quite see you as being nice, Jo. You're not at all that way. You're really a very bad girl."

"That's how I mean," she agreed. "I'm nice and bad."

"Just plain bad," he said. "Why did you tell Aunt Sophie and Sanders and all those people that you were going to have a baby by me?"

"Well, aren't I, sometime, maybe?" she asked. "I thought I could read the writing on the wall."

"To begin with you're not," said Peter, "and in the second place if you were going to have one of my babies there'd be no writing on the wall about it."

"All right, mister," she answered with a little shrug. "Perhaps the wish was father to the thought."

"Your prospective babies are none of my business."

"You're a hard man, Peter Van Dyck."

"But a just one," said Peter.

"Can't you find a little moral weakness somewhere about you?"

Silence. Jo moved her tireless young body closer to the man's good arm. She liked being there. He was such a clean man. Daring little dreams came to her across the water—half-formed hopes swaddled in fog. But deep in her heart Josephine did not have any too much hope. Her confidence was all on the surface.

"Peter."

"Well?"

"You're letting me stay mighty close to you."

"Why bring the matter to my attention?"

"Do you like us this way, Peter, all scrunched up?"

"The way you phrase it hardly presents an idyllic picture to my eyes. Scrunched up—no. Make it better."

"I suppose you're such an old stick you just can't help being a stickler. Scrunched up is a fine way. It's so cozy."

"Sounds almost immoral."

"Your mind is much worse than mine, Peter."

"Wouldn't be a bit surprised, young lady."

"I'm glad you told me, Peter. I like your mind that way."

"You deliberately make it that way. I think I'll call you a trull."

"Oh, what a word to call me! I rather like it, too. I'd have done well in the days of Falstaff."

"You'd have run the fat knight ragged."

"Sir John was ragged most of the time—spiritually as well as sartorially."

"You and Sir John have much in common," said Peter, considering her thoughtfully. "Do you read books ever?"

"Mostly pornography," she told him. "I read until I come to the nasty parts, then I stop to think of you."

"Please spare me your thoughts."

Silence again. The slow indolent churning of propellers and the crinkling splash of waves gossiping sleepily under the bow.

"Peter."

"All right. What now?"

"Isn't it funny about being in love and all?"

"I don't know. What are you trying to drag me into?"

"I mean about being in love," the girl went on in a small reflective voice. "When you are in love, I mean. It's so swell if everything's okay. Not quite so lonely any more, and everything takes on a fresh meaning—becomes much more interesting. Even dull things. Happy days waiting just round the corner. And all the time you're kind of quiet and still inside. It's like waiting for the curtain to go up or just after it's gone down. And you have private thoughts about God, and wonder if you're all right with Him and if He's going to see you through. Whenever you pass a furniture store you stop to look at the beds. I like a nice bed, Peter. Don't you?"

"I feared you would end up on some lewd note," he remarked, secretly feeling the mood behind her words. "What have we in common with a bed?"

"I don't mean right now, Peter. Not this very minute. But some day we might own a bed between us, don't you think?"

"How should I know? We might own a flock of beds."

"Oh, you mean the babies. About how many babies would you like?"

Peter grinned at the fog.

"Oh, anywhere between five and ten," he told her.

"I might manage five," she said, "but ten—oh, why bother about that now? We'll see how we stack up after the first five."

"Sure," replied Peter. "We'll take stock of ourselves then, but in the meantime, has it occurred to you that we're not even married yet?"

"It has," Jo said regretfully. "And what about Yolanda?"

"Yes," said Peter in a flat voice. "What about Yolanda?"

"Is it all fixed about our loving each other?"

"You seem to have arranged it quite nicely," said Peter.

He was more in earnest than he cared to admit even to himself.

"Go on, then," she urged in a low voice. "Say it just once. You can lie a little if you have to."

"You mean tell you in cold blood—in so many words—that I love you?"

"I don't care how many words you use, but I would like you to do a little something about your blood. Can't you warm it up a bit? I've been like that about you for a long time."

"How do you mean like that about me?" he asked. "Go on and say it yourself."

"I love you, Peter," she said in a small voice.

Jo was no longer a bold girl. Rather crushed and subdued, if anything. A little timid. She had thought a lot about love, talked a lot about love, and practised it a little, but never before had she told a real live man she loved him and meant it as she did now. And Peter, looking down at her, whether it was because he was becoming a trifle delirious or just beginning to realize what previously he had vaguely suspected, decided it would not be at all difficult to tell Jo he loved her, provided he said it very quickly and slurred a little on the edges.

"IloveyouJo," he said at full speed ahead. "Damned if I don't."

"God, how quick!" gasped Jo. "Where did it get to? Never mind. It sounded swell while it lasted. And now?"

She held her face up to his. Peter complied. He was at it quite a while. Long enough to let the freshly risen Yolanda witness more than enough.

"Peter!" she cried. "Are you mad?"

"Through and through," he muttered, removing his lips from Jo's slightly parted ones.

CHAPTER ELEVEN

Six Characters Embark in More Fog

FOR A BRIEF MOMENT PETER STOOD CONFRONTING YOLANDA, his face shocked expressionless; then, remembering her question, he actually feigned madness. Waving his hands about as if leading a multitude in song he burst out in a high, quavering voice with:

"My country 'tis of thee,
Sweet land of liberty—
God help the king."

"Stop that awful noise," Yolanda commanded imperiously. "It's bad enough to be caught doing what you were doing without singing about it."

"He's a little light in his head," Jo said in a quiet voice. "And he's not singing about it."

"He's crazy in the head if he thinks he's fooling me," ripped out Yolanda. "He acts more like a drunken man than a delirious one."

To force conviction home on Yolanda, the quavering voice redoubled its efforts, this time running short of words:

"I love your rocks and brooks
Gangsters and dirty crooks—
Who's got the king?
I——"

"Peter Van Dyck, if you don't stop making those sounds you'll wake the whole ship up," said Yolanda.

"Spangles," said Peter inanely. "Pretty spangles and banners by the score."

"Do you think he's really gone?" Yolanda asked doubtfully.

"Must be," Jo replied. "He mistook me for you. Didn't you notice how he was acting?"

"I hope you don't imagine I let him carry on like that?"

"I sincerely hope not," said Jo. "But just the same, it was pretty nice. Hadn't you better get him inside? He might suddenly take it into his head to go in swimming."

"Heavens!" exclaimed Yolanda. "He appears to think he's a seagull now."

Josephine considered the man seriously.

"Either that or a dog," she said at last. "Come here, Fido."

"There's not much similarity between a seagull and a dog," Yolanda remarked in a superior voice.

"Not much," replied Jo, "but a little—just enough to make it interesting. *Couchez-là*, Fido."

"*Avec vous*," snapped Peter. "I know French. Ha, ha! Thistledown!"

Yolanda took the fluttering man by the arm and led him babbling cheerfully into the cabin. Jo turned back to the fog. There was a happy mist in her eyes. If that kiss had lasted thirty more seconds she would have been sure of the man for life. As it was, she felt reasonably safe. She had even room enough in her heart to feel pleasurably sorry for Yolanda.

Dawn, instead of dispersing the fog, drew it closer together. From the air above her the voice of the fog horn sounded wearily. Josephine did not mind. The fog could solidify for all she cared. She felt herself authentically in love, and she was ready and willing to fight it out along those lines. She tossed all scruples into the face of the soggy day.

Morning became evening and evening became night and the commuters became bored. Beer seemed so far away to Aspirin Liz that she found it almost impossible to think of it in the abstract. Whatever good works the Bishop had set out to perform in New Jersey—a state which can stand a lot—remained unaccomplished. Drawers no longer played an important part in Little Arthur's life. Even Yolanda had forgotten about the house party. She was in the presence of grim reality. Having slept in public, an object of desirous scrutiny from God knows how many pairs of vulgar eyes, the fastidious young woman felt herself slightly deflowered. As for Peter Van Dyck he was far from well. Unlike the others he had been unable to get any real sleep. His arm was swollen and feverish. The Bishop feared infection, but kept his fears to himself. Alone of the little party Josephine seemed unperturbed. Yolanda gained the impression that her fiancé's secretary was actually deriving no little ill-bred enjoyment from the situation. Yolanda was not far wrong. Jo had decided that so long as she could be near Peter it did not make much difference what the ferry did on the surface of the sea. Her only anxiety was that the boat might take it into its head to do things beneath. The way the situation stood between herself and Peter gave her a strong desire to live. So she contented herself with bathing the man's arm and enjoying the assaulted truckman's attempts haughtily to disregard her hateful presence. She even grinned at him.

Commuters were spread out all over the place. The decks were littered with bodies in action or repose. Several packs of cards had mysteriously appeared, and little groups of gentlemen were playing pinochle as happily and as stolidly as if they had been seated opposite one another on the 5:15 or the 5:32.

Fresh water was running low, and faces were growing dingy. Yet it may be surprising to learn that many of the passengers on that long lost ferry were not so distressed as it might seem. Men and women with serious obligations to meet, debts to pay, dull engagements to keep, too familiar faces to look at and voices to hear, stockings to wash, furnaces to stoke, dogs to walk, and even letters to write found in the fogbound ferry a good excuse ready to hand.

In one quarter of the cabin a harmonica had broken out in spasm of lippy rhythm to which several stenographers danced from time to time. Jo finally succeeded in dancing with the assaulted truckman, a development which surprised the man as much as it pleased Bishop Waller, who enjoyed seeing people happy and on amicable terms.

The few encounters they had with passing but unseen ships led only to further unpleasantness and deepened the captain's misanthropic attitude towards life in general and seafaring men in particular.

"What sort of ship are you?" he was once so ill advised as to inquire of a wandering vessel.

"Oh, I'm just the loveliest sort of ship," came back the derisive reply, and the captain almost swooned from humiliation in the privacy of his pilot house.

"Go to hell!" he shrieked through the fog as soon as he had collected his scattered faculties.

"Can't even find that," the fog retorted in tones of deep dejection.

"Have you no idea where you are?" asked the skipper, a little mollified by the other's obvious discouragement.

"Yes," came the ready reply. "I have no idea where I are. How about yourself?"

"I have no idea, too," yelled the ferry captain.

A moment of brooding silence.

"Well," came the voice from the unseen ship, "this conversation doesn't seem to be helping either one of us. You have no idea and I have no idea. That makes two no ideas. Wonder who's cornered them all?"

"God knows," retorted the skipper.

"I guess He'd have a high old time putting his finger on me at this moment," observed the other. "It's a hell of a helpless feeling for a great big ship."

"Think of me!" exclaimed the skipper. "I'm only a little ferry."

Silence, then muffled laughter.

"You're only a little what?" asked the fog.

"I'm only a little ferry," declared the skipper in a voice soft with self-pity.

"Fancy that!" came back the other voice in most insipid tones. "I thought you sounded queer all alone out there in the fog. You poor dear! Just a little ferry—a pansy, as it were."

The next minute a deckhand had caught the maddened skipper just as he was on the point of hurling himself from the rail of his ship. The man was blue in the face, and the fringes of the fog round him were curling up beneath the violence of his obscenities.

"Tell 'em you're an ocean liner next time," the deckhand said soothingly to his captain. "Don't let on you're a ferry."

The captain turned on him a face in which remained only the remotest suggestion that it had once been human, then staggered to his pilot house.

"And so are you," he mouthed as he slammed the door behind him.

Wondering so was he what, the deckhand sat down on a packing box and breathed heavily into the fog.

Josephine in the wet darkness was leaning over the rail of the slowly drifting ferry. Her ears and eyes were strained to the point of exhaustion in their efforts to tear from the fog the secrets that lay behind. Her eyes failed utterly, but her ears gave food for hope. From somewhere far away in that mysterious chaos of night and fog sounding vaguely like rustling leaves in a fast receding dream, came the faint, rhythmical cadence of water washing against rocks. From what great distance the sound came, the girl was unable to estimate, but that it came from land she was convinced. To Jo at that moment land was all-important. Peter was getting no better. If anything he was worse. She disliked the feverish glitter in his eyes and the tight discolored skin round the wound. Exhausted as he was, he had been unable to go to sleep. The realization of Peter's condition had forced Josephine to revise her opinion of the ferryboat. It was no place for a wounded man. She wanted him safe on dry land, and in some desperate way, unknown at the time to herself, she intended to get him there. For a few seconds longer she listened. That distant murmur still crept to her through the fog. Rapidly she made her way to the pilot house.

"Captain," she began without preamble, "there's land somewhere about."

"Yes?" grunted the brooding man. "About what—the North Pole?"

"Maybe," said Jo. "But there's land nearer than that. Listen."

The captain thrust his head out of his door and listened. Several times he nodded, then closed the door and returned to his brooding.

"Well," asked Jo. "What are you going to do about it?"

"Nothing," replied the skipper. "It ain't near enough yet to do us any harm."

"Harm!" cried Jo. "What do you mean, harm? Aren't you going to land this ferry?"

"You mean run my ship aground on an unknown shore—maybe a reef or a mud flat? Don't be silly, lady."

"But if you don't land somewhere," Jo protested, "We may end up in Cape Town."

"What's wrong with Cape Town?" inquired the captain.

"Who said anything was wrong with Cape Town?"

"You don't appear to want to go to Cape Town."

"Would you want to go to Cape Town?" Jo flung back.

"If what?" asked the captain.

"If what?" she demanded. "How do you mean, if what?"

"I don't understand the question," the captain replied hopelessly.

"I didn't understand yours," she told him.

"Then let's begin again," he suggested. "You asked me would I like to go to Cape Town, and it seemed to me you hadn't finished what you wanted to ask and that you meant to say, would you like to go to Cape Town if something or other happened, or words to that effect. Anyway, I'm tired of Cape Town now and I don't want to go there any more."

"Neither do I," Jo agreed. "But that place we hear might be Atlantic City for all you know."

"Well, I certainly don't want to go to Atlantic City," replied the skipper in exasperation. "Of all places to land up in!"

"Will you tell me, in God's name, what's wrong with Atlantic City?" she asked in a tired voice.

"Will you tell me what isn't wrong with Atlantic City?" he retorted.

"I don't know," she said.

"It's nice we agree about something," he replied bitterly. "Some little thing."

Jo felt inclined to ask him how he would like to go to hell, but instead she tried to find out where he did want to go.

"I want to get back to my slip," the captain told her. "I'm not an excursion boat, lady. I'm a——" He stopped suddenly, remembering his recent encounter with that tormenting voice in the fog.

Jo felt stumped and discouraged. It was not that she and the skipper spoke two entirely different languages. They spoke too much alike. That was the trouble. Probably the fog had driven both of their minds off on a spur line. Glancing through one of the pilot-house windows, her eyes encountered a small boat lashed to the deck. And whether or not her mind was off the main line, it still continued to function.

"If you don't want to go to Cape Town or Atlantic City," she said in a stipulating voice, "or any other nice, reasonable seaside resort, will you let me borrow that little boat?"

"Anything to get you out of this pilot house, lady," the captain replied with sincere dislike. "I'll get her into the water for you and bid you good-bye with the best of feelings. As soon as the fog gets you out of my sight I'll try to get you out of my mind."

"You don't have to go as far as that," said Jo. "What's to become of the rest of the passengers?"

"You can take every damn one of 'em with you if you want," he assured her. "If not, they can stay here until somebody comes and drags me home."

"I suppose you expect the grand fleet to escort your damn scow to its slip?" said the girl annoyingly.

But the captain was past being annoyed.

"I don't care if it's the grand duke," he replied. "I ain't going to endanger my ship for a handful of commuters."

A few minutes later Jo addressed herself to Little Arthur.

"Can you row, shrimp?" she asked him.

"No," replied Little Arthur. "I never learned how."

"Only how to pick pockets, eh?"

"I'm trying to forget that," he said.

"I used to row," put in Bishop Waller. "Very fond of the exercise at one time."

"You never will be again," said Jo. "Not after tonight." She turned back to Little Arthur. "Little man," she continued, "if a man of God and honest ways is willing to row, you can at least try. And that's just what you're going to do if you want to come along with us. You're going to row us to land if you have to get out and push."

"I can bear a hand with one arm," said Peter.

"It's a silly-sounding sentence," she told him, "but I guess your heart's in the right place."

"A sailor once rowed me round Central Park," Aspirin Liz contributed reminiscently.

"Yeah, and after that treat what did he do—collapse?" Little Arthur inquired.

"Are you looking for trouble?" the lady asked with terrifying quietness.

"No," said Little Arthur quickly. "We've got trouble. I was just thinking——"

"Don't," Aspirin Liz admonished him. "That is, don't think about me."

Up to the moment of departure Yolanda Wilmont protested against this new and dangerous venture. She could see no good resulting from going rowing at night in a fog. However, as the others gave every indication of abandoning the ship as well as herself and the luggage unless she altered her attitude, Yolanda reluctantly tagged along with the strangely assorted party.

"If you hadn't insisted on bringing that dangerous criminal along," she told Peter, "you never would have been shot. Obviously the murderer was aiming at him."

"Can't say as I blame the murderer," said Aspirin Liz, heaving herself over the side of the ferry to the small boat below her.

"I blame him for missing," put in Jo, following the ex-model down into what impressed her as being illimitable space turned uncompromisingly black.

"Ain't you all ever going ter stop nagging at me?" asked Little Arthur. "Everybody should be friendly and all at a dreadful time like this."

It required the close coöperation of both the Bishop and Peter, wounded as he was, to lower the small crook into the bobbing boat. Passengers shouted advice while from the upper deck the captain peered down at them sardonically.

"For a worthless thing, Little Arthur," grunted Peter, "you place too high a value on that damned life of yours. Pardon the word, Bishop."

"Perhaps it would make us all feel better if we called a temporary armistice on the niceties of speech," observed the Bishop as his foot searched thoughtfully for something or anything in the darkness below him. "At the moment I feel like expressing myself in terms employed by only the most recondite students of obscene language."

"So long, chief," called Jo from the boat to the black-faced man who was looking gloomily over the side. "Next time I steal a chicken I'll let you cook it for me."

"Hope I never see a chicken again," said the chief. "Good luck, lady."

"Hope you never see one of mine," put in the truckman. "Here, little miss," he called down to Jo, and stooping, passed her several packages. "You forgot to take these when you and the rest of this ship's company were robbing my truck. Thanks for the dance."

"Thank you," replied Jo. "How did you know I liked cheese and crackers?"

"I sort of hoped you didn't," said the man, grinning down at her.

"Shove off," Peter sang out to the Bishop, who was resolutely manning the oars. "And, ladies, please stop milling about so blithely. The boat might lose its patience."

As the little boat shoved off into the fog and darkness, a cheer broke from the passengers lining the rails of the ferry. Individual voices quickly became indistinct and merged with the general babble. Suddenly a parting impulse of malice warmed Little Arthur's chilled breast.

"What did you say you were, Captain?" he called in a high-pitched voice. "Only a little what?"

Immediately the fog was made hideously vocal by the voice of the now invisible skipper. Jeers and catcalls broke from the passengers. They seemed to be directed against their own ship's officer. The Bishop increased his stroke.

"If you're trying to row us out of the way of all that bad language," said Josephine, "you might just as well save your strength, Bishop. We don't mind it in the least."

"It's odd, but neither do I," Bishop Waller got out between strokes. "It gives me a kind of vicarious kick—I think that is the word."

"Listen," Jo commanded. "It would never do to lose that

offshore sound or whatever it is." For a moment the voluntary castaways held their breath in anxious silence. "All right," said Jo at last. "It's coming from dead ahead."

"Can't you say straight ahead?" asked Little Arthur. "We're too close ter being the other."

CHAPTER TWELVE

From the Nowhere Into the Unknown

"THINGS ARE NOT SO DESPERATE," SAID JO, BREAKING A heavy silence made a little less awe-inspiring by the heaving of the indomitable Bishop. "Here we all are, the six of us.

Three men and three women—just as it should be. There's Peter and myself, Yolanda and Little Arthur, and——"

"Just call me Liz," supplied the retired model. "Everybody does. Aspirin Liz—the former being one of my vices."

"A name in a million," said Jo. "I like it. Well, then, there's Aspirin Liz and the Bishop. All cozy in a little boat."

"With more than enough water under our feet," put in Little Arthur miserably, "to swaller us all in the blink of an eye."

"Are you by any chance bracketing my name with that unwashed mite of a criminal?" Yolanda demanded arrogantly.

"I knew he was a criminal," replied Jo, "but I didn't know he was an unwashed one. How did you find that out?"

"I am accustomed to clean men," Yolanda asserted coldly. "Clean men with fresh linen."

"Have you gone as far as that with Little Arthur already?" inquired Jo. "You must have worked fast and deftly."

"One needs only to look at the man to get an unpleasant conception of what lies beneath," vouchsafed Yolanda.

"Is that any way to talk?" Little Arthur was on the verge of tears. "Call yourselves ladies, do yer? If you'd like to know it, I am washed, and if I hadn't been looking for a—a——"

"For clean linen," said Jo helpfully.

"Yes," said Little Arthur. "If I hadn't been looking for a fresh pair of those I'd of been taking the old ones off right now in the privacy of my own kip."

"Do you?" inquired Jo.

"Do I what?" asked the pickpocket.

"Take 'em off?" the girl replied.

"Of course I do," the small man lyingly stated.

"I didn't know," Jo told him. "Some men don't. You impressed me as being such a type."

"Don't see why you should be discussing my habits at all right out loud in this fog and weather," Little Arthur complained. "Ain't we got no private lives?"

"Thus far," observed the red-headed girl, "my life has been much too private. I have decided to take steps."

"We won't have any lives at all," Peter put in, "if you two charming young things don't abandon Little Arthur's drawers as well as what's in them, and listen like hell for the shore."

"Well meant but indelicately expressed," replied Jo. "In moments of great danger the mind has a way of fixing itself on trifles. Should we sing, perhaps? People always do in little boats."

"Not a bad idea, that," Bishop Waller pronounced. "Singing lightens the spirits. Why not try a snatch of a song while I row?"

"I know a song," said Aspirin Liz.

"Let's have it," suggested Peter.

"Anyone got a pill?" she asked.

"Might have one in my bag," said Jo. "I'll look."

The girl succeeded in finding a rather soiled aspirin tablet and passed it to Liz.

"What are you going to use for water?" Little Arthur asked.

"Never use water," she said. "Keep it under my tongue. It's better that way."

Little Arthur shook his head in the darkness. This woman was hard indeed.

When the tablet had been satisfactorily adjusted under Aspirin Liz's tongue, she broke suddenly into violent song, her voice floating mournfully across the water:

> "*O bury me not on the lone prairie-e-e*
> *Where the wild coyotes will howl o'er me,*
> *But lay me out in a quiet churchyard*
> *In a grave dug six by three.*"

So sang Aspirin Liz as a depressed silence fell upon the occupants of the little boat. Their spirits were not lightened.

"Golly," said Little Arthur with a slight shiver. "That's an awfully sad song. Them howling coyotes. I can hear 'em now."

"Wish I could," replied Jo. "I'd let a chorus of wild coyotes howl o'er me if they'd give me a prairie to park on. There must be something solid behind all this fog and darkness."

"Wonder what it is," said Yolanda in a subdued voice.

"Africa, maybe," Jo answered.

"Wish it were the Riviera," observed Peter.

"Ain't we got enough water already without adding some foreign river to it?" the ignorant little felon demanded.

No one paid any attention to him, each being occupied with his or her thoughts.

"It's a miscellaneous cargo we have aboard," observed Aspirin Liz at last. "A bishop and a crook and a lady of fashion—what are you, Mr. Van Dyck? I'm a model, myself—that is, I was one before I lost my shape."

"Don't know what I am exactly," Peter replied, somewhat in doubt himself. "What am I, Jo?"

"An indifferent coffee importer," answered Jo. "And I'm his invaluable secretary."

"He's the only surviving male of one of New York's oldest families," Yolanda Wilmont proclaimed, not without pride.

"Go on! Is he, now?" said Little Arthur. "Well, I'm proud to be wearing his drawers, but if we don't find a scrap of dry land soon it looks like that old family is about due to lose its last male survivor."

"Right, Little Arthur," Jo maliciously agreed. "Instead, they can lay claim to having the soggiest nonsurviving male of any old family anywhere."

"That, at least," remarked Peter, "would lend me a little distinction."

"I like you better dry," said Jo, "and very much alive—pulsating, in fact."

"What do you mean by that?" asked Peter.

"My dear," Jo replied. "Spare the Bishop's feelings."

"You're a wicked lady," declared Little Arthur. "And you use horrid words—pulsating."

"I'll use horrid words on you," Jo told him. "Change places with the Bishop or this skiff will ride higher from the loss of one feather-weight crook."

"Which end of these sticks do you pull?" gasped Little Arthur after the perilous exchange of seats had been made, not without endangering the safety of all hands. "Just to hold 'em still is hard enough, much less waggling 'em about."

"Don't make yourself out any dumber than you are," replied Jo. "Put the wet ends of those sticks in the water and pull your small but black heart out."

"Sure, sonny," said Aspirin Liz encouragingly. "Find a pocket in the fog and pick your way through it."

"I can't stand wisecracking women," Little Arthur remarked to misty chaos. "Bad taste and worse manners."

Slowly the rowboat moved ahead, but very slowly—too slowly. Peter critically watched his valet.

"Little man," he said, "you're not pulling those oars. They're pulling you. Put your shoulders into it."

"Put my shoulders into what?" groaned Little Arthur. "Wish I could put them into a bed."

"Use your back, man," the Bishop commanded somewhat impatiently.

Little Arthur laughed hysterically.

"Use my back," he sneered. "Can't even use the mere end of my back. Every time I try to put it down on the seat these here oars deliberately flip it off as if it was a moth. First thing you know I'll be flying. And you ask me to use my back."

"If you don't use your back I'll kick it," said Jo.

"Want me to sit on your lap?" asked Aspirin Liz. "That would hold it down."

"That would break it down," he told her. "Let me alone for a minute. I'll get the hang of it soon. What do you expect a pickpocket to be—a motorboat all of a sudden?"

"I expect you'll be a sinking body if you don't get a move on," Josephine declared.

"Have a heart, lady," he pleaded. "This was your idea, having me row. I didn't ask for the job."

"I think he talks too much," said Peter. "Let's gag the little blighter."

"I'm gagging already," the little blighter complained. "No need to help me. Fair sick I am, what with all this brutality and bobbing about."

"Pipe down, everybody," Jo commanded. "I hear something."

Something was wallowing close by in the fog.

"Who's there?" called Peter.

"Only us," replied a familiar voice ironically.

"You mean the ferry?" Peter almost screamed.

"Yoohoo!" called the voice. "That's who we are."

"For God's sake go away," yelled Peter.

"What for?" said the voice. "We like it here. Want to come back home?"

"No!" shouted four voices from the rowboat, Little Arthur being too discouraged to answer and Yolanda too disgusted.

All sorts of unpleasant noises were launched from the ferry. Personal insults fell thick around them. Even Little Arthur was stung to life and action.

"How's our dear sweet captain?" he inquired, with an astounding vocal inflection.

Immediately the captain told them not only how he was, but also how he hoped they were and where he hoped they would go. He referred individually and collectively to the characters, antecedents, and habits of everyone in the rowboat, and finished up by threatening to run the small craft down. It was too much for Little Arthur. He stood up suddenly, and like Ajax defying the lightning, impotently thumbed his nose at the fog in the direction of the ferry. There was a loud cry and a small splash. Little Arthur was no more with them.

It required some minutes to drag the wet snatch-purse back over the side. He was delicate about it. His fear of rough handling was equal to his fear of cold water. He was a small, soggy mass of moist lamentation, the utter futility of ever changing one's undergarments being his chief source of complaint. At last he lay panting in a puddle in the bottom of the boat.

"Bruised, body and soul," he muttered. "A nervous breakdown, no less. A mangled man."

"If you ever try to give us the slip again," Jo gritted at him between her small white teeth, "you'll be a mutilated man."

"What!" he choked. "Do you think I tried to do it?"

"Of course you tried to do it. Wanted to run away," said Jo.

"Across the bottom of the sea, I suppose?" he retorted. "I ain't no blarsted mermaid."

"Well, if you're not a mermaid," she continued, "I'd like to know what you are. Certainly, you're not human."

"Might not be human," the man admitted, beginning to doubt it himself. "Don't feel like it right now. But I ain't no mermaid, at any rate, and I ain't no trained seal, either, like you think I am, making me do boat-racing all over the fog."

"Little valet," put in Peter with calm conviction, "if you don't get up quietly and quickly and stop all that yapping, I'm going to put you beyond the reach of the law forever, and that with this one hand."

Little Arthur took a look at the one clawlike hand extended over him and thanked his God it was not two.

"Yes, sir," he muttered. "Can I sit down by you?"

"I'm going to row," said Peter. "Rested up, Bishop? I'll take the starboard oar."

When this arrangement had been worked out, the rowboat once more got under way. The gratuitous but hardly constructive suggestions of the ferryboat's passengers followed them through the fog, then gradually died away. Silence settled down on the occupants of the rowboat. Peter and the Bishop were too deeply occupied to speak. Little Arthur was too miserable, Yolanda too aloof. Josephine listened for offshore sounds, and Aspirin Liz seemed content to sit and do nothing. The minutes piled up and drifted by until time became as nebulous as the fog. Still the two rowers stuck to their oars. Peter was cracking under the strain. His face had grown a little more haggard, his cheeks flushed. Josephine quietly removed the oar from his hand and seated herself by the Bishop.

"Give way," she said. "I hear waves washing on something more substantial than fog."

Peter sank down by Aspirin Liz and again the boat moved forward, tunneling its way mole-like through the fog. Sounds of a chugging motor came from the port side.

"Who are you?" called the Bishop, resting on his oar.

"A group of American citizens, sir, running rum into their native land," came the prompt reply.

"You're frank about it," Bishop Waller declared.

"We can afford to be in this fog," the voice answered cheerfully. "We're more than frank—we're abandoned."

"We're abandoned, too, but without any rum," Josephine informed the American citizens.

"That's bad," came the sympathetic reply. "Perhaps you would care for a bottle?"

"We'd devote our lives to it," yelled Peter. "Dedicate them to the bottle."

"Have you a corkscrew?" called Jo.

"You all can't be American citizens," came back the voice, "if you haven't one of those things. Stand by to break the Eighteenth Amendment, and keep on shouting."

The chugging of the motor grew nearer, and presently a hand holding a quart bottle, and reminding Peter of a picture of Excalibur in some long-forgotten book, was thrust through the fog.

"It is open," said the hand cryptically. "Remove the cork and drink."

"Awfully good of you," said Peter, plucking the bottle from the fog.

"Don't mention it," replied the voice, equally courteous.

At this moment a stealthy breath of wind blew the fog aside. The moon swam through the mist. The night became vivid.

"Why, you're all naked," said Peter, too stunned to be surprised.

"Yes, quite," said the man in the motorboat. "We all are."

A synchronous gasp broke from the rowboat.

"God send back the fog," prayed the Bishop, in a fervid voice; then added, with a note of prudence: "Temporarily, at least."

Although there were only five naked figures in the motorboat, they were quite enough for those in the smaller craft. To them the motorboat was fairly swarming with naked figures. It was by no means difficult to distinguish between three men and two women. It is a singular thing yet nevertheless true that there seems to be a lot more to five naked persons than to five persons either fully or partially clad. There was certainly more than enough to those five naked bodies.

"Gord," breathed Little Arthur. "How come you lost all yer clothes?"

"We didn't lose them," the naked spokesman replied. "We took them off."

"Whatever for?" the crook asked incredulously.

"Don't ask such silly questions of the gentleman," Josephine primly told the pickpocket.

"I see no good reason for asking him any questions at all, silly or otherwise," put in Yolanda, her eyes averted but not closed.

"Oh, don't mind us," said the man easily. "This is our way of doing things, that's all."

"It's a poor way, indeed," said Bishop Waller. "Wouldn't it be more thoughtful to do such things elsewhere?"

"We don't mind where we are," declared the man.

"You seem to think we're considering your plight," replied the Bishop, "whereas in reality we're considering only ours. It's distressing enough to be investigating an unknown body of water without the enforced companionship of five naked ones."

"Oh, you'll get used to all that," said the man prophetically.

"Do you mean by that," inquired the Bishop, "that you plan to continue this close association?"

"If that great big strapping woman with the mole on don't stop grinning at me," chimed in Little Arthur, "I'm going to jump clean back in the ocean."

"Where's the mole?" demanded Jo.

"What a thing to ask," the valet retorted indignantly. "It's where nobody should see it, that's where it is."

"Then why look?" asked Bishop Waller.

"Nonsense," Aspirin Liz observed with the utmost calm. "She's a fine figure of a woman. I was very much like her myself in my day."

"What do yer mean?" cried Arthur. "Mean ter say you ran about naked?"

"I usually stood or lay," replied the imperturbable Liz.

"And you openly admit it in public?" the small crook got out in a scared voice. "Oh, you are a one, you are. A regular broad and no mistake."

"Fiddlesticks!" snapped the retired model. "I made my living that way."

"It ain't a thing to dig up out of the past," Little Arthur told her, "much less to brag about when we're all in danger."

The naked man and his companions had been enjoying this conversation. One of the women now spoke.

"Why don't you get naked like us, midget?" she asked Little Arthur with a touch of malice. "Or are you afraid you'd fall apart?"

"Mind your own business," the small man answered stoutly. "Should be ashamed of yourself."

"I've lost all shame," said the woman.

"Madam," pronounced the Bishop, "if you'll pardon me, you've lost a lot more than that, and if you don't do something about yourself rather soon I'm afraid I'll lose the training of years and go a little bit mad."

What the woman could have done about herself will never be learned, because the fog intervened at that moment and devoured her nakedness.

"Mr. Van Dyck," resumed the Bishop when the unique group had faded from view, "I think it would be just as well if someone else tried that bottle other than yourself."

"Pardon me," said Peter, passing the bottle to the Bishop. "The incident rather unnerved me."

"I'm hardly tranquil myself," replied the Bishop. "And then, of course, there's the fog. That is equally or, rather, almost as dangerous."

He raised the bottle and drank, then passed it to Jo, his rowing partner.

"My child," he said in a hoarse voice, "this will strengthen your arms."

It must have had that effect, for no sooner had the girl

polished off her drink and passed the bottle to Aspirin Liz than she and the Bishop began to row with surprising speed and irregularity. The boat darted capriciously through the fog. Once it pivoted crazily round, then started off at its mad pace. Evidently Josephine and the Bishop were intent on seeing which side of the boat would get anywhere first.

"How far is the nearest land?" called Peter after the motor boat.

"That depends on which way you're heading," came the rather disturbing reply. "Not far in one direction, but thousands of miles in the other."

"Which way are we going?"

"Just about the middle," the voice drifted back.

"A lot of help that is," grumbled Little Arthur. "Can I have some of what's in that bottle?"

"Give the little convert a dram or so," puffed the Bishop. "It will do him a world of good."

"I don't want to do him any," said Aspirin Liz. "Here you are, crime wavelet, choke yourself to God while you're still redeemed."

"No need ter get nasty about it," objected Little Arthur, accepting the bottle with an eager hand. "If a bishop can keep this stuff down I ought ter be able ter *get* it down, at least."

With a feeling of fascinated revulsion Yolanda watched the Adam's apple as it bobbed and quivered, paused, then bobbed again in Little Arthur's throat.

"There seems to be even less sex distinction in this boat than in the other," she observed bitterly.

Little Arthur took the bottle away from his lips and eyed the young lady reprovingly.

"Shouldn't talk about sex," he rebuked her. "We've seen too much of that already. Have some of this?"

"After watching you," she informed him, "I find it easy to refuse."

"Ain't nobody civil in this here boat?" the small man asked hopelessly.

"I'm just sufficiently civil to accept a drink from you, Little Arthur," Peter told him, reaching for the bottle.

"Even though I am trying," remarked the Bishop, resting a moment on his oar, "still I can't quite forget that singular encounter of a few minutes ago."

"Wouldn't have been more surprised," remarked Aspirin Liz, "if that boat had been chuck-full of bounding lions."

"No doubt we'll never learn the beginning or end of that story," Josephine said. "This whole business has a dreamlike quality."

"I don't mind it," replied Peter drowsily. Fatigue, grog, and fever were assaulting him with sleep. Soon he was well off, half drunk and half in dreams.

"It certainly wasn't no way for American citizens to act," put in Little Arthur with an air of one who had always done a little more than his duty to his country.

"Look! What's that?" cried Aspirin Liz in a startled voice pointing to a white strip lying pallid beneath the filtered light of a moon swinging high above the fog.

"That's dry land," Josephine informed her. "Ever hear of it before?"

"It seems to have been connected with my far-distant past," said Aspirin Liz, her eyes devouring the smooth beach. "That and beer."

A few minutes later the rowboat scratched its nose on the sand, but Peter Van Dyck never knew it. He was unconscious of what lay behind him as well as of what lay ahead. Had he not been so, he might have put back to sea.

CHAPTER THIRTEEN

The Naked Physician

PETER VAN DYCK AWOKE TO FIND A NAKED FIGURE STANDING by his bed. This hardly placed the figure in Peter's mind. To him almost any naked figure would have been a considerable shock. This one was. In the course of his thirty-four years Peter had scarcely associated at all with naked figures. From what he saw of this one, he had no desire to take up the practice at this late date. Therefore it was with a feeling of mingled constraint and alarm that he swiftly cast his eyes over this unclad body before resolutely looking at something else. The man was carrying a small black bag. This added to the shock, this bag. Its owner was standing in an attitude of negligent but well-bred repose which struck Peter as being rather incongruous in view of his appalling condition.

Could this stranger be, by any remote chance, the telephone man gone a little mad, Peter wondered, or a skilled artisan subject to one of those embarrassing mental aberrations popularized by Freud? Could he possibly have called to do things to a typewriter or a drain pipe or to perform some other highly specialized operation involving the removal of his clothes? Far simpler it was to assume that the man had been on his way to take a bath when he had suddenly been seized by a desire to look on another human face. But why the black bag? Peter decided to ask rather than to wonder.

"Hello," he said. "Who are you?"

The man smiled much more naturally than Peter had believed a naked man with a black bag could smile.

"I am the doctor," he said in a well-dressed, cultured voice. "The doctor of the house."

Peter gagged a little at this.

"What," he began rather fearfully, "what sort of a house is it?"

"A delightful one, my dear sir," said the doctor.

"In what sense?" asked Peter.

"In every sense," the man assured him.

Suddenly Peter remembered. His arm. He must have grown worse during the night.

"Listen, Doctor," he said anxiously, "I must be sick as hell if you didn't stop to put on your clothes."

"Nonsense," replied the doctor shortly. "Your arm is perfectly safe. I call on all my patients like this."

Peter shrank back among the pillows.

"Oh," he said faintly. "You do?"

"Why not?" snapped the doctor.

"Why not, indeed?" repeated Peter with a sick smile. "Being a doctor and being used to naked bodies and all, I suppose you don't mind . . . much."

"Much!" exclaimed the doctor, laughing scornfully. "Why, my dear chap, I don't mind at all. Like it, in fact."

"And your patients?" inquired Peter.

"They like it, too," said the doctor complacently.

"They do?" asked the incredulous Peter.

"Certainly," replied the doctor. "Why not?"

"I wish you would stop asking me why not," Peter complained, once more running his eyes rapidly over the naked man. "From where I am I can see any number of reasons why not."

"What's wrong with me?" demanded the doctor. "Tell me that."

"Merely that you're as naked as the palm of my hand," Peter observed. "Apart from that small item you look perfectly natural."

"My patients don't seem to mind," retorted the doctor.

"I can't understand that," said Peter. "I should think they'd all pass out from sheer panic."

"My dear young man," said the doctor, striding over to the window with his little black bag, "don't be childish."

"Come away from that window," cried Peter. "Don't make this a public scandal."

"Why worry about that?" said the doctor carelessly.

"Somebody has to worry about it," replied Peter. "I have no desire to have you seen in my room. It's not at all nice, Doc. Wouldn't be quite so degrading if you happened to be a woman, although that would be bad enough."

"Naked women," answered the doctor, flexing his limbs by squatting suddenly. "You'll have more than you want of those in here."

Peter was too alarmed by the man's words to be revolted by his actions.

"What!" he exclaimed. "Naked women in here?"

"Why not?" asked the doctor, turning from the window.

"Let's be reasonable," said Peter. "You know why not without asking me. You're a bit of a joker, aren't you, Doc?"

"Not at all," the doctor answered coolly. "Some of my favorite patients are women, if you'd like to know."

"You mustn't get much work done," Peter remarked thoughtfully.

"Just what do you mean by that, young man?" asked the doctor.

"Everything," said Peter. "All."

"You're vulgar," replied the doctor severely. "Lots of my patients are ladies, and all of them are naked."

"I know," said Peter, "but at least they have bedclothes over them."

"I pull those off," snapped the doctor.

"Good God!" said Peter. "What a doctor!"

"As a matter of fact," the doctor went on meditatively, "the ladies seem to take to it quicker than the men."

"Take to what?" asked Peter fearfully.

"Being naked," replied the doctor.

"Do you mean to your being naked or to their being naked?" Peter wanted to know.

"To our being naked together," said the doctor, neatly dislodging with his left foot a spring fly from his right shin.

"Well, that seems natural, at least," went on Peter, "although I rather boggle at the term 'ladies.' "

"That's what they are," said the doctor. "Perfect ladies."

"Perfect in what sense, may I ask?"

"In the right sense, of course."

"You seem to have a rather distorted conception of just what is right," observed Peter. "For example, I don't think it's at all right for you to call naked on equally naked ladies."

"Why not?" demanded the doctor. "I cure them, don't I?"

"I know," went on Peter reasonably, "but curing them of one complaint might easily give rise to another."

"There are never any such complications, I assure you," said the doctor with great dignity.

"Then there must be something funny about the whole business," muttered Peter, thinking of Josephine's legs. "Or else you're a little more than human or 'way below par. I don't understand it at all."

"No," replied the doctor. "You're too much a creature of the flesh."

Peter laughed sarcastically.

"You're entirely a creature of the flesh," he retorted. "I, at least, am part bed."

At that moment, his troubled gaze straying through the door carelessly left open by this mad or abandoned doctor, Peter witnessed a little incident not given to every man to behold. A naked man, blithely carrying a ladder under one arm and swinging a pail of paint in his free hand, was footing it silently along the hall from one direction. From the other came a woman, equally innocent of clothing. She was bearing a breakfast tray. Peter's natural assumption was that the woman upon seeing the man would drop her tray and run like hell while the man would do likewise. Instead, he was shocked to see them dexterously pass each other with an agreeable nod and continue calmly about their business. The man in the bed drew a deep breath, then his eyes sought the doctor's.

"Do all the servants in this place go about like that?" he asked. "And for God's sake don't say 'Why not?' "

"I feel like it," said the doctor. "How else would you have them go about?"

Peter momentarily thought of the Bishop, then a small grin relieved the tenseness of his lips.

"Couldn't you dig up a couple of towels for them?" he asked.

"And what, pray, would they do with the towels?"

"Hang them about themselves somewhere," said Peter. "Even you should see a little sense in that, Doc."

" 'Fraid I'm a trifle dense," remarked the doctor, now busy with Peter's arm. "Can't see it at all. Exactly where you would want them to hang the towels is beyond my comprehension. However——"

"You are sadly lacking in imagination," said Peter, a little bitterly.

He said no more for the reason that he had suddenly disappeared beneath the bedclothing. A naked woman, bearing bandages and a basin of warm water, had come briskly into the room.

"Here you are, Doctor," he heard her say. "Sorry I was a little late. There's a gentleman in Seventeen who refuses to give me his drawers."

"Sit it down, sit it down," replied the doctor testily, and Peter wondered under the blankets how a naked man was able to talk like that to a naked woman.

The doctor was struggling with the coverings. He was trying to pull them off.

"No, you don't," grunted Peter. "You didn't give me any pajamas."

"Have we any pajamas on?" cried the doctor, panting a little from exertion.

"No," replied Peter. "You have not. You're both naked as hell and you're trying to make me like you."

He heard the girl laugh horridly, then fresh hands were laid on the coverings. It was an unequal struggle. What with Peter's wounded arm there were four hands against one.

"How far are you going to pull those coverings down?" he gasped.

"All the way," gritted the doctor. "Clean off."

And he did.

Peter, wild-eyed, gazed helplessly up at the two bodies bending over his. The girl's eyes were merry while those of the doctor were mad.

"No more of this larking," the man snapped, skillfully bathing Peter's arm.

"Larking," said Peter, amazed. "Did you think I was doing that?"

"Either that or making a lot of fuss over nothing."

"Nothing!" cried Peter in a frenzied voice as he ran his eyes down over his body. "Oh, God, he calls it nothing."

"Stop trying to attract attention to yourself," rasped the doctor. "You're not so hot."

Peter was almost speechless with indignation.

"Call attention to myself?" he repeated. "I ask you—could I be any more conspicuous than I am?"

"Certainly," replied the girl, her blue eyes dancing with unholy merriment. "In evening clothes you might pique my curiosity. Even in a pair of drawers you might give me a little thrill."

"Aren't you ashamed of yourself?" he asked her in a wounded and wondering voice.

"Not a bit," she replied. "It's all in the day's work."

"Then God knows what you must do at night," he answered. "There's no use for me to try to look somewhere else, because wherever my eyes turn one of your naked bodies manages to get in the way."

"Why not look at yourself?" suggested the doctor.

"That sight is even harder to bear," said Peter.

"Funny," remarked the girl. "I don't seem to mind you at all."

"Why don't you both crawl in bed with me and make it a clean sweep while you're at it?" Peter asked sarcastically. "You don't seem to mind anything."

"I'd hate to do that," said the doctor fastidiously.

"Is that so?" said Peter. "May I ask what is wrong with me?"

"I believe you're a thoroughly evil-minded man," replied the doctor. "You'll have to watch your p's and q's round here."

"Strikes me I'll have to watch a damn sight more than that," muttered Peter.

"Don't fret," put in the girl soothingly. "We'll keep an eye on you."

"That's just what I'm worrying about," said Peter. "There'll be too many eyes on me."

"You'll have quite a lot to do with your own eyes," said the girl. "Don't forget that."

"Not for a minute," Peter answered.

There was a scuffling sound at the door as Little Arthur, armed with a mop and pail, scrambled nakedly into the room.

"Boss!" he cried wildly, running up to the bed. "They've taken away all my clothes and I'm as naked as a babe."

"Naked as a what?" asked Peter.

"A babe," replied Little Arthur, a strange and awful sight. "A small child."

"You impress me as being much nakeder than even the smallest child," said Peter. "You're simply epic."

"Don't know what that is, but how about yourself?" asked Little Arthur. "And look at that brazen hussy."

"At least I've a bandage on," replied Peter. "And don't ask me to look at anything. Never thought I'd see so much in all my life."

"What the hell good is a pickpocket in a nudist colony, I ask you?" the little man tragically demanded.

"That is something to ponder on," observed Peter. "I should imagine you'd have to be far cleverer with your hands than you've ever been before."

"Might just as well have no hands at all," Little Arthur answered bleakly.

"So far as pockets are concerned," added Peter. "However, I should imagine that many men in a nudist colony would find one pair of hands hardly enough. By the way, are we in a nudist colony?"

"Either that or among the white-slavers," breathed the little crook. "It all comes to the same thing."

"Which is?" inquired Peter.

Little Arthur blushed.

"Don't ask that," he stammered, "in front of this here woman."

"Oh," said Peter. "Have you met these nudes already?"

"If not them, I've met a dozen just as bare," Little Arthur lamented. "Can't keep my eyes in one place long enough to tell one of 'em from the other. Don't know which way to turn."

"Why not crawl into your pail?" asked Peter.

"Wish I could," the naked felon replied. "If it wasn't full of water I'd stick my head in it."

"Do it anyway," snapped the doctor, speaking for the first time since Arthur's arrival, "and hold it there awhile."

"Nice way for a doctor to talk," said Little Arthur, offended. "It's a murder house, that's what it is, and worse."

"I was speaking personally rather than professionally," the doctor told him. "Speaking professionally, I'll have to ask you to get about your business, whatever it may be."

"They want me to swab up the bathroom," the undernourished snatch-purse complained with a sob in his voice. "Think of it. Me swabbing up a bathroom the way I am."

"I should think the way you are would be ideal for bathroom swabbing," allowed Peter.

"You're almost as bad as they are, boss," the little man replied. "Don't you feel sort of funny lying there naked and all?"

"Sure," said Peter. "I feel so funny I think I'm going to cry."

"Hurry," commanded the doctor. "If you don't want to get into any trouble, do exactly as you're told. Otherwise, things will go hard with you, let me assure you of that. We stand for no nonsense."

"If you ask me, that's all it is," said Little Arthur, moving slowly towards the door. "Too damn much nonsense. Running around naked and carrying on. I suppose you think that's sensible? Well, it isn't. It's just plain childish, I calls it. It's worse than that—it's nasty, that's what it is. It ain't even human."

The doctor pointed a sharp instrument at the scolding crook.

"Want me to operate on you?" he asked.

Little Arthur instinctively glanced at himself.

"Oh, no," he breathed. "No indeed."

Peter chuckled in spite of his own unprotected state. He had never seen this mite of a man so utterly sincere.

"Then be gone!" thundered the doctor.

"See here," protested Peter. "You can't talk to my man like that."

The doctor looked darkly at Peter, then suddenly snipped the gleaming blade at him.

"How would you like that?" he asked in a gloating voice. "Or this?" Here the doctor made an even more excruciating snip at Peter as if visualizing the horrid deed.

Peter shrank visibly in every fibre of his body.

"There's no need to be so vivid about it," he muttered. "So

garishly dramatic. I'd do exactly as he says, Little Arthur, if you want to remain intact. This man is sort of crazy."

"Can't I stay here with him?" pleaded the little man. "Naked as he is I can at least recognize his voice."

"Go," said the doctor, and Little Arthur, mop and pail, disappeared from the room.

"Listen, Doctor," began Peter when his valet had gone nakedly to whatever lay ahead. "I've been hesitating over this question for some time. Tell me honestly—am I in a madhouse or a socially prominent brothel, or in the shrine of some fanatical cult, or just where am I?"

"I am not in a position to satisfy your puzzling curiosity," replied the doctor, repacking his little black bag.

"Then it certainly must be terrible," observed Peter, "because you apparently stop at nothing."

"Come," said the doctor to the girl. "We must be skipping."

"Don't skip before me," put in Peter. "I don't think I could bear the sight and still retain my reason."

"Your wound, which luckily is slight," continued the doctor, ignoring Peter's remark, "will be dressed again this evening."

"Couldn't you leave me a little extra dressing?" Peter asked. "Just a bandage or so? I've got an idea."

"That would be cheating," said the girl, following the doctor from the room. "Besides, it would look extremely silly."

"I feel extremely silly," Peter called after her as she left the room without closing the door.

No sooner were his two visitors gone than Peter sprang from the bed and tiptoed to the window. Protected by a curtain he discreetly peered out upon a green, rolling lawn splashed with sunlight and early flowers nodding up encouragingly at him in a breeze blowing fresh from the sea. And there was the sea itself, the sea looking a little unfamiliar now that it was clear of fog. Forever and forever it seemed to run, that flat, streaming surface, into a cool blue solitude untroubled by voice or wing. In his present naked predicament Peter very much wished he could enjoy a reasonable quantity of that solitude himself. Shifting his fascinated eyes from this ever-reaching expanse, he turned them on the dense, deep green of trees sweeping round the house in a half-moon of leafy protection. Branches waving in the wind, white clouds above, and white bodies on the lawn, white and gleamingly naked. An appalling sight, this, and yet not unpicturesque. Peter drew a deep breath. A little of his profound belief in the established order of things began to drop away from him. In the face of so much nudity he found himself doubting the reality of such terrifically reiterated facts as the Empire State Building, Tammany Hall, and crooning. Had the bodies been black instead of white, he would have felt a little better about it. Black bodies and brown ones had a way of getting naked. But, then, the black races were not essentially interested in things of the flesh like the white race. No. Black people took the flesh at a stride and passed on to the supernatural and other things of the spirit with only an occasional fleshly picnic—a good rough-and-tumble sort of orgy that cleared up a lot of nonsense and left their thoughts free for other and more important considerations.

A period was put to his confused meditations by a furtive sound in the room behind him. Turning, he beheld still another naked body. But this naked body was by all odds more disconcerting than those he had previously encountered, and this in spite of the fact that it was the most alluringly fashioned body it had ever been his good fortune to behold.

For a moment there was a tense, watchful silence in the room as wave upon wave of emotion dashed over Peter, but before he went down for the third time a bright little idea came to what he hoped would be his salvation. With nerveless limbs he staggered to the bed and disappeared beneath its coverings. However, the same bright idea seemed to have found an opening in Josephine's demoralized mind. Stopping only to close and lock the door, she rushed across the room to the bed and, dragging the clothes off Peter, promptly emulated the example he had so brilliantly set.

"Give me those bedclothes," grated the gentleman, laying frantic hands on the coverings, "and get out of my room and bed."

Josephine hung on grimly.

"I won't!" she gasped. "I won't!"

"But you've left me naked as a coot," cried Peter.

"That's your worry," she said. "Better you that way than me."

"I don't know," replied Peter distractedly. "I can't say. Both ways are pretty awful. I do know, however, I'm not going to lie here like this and argue about it with you."

So saying, he gave the coverings a brutal tug, and Josephine's naked body appeared as Peter's burrowed under. It was a scene of desperate activity and concentration. Chivalry and gentleness were sacrificed to meet the demands of modesty.

"A nice man," Josephine panted. "A lecherous little mole of a man. Snatch all the clothes from a naked woman, will you? Well, we'll see about that. I'll have you stripped in the shake of a lamb's tail."

"Mine's shaking enough for a whole flock," came Peter's muffled voice. "Go away and stop all this talking."

"I should worry how much it shakes." Jo flung herself at the coverings and neatly twisted them from Peter, wrapping them round herself.

"This can keep up forever," muttered Peter, "until we're so exhausted we won't be able to cover ourselves at all."

"If you hope that's going to happen you're very much mistaken " said Jo. "I'm under these coverings for good."

"Don't see why you're under them at all," he protested, churning the air with his hands. "An astonishing thing to do —crawling nakedly into bed with a man."

"You crawled nakedly into a closet with me."

"I know, but a closet's different."

"Why, may I ask?"

"Obviously a closet is not arranged."

"What in the world do you mean?"

"I mean that a bed is always associated with vice and carrying on," he told her. "You should know that yourself."

"I sleep in my bed," she replied.

"Well, you're not going to sleep in mine, and that's flat."

"I'm not going to do anything else."

"Who wants you to do anything else? Go on. Go back to your own bed and sleep."

"I can't," she protested. "Perfect strangers keep coming in. I was looking for Aspirin Liz when I saw you. Then I said to myself, 'Any port in a storm,' and here I am."

"Let me assure you, my girl," said Peter, hoping to frighten her, "you picked far from a safe anchorage for your body. I'm drifting into danger myself."

"With you, Peter," she replied in a voice he both feared and suspected, "I can face any danger."

"Sure," said Peter, "you might even think up a few. No fooling now. Give me back those bedclothes. It's your turn to be naked for a while."

"Let's compromise," suggested Jo.

"We are compromised," he retorted. "If this gets out we'll be ostracized for life."

"If what gets out?" asked the girl, popping up her head interestedly.

"This situation," chattered Peter, flipping over on his stomach like a netted fish without having the comfort of knowing whether he had improved himself any. "Please throw some coverings on me."

"He wants me to cover him, no less," she said with nasty derision. "Cover your own vast nudity. I'm too busy with mine."

By a miracle of contortion Peter succeeded in worming his body beneath the bitterly contested bedclothes only to find himself face to face with his disconcerting bedfellow.

"Aren't we in a terrible fix?" he asked her in an awed voice.

"I don't know," said Jo. "Some persons might not think it so bad."

"You're awful," he breathed, looking at her almost with admiration. "I can't stand things like this. Actually, I'm nearly exhausted from excitement. Might swoon at any moment."

"You're far from complimentary," she told him, her red head thrust out of the clothing within three inches of his. "What did you think of my one-piece, Peter?"

"From the glance I got," he said, "you weren't wearing any."

"I certainly was," she declared. "One piece of skin."

Peter shivered at this.

"How you put it!" he muttered. "Would you ever have believed two days ago that we'd be like this in the same bed?"

"Yes," she said without batting an eye.

"What!" exclaimed Peter.

"Certainly," she replied quite calmly. "Why not? Other people have."

"Not nice people," he argued.

"Very nice people," she told him. "Some of the best."

"You mean married, of course."

"Well, that would tidy up the situation a bit," she replied thoughtfully, "but in view of the extraordinary circumstances in which we find ourselves through no fault of our own I, for one, am willing to waive certain little formalities, or at least to delay them."

"You talk too much," he answered, "altogether too much, and you don't mean one eighth you say—that is, I hope not."

"I'm not so sure," said Jo. "Anyway, I know I love you."

"Is this a nice place to tell me that?"

"If I didn't tell you that," she retorted, "the situation would be just plain wicked."

"I've never been in a wickeder," he confessed.

"Well, I've been a shade more remote myself," she admitted. "When one's in Rome, however, I suppose one might just as well make hay while the sun shines."

"I'm under the impression these particular Romans don't," said Peter. "The doctor seemed very snooty."

"Don't what?" she asked.

"You're always so damn blunt," he complained. "I mean they don't make hay."

"Then they don't sound like Romans to me," said the girl. "Those old devils were always making hay."

"You carry logic to the point of depravity," he objected.

"I don't understand," said Jo.

"Well," he began with an effort, "I don't quite understand myself, but it's like this: Logically speaking, this situation calls for a certain line of conduct, whereas——"

"Almost demands it," said Jo.

"Don't interrupt. Whereas, morally speaking, if you were a lady you'd get the hell out of here and go back to your own bed."

"But, morally speaking, suppose I wasn't a lady?" she asked.

"Then naturally we couldn't continue to speak morally," he replied.

"I'm glad of that," said Jo, running her fingers through his hair.

"Don't do that," he told her. "Don't make the slightest move."

"Shouldn't I do this?" she asked, a white arm slipping snakelike round his neck.

"No," he replied. "Not that nor anything like it."

"What will you give me if I don't?"

"I haven't a damn thing to give," gloomed Peter. "They didn't even leave me a check book. If they had I'd tear out the checks and rig up a girdle for myself."

"You'd look sweet," said Jo.

"Might not look so well," he told her, "but I'd feel a lot less public."

"You know those women?" Jo asked in a conversational voice.

"No," Peter replied. "I don't. What women?"

"Those women," Jo went on, "who claim that if their husbands came home unexpectedly and found them in bed with some man, the husbands would show how evil-minded they were if they thought anything wrong about it—do you know those women, Peter?"

"There may be longer and less ably stated hypothetical questions," replied Peter, "but I never answered one. No. I don't know those women, thank God."

"Well, what I was trying to say," she continued, her arm tightening round his neck, "is that I'm not at all like those women."

"And if I happened to be your husband," said Peter, "I wouldn't believe you if you were."

"Then that clears away a lot of obstructions," she observed.

"May I ask what all this is leading up to?" asked Peter.

"To this," said Jo.

She kissed the man and forgot to stop.

CHAPTER FOURTEEN

In Pursuit of Privacy

"YOU HAVE THE MOST EVIL-LOOKING HEAD OF RED HAIR I ever saw," Peter vouchsafed lazily some time later. "Just like some of the smaller flames of hell or those snake-like locks of Medusa. And your face is baleful, too, in a beautiful sort of way."

He was lying on his right side, critically surveying the girl's face, touching it here and there with an inquiring fingertip.

"I don't know how I can lie here in bed and look at yours," she told him with a small companionable yawn. "God must have run out of color or lost interest when He came to your hair and eyes. You're merely tinted. To me you are singularly rabbit-like."

"In what sense, may I ask?"

"In appearance," she said. "I daresay you consider yourself the Casanova of the coffee world now."

"No," he replied. "I have no such exalted aspirations. I am merely a man who will stand for so much and no more."

"It's too bad you're not the kind who will go just so far and no further," Jo retorted.

"One can hardly do that with you," he said easily. "You'd drag them the rest of the way."

"Oh, so I'm the responsible party," she observed, gouging him in the cheek, "while you, you poor dear, are the wronged one."

"Exactly," was the complacent reply. "I look upon myself, thank God, in the most detached light. Only in a remote way, like an extra on a crowded stage, am I connected with the drama of your inevitable downfall."

"I don't like that crowded-stage crack," the girl replied sombrely. "You were the first player in my young life. And as for that downfall stuff, don't confuse life with fiction. There're more ruined women in the world today eating three square meals with an easy conscience than there are homes for wayward girls."

"You're hard," said Pete.

"No, I'm not," she retorted. "I'm reasonable. And I'm not at all unromantic. For instance, I think it's quite beautiful being here with you like this. Won't forget it for some time."

"When you feel that you're beginning to, just drop round

when you're not busy and I'll try to refresh your memory," said Peter.

"You see," asserted Jo triumphantly, "you're really the hard-boiled member of this team. Men usually pretend to make quite a fuss over the women they've ruined. You strike me as being a little proud, a little strutty."

"I confess I don't know," he admitted. "No man ever attempted to ruin me, but as you say, I do suspect myself of a slight feeling of elation."

"As much as I hate to take the wind out of your sails," she said, "in justice to myself I must remind you that far from being your victim you're jolly well mine."

"Stuff and nonsense," scoffed Peter. "You're merely a butterfly on the wheel, crushed and broken—another conquest, no more and no less."

"You'll be crushed and broken, you little coffee bean," she retorted hotly, "if you don't watch your step. I ruined you, my lad. You didn't ruin me."

"It hardly seems sensible to be lying here disputing over which of us ruined the other," he remarked. "It's a highly technical question."

"My eye, it is," exclaimed Jo. "You're damn well seduced and I did it."

"Have it your way," he said amiably. "Just so long as one of us was seduced, I don't care much who it is."

"Oh, you don't," she snapped. "Just like a man. Ruination means nothing to you."

"Inasmuch as you insist on me being the ruined party," he mildly protested, "I'm doing my best to be as cheerful as possible among all the débris."

"And succeeding almost too well," she retorted. "One would think you actually enjoyed it."

"Well," confessed Peter ruminatively, "you must admit it has its lighter side."

"I admit nothing," she said.

"Under the circumstances that would perhaps be best," he agreed. "In fact, I'd deny everything, if you don't mind an impersonal suggestion."

"I'm telling Yolanda right off," she told the man with malicious enjoyment. "Then I'm going to tell the Bishop, and after that I'm going to get him to marry you to me."

"How are you going to manage that? Seduce him, too?"

"If necessary."

"Rather than that should happen, I'll marry you, if not of my own free will at least without public lamentation."

"Then you do care!" cried Jo, impulsively flinging herself upon him. "How sweet!"

"I was thinking of the Bishop," he protested, making a poor showing of warding off her flashing arms.

Fortunately for this record Josephine's hoydenish activities were interrupted by a peremptory knocking on the door which was followed by the command of a stern voice. The sound of the knocking returned to Peter a terrible realization of the situation in which he found himself. And with the arrival of this realization his presence of mind departed. In a naked panic he sprang from the bed.

"Open the door!" cried the voice. "This is strictly against the rules. Open the door immediately."

"I don't know the rules," chattered Peter.

"You should know enough not to do a thing like that," the voice replied in high reproof.

"My God," muttered Peter, his face blanching. "The whole world seems to know already. Like what?" he asked aloud.

"Don't quibble with me, young man," said the voice. "If you don't open this door I'll have it broken down. Is there a woman in there with you?"

"What made you get that quaint idea?" asked Peter, motioning Jo to silence.

"There's a girl missing," came the answer. "And sometimes new arrivals carry on."

"Carry on how?" called Peter, sparring desperately for time.

"When were you born?" queried the voice.

"This is hardly the proper moment for vital statistics," retorted Peter. "Go away and leave that door alone."

Fresh voices could be heard in the hall—the patter of bare feet. There were sounds of suppressed laughter and giggling—frolicsome slaps on bare flesh. Peter closed his eyes and shuddered. He pictured a mass of naked bodies waiting outside the door to witness his disgrace. The pounding was resumed. In his desperation he forgot his wounded arm and began to tear a sheet in strips, thoughtfully putting one aside.

"What are you doing that for?" Jo asked in a low voice.

"Through the window," he told her. "Tie the blankets together."

"I mean the sheet you put aside," said the girl.

"I'm going to wear that," he replied briefly.

"What about me?" she asked.

"Haven't time to think of that now," he muttered. "I'm much too busy."

"Sir Galahad in the flesh," she said in an awful whisper as she sprang from the bed. "A little nude coward."

Busily she began to tie the blankets together as the pounding was redoubled on the door.

"Open this door, I tell you!" cried the voice. "What are you doing now? What can you be doing?"

"Use your imagination," snapped Peter.

"It seems fairly obvious," shouted the voice on a note of bitterness. "Here goes the door."

A resounding thud shook the door as Peter grabbed the blankets from Joe, added his strip to them, and, securing one end of the rude line to a leg of the bed, tossed the other end out of the window. Twisting the remaining sheet round his body in bizarre tufts and slashes, he hurried to the window.

"One moment, my small Mahatma," said Jo in a low, unpleasant voice. "Are you planning on leaving me behind?"

"Not making any plans for you," he replied. "I'm simply taking care of myself."

Without even glancing down to see what fate lay below him, Peter seized the knotted bedclothing and disappeared through the window, his wounded arm paining unnoticed beneath its bandage.

"Damned if I'll let him get away with that," Jo muttered, her eyes searching in vain for some garment to wear in her flight. "Honor is lost, but pride dies hard."

She ran to the window, and with a prayer in her heart to the god of impulsive maidens, lowered herself on the strip. Peter, glancing up with a strained face, almost lost his grip. More stunned by what he saw above than by what he feared below, he continued on his way, grimly wondering the while if the world had ever witnessed so indecent an escape staged in any language.

Jo speedily overtook the queer-looking object below her. Soon she was ready to pass him, but hardly in a position to do so.

"Can't you find some place to sit on, other than my head?" Peter inquired wanly.

"How can I?" she called down.

"I don't know," he replied. "That's what I'm asking you."

"I'm doing my best," she assured him.

"You're doing too damn well," he grunted. "if you want to know, you're doing your best to crush me to earth."

For answer Jo reached down with a momentarily freed hand and snatched the sheet from his body. Peter emitted a small shriek of dismay.

"There are too many people on the lawn," she told him. "I need this."

"Can't see a thing for your feet," he got out. "They're dangling in my eyes."

"You must look pretty from down there," she retorted.

"From here you're nothing to sneeze at, yourself," he retorted.

"A lot of people are looking down at me," said Jo. "A lot of faces from your window. They're furious."

"They'd be frozen from this end," he assured her. "Wish I were back in the fog."

His wish was almost granted, for Jo, twisting the ends of the sheet round her neck, allowed the covering to flow down over her body and continue on over part of Peter's. The effect was astounding. It was that of a creature or thing that had started out in life as a red-headed woman and who at some time during the stages of a strangely attenuated evolution had decided to finish off her already sufficiently bewildering body with the long and skinnily dangling legs and feet of a man. The great expanse of mysteries that lay between the flaming head and shrinking feet was luckily more or less hidden from view by the frantically fluttering sheet. As this weird, synthetic figure crawled lumpily down the strip of bedclothing, new arrivals on the lawn were almost too frightened to ask what it was. They seemed to prefer to remain in ignorance rather than to face what could not be otherwise than a decidedly unpleasant fact.

"How much farther do we have to go?" asked Josephine, her strength rapidly failing.

"By this method not much farther, I fear," Peter drearily communicated through the sheet. "I'm about ready to fall to my death at any moment now. And, by the way, before I go I'd like to say how greatly I've enjoyed your comfortable rest on my head. You seem to think I'm an elevator."

"Hurry up!" cried Jo. "If I start to fall I'm going to take you with me."

"There is a sea of faces below," he informed her. "I'd like

to fall on all of them, but their mouths are shockingly filled with teeth."

"You mean dogs?" asked Jo.

"Worse than dogs," said Peter. "Naked bodies that once were human."

As if by special arrangement the sheet parted a moment, and Peter found himself gazing in through a window on a scene of domestic activity. A lady was drying herself with a towel while her husband, or rather, one whom Peter piously hoped was her husband, was busily combining the worst features of a setting-up exercise with those of an interpretive dance. Upon seeing Peter, they both nodded casually. Then as he seemed to continue on indefinitely they decided this manifestation was sufficiently interesting to justify closer examination. They hurried to the window.

"I thought you were one," the man called down to Peter.

"Oh, no," replied Peter, halting his descent. "I'm at least two."

"I mean," said the man, "there's something above in a sheet."

"There is, indeed," answered Peter. "You don't know what all there is in that sheet."

"Are you exercising?" asked the dripping woman. "Is this some new wrinkle?"

"I'm wrinkled all over, lady," came the voice of Jo, "and every wrinkle hurts."

"If you really want to know," called Peter, "we're trying to escape."

"From what on earth?" asked the man.

"Oh, everything," said Peter. "All things on earth."

"From our thoughts," put in Jo.

"Just mentally run down," said the wet woman to her husband. "This place will do them a world of good."

Peter laughed wildly. "It's helped us a lot already," he

said. "Morally as well as physically we feel like giants refreshed—like a couple of shooting stars, in fact." Suddenly his voice took on a note of anguish. "I'm going, Jo," he called. "Here drops nothing. My arm's gone bad."

As Jo reached down to grab him, she felt herself being dragged from the line, and even as she fell through space she managed to find some comfort in the thought of what a low hound Peter Duane Van Dyck was to have pulled her with him.

They landed amid a lot of naked bodies, bearing some of them with them to the ground, upon which they lay for one startled moment; then, springing up, dashed across the grass in the direction of the nearest trees. The naked bodies capered after them, laughing and shouting to one another like sportive maniacs. And that was more or less what Peter judged them to be, only he was not so sure how long they would remain in a state of amiable hilarity. The pack of them might undergo a sudden change of mood and rend him limb from limb. There was no room in his thoughts at the moment for the safety of Josephine's limbs. Embarrassment added to fear forms a sufficiently strong combination to demoralize the stoutest of souls. Dressed, Peter might have been willing to turn and face the world. Naked, he had only one idea, and that was to let the world and all its works very much alone.

Peter might have achieved his burning ambition—the blessed protection of those trees—and so might Josephine, his nearest rival; this temporary relief might have been vouchsafed them had it not been for the intervention of an unkind fate in the guise of ebullient flesh and lots of it. It so happened that as Peter was passing a large, formal flower bed, a large but informal-looking gentleman materialized from it and with amazing agility set himself in motion to spoil Peter's plans.

"A chase!" cried the man, dancing delightedly after Peter. "Watch me catch you."

"Not for a moment," Peter jerked out. "Go chase yourself."

"This," replied the man, leaving the ground and landing on Peter's back, "is much more fun."

"Damned if I see it," muttered Peter as he fell earthward on his nose.

"Caught!" cried his excited antagonist. "Now you chase me."

So saying, he sprang up and, taking a return pursuit for granted, sprinted busily across the lawn. Peter followed the man's example but not his direction.

"If he's foolish enough to think I'm going to chase him," Peter reflected, "he's due for a bitter disappointment."

At this moment his speed was checked by the sound of a desperate cry.

"Help, Peter!" screamed Josephine. "If you don't come back I'll tell them what you did."

Peter came back. In fact, he hurried back. Although he could not see Josephine, he had, from the noise she was making, a general idea of her whereabouts. She was under the large body of an exceedingly active woman. The mere thought of laying violent hands on so much bare flesh to which he had never been properly introduced somewhat retarded Peter's celerity of decision. Tentatively he grabbed the twisting woman, then quickly withdrew his hand. The physical contact had been too much for his nerve centres.

"Come on," panted the woman, seizing his ankles. "I'll get you down, too."

And get him down she did. She got him down and literally incorporated him into the gyrating mass of bodies, arms and legs. He had never realized before that there could be so much unclad flesh in any given quarter of the universe. Even then in this primitive struggle Peter strove to conduct himself as he thought a gentleman should under the circumstances, although exactly how a gentleman should accomplish this was beyond his conception. However, as the woman's grabs and thrusts became more careless and at the same time more telling, Peter began to realize that if the last surviving male of one of New York's oldest families desired to acquit himself with honors he must abandon the restraint of a lifetime and do his level best. He must fight fire with fire, which in this situation meant to seize upon whatever part of the woman lay most convenient to his hand. Comforting himself with the reflection that she had exercised little restraint in the handling of his body, he rose and, taking hold of the woman, threw her several feet away. She landed with a gurgle of laughter and promises of further endeavors.

"Listen, lady," said Jo, hoisting herself up wearily from the grass by means of Peter's leg, an action which in other surroundings would have filled him with consternation, but which in these he scarcely noticed. "Please, lady," she continued, "we're not playing. Honest, we're not."

"You give in?" cried the woman, gathering herself for a fresh assault.

Then the Van Dyck blood rose rebelliously in Peter's veins. Naked or fully clad, a Van Dyck would never give in. Either naked or clad, it was a rare Van Dyck indeed who had ever given anything. Van Dycks always took. So would this one. He took to his heels without further parley, and Josephine took right after him.

"They're trying to play with us, Peter," she explained, a shade above her labored breathing. "It's all a game to them."

"It may be a game to them," he flung back, "but it's serious as hell to me. Hurry up. Get a move on. That woman was simply awful. She was all everything."

"Wasn't she lots?" agreed Jo. "Where're we going, Peter?"

"How should I know?" he asked her. "By rights we should be dashing gayly from the wings of the Follies."

"The seduction scene in this drama," said Jo, "was enjoyable if not edifying. I can see some sense in a thing like that, but this naked chase is beyond me."

"If you hadn't sneaked into my room," complained Peter, "this would not have happened."

"Then do you admit you were seduced?" she asked.

"Is this a time to argue about that?" Peter demanded, glancing over his shoulder at their pursuers, now close at their heels. "It's no go," he continued, pausing to let the girl overtake him. "Those naked fanatics can run like hell. We'll never make the woods."

"I don't see what good it would do if we did," Josephine asserted.

"We could climb trees," Peter suggested dubiously, "or dodge about behind them."

"Playing Adam and Eve among the trees is about as comfortable as making love on a beach," Josephine assured him crisply. "Both are exploded theories."

"My education along certain lines is less extensive than yours, it seems," was Peter's tart rejoinder.

"Well," replied Jo, "be that as it may, but if anyone had told me a few days ago I'd be spending the week-end arguing about such matters with a naked gentleman in the face of an onrushing multitude of naked lunatics, I'd have said that only the first part was either possible or desirable."

"Occasionally I've dreamed about situations just like this," said Peter.

"Was I along in those dreams?" Jo asked. "Don't let's run any more."

"Those dreams were bad enough," he replied, "without you making them any worse. And we're not running, if you care to know. My arm hurts like hell."

"It's bleeding," said Jo, a spark of concern in her eyes.

"And the bandage is coming off. If I wasn't so worried about my own condition I'd be worried about yours."

"I'd like to wind the bandage around me," said Peter.

"It's not doing any good where it is," replied Jo. "Want me to do it for you?"

"God, no!" exclaimed Peter, bending on her a pair of agitated eyes. "What a suggestion to make."

"Why don't they come and get us?" asked the girl. "Look! They've gone into a huddle."

"A pretty sight," mused Peter, gazing upon the nude grouping. "Wonder what they're cooking up?"

He was not long in learning. Suddenly the intimate little mass of bodies resolved itself into individual nudes who galloped towards Jo and Peter. In a moment the two of them were surrounded by a dancing garland of men and women, all singing lustily a song which even in his own embarrassment made Peter feel a little embarrassed for the singers.

"I am coming, I am coming, for the dew is on my feet," the singers informed the semi-crouching couple in the centre of the whirling circle of arms and legs and everything else.

"I don't give a damn what's on your feet," Peter yelled back, "if you'd only let me stagger away on mine."

"I am coming, I am coming, where the little birdies tweet," the naked dancers went on melodiously to explain.

"Aren't they silly?" Peter asked, turning to the girl beside him. "Honestly, they almost make me forget the figure I cut."

"The trouble with this arrangement," Jo complained, "is that when you turn your back on some of them you turn your front to the others. It's the viciousest damn circle I've ever been in."

"Then why not stand still?" said Peter.

"I'd like to lie down," she told him.

"All right, let's," he replied. "Flat on our stomachs."

"I think I'll curl," said Jo.

"I'd like to wither," said Peter.

And to the surprise of their prancing entertainers, Jo and Peter thereupon lay down on the grass and arranged their respective bodies according to their conception of what the occasion demanded and what was best to conceal.

CHAPTER FIFTEEN

The Bishop Insists on His Drawers

THE NAKED PEOPLE, WHEN THEY SAW THEIR QUARRY GO to earth, promptly lost interest in dancing and stood gazing down at the two strangely twisted figures with friendly concern.

"What's the matter?" one of them asked. "Resting?"

Peter groaned aloud at this, and Josephine, a small white ball, giggled to herself at the questioner's simplicity.

"No," she replied. "We're looking for edelweiss."

"Edelweiss grows in the Alps," the man informed her.

"Does it?" Jo said innocently. "Then if you'll go your way we'll go ours."

"There must be something wrong," another voice declared.

"I suppose it would be quite hopeless," said Peter, bitterly addressing his words to a cluster of bare feet. "I daresay it would be positively ridiculous to try to make you understand even the most obvious things that are wrong with the situation."

"Not at all," a pair of feet replied. "We're an exceptionally intelligent group."

"I don't see how that can be," protested Peter. "Tearing about all exposed isn't especially intelligent."

"In pairs it might be, Peter," said Jo, "but not in large, impersonal masses."

"So that's it!" cried a voice. "You don't like being naked, eh? Embarrasses you?"

"Worse than that," said Peter. "It paralyzes me."

"If you can't guess what's wrong with us," Josephine offered, "I'll tell you under three separate and distinct headings so you won't get confused. A: We're naked. B: You're naked. C: We're all naked together. And if that doesn't make it clear, I'll toss in another letter. D: There isn't so much as a doll's handkerchief to cover a dozen adult members of the male, female, and indeterminate sexes."

"There's more of us than that," someone remarked.

"Well, after you've reached a dozen naked bodies," replied Jo, "it takes a cooler brain than mine to keep an accurate count."

"Tell 'em to go away, Jo," said Peter. "I don't like it here."

"Go away," Jo told the naked people. "He doesn't like it here. The grass tickles."

"I didn't say that," said Peter. "However, it does."

"What's wrong with him now?" asked a female member of the party. "Has he lost his voice?"

"I've lost everything but an audience," Peter retorted. "And I don't want that. Honor, hope, and decency are gone, all gone. I wish you would go, too."

"If you don't like being naked," inquired a hitherto silent member of the group, "why did you come here?"

"Didn't know anything about it," declared Peter. "I was partly drunk and partly delirious, and I wish to God I was in that happy state right now."

"Yes," supplied Josephine. "We were lured into this fix. A fully clad gentleman met us on the beach and offered us the hospitality of his home overnight. When I woke up, my clothes were gone. Immediately I suspected a bad house. I still do, a little."

"Mine were gone, too," proclaimed Peter dramatically, "and in their place was a man—a naked man with a funny little black bag. What a pretty sight that was, first thing in the morning! A naked man with a black bag. My word!"

"That would be our doctor," a voice said proudly.

"He pretty nearly made a wreck of me," snapped Peter.

"Yes. That was Dr. Wolf," another voice declared.

"He looked like one," replied Peter, "without the sheep's clothing."

"He's a very nice doctor," cried a girlish voice. "He believes in nuts."

"So do I," said Peter, "after this morning."

"You're actually brilliant, Peter," Josephine told him. "If they'd provide us with a pair of blankets we could talk like this indefinitely."

"Then you are not voluntary nudists, we take it?" a lady inquired.

"That's right, lady," put in Jo. "You can take it or leave it. Lying here naked like this is one of the most involuntary acts in my life. It's almost instinctive."

"Well," announced a new voice authoritatively, "you'll have to come along now voluntarily or otherwise. The leader wants to see you."

"The leader?" laughed Jo sarcastically. "Do you mean that smooth little snake in the grass who lured us into his establishment? If so, I'm anxious to see him, too. I'll claw the clothes from his body."

"He doesn't wear any," continued the man.

"He did last night," said Jo.

"I know," continued the other impatiently. "He had just returned from a trip to town. Now he's like the rest of us."

"He won't be long," cried Jo, thoughtlessly springing up in her eagerness for action. "His skin will be in shreds when I get through with him—in tatters."

"I won't get up," groaned Peter. "I can't get up. It's against every instinct in my being. Can't we call on this procurer alone?"

"You seem to have got used to the little lady," said an insinuating voice.

"She's an old friend," explained Peter. "She knew my father."

"And I fancy he would approve of your conduct?" the voice continued. "You were in the same room together behind a locked door."

"Sure," retorted Peter. "My father used to do that himself."

"How do you mean? He used to do what?"

"Why go into details?" cried Peter. "He was a man who craved privacy—liked naked bodies and everything behind locked doors."

"We go in for naked bodies here," the man replied, "and leave everything else alone."

"That hardly seems logical," said Jo. "If true, why the naked bodies? Strikes me as living in the lap of an anticlimax."

"We dance and exercise as God intended us," the man explained.

"Don't tell me that," declared Jo, warming to the argument. "When God made a man and woman He had a lot more in His mind than dancing and silly exercises. He might not have said it in so many words, being quite content to leave a few things to the imagination."

"I won't attempt to explain," replied the man with offended dignity. "I fear it would be quite useless." Here he paused and turned to two companions. "If you two," he resumed, "will be good enough to drag that body up from the grass we will bring it along with us."

"Keep your hands off of me," cried Peter. "If I must get up I'll do so under my own steam."

Painfully Peter rose from the grass and stood huddled up beside Josephine, his eyes ruefully fixed on his feet. A realization of the ordered madness of life was growing in his mind. He had started this naked business himself by dashing unclad down his own stairs in pursuit of a siphon-squirting pickpocket. Destiny, seeing in him a willing subject, had since that unconsidered moment done with him as it pleased. What, exactly, would Aunt Sophie or Sanders do under similar conditions? It stultified his imagination to think of them standing naked on a lawn in the presence of a group of equally naked strangers. How was Yolanda taking it? Not at all well, he felt sure. Not nearly so well as Josephine, but then the latter was of different clay—much coarser and nicer.

The naked people gathered companionably round him—too companionably for Peter's comfort. In spite of his morning's introduction to the flesh he still shrank from promiscuous contact with it, still objected to being bumped and jostled by naked bodies. Such alarming experiences were occurring with increasing frequency as the party approached the long white house. Deep verandas flared from its sides upon the cool green of the lawn—deep verandas with well-tailored awnings picked out in stripes of white and orange.

"Not unlike your drawers," observed Josephine, pointing to the awnings.

"Wish I had a pair right now," was Peter's wistful answer. "They would give me a slight shade of moral ascendancy at least."

"If you can't maintain your morals naked," a tall scholarly individual cut in, "you will lose them entirely when dressed."

"That," said Peter, "would disturb me very little. I don't care how many morals I lose so long as I retrieve my clothes."

"Not an edifying attitude," replied the man. "Why don't you stand erect like the rest of us? Why not throw out your chest and shoulders? You walk like a man with knots in his bowels."

"What!" Peter almost screamed, recoiling from the speaker's side. "A man with knots in his what? No. Don't speak. I'd rather you wouldn't."

"My friend finds your words even less comforting than your body," Josephine informed the man. "And so do I."

"It's disgraceful," muttered Peter, "the way these men and women strut along just as if nothing was wrong with them. They throw everything out—chests and all. Wherever I turn my eyes some horrid section of anatomy fairly leaps into view."

"But you really are walking like a camel in labor," Josephine reminded him.

"If I could walk with my head between my legs I'd feel all dressed up," said Peter.

"That sight would be even more memorable than the present one," his red-headed companion replied.

By this time they had reached the house, which they entered, only to find themselves in the presence of a fresh burst of nudity. Naked people were sitting, squatting, and reclining wherever Peter tried to rest his eyes from the sight of flesh. Had he been able to discover the Bishop bereft of garments he might have found some comfort there. Even an unclad Aspirin Liz would have provided a slight kick, but the only member of the party who was present was his valet-pickpocket, Little Arthur. This small individual was standing miserably behind a high-back chair, and Peter could not but envy the felon's tactical position.

The room was long, low, and raftered. It was luxuriously furnished and decorated with quiet good taste. There was nothing mad about the room, a fact which rather than comforting Peter increased his sense of alarm. Perhaps these people instead of being crazy were merely depraved. A stout bronzed gentleman, Peter noticed, was reading the financial section of the morning paper with as much absorption as if he had been fully clad. Peter could not understand it. At a small table a huge gray-haired lady whose seemingly endless expanses of flesh should have been covered by yards of black brocaded satin was diligently cheating her way through some involved game of solitaire. True to form, reflected Peter, if not to convention. Still another figure—a sharp-cornered gentleman dressed only in a pencil—was engrossed in a crossword puzzle. He was entirely unconscious of his surroundings.

Scattered here and there on pillows, young women were combing each other's hair and twisting it in odd fashions. A man wearing only a pink beret was making a sketch from which Peter promptly turned his eyes. Several men were standing in a group by a large buffet. They were engaged in drinking coffee, and one of them was asserting that Al Smith might still have a chance to be President if he would discard his brown derby. In view of the fact that the speaker had discarded everything himself, Peter decided he was exercising admirable restraint in regard to the ex-governor's wearing apparel. Peter would not have been at all surprised had the man stated that if Al Smith discarded all his clothes he could walk into the White House, the unanimous choice of all parties. Through a long window he could see a number of naked children wandering about the lawn. They did not seem elated. Some of the older ones, Peter thought, looked far more self-conscious than their elders. Evidently they had not yet been entirely claimed by the general depravity. This was quite natural, children being instinctively conservative like all other self-respecting animals.

But by far the most arresting figure in the room was that of a young man reclining a little apart from the others on a large divan. Even in his unclad state there was a sense of satanic polish about this person. In his eyes dwelt a dangerously amused light, and his agreeable-looking mouth seemed capable of uttering quite acceptably the most objectionable blasphemies. Dark hair and dark eyes, remarkably fine, white teeth. The only suggestion of degeneracy about him, Peter concluded, was a duck, a large, self-possessed-looking bird squatting by its master, its long purple neck extended snake-like across the man's flanks. This duck had a pair of the most disconcertingly probing eyes Peter had ever seen in the head of man or beast. These bright beady eyes were now turned on Peter, who felt with an uneasy pang that they were reading him through and through and not altogether approving of the subject matter. Nor was there anything degenerate in either the duck's manner or appearance. It was the bond of perfect understanding that seemingly existed between master and fowl that impressed Peter unpleasantly. About both of them there was something severely sinister. For some reason the man's naked body suggested a perfectly fitting dress suit, while the duck brought to mind visions of some especially discreditable form of witchcraft.

"My name is Jones," said the suave-looking individual on the divan in a detached yet decently cultivated voice. "You are perhaps wondering, my dear sir, and also you, my red-headed young lady, how a person as naked as myself could bear such a simple name as Jones. However, as you grow to know me better you will understand that simplicity is the keynote of my character. My duck waddles through her days quite cheerfully with the name of Havelock Ellis. A pardonable whim of mine. Her attitude is so opposed to the Dance of Life."

"All this information may seem important to you," Peter replied in the true Van Dyck manner, "but to us it is ponderously superfluous. What is important to us is the whereabouts of our clothes and our friends."

Jones made a smooth gesture in the direction of Little Arthur, while the duck, slightly elevating her sleek head, looked directly at the partly concealed criminal as if he were one bug too many.

"Is that one of your friends?" asked Jones. "Don't hesitate to admit it if he is. Almost any peculiarity passes uncriticized here."

"That's just as well," Josephine spoke up. "Otherwise you'd be too busy."

"Yes," agreed the gentleman called Jones. "We would. But to return to that strange, almost human object——"

"Cut out yer wisecracking," retorted Little Arthur. "You're no better than a naked lounge lizard yourself."

"If as good," replied Jones easily; then, turning once more to Peter: "Your other three friends seem disinclined to leave their rooms. You two, I understand, succeeded in visiting each other. For your sakes as well as ours we won't go into that. We will try not even to think about it. However, I see no reason why we should longer deprive ourselves of the company of your friends. We shall send for them."

Jones clapped his hands, and two oppressively large-looking individuals appeared at his summons. They were innocent of garments but not unconscious of their absence. At that they were more fully clad than the others, being decorated with light blue armbands, the uniform dress of attendants.

"Drag 'em down, boys," Jones told them briefly.

The boys paddled heavily up a long flight of stairs, and presently sounds of vituperation were heard in the hall above.

"Keep your nasty talons off me," came the voice of Aspirin Liz. "I've been naked in front of real gentlemen, I'll have you to understand, and they never laid a hand on me unless——" At this point in Liz's narrative there was a momentary pause, then she resumed: "It's none of your filthy business. I've learned some mighty dirty tricks in my time, you pot-bellied bucks, and unless you take your hands off me I'll play them all at once."

Apparently the boys must have doubted the extent of the model's learning, for the next few moments were devoted to deep-throated cries of anguish and indignation.

"I wonder what she could have done to them?" Jones mused aloud to his duck, who significantly lowered the lids over two yellow eyes.

At this moment Aspirin Liz, shaking with coarse laughter, appeared at the head of the staircase. Holding with one hand to the banister, she slapped with the other enough thigh to make at least three of the average large woman, which, it must be admitted, is a stupefying amount of thigh.

"For once I don't need an aspirin," she announced mirthfully to the company below. "That did me a world of good."

"May I ask what you did to my men?" Jones asked, considering the figure with respectful eyes.

This question produced in Liz another spasm of mirth.

"Better ask them," she said at last, "but believe me, mister, I did plenty. And I'll do the same to you if you lay a hand on me."

Even the imperturbable Jones appeared to be momentarily disconcerted by this possibility.

"I shall endeavor to restrain my eager hands," he assured her as the mountain of a woman moved down the stairs.

"Oh, dear," she exclaimed, catching sight of Josephine and

surveying her with critical approval. "What a glorious figure you have, child. Why, you should go naked all the time. And if it isn't Mr. Van Dyck himself all undressed and no place to go."

"That's just the trouble, Liz," said Peter. "There's no place to go—nowhere to turn."

"Cheer up," Aspirin Liz replied in her hearty voice as she joined them before the divan. "Look at me. I'm three times as naked as you are—that is, I'm showing three times as much—and I don't mind at all."

"You're fortunate," Peter told her. "The relatively small amount I am showing bothers me a lot."

"That's because you never posed in the nude," Liz assured him. "You'll quickly get used to all this. It doesn't matter at all. And who may this naked reptile be? Did he send those heels after me?"

"I realize my mistake too late," murmured Jones. "I'm sorry, madam."

"It's too late for them," Liz retorted. "They'll never be the same."

Looking as if Liz had spoken nothing but the truth, the two attendants weakly appeared on the stairs and stood looking down with pain-ravaged eyes upon the room below. The two men were in turn subjected to the interested scrutiny of many pairs of eyes intent on ascertaining the full extent of the calamity that had befallen them.

"The lady is locked in her room," said one of the men in a hoarse voice, "and we're too weak at present to drag her out, Mr. Jones. The other party who calls himself a bishop says he won't come down unless we give him back his drawers."

A lean, sun-tanned person bearing the head of a Greek philosopher now spoke.

"If the gentleman is a bishop," he observed in a deep musical voice, "I think he should be allowed his drawers if only out of respect for his cloth."

"It does seem as if the situation justifies a slight deviation from our usual custom," Jones replied. "We have never had a bishop with us before, and I say better a bishop in drawers than no bishop at all."

"Give the Bishop back his drawers," several voices readily responded. "We want to see him."

"It seems agreed," continued Jones, "that the Bishop should retain his drawers. Very well, boys. Give him back his drawers and leave the lady alone until you feel a little stronger. Sorry about that other business. Women have rather —er—let us say, painfully primitive methods of retaliation."

A short time thereafter the Bishop, clothed in jaegers and righteous wrath, stood at the head of the stairs and like Moses from the mountain looked scornfully down on his naked audience.

"Although they are only drawers," Mr. Jones observed coolly, "there seems to be no end to them."

"My dear Bishop," exclaimed a lady volubly, "what a remarkable pair of drawers you are wearing. Tell me. Don't they tickle?"

"Probably the Bishop is thick-skinned," put in Jones, thoughtfully scratching his duck's head. "Bishops usually get that way."

"There is nearly enough material in those drawers," drawled a voice, "to make all of us in this room feel almost overdressed."

"There's not enough material in all the world to make me feel overdressed," said Peter. "As silly-looking as those drawers may be, I long to have them on."

"If I ever found you in drawers like those," Josephine declared, "there'd be no room for you in my life."

"I'm not usually found in my drawers," replied Peter.

"No," Jo admitted with confounding simplicity. "I never found you in a pair except once in the office."

"Don't let them kid you, Bishop," Aspirin Liz called encouragingly. "I've seen more peculiar-looking drawers than those in my day."

"Thank you, madam," said the Bishop icily.

"It must have been a mirthful day," the philosophical gentleman observed.

"There ain't a thing funny about them drawers," Little Arthur suddenly and sincerely proclaimed from behind his chair. "If anyone gave me my choice of drawers, I'd pick out a pair exactly like them—only lots smaller!"

"Of course," murmured Mr. Jones politely. "The mere sight of them makes me feel like panting."

Bishop Waller cleared his throat and raised an admonitory hand. It was a gesture that had silenced many a godless congregation before as it now silenced this one spread out nakedly at his feet.

"It is a sad commentary indeed," he said in a voice vibrant with emotion, "on your good taste as well as moral character that of you all only a recently converted criminal has sufficient discernment to recognize an honest pair of drawers when he sees one."

"What did I tell yer?" put in Little Arthur complacently. "You said it, Bishop. Them are good, honest drawers, yer reverence."

"Even better than that, Little Arthur," amended Bishop Waller, his voice rich with pride and approval. "They are quality drawers, my man. No finer jaegers made."

"And certainly no funnier," a brazen voice put in.

"Don't listen to them, yer honor—I mean yer reverence," the small crook continued heavily on the side of righteousness. "They ain't got a pair of drawers between 'em. Why, there ain't even a blessed pocket in the whole horrid outfit."

"Ah!" exclaimed the Bishop, beaming brightly upon his disreputable little convert. "No pockets at all. What a relief that must be for you, my fine fellow. No pockets at all—a blessing in disguise."

"This lot don't even trouble to disguise," Little Arthur muttered as his glance drifted disgustedly about the room.

"Nevertheless," went on the good Bishop, "God moves in a mysterious way His wonders to perform."

Little Arthur looked a trifle shocked. He hated to think of God as having had anything to do with this stark naked household.

"Perhaps," he agreed rather gloomily. "He's certainly made it impossible for me to perform any of my wonders. Yards and yards of naked flesh where pockets ought to be. What a place for a dip!"

"An ex-dip, Little Arthur," heartily replied the Bishop. "Never forget that, my fine fellow. An ex-dip."

At this point in the conversation Mr. Jones rose gracefully from the divan and, carrying Havelock Ellis carelessly under one arm, advanced to the foot of the stairs, where he stood looking courteously up at the Bishop, who in turn had descended a few steps.

"Bishop Waller," said Mr. Jones in a voice of the most convincing sincerity, "believe me, sir, we consider ourselves greatly honored to add one of your exalted station to our little group."

"Your naked rout," the Bishop corrected. "I refuse to be added to it."

"I hope you will later revise your judgment," said Mr. Jones. "And I trust you will also believe me when I say that it was not our intention to imply that your drawers were not strictly honest."

"Of course they're honest," exploded the Bishop. "But why waste time discussing my drawers when you are not wearing so much as a glove?"

"Quite," continued the smooth nude known as Jones. "Naturally your drawers would be unusually honest. As you say, there is really no need to discuss them."

"I don't hold with you there," broke in the man with the

philosopher's head. "To advance as a premise that, because a man is honest himself, the drawers he is wearing are equally honest, is entirely false and indefensible. In actual fact the wearer of the drawers may have a character of the highest integrity, whereas the drawers themselves may be utterly vile."

"I beg your pardon," expostulated the Bishop.

"By that I mean, my dear sir," the philosopher continued, "the drawers may be the product of non-union labor, of intolerable factory conditions, of unfair price competition, sweat-shop methods, horrid industrial slavery—who knows? There are more ways of making drawers dishonest than one."

"There's only one really diverting way," Josephine vouchsafed.

Aspirin Liz looked at the girl for a moment, then shattered the uncomfortable silence with her laughter. Peter sank down on the divan the impeccable Jones had abandoned and covered his face with his hands. He was too much of a coward to show in public his appreciation of Jo's unconscious revelation. The duck was looking at Aspirin Liz with glassily staring eyes. As accustomed as the bird was to flesh, she found it objectionable to contemplate so much of it in one body, one huge, swaying, cascading figure.

"That last remark may be stricken from the records," Mr. Jones resumed imperturbably, "if not from our minds. Let me go on to state, Bishop Waller, that the subject of your drawers would not have been brought up at all had it not been for our realization that to ignore totally a manifestation so peculiar—perhaps unique would be a better word—would have been so unnatural a suppression of emotion as to become in itself noticeable. You yourself, sir, might have experienced a sense of having been cheated, and that would have been too bad. Will you join our little gathering?"

Bishop Waller, not at all sure in what spirit to accept the invitation of the polished speaker, was about to comply rather than to stand isolated any longer on the stairs, when further independent action was taken out of his hands.

The wild cry of a desperate woman suddenly rang through the house. Turning, he was electrified to see Yolanda Wilmont, in a disheveled condition, appear waveringly at the head of the stairs hardly a foot in advance of an extremely active and naked man. After this the good Bishop saw nothing save a swiftly revolving universe composed entirely of stairs and contorted members of the human body. He was brought back to an unpleasant awareness of his surroundings by a sensation of insecurity round his waistline and a violent tugging at the back. Havelock Ellis, the duck, excited beyond endurance by the turmoil of the triple descent, had launched herself into action which centred itself on the rear part of the excellent Bishop's jaegers. Also, in the course of his swift passage down the stairs the Bishop had sustained the loss of his most invaluable button. Unable to rise for fear of losing his only protection, yet disinclined to remain prostrated and endure the envenomed assaults of the duck, Bishop Waller found himself in the unique position of one being torn on the horns of a dilemma about midway between Scylla and Charybdis. It is a position that even a bishop can scarcely face with an overabundance of fortitude. Bishop Waller feared that his supply was being rapidly exhausted.

"Will someone give me a safety pin," he asked in a weak voice, "and at the same time remove this infuriated duck?"

"Why, Havelock Ellis is actually pecking at the Bishop," a voice exclaimed.

"Both actually and viciously," gasped the Bishop. "And in an exceedingly mortifying spot, let me assure you."

"There could be worse," the philosopher observed.

"Let's not become involved in a long academic discussion as to what part of one's body is the most mortifying to have pecked by a duck," protested the Bishop, becoming slightly involved himself. "Suffice it to say that the spot this duck is at present pecking with the utmost determination is both mortifying and painful enough to convince even the most skeptical observer that something should be done about it. And," added the Bishop, "done without delay."

"You have convinced me," said the philosopher.

"Thank God for that," murmured the Bishop. "And the pin? The pin is most essential."

Now, to find a safety pin in a nudist colony is a task that would baffle the best minds of Scotland Yard. So hopeless was it that no one present made any attempt to look for one. Instead, Peter removed what remained of the bandage from his wounded arm and passed it to the red-headed girl who in turn conveyed it to the Bishop.

"Thanks, my dear," said the Bishop, eagerly snatching the bandage from her hand. "God will forgive you much for this."

"There will still remain plenty to be forgiven," said Jo with a pretty show of humility.

"No doubt," replied the Bishop, securing his jaegers with the bandage. "We will deal with that later if someone will collect this bird whose egg was indubitably hatched in hell."

Mr. Jones thereupon collected the squawking Havelock Ellis and at the same time assisted the Bishop to stagger to his feet.

"There are holes in the back, perhaps?" the Bishop delicately suggested in a low voice.

Mr. Jones, cocking his head at an angle, took a quick survey of the recent scene of action.

"No holes," he murmured to the Bishop.

"I find that difficult to believe," said the reverend gentleman. "There would have been soon—a great many, I feel assured. These jaegers, my dear Mr. Jones, are but recently purchased."

"They are exquisite," replied Mr. Jones.

Yolanda furiously confronted the speaker. She had been too long neglected.

"Does it matter to you if I'm assaulted beneath your own roof?" she demanded.

"Not at all, my dear lady," Mr. Jones replied with admirable urbanity, considering the nature of the question. "Make yourself entirely at home."

CHAPTER SIXTEEN

The Advantages of Nudity

"SIR!" CRIED YOLANDA. "ARE YOU TRYING TO INSULT ME?"

"Far from it," replied Mr. Jones, striving to bring his mind to grapple with the situation. "So many things are going on. Too many things. Aren't you the young woman who wanted to be assaulted?"

"Certainly not," retorted Yolanda. "This is too much. I was nearly assaulted."

"And someone interrupted you," exclaimed Jones, as if suddenly seeing a light. "How extremely trying! Who was the boorish party?"

"That man!" cried Yolanda, pointing to an excited-looking gentleman now being firmly held in check by two attendants.

Mr. Jones looked quickly at the man, smiled ever so faintly, then elevated his eyes.

"No," he said. "You misunderstand. I mean the interrupter."

"Heavens!" exclaimed Yolanda. "Have you taken leave of your senses? There was nothing to interrupt."

"But my dear young lady," protested Mr. Jones rather wearily, "I thought you said 'nearly'?"

"Listen," explained Yolanda, her own voice taking on a note of weariness. "That naked creature—that chattering baboon—climbed through my window and attempted to attack me. I fled down here. That's all there was to it."

"Not much, I'll admit," murmured Mr. Jones. "Scarcely anything at all." He paused, then looked startled. "Is it possible," he asked, "that you did not want to be assaulted?"

"Of course I didn't," replied Yolanda, too frustrated to be offended.

"Then why are you dressed?" asked Jones, elevating his upturned palms. "Don't you realize that the presence of clothes here is an open invitation to assault?"

"Do you mean that to protect her honor a woman here must first abandon her modesty?" the girl inquired bitterly.

"From your point of view," replied Jones, "you have stated the case concisely. Even those extraordinary garments the Bishop has on would make him subject to assault were it not for his high calling. Of course, in the case of the Bishop the assaultress would have to be a woman of great determination."

"I don't understand it at all," Yolanda uttered helplessly.

"Then let me explain," said Jones, leading her to the divan wnere they seated themselves beside Peter.

"Hello, Yolanda," muttered that individual huskily.

"Don't speak to me," snapped Yolanda, "you naked little nitwit. Should be ashamed of yourself."

"He's not subject to assault like you," retorted Jo, sitting down on a pillow at Peter's feet and resting her red head against one of his shrinking legs.

"I'm not so sure of that with you around," replied Yolanda.

"Well, just to add to your happiness," Jo answered, "I'm not so sure of it myself."

"Ladies," Mr. Jones interrupted. "Please let me explain."

"Go on, Mr. Bones," said Josephine. "That's about all you are—Mr. Skin and Bones."

Jones looked at her for a moment with pensively elevated eyebrows, then cleared his throat as if to rid himself of some disturbing impression.

"Mr. Jones," asked Peter, "can't you do a little something about this arm? It's had a hard morning considering it's been shot full of holes, or practically."

"Certainly, Mr. Van Dyck," replied Mr. Jones in great concern. "Call Dr. Wolf," he cried.

"Wolfie! Wolfie! Wolfie!" sang out a chorus of voices, and presently the naked physician, looking strangely out of place what with his professional air and incongruous little black bag, appeared, and with the help of a pretty assistant did things to Peter's arm.

"Well, you see," began Mr. Jones at length, "this little endeavor of ours, this small gathering of nudes, so to speak, is the result of too much reading, although the germ of the idea sprang from an age when books were not even printed."

"I can well understand that," rumbled Bishop Waller. "The history of the world is littered with examples of the most reprehensible attempts to imitate the more shady side of the Garden of Eden."

"No doubt," continued Jones smoothly. "All planets have had their pasts—their giddy moments in time. Yet, my dear Bishop, had it not been for such moments this world would not be populated today."

"Is it the aim of this small gathering of nudes, as you put it, to add to the world's population?" Peter enquired.

"Not its chief aim," replied Mr. Jones. "We would rather raise the standard, but of course we haven't got going in earnest yet. We have only been established a short time."

"For a short time you've done pretty well," interposed Little Arthur with a slight sniff. "There ain't any more left to take off unless we skin ourselves alive."

"Jean Jacques Rousseau, Havelock Ellis, Craft Ebbing, and even that indefatigable humanitarian, Mr. H. G. Wells, not to mention innumerable other great thinkers," resumed Mr. Jones, ignoring Little Arthur's interruption, "have all at one time or another been preoccupied with the idea of nudity."

"If them guys you mentioned spent their time thinking about naked bodies," Little Arthur declared, "they weren't great thinkers at all. Just plain nasty."

"It was not their desire, Little Arthur," Jones explained patiently, "to think about nude bodies. Nude bodies meant nothing to them. They——"

"Yeah," scoffed Little Arthur. "They must of been old hands at it—all worn out. Why, I'm just as great as they are. Don't even want to see nude bodies, much less think of 'em."

"Sex is entirely forgotten here," said Mr. Jones with crushing simplicity.

"With all the reminders on every hand," observed Josephine, "you must have exceptionally short memories."

"Sure," agreed Little Arthur. "Ain't we supposed ter use our eyes?"

"If you use no more than your eyes," replied Mr. Jones with a significant look at the little crook, "everything will be quite all right."

"Ain't we supposed ter be even human?" protested Little Arthur.

"We are supposed to be," said Mr. Jones coldly, "but I find it hard to believe that you are."

"If you ask me," put in Aspirin Liz, "when I look at some of the samples hanging about here I don't want to remember sex at all. If I had my figure back for five minutes there'd be a riot in this room."

"It ain't patriotic," the little thief asserted. "A lot of American citizens going around without even a pair of drawers."

"Look at it philosophically, my man," said the gentleman with the fine head.

"Look at what that way?" asked Arthur.

"At everything," replied the philosopher. "Everything."

"Well, if you can extract one grain of constructive philosophy from some of the things I'm looking at," declared Josephine as she glanced round the room, "you've got a more godlike mind than I."

"I have," said the philosopher.

"Please, mister, give me a pair of drawers?" the snatch-purse pleaded.

"If a bishop rates only a pair of drawers in this outfit," Mr. Jones replied, "where do you think you get off, you small unpleasant knave? Did you bathe this morning?"

What could be seen of Little Arthur was turning delicately pink. The small unpleasant figure was evidently engaged in blushing all over itself.

"What a question ter ask," muttered the unhappy man.

"It was unnecessary I'll admit," replied Mr. Jones. "Will a couple of you girls take him away and bathe him?"

Little Arthur's jaw fell, then disappeared with the rest of

his head behind the chair. Sounds of merriment were heard in the room as several girls and a male attendant dragged the struggling figure up the stairs. Little Arthur did not contribute to these sounds. He was all for having the law on the sleek head of Mr. Jones. He went even so far as to assert that he would never rest easy until the police had raided the place. At last his threats became incoherent, and when finally seen he was babbling like an idiot and endeavoring to prostrate himself on the floor of the upper landing.

"Perhaps we may be able to talk now," remarked Mr. Jones with one of his faint smiles when Little Arthur and his fair bath attendants had disappeared. "You see, Yolanda—I trust you will forgive me, but I cannot resist using such a pretty name—you see, my very charming young lady, I misunderstood the situation altogether. I assumed because you were dressed you naturally had certain ideas in your mind. So many women have, you know."

"No," replied Yolanda. "I don't know. I don't care to hear."

"But you must," persisted Mr. Jones. "It will do you a world of good." Here he held out the duck to an attendant standing near by. "Will you kindly take Havelock upstairs and toss him in with the person being bathed?" he said to the man. "The poor bird dearly loves a little romp in the tub."

A short time after the departure of the duck, screams of anguish drifted down to those in the room below. From the sounds Little Arthur was making, Havelock Ellis was having more than a romp in the tub. He was having a regular tussle.

"A lovable duck," observed Mr. Jones with a smile of rare sweetness. "So fond of snapping about in a tub—catching things under water."

With an expression of horror Peter gazed at the speaker, then looked down into Josephine's amused eyes.

"Oh," said Peter in a low voice. "Oh, for goodness sake! Poor, poor Little Arthur."

"Don't worry about that crook," she said reassuringly. "He's picked enough pockets in his time to be picked on a little himself."

"The fact is," Jones broke in, fixing the group with his enigmatic black eyes, "in this colony nudity leaves us emotionally cold, or should leave us cold. Of course there are occasional localized rises in temperature which are due, we hope, entirely to lack of training. On the other hand, the average well-built woman—and you are far, far above the average, my dear Yolanda—the average well-built woman, dressed as women dress today, which is a little more than demi-nude, arouse our gentlemen nudes to outbursts of simply amazing ferocity. To look at them now you would be surprised."

"I would not," Yolanda told him. "You forget I was the subject of such an outburst already."

"To be sure," exclaimed Mr. Jones. "It was fortunate indeed you managed to save as much of your honor as you did."

"First time I ever knew a woman's honor could be partially saved," Josephine remarked. "I always thought it was something you either lost outright or just couldn't give away."

"Not only are your thoughts painfully crude," Jones replied, "but also crudely expressed."

"Listen here, naked," Aspirin Liz asked from a pile of pillows upon which she was ponderously wallowing. "What's so wrong about a man and a woman having a little fun when they feel like it?"

"Nothing at all," Jones hastily replied. "I think it's both commendable and diverting—essential, in fact. What we do object to here is the undue emphasis placed on sex. Sex preoccupation day in and day out. Sex consciousness morning, noon, and night. What is the dress of woman but an invitation and a challenge to the eye, to the senses? Do women dress to keep warm? Certainly not. Do they dress to cover their nakedness? Certainly not. They dress to reveal it, to suggest it, to enhance it. A pair of high-stockinged legs against a background of frills is a far more provocative sight, with a few exceptions, than the same pair of legs nude, hairy, and garter-stripped."

"Say, young feller," Liz put in, a shade of respect in her voice, "You've been round a lot."

"And I hope to go round a lot more," he assured her, "but I have no intention of forgetting the fact that there are ever so many other things to do. Nor do I wish to be constantly reminded by fresh relays of sex-dominated women that there is only one inevitable end to social mingling of the sexes."

"A guy like you doesn't have to be reminded," Aspirin Liz declared.

"That's just the point," agreed Mr. Jones. "I need no reminders of sex to be brought to my attention. Very few men do. What we do need is something to get our minds on other things."

"How about drink?" asked Jo.

"Drink is a stimulant," Jones replied, "and would therefore defeat its purpose."

"I never expected to hear a naked man preaching to a naked audience words laden with so much practical morality," observed Bishop Waller. "I almost feel like taking off my drawers and leading you all in prayer."

"Let me ask you a question, sir," continued Jones, turning directly on Peter. "What is the good of a woman spending hours and hours in scenting, annointing, and dressing her body only to undress it again in from three to five minutes—in some cases even less—for the sake of some damn fool man who probably never knew what she had on to begin with and who would have reacted the same no matter what she was wearing?"

"You said from three to five minutes," Peter observed musingly. "In some cases less."

"Exactly," said Mr. Jones. "Sometimes even less."

"Have you gone round timing women at it?" asked Peter.

"That is neither here nor there," Mr. Jones replied impatiently. "I make five minutes the maximum because I don't think the average man will wait any longer than that."

"I know," agreed Josephine wisely. "Just great big, grown-up babies. After five minutes I suppose they begin to cry."

"Should we continue this conversation?" interposed the Bishop. "Should we?"

"Why not?" replied Josephine innocently. "Didn't you say he was speaking words of practical morality, Bishop Waller?"

"His words were safe," said the Bishop, "but I very much suspect yours."

"We order things better here," Mr. Jones resumed. "By taking off our clothes we forget about our bodies."

"What's the fun in that?" asked Jo.

"I'm afraid you'd find it difficult to understand," Mr. Jones replied, and this time his smile was a trifle too pleasant.

"I don't want to understand," said Jo. "Frankly, I'm very fond of my body. So much so, in fact, that if I did not have it I think I'd lose my mind."

Mr. Jones restrained the impulse to inform the red-headed girl that her total disappearance would not be so great a loss that he personally would be unable to survive it. Perhaps, upon considering her delicate yet not reluctant proportions, as he did now, he decided he would not be speaking the exact truth. Few men could look on Jo and wish her absent.

"Here," he continued, "we endeavor to retain both mind and body. However, we are making an attempt to give the mind for once an even break. In the old days when people went naked they were too busy either fighting things or each other to notice the absence of clothes. Today, when so many things are done for us, we have much more opportunity to take advantage of any sudden burst of nudity. Therefore, it is my belief that any attempt to introduce sustained nudity is as impractical as it is undesirable. In view of this we have made arrangements to enjoy at our little colony certain seasons and occasions. We have thought up names for them. They are to be called Seasons of Forgetfulness and Civilized Occasions."

"Go on," murmured Jo. "You interest me strangely, Mr. Skin and Bones."

Now, strange as it may seem, Yolanda, upon hearing Josephine's remark, allowed her eyes to pass swiftly over the tanned, youthful figure of Mr. Jones. Instinctively she felt inclined to take issue with the girl. There was something about Mr. Jones that pleased and attracted Yolanda almost too much. Perhaps it was because she was fully clad, or it might possibly have been because he was not clad at all. Whatever it was, the fact remained that Yolanda felt herself slipping, and for the first time in her life admitted to herself a sensation of healthy depravity.

"During Seasons of Forgetfulness," Mr. Jones explained, "it is our intention to get all dressed up and to conduct ourselves as men and women ordinarily do now under this regime of prohibition. In other words, we intend to drink bad gin in garish and cleverly faked up surroundings. Women will dress as provocatively as possible and men will pursue them without stay or hindrance. The cost of destroyed garments during these seasons will be extremely high. Husbands and wives will fight with each other in the old traditional way and promptly console themselves with husbands and wives to which they are not entitled. And because I have noticed that at all rough parties pulled by nice people there is always a certain percentage of women who are not thoroughly happy unless they have attracted the eyes of all men by an exhibition of orgiastic dancing, a stage will be provided for this special purpose. Ladies suffering from exhibitionism which cannot be satisfied by one man alone can use this stage to their hearts' content and be sure of an appreciative audience. During these little seasons, which should be limited to a week's duration, we will all of us become highly civilized human beings such as exist in the world today. There will be very little reading except from delightfully illustrated pornographic books, no thinking whatsoever, no really constructive or artistic effort, no loyalties nor friendship. In place there will be a tremendous amount of smart talk and wisecracking in the accepted manner. Ladies will display their wit by saying brilliant things at the expense of each other and everything else. Men and women will make screamingly funny speeches and tell each other all about the plays they were unable to sit through. In short, every little cankerous growth will have its day, and when it's all over and the attendants, somewhat wearied themselves, have dragged the exhausted bodies away we hope to be able to settle down to a period of calm, uneventful living in which the mind will have a chance as well as the body. When, after careful observation, I discover that the majority of colonists are becoming a trifle nervous and repressed from this sort of existence, we will declare another Season of Forgetfulness and return to civilized conditions."

"You're a bit of a wisecracker yourself, Mr. Jones," Josephine remarked after a thoughtful silence, "but I don't mind saying I'd feel a lot more at home if we had arrived during one of your Seasons of Forgetfulness than during this present one of embarrassment."

"You don't appear to be so desperately embarrassed," Mr. Jones told her.

"No," the girl answered. "I get used to things quickly."

"As bad as this is," said Bishop Waller, "I am heartily thankful we escaped arriving at a period such as has been described."

"I am inclined to believe," remarked Mr. Jones, looking with significant appreciation at Yolanda, "that a Period of

Forgetfulness is rapidly approaching, or perhaps it may be merely a Civilized Occasion."

"And what is a Civilized Occasion?" Yolanda asked under her breath.

"The same thing on a smaller scale," Mr. Jones confided to her. "It's more like an individual tour and is usually confined to two persons who find themselves unable to stand the strain of continuing under present conditions. You see, we have taken really every eventuality into consideration."

"I think," Yolanda murmured, the lids dropping demurely over her beautiful eyes, "that I might be able to understand a Civilized Occasion. The present one is extremely trying and I do so hate publicity."

"Arrangements can be easily made," replied Mr. Jones, in a low and hypocritical voice. "It is one of my duties to conduct ladies through such occasions when their companions do not feel up to it."

What Yolanda would have said to this will never be known, for at this moment Little Arthur, pursued by a duck and a flock of women, leaped nimbly down the stairs.

"What do yer mean," he cried out to Mr. Jones, "by having your nasty duck chucked inter my tub? It fair gave me gooseflesh, it did!"

"How can a duck give one gooseflesh?" the philosopher wanted to be told.

"Why did God give you brains?" Little Arthur tossed back.

"Certainly not to credit the ridiculous assertion that a duck can give one gooseflesh," the philosopher replied impassively.

"What's the difference between 'em?" demanded Arthur.

"I don't know," admitted the philosopher. "I have never compared the flesh of duck with that of goose. They don't taste very much alike."

"Well, drag the feathers offa this duck and take a taste of

it," Little Arthur retorted. "Gnaw its black heart out, for all I care. What's it doing with feathers on, anyway? Ain't we all naked?"

"Little Arthur," put in Jones in his quiet way, "I urge you not to suggest liberties being taken with my duck."

"The old hooker took liberties with me," the little crook protested. "Just look at all them welts."

Here Little Arthur turned and dramatically displayed the place of the welts. Even Mr. Jones was moved.

"There are some exhibitions," he observed, "that are difficult to bear with even in a nudist colony. Take your welts away, Little Arthur. You are dripping all over the place."

Little Arthur, looking as if knots had been tied in all parts of his body, moved painfully towards the door and God's open spaces.

"Talk about being put on the spot," he muttered. "Why, a machine gun's a mere mersage compared ter the bill of that duck."

CHAPTER SEVENTEEN

Reactions and Routine

LIFE IN A NEWLY ESTABLISHED NUDIST COLONY IS NOT SO restful as one might suppose, especially when punctuated by various little infringements of nudist ethics such as those which it is only natural for ladies and gentlemen to make who have not become quite accustomed to the big idea. These infringements were at times sufficiently serious to cause nice-mannered spectators to hurry away from the scene of action. The sound of a great deal of unnecessary slapping was heard, usually followed by cries of indignation or gasps of sheer astonishment. Some men found pinching a playful habit very difficult to break. There was more or less unseemly giggling among the women. Innumerable tentatively advanced suggestions by enterprising males were being steadily rejected by the more conservative females. Man is an animal in which the most extravagant hopes die extremely hard. He is difficult to convince on certain points. He always tries.

The little party of involuntary nudes was more or less disconcerted all of the time. Even after the passage of several days Bishop Waller and Little Arthur seemed still inclined to keep their eyes steadfastly fixed on the relatively innocent reaches of the sea. Peter and Josephine were much together—too much together. Inseparable, in fact. Mr. Jones, who was liberal to a fault in such matters, and especially so where new arrivals were concerned, was forced to ask Josephine to be a little quieter about it when she called on Peter at night. Peter himself objected to the way the red-haired girl came thumping into his room. Of all the party she seemed to be enjoying herself the most. There was something either innocently pagan or healthily unmoral in the way she accepted the situation and contrived to take advantage of it. Jo was outrageously forthright. She seemed to consider this little interlude in the drabness of her circumscribed existence as a sort of virgin's holiday—an escape from the conventions and inhibitions which to her way of thinking would never have been imposed on men and women in any normally constituted world. Her conception of a nudist colony and that of Mr. Jones were greatly at variance, for the simple reason that the colony had been established for the benefit of sex slaves instead of executives. Josephine was a past master at sex. That is, she was so frankly and honestly a creature of sex that its freedom of expression appeared to her as being neither especially wild nor wicked. To her it was merely a fact which once accepted, did not require a lot of hypocritical trimmings and tortuous divagations to make it socially presentable. For this reason she was able to think of other things, which she did quite frequently. Life to Josephine was divertingly improper and more than a little grotesque. It was always amusing even at its worst moments, many of which she had experienced without too much self-pity during the brief period she had beautified the world.

While the ladies and gentlemen of the colony were engaged in performing esthetic dances on the lawn, Josephine would imitate their movements with contortions that caused them to pause in wonderment and disgust. Knowing she was already sufficiently beautiful, it was her desire to pass on to higher things and to make herself also funny. Women found this attitude difficult to understand, and the more the men were amused the less the ladies appreciated the object of their mirth. Mr. Jones was forced to withdraw Josephine from participation in the community dancing.

To the children of the colony Josephine was the most acceptable adult nude. It was strange to hear these small naked creatures trying to persuade their mothers and fathers to go back to the house and put on some clothing. The conservative attitude of children is strongly marked in a budding nudist colony. Here the disastrous results of endeavoring to inculcate the youthful mind with a sense of decency before a knowledge of indecency has been acquired became accusingly apparent. For the first few days the lives of the little people were quite miserable. They spent much of the time in hiding.

Josephine, however, they accepted at her flesh value. In her company they began to thaw out a little, to forget the shame of it all, and to take an interest in their naked world. And although the dances she created for them were far from being the seriously ludicrous affairs their elders fondly believed to be esthetic, they were danced with a great deal more enjoyment and a lot more noise. After telling them the story of

Pandora as told by Mr. Eustace Bright in Hawthorne's *Wonder Book* she eventually succeeded in reconciling the children to their own nudity if not to their parents'.

In short, Josephine was both busy and contented. And one of the reasons for this was that she was considerably in love with Peter Van Dyck and growing daily more confident of keeping what she had taken. That she had used shock-troop methods to achieve her ends did not trouble her in the least. Yolanda had enjoyed even better opportunities and had failed to take advantage of them.

In the nudist colony Yolanda had become the major exception to the rule, and the Bishop the minor. Mr. Jones, for reasons known only to himself, had allowed her to retain everything while Bishop Waller moved through his paces nattily attired only in his drawers. Whether Yolanda was deliberately inviting assault will never be known. It was a subject of open comment that both she and the suave leader of the colony appeared to find much in common. The degree or amount of commonness was also a matter of considerable speculation.

Aspirin Liz had settled comfortably into her niche, as that lady would have settled in either heaven or hell, or in any way station between those two points. And she had found certain cronies, as ladies of the disposition of Liz inevitably do—cronies who played cards and talked about little things having to do with this and that and mostly about food and drink. In spite of the vast expanse of flesh she presented to the world, when one saw Aspirin Liz engaged in a game of cards with her friends it was difficult to think of her as being naked, so casually had she accepted the situation. Mr. Jones, who seemed fond of exceptions—stimulants being prohibited save during Seasons of Forgetfulness—had managed some beer for Liz and supplied her with a quantity of aspirin. In view of these little attentions and because of the absence of her corsets life seemed good to Aspirin Liz. She was the only woman in the colony with whom the Bishop conversed with any degree of comfort or feeling of security. She was essentially a home body, even though a naked one.

Peter spent most of his time fluctuating between a sense of guilt and a mood of dark rebellion. Van Dyck bodies had been concealed beneath silk, satin, and furs for so many generations that sunlight and fresh air had become almost alien elements to them. He disliked exceedingly the idea of being peered at and scrutinized. His modesty was far less outraged than his personal dignity. He had soon discovered to his profound relief that he possessed no really decent scruples which could not be easily overcome. In this he was a true Van Dyck. But he did strongly object to being a naked unit in a seething mass of flesh—in a colony of what he stoutly maintained was composed of weak or simple-minded cranks. Pictures of himself in the paper surrounded by a flock of naked men and women kept reappearing before his mental gaze. He wondered what the captions beneath these pictures would be. "Head of Old New York Family Enjoying a Short but Naked Holiday With His Friends," unreeled itself before his eyes. Or: "Peter Van Dyck Abandons Silk Hat for Simple Life and Naked Dancing." Or—and this from the tabloids: "Mad Van in Naked Dance."

"Pretty," he muttered to himself. "They'd probably strike out 'dance' and put in 'orgy.' "

He was especially annoyed with Mr. Jones because that gentleman would neither allow him his clothes nor appoint a definite date of departure. Nor would the naked leader permit any of the party to communicate with the outer world. For all Peter's office or Aunt Sophie knew, he might be in China with Yolanda or at the bottom of the sea. Whenever he brought up with the unfailing attentive Jones the subject of departure, that gentleman looked hurt and then asked him with disconcerting significance if he was not having a good time.

As a matter of fact, had Peter been honest with himself he would have admitted he was having the time of his life. But he did not like Mr. Jones at all when the leader slapped him too low down on the back and assured him that he, Peter, was holding out splendidly under the circumstances and that many a man would envy him his good fortune. No. Such remarks were most decidedly in bad taste, especially when one was too alertly conscious of the thoughts passing through the other's mind.

"The red-headed girl isn't doing any complaining," Mr. Jones once went so far as to remark, looking Peter in the eye with a subdued leer. "I should think you would find some comfort, not to mention cause for a little pride, in that. Now, from my experience with red-headed women . . ."

Peter did not stay to listen to what he had every reason to believe would be a highly objectionable recital of the leader's amorous adventures with red-headed women. He had a red-headed woman of his own on his hands, and she was quite enough.

Of all the members of the band of castaways Little Arthur, surprisingly enough, was the most popular with the nudists. He was perhaps the noblest nude of them all—the most unimpeachable, the most impenetrably clad in the armor of righteousness. Although the object of no little jest and levity he was nevertheless held in considerable affection by his fellow nudes. He was always so ready and willing to explain to them just how depraved they all were and how especially depraved Mr. Jones was because he would not give Little Arthur back either one of the pairs of drawers he had been wearing when lured into this sinkhole of iniquity. If a bishop was allowed a pair of long drawers, Little Arthur argued, a retired pickpocket should be allowed at the very least a pair of short ones. As a matter of fact, a naked bishop most likely would stand more fully clad in the eyes of God than a pickpocket in a fur coat. The strength of Little Arthur's claim on drawers was fully and freely discussed. Much sympathy was extended him, but no drawers. The small crook, because of his social triumphs, grew to enjoy the very indignities against which he leveled his artless tirades. Also, for the simple reason that the ladies and gentlemen whose morals and manners he so severely criticized invariably—almost callously—agreed with him, Little Arthur, after a few days, actually became quite fond of them. Without a naked body knocking about somewhere on the horizon to become moral about, Little Arthur would have found his life a dull thing indeed.

When the colony forgathered at the long tables in the dining hall, it was a sight to make the most daring producers of Broadway Glorifications think several times more than twice—to pause and rub their jaded eyes and wonder if they had ever before really witnessed life in the nude. Yet nothing more exciting happened than a tremendous consumption of food.

When Peter had first been induced to attend one of these communal meals he had cagily asked for a napkin, hoping to be able to cover some part of his body at least. His almost pleading request had been scornfully rejected.

"Napkin," sniffed the maid. "They don't even let us girls wear aprons, the nasty naked things. If it wasn't for this depression . . ."

The rest of the maid's lament was drowned in a babble of hungry voices.

Peter, surveying the multitude, found it impossible to understand how all these people were able to sit thigh to thigh, rib to rib, and consume huge quantities of food without being convulsed by the severest pangs of indigestion. Seated between two blandly naked ladies, he was continually being forced to shrink fastidiously into himself to keep from being overpowered by their swaying torsos and gesticulating arms.

At that first meal Peter ate very little. He had accustomed himself in business to seeing a number of people use their jaws, temples, eyebrows, necks—in fact, their entire faces—when engaged in the horrid business of mastication. It had been not easy, but he had brought himself grimly to bear with this, realizing that time was short in a business day. But to see a gathering of naked individuals eating not only with their faces but also with their bodies was too vivid a demonstration of greed for him. He found his fascinated eyes dwelling on various parts of these bodies—on necks, diaphragms and stomachs—as if they were endeavoring to ascertain the exact location of the last mouthful of food the person under observation had swallowed.

The routine observed at the nudist colony was simple to the point of idiocy. At least it seemed so to Peter. In the morning the household was awakened by the tinkling of many bells which announced that everyone was supposed to spring out of bed, rush downstairs, and dash around the lawn in mad pursuit of Mr. Jones, who usually, because of pressing business, delegated the task to the philosopher, who seemed to extract from it a certain amount of sardonic amusement. Going downstairs late one morning, Peter discovered that Mr. Jones's pressing business consisted of dashing from his own room to another's. Peter put the man down as a thorough-going hypocrite. He would have put him down as even worse had he realized that the room into which Mr. Jones had so eagerly disappeared was none other than Yolanda's. That unassailable young lady, under the direction of the leader, was beginning to take more and more interest in his Civilized Occasions.

On the other hand, had Peter been aware of the extra service Mr. Jones was performing to make Yolanda a thoroughly contented guest, he, Peter, might have felt grateful to the diligent young leader. Realizing how the situation stood between himself and Josephine, it was with a sensation of profound uneasiness that Peter considered Yolanda and the future. This sensation alone would have reconciled him to the nakedness of his life had not certain little indications warned him that the Season of Forgetfulness was rapidly approaching. Peter had no intention of being one of the colony during the festivities of this season. He had collected enough moral turpitude already to last him for a lifetime. He had no desire to join in a public demonstration.

Bishop Waller was equally determined to escape from the colony. Josephine, much to Peter's surprise, showed no disposition to remain. It was her conviction that once a good man had fallen, one never could tell where he was likely to bounce. She did not intend to let Peter bounce into some other woman's lap. He had in his composition all of the potential vices engendered by a clean past. It was well enough —in fact, it was a commendable thing—to share these vices with Peter, but it was not at all desirable to place them at the disposal of the temporarily dressed and drunken ladies of a nudist colony. Therefore Josephine had good and sufficient reasons to join with the Bishop in his determination to escape from the nudists no matter how difficult or embarrassing such an endeavor might prove to be. Little Arthur was of a similar disposition. So was Aspirin Liz, who in spite of her contentment still maintained that, of all the pleasant places in the world in which to drink beer, the Hoboken waterfront was by far the pleasantest. Yolanda alone seemed a trifle vague when approached on the subject of escaping. And this was exceedingly strange in view of the fact that she was the only member of the party who had been allowed to retain her garments and who therefore had nothing to fear from a flight back to the world of covered flesh. True, she was careful enough not to give the impression that she was anxious to remain where she was, yet even Bishop Waller suspected her of being more than a little on the fence.

And the exact location of the colony was also a subject of

no little speculation among the members of the party. Mr. Jones had mentioned so many different places when questioned that even the most gullible person would have been forced to conclude that the man was a well-meaning but absent-minded liar.

"I feel we're safe in figuring we're somewhere on the seacost of the North American continent," Peter remarked to his fellow castaways.

"Wherever we are," allowed the good Bishop, "somewhere else couldn't be so much worse. We must get away at all costs."

At this moment Yolanda, accompanied by Mr. Jones, strolled up to the group.

"Setting-up exercises in five minutes," the naked leader announced with a bright smile in which Peter detected a glint of vicious amusement.

"I can't join in today," Yolanda murmured. "I'm too utterly weary. It must be the ocean."

Josephine's large brown eyes were fixed on the girl.

"I'm beginning to admire you, Yolanda," she said amicably. "And that shows how bad I am."

Even Peter wondered why Yolanda did not ask Jo exactly what she meant by that.

With a sigh Little Arthur uncoiled his thin body.

"Always setting up," he complained. "Always exposing something or other. Why can't you let a guy crouch in peace by hisself?"

The naked party trailed across the lawn in the direction of even more nakedness—a multitude of prancing nakedness singing loudly about dew being on its feet.

"Look at 'em," muttered Little Arthur. "All bare and all crazy as hell in the head—begging your pardon, Bishop. Singing about dew and their great feet. Who cares, I ask you? Who cares? I'm tired of naked bodies. They hurt my eyes."

"Well spoken, Little Arthur," said Bishop Waller, "in spite of your choice of words. If those bodies were only black or brown, I might at least succeed in getting drawers on them as I have in the past. With white bodies it is sadly different. Once they have abandoned their drawers, they seem also to have abandoned their reason."

"You forget, my dear Bishop," observed Peter, "that drawers are a bit of a novelty to your dark-skinned converts, whereas no drawers are equally novel to these deluded people."

"No drawers aren't novel to me," remarked Aspirin Liz. "It's an old, old story."

"Well, no drawers ter me," said Little Arthur earnestly, "is simply frantic."

"Without my jaegers," remarked the Bishop a trifle complacently, "I fear I would find it difficult to turn even to God in my distress."

"I want my step-ins," said Jo with devastating frankness, "more because I like their looks than because I feel their loss."

Bishop Waller looked sadly at the red-headed girl, opened his mouth to speak, closed it again, then hopelessly shook his head.

His God was too greatly handicapped in the presence of so much beauty unadorned.

Peter and Jo on the sand dunes. Havelock Ellis had accompanied them for a little sunshine and salt air. The duck was actually trying to sleep on its side like a dog. It was not a pleasing sight. Nor was Havelock Ellis comfortable. No duck should be seen that way. She was clucking bad duck language deep down in her throat. Peter, taking advantage of the sand, had dug himself in. For the moment he felt almost well dressed. At the water's edge the Bishop was conversing with the philosopher. The Bishop was dressed in his jaegers, which by now were looking sorely tried. The philosopher wore simply a pipe. Havelock Ellis flipped her wing disgustedly, sending a spray of sand across Peter's face. Peter submitted patiently. He had grown fond of Ellis.

"It's too bad you're not married, Peter," said the girl, kicking her legs up behind her, thus sending more sand in Peter's face.

"Why?" asked Peter, still patient because he had also grown fond of Jo.

"Because," she answered, "the situation would then be more desperate—more dramatic. You might even leave me with an unnamed child for which I would have to slave in silence while treasuring your memory deep in my heart."

"You're breaking mine," Peter told her. "I've decided to marry you even though such a step is entirely unnecessary."

"It would be far cheaper than keeping me," the girl replied calmly. "I'd work for you for nothing and we could spend my pay."

Peter thought this over.

"It's too involved," he said at last. "Yet I sense something in it somewhere."

The Bishop strolled up with the philosopher. Both stood moodily looking down upon the couple in the sand. Then the philosopher turned to the Bishop.

"You, I contend, my dear Bishop," he stated deliberately, "look more ridiculous in those weird pantaloons of yours than I do in my pipe."

"But you look far more naked," replied the Bishop. "Even though I cut a sorry figure in the eyes of man and God alike, I have the comfort of knowing I am not childishly exposed."

"Do you consider me childish, Bishop?" the philosopher inquired.

"I endeavor not to consider you at all," replied the Bishop, "although I know full well that the memory of your gaunt figure will haunt my dreams for years. I think it's the addition of the pipe that makes you look extra naked."

The philosopher smiled appreciatively.

"Not a bad point, Bishop Waller," he said. "No doubt the pipe is an incongruous touch. However, I'd rather have my pipe than your drawers."

"I wouldn't relinquish these jaegers for all the pipes in the world," the Bishop told him.

"Don't you feel at all funny," Peter asked the philosopher, "being naked like that before everybody?"

"How do you feel, my dear sir?" the tall man inquired.

"Like a suddenly evicted Turkish bath," said Peter. "Even worse than that."

"And the young lady?" the philosopher pursued.

"I feel great," said Jo, "but I still find grounds for complaint. They're not moral. Sorry, Bishop. I miss my nice things—silk stockings and all. You should know, Mr. Pipe, that all pretty women like to show their bodies but most of them prefer to select their audiences. Uniform nudity does not appeal to our sex."

"A good point, too," observed the philosopher. "Even the most primitive members of your sex instinctively decorate their bodies."

"Also the men," said Peter.

"Come," said the Bishop hastily. "We must continue our stroll."

The two strange figures walked off across the dunes. Suddenly the philosopher turned back.

"I forgot to answer your question," he called. "I think this show is a lot of bunk, if you want to know my frank opinion. And if it wasn't for a disciplined and inquiring mind, I'd feel simply awful. Good-day, sir."

Peter waved a hand, and the two gentlemen continued on their way.

"I suspected that," said Peter. "All the time I knew he wasn't an honest nude."

"Listen, sweetie," replied Josephine. "Taking off your clothes doesn't make you honest any more than putting them back on again makes you respectable."

"Taking them off certainly did things to us," he observed.

"Are you complaining because I ruined you?" Jo demanded scornfully.

"My dear girl," said Peter wearily, "must we go into that again. You were putty in my hands. Putty."

"You poor fish," she answered angrily. "You haven't nerve enough to seduce an alligator."

"Not one man in a hundred has," he assured her. "Not one man in a thousand. Even less have the inclination."

"You are very fond of me, Peter—love me, in fact?" asked Jo.

"Oh, very fond indeed. I dote on you, Jo. Love you as much as a coffee importer can. I've a dull background, though."

"But an aromatic one," she said. "I'm deeply in love with you, too, but I feel quite ashamed of my lack of discrimination. You're awful, Peter."

"You're not, Jo. You're beautiful. When I think of those brown eyes and all that red hair and all——"

"I suppose you're quite overcome by the sheer quantity of things."

"More or less. I just can't see how you can care for me—don't understand how you can do it, that's all."

"I don't see how I can do it myself," she told him. "When I see you lying there in that cowardly sand-draped position with your unlovely feet sticking out, all my finer instincts tell me to get up and walk right away, but just the same I stick around. Love must be able to stand for 'most anything, and I'm that way about you."

"Does it come over you in waves?" he asked her. "You know, in—in waves. A lot of waves coming over you?"

"Do you mean do I feel as if I were drowning?" she wanted to know.

Peter shrugged his shoulders hopelessly. Romance did not seem to be in his line.

"Just waves," he muttered moodily, wishing he had never attempted analogy. "Coming over one in waves, you know."

Jo looked him steadily in the eyes. There was a strange glint in hers. Suddenly she grabbed his head in her arms and hugged it roughly against her breast.

"What a fool," she said. "Inarticulate—driveling. No sort of a lover at all, but don't worry about those waves of yours. I feel them, too." She gave a sudden start and flung Peter's head away. "You reptile," she gasped.

"What's up now?" he asked her.

"Why, look what you did," and she proceeded to show him. "You pinched me with all your might—a regular nasty pinch, it was."

"Nonsense," he retorted. "I don't do things like that—not in public."

Jo regarded him intently, then unleashed a wild whoop.

"There you go again," she cried.

From behind her came the exultant squawk of the duck, Ellis.

"Why, you old bitch," exclaimed Josephine. "Let's leave her flat. She's pecking me."

"Oh, let her tag along," said Peter. "She's a good duck in her quaint way."

"Very well, then," replied Jo, springing up from the sand. "But not if she bites my—me there every time I hug your head. That's going from the sublime to the ridiculous."

"Snap to it, Ellis," said Peter, reluctantly removing the sand from his body. "Get a waddle on."

CHAPTER EIGHTEEN

An Unassaulted Lady

FACTS WERE THE ONLY CLOUDS THAT TROUBLED YOLANDA'S unextensive spiritual horizon. She was upstage about facts—arrogant. And this was just too bad for Yolanda, because these small wings of reality, even when far outstripped, have a nasty habit of overtaking the most evasive feet.

She was one of those imperious creatures, was Yolanda, who can face anything—and outface most things—except facts of the unpleasant variety. To her way of thinking, they did not belong. And naturally. All her years of maturity had been devoted either to distorting or sidestepping the less agreeable facts motivating her self-indulgent conduct. In this she had been ably assisted by fond parents and flattering friends. She alone was not to blame.

For example, Yolanda could never be wrong, and all the facts in creation were never going to make her wrong. They might make her angry, of course—shockingly and shrilly angry for a girl of Yolanda's breeding—but certainly not wrong. Had she been confronted with the facts of her relations with Mr. Jones, rather than admitting them quite cheerfully she would have done an intellectual tail spin and laid the blame on Peter or God or her high-strung nature or on any other convenient person or cause. She had one of those twisty minds that find no difficulty in sublimating their meanest little impulses to almost dizzily ethical heights. So much for her mental equipment.

As she stood now a little apart from the others on the beach, following with clouded eyes the antics of the bathers, she found herself confronted by several facts she would much rather have avoided. However, even the slipperiest mind cannot easily get around the various glaring facts associated with a lot of naked bathers, especially when, as in this case, the men insisted in striking terrifically heroic attitudes as they leaped high in the air from the sand and the women kept dancing round jouncilly in almost human garlands, while a number of small children stood about and regarded the antics of their naked elders in bewildered disapproval.

If the truth must be known, it was not the fact of nakedness that disquieted Yolanda's reflections as she stood there fully dressed on the sun-bright beach. It was the acceptance of the fact of nakedness that did things to her vanity—the incredible disregard of sex distinction all these naked men and women were displaying before her outraged eyes. The thing just could not be true. These people were pretending.

Yolanda would not believe that a man could so far forget his place in life as to look on a naked woman with anything other than covetous eyes. Not that women desired this reaction—far from it—but men were that way about women. It was very annoying, but women had learned to expect it, some even endured it with a splendid display of fortitude. As a matter of fact, she herself had learned to endure the lascivious glances of men. Let the poor beasts ogle if it did them any good.

At this moment, confronted by factual evidence of her own eyes, Yolanda still refused to believe that these men would remain insensible to her fair body should she remove the clothes from it and display it along the beach. She did not go so far as to say to herself that a riot would break out, but she did admit the possibility of a series of serious assaults not to mention innumerable insulting invitations. How could it be otherwise? And the women. How annoyed they would be —how enviously sympathetic. It was a fascinating idea. It crept inside Yolanda and gradually took possession of her.

And in this the girl showed herself to be a little less than clever not to have realized the horrid fact that men, when engaged in striking heroic postures, cannot be induced to assume any others no matter how entertaining they promise to be. It is only after they have convinced all admiring females of their virility and physical perfection, of their masculine grace, fleetness, strength, and agility, that they will deign to consider the ultimate object of their peculiar behavior. Certain types of men when confronted by a beach suddenly become the silliest of God's creatures, also the most annoying. Show them a ball of any size, and what was a moment ago a paradise of sun-warmed contentment becomes a living hell. Contemplation and repose are shattered, bodies are endangered, eyes, mouths, and ears filled with sand. One can only rise wearily and stagger away. Boyishness in man is a much overrated attraction. It is even less endurable than manliness. Both deserve capital punishment.

For the first time since she had become an involuntary guest of the nudist colony, Yolanda was moved by an impulse to emulate in public the example set by its members. She was more than moved by this daring impulse. She was actually impelled by it. As her dress fell to the sand and she stood in her low-cut slip for all the world to see, she felt herself on the threshold of a revolutionary experience. With the slip gone, little remained of Yolanda's clothing, but what little there was, that went, too, falling like foam round her feet on the yellow sand. For a moment she experienced the sensation of being blind. The pores of her skin were startled by the light. She gasped. She shrank a little. Then, for a moment, before self-consciousness shut down on her, she raised her arms to the sunlight and gave herself to its warmth—one of the few honest, unstudied gestures she had made since she had last been unaware of her naked body some twenty-odd years ago.

This sudden, spontaneous gesture ended in a startled crouch as Yolanda realized her condition. Half frightened, half expectant, she glanced about her. As the warm air bathed her body and the shouts of the bathers drifted to her from down the beach, her thoughts were spinning dizzily. This was an even more difficult experience than any she had passed through under the skillful tutelage of Mr. Jones. Now she was so much alone, so definitely her own woman. Only her stockings remained between herself and complete nudity. Glancing down, she noticed that these sheer, well-filled sheathes of silk had become wrinkled since being detached from the garters. This would never do. Fastidiously she seated herself on her abandoned clothing and slipped off the stockings. Now she had done it, irretrievably committed herself to the official costume of the colony—bare flesh. Slowly she stood up, and as she did so the air and sunlight flooded round her body like the soft, clear waters of a pool. Dimly she felt all this, felt herself a living part of the beach, a little more intimate with the ocean and less remote from the gulls in the air. But dominating her consciousness was the thought of how she must look in the eyes of men, the effect she would have upon them. She knew she was fair to behold, a creature altogether lovely. Then another thought crossed her mind. Should she walk or run in her present nude state? Should she move along in maidenly aloofness, modest, subdued, and enticing? It was too bad they were all playing those silly games. All those men. All those naked men. Really, they were ridiculous. She would take their minds off their occupations. She would arouse them to an awareness of themselves. And the women? She would show the women that the feminine form was nothing to be taken lightly, to be accepted and dismissed by a flock of prancing males. For the life of her she could not understand why these women allowed themselves to be regarded as so many bits of landscape, why they seemed content to make garlands of themselves as indifferently as if there was not a man in sight. Surely this was depravity—this total lack of recognition of the difference existing between the sexes.

Haltingly the girl moved along the beach in the direction of the bodies. Each step cost her an effort. Mental readjustment was coming in fits and starts. At times she found herself timid, at others bold and challenging. Once or twice she was tempted to turn back and put on her clothes. So far no one had looked her way. She had not been spied. But had she? That was a nagging question. Suppose she had been seen and taken for granted? Impossible. At least out of mere politeness a new naked body in their midst should give rise to a little display of interest. A fresh nude female figure among all these men should occasion some slight comment, cause eyes to peer and heads to turn. She would see about that.

When she had approached still closer to the bathers, Yolanda decided she would feel somewhat more assured if she ran a little. Accordingly she gathered her courage and ran lightly and with heroically assumed casualness through the naked group, her eyes apparently fixed on space. Her first passage through failed to arouse the comment she had expected. She was still unassaulted as well as uninsulted. Had she imagined herself bathed in daring glances, or had her presence really passed unnoticed? She would try again.

This time as she ran back she unfortunately tripped over a gentleman's leg and found herself sprawling in the sand. It was not a position in which she was anxious to be found. Certainly it failed to do her justice. Rather grotesque, she thought with a little shiver of revulsion. She was not doing well by herself. Before she could rise of her own accord, two huge arms picked her up and plopped her down again on the sand. The contact had been so forcible it made her teeth click. For a moment she sat there stunned. Was the assault about to begin? If so the aroused male was going about it in a surprisingly leisurely manner. She waited a few moments, then looked up over her shoulder. No one was paying the slightest attention to her. Strange—unbelievable. She rose and hurried through the group.

As much disgusted as she was disturbed, Yolanda braced herself and returned to the battle. This time her passage was interrupted by the arrival of a basketball in the pit of her stomach. It bounced off with surprising speed, and Yolanda found herself on her back, getting a crab's eye view of seemingly endless nakedness.

"Lucky it wasn't the medicine ball," said a man's voice above her. "That would have taken the wind out of your sails."

Yolanda regarded the man hatefully even though she agreed with him. Lucky, indeed, it had not been the medicine ball. Its smaller and less weighty edition had been quite enough. Yolanda thought of the involuntary grunt it had surprised out of her. She found no pleasure in this thought. How horrid! Then, suddenly, it came to her that this was no way for a prominent young member of that high social circle, the Junior Daughters, to be found lying on a beach. She was altogether too prominent.

Once more she picked herself up and scurried to the outskirts of the nudists. She was on the point of abandoning the experiment. She was beginning to feel that the proof of her point might involve too much wear and tear on the flesh as well as spirit. Still she was not convinced. Her failure so far had been due to accidents and not to any fault of her own. She would try again. This time, rather grimly, she launched her body into the naked mass of humanity. An old gentleman pushed her rudely.

"There you go!" he exclaimed with the petulance of the aged. "Spoiling my One Old Cat."

Vaguely Yolanda wondered what part of him he meant by his One Old Cat; then, as a tennis ball came flying through the air, she realized the old man was referring to some childish game.

"Why don't you take your One Old Cat and play it somewhere else?" she inquired bitterly.

"Beach free," grunted the old man. "Play One Old Cat where I like. You butted in."

Obviously there was no danger of assault from this infirm direction, decided Yolanda. All that aged creature's life seemed to consist of was his One Old Cat. She turned away and experienced the electrifying sensation of putting her foot down on a living being who had somehow managed to get itself tangled up with her legs. A yell of pain smote the air.

"For God's sake, lady," said the living being, "be more careful where you put your feet. That might have been very serious. As it is——"

Yolanda turned away from the investigating creature beneath her feet, but his voice still pursued her.

"You've got to watch your step in a nudist colony," he called after her. "If you think it's any fun——"

A sudden resounding and extremely smart slap from the rear made Yolanda freeze in her tracks. Perhaps at last this was the prelude to an assault. Rather a common way of going about it, but she understood men were that way. In spite of her pain and indignation Yolanda kept her poise. Assuredly that slap—such a familiar, whole-hearted slap—must have denoted some slight show of interest on the part of the slapper. She turned and looked. A large, splendidly proportioned gentleman was confronting her.

"Sir," she said, "did you slap me?"

"Where?" he asked good-naturedly.

"Need we go into that?" she inquired coldly.

"Oh, there," replied the man with a friendly smile. "Perhaps I did. I slapped someone a moment ago. Might have been you."

"It was me," said Yolanda.

"Do you mind?" he asked. "It's a habit of mine. Sort of playful. I see something and I slap it. That's all."

"That's all?" said Yolanda, greatly surprised. "Isn't that enough—too much, in fact?"

"Sure," agreed the man pleasantly. "If you want to get even I'll let you slap me back."

Here he turned round and waited expectantly. Yolanda, as she looked, felt strongly tempted to kick. In a sudden burst of exasperation she did kick. And this was her second honest and natural gesture in years. It was a terrific kick. Every toe on her foot was crumpled. Also it hurt the man, or at least surprised him mightily.

"That's not fair," he declared, turning round sharply. "I wasn't expecting that."

"Neither was I," said Yolanda. "I wasn't expecting what you did. I forgot myself for a moment."

Upon hearing this, the man reached out and unceremoniously spun Yolanda about.

"Well, here's one you won't forget in years," he assured her, and he gave her a smart kick with his foot.

Yolanda, whether she liked it or not, buckled outward and shot through space. She caromed off several naked bodies, barely kept her feet, and continued on to the outer fringe of the circle.

As she stood looking back at her assailant, she was surprised to find that the incident had passed unnoticed. Apparently these men and women were accustomed to indiscriminate kicking. She wondered how they could be. To her way of thinking, it was far worse than being assaulted, far more of a blow to one's self-respect. Yolanda's was completely gone. With a mad light in her eyes she hurried right back, and when the man was not looking she pounced like a cat into his flesh with her long, sharp fingernails. This was one of the most satisfying experiences in Yolanda's life. The man uttered a scream of anguish and struck out instinctively. Unfortunately—that is, unfortunately for a small, thin lady, who chanced to be passing at that moment—the man's arm caught her under the chin and catapulted her through the air into and upon the stomach of a reclining body which immediately became passionately active. It seized upon the thin woman and threw her in the general direction of the sea. She failed to attain her objective, however, because of a forest of legs into which she plunged forthwith, only to find herself being sat upon from several different directions.

From this moment on, the beach became the scene of the most irresponsible activity. It was nude against nude irrespective of sex or size. Yolanda felt herself rapidly being smothered by the dead weight of flesh bearing down upon her face. The girl was forced literally to bite her way to freedom and fresh air. As she rose weakly to her feet, her speed was accelerated by the feet of others pushing her violently from behind. As a result of this gratuitous boost she continued on in a graceful arc and landed on her face.

"Pardon me, madam," said a courteous voice. "I intended that for someone else."

"That's no comfort to me," replied Yolanda, grabbing the voice by its leg and giving it a vicious tug.

The leg straightened and a body followed it out of the struggling mass of humanity.

"Be careful of my scar," said the small creature she was pulling over the sand. "My operation is scarcely ten weeks old."

Wishing the operation had been performed on his throat instead of his appendix, Yolanda dropped the leg where it was and walked disgustedly away. She returned to her abandoned garments and wearily dragged them on her bruised and battered body. They could tear one another limb from limb for all she cared, those wild, infuriated nudes. Entirely disregarding the fact that she alone was responsible for making the nudes wild and infuriated, she hoped that the contest would spend itself in a homicidal draw, that it would end only because of a lack of live bodies. She was a bitterly disillusioned girl. Her experiment in public nudity had turned out miserably. She had discovered that there could be assaults and assaults. She had been subjected to the worst kind, the most unsociable and least flattering type. There had been no intent to please, but merely to maim. She would never attempt the experiment again, she decided, as she snapped the garters of her girdle to her stockings, flipped herself irritably into her brassière, yanked on her step-ins, dropped her slip over her head, and covered all with a dress.

Once more she was clothed and in her right mind. Her

thoughts turned to Mr. Jones. She would return to the house and look for him.

When she entered the long, low lounging room she found herself plunged into a scene that rivaled the beach in indignation if not in action. Little Arthur appeared to be occupying none too happily the center of the stage. At least five excited nudes were pointing at him accusingly. Mr. Jones was endeavoring to bring the vociferating members to order while Peter, Josephine, Aspirin Liz, and Bishop Waller were lending attentive ears. As Peter regarded Little Arthur, Yolanda read in his expression a mixture of admiration and pride. What had the little man done thus to gain the approval of his master and the enmity of this small but earnest group of bodies?

One of the first things Yolanda noticed was that Little Arthur's accusers seemed to be finding difficulty in putting their thoughts into intelligibly articulate words. It was as if they had found a bottle somewhere and punished it severely. An amazing amount of slurring and mouthing was going on. Several of these angry people were almost whistling. Some words never managed to get themselves pronounced at all, others only partially, imperfectly, much as if they were swimming under water.

Her interest in this little scene made Yolanda forget for the moment her own distress and indignation. That she was an unassaulted lady no longer seemed to matter. Here was real anguish. Here was the stuff of authentic drama. Mr. Jones was speaking.

"Little Arthur," he was saying in a voice which strove to express patience, "because members of a nudist colony are required to remove their clothes it does not follow that they must also remove their teeth if they chance to be wearing the removable type."

So this was the explanation of the mouthing. Yolanda shuddered a little. The five indignant nudes by sound and gesture made it clear that they were in complete agreement with their leader.

"Then why do they go sleeping about the place with their mouths open?" demanded Little Arthur.

"Little Arthur," continued Jones, "you don't seem to realize that a person has a right to sleep with his or her mouth in any desired position. Shut, of course, is more acceptable to the public, but the fact remains that an individual can sleep with his mouth set grim or gay, swinging like a gate or closed like a trap."

"According to his theory," put in a large gentleman indistinctly, "no open mouth in the colony would be safe."

"Some of 'em weren't open," Little Arthur said, not without pride. "They was almost gritted. That's where I showed my craft."

Cries of rage greeted this bragging statement.

"No doubt you were deft," agreed Mr. Jones equably. "I cannot help admiring your technique myself, but it was used in a very low, a very degrading manner. You should leave other persons' mouths alone as well as what is in them, Little Arthur.

"In Gord's name, Mr. Jones," exclaimed the exasperated little felon, "what's a high-class pickpocket going to do with a lot of naked thighs? He's gotter have some outlet."

"As regards the naked thighs," observed Mr. Jones, "your question rather embarrasses me. I would suggest that you consult the owner of the thighs. Mouths, however, are different. Once more I say, leave them entirely alone. I must protect my guests and their teeth."

"I had ter keep my hand in, didn't I?" demanded Little Arthur.

"You didn't have to keep it in my mouth," lisped a lady with artificially flaming hair.

"Nor in mine," cried the large gentleman.

"Why don't you keep your hand in your own mouth?' asked a third nude.

"What would be the fun in that?" retorted the small crook.

"You might snap your tongue out," suggested Jo.

"Yes," put in Peter, "or bite off your pilfering fingers. Like Mr. Jones here, I admire your craftsmanship, Little Arthur, but I'd hate to let it be noised abroad that I employed a tooth-snatching valet. A pickpocket is bad enough, but a pick-mouth is just too much."

"You're all against me," Little Arthur replied sorrowfully.

"I'm not," announced Aspirin Liz surprisingly. "Although I don't hold with mouth-picking or tooth-snatching, I do know that a habit of years can't be dropped in a day."

"But teeth, my dear lady!" protested Mr. Jones. "Of all things teeth! Let him steal anything in God's world but them. I'll tuck coins about the place for him to snatch if he'll only leave teeth alone."

"I'll give him five dollars if he'll give me mine back," said the large man.

"Don't want money," Little Arthur replied. "Don't want teeth. Just a little sport."

"It's about the lowest form of sport ever indulged in by man," commented Mr. Jones to the group. "In my mind it's worse than body-snatching. He leaves his victims bereft of pride and self-respect. Listen to the inhuman sounds the poor things are making."

"I wish we didn't have to," replied Jo.

"So do I," agreed Mr. Jones, "but this question of teeth has to be settled for once and all."

Bishop Waller spoke for the first time. It was clear to see he was deeply moved.

"Not only is the theft of the teeth a crime in the eyes of God," he said, "but also it is in shockingly bad taste. Of the two, bad taste is the harder to forgive. Little Arthur, I thought you had resolved to mend your ways."

"Bishop," replied the little man contritely, "you don't understand. You can no more keep from trying to save my soul than I can from picking your pockets while you're doing it. Here's one of your buttons."

"Oh, miserable sinner!" cried the Bishop, snatching the button from the extended hand. "Now where does this belong?"

Jo promptly started to look.

"There, perhaps," she said, pointing.

With a startled exclamation Bishop Waller turned sharply away.

"I will find the spot myself," he said. "You take my question too literally."

"It was merely a suggestion," replied Jo.

"A most improper one," muttered the Bishop.

"From where I was standing," said Jo, "it was the most helpful one to make."

"As bad as that?" murmured Bishop Waller, his eyes darting over his jaegers. "I must go in search of a pin. Perhaps I might even find a needle and a bit of thread. Pardon me."

Stepping cautiously, the Bishop ascended the stairs to interview the housekeeper.

"To return to these teeth——" began Mr. Jones.

"Must we?" inquired Jo.

"I wish somehow," said Peter, "we could manage to drop the entire subject."

"I say return the teeth to their various mouths," suggested Jo, "and hang up an old pair of trousers for Little Arthur to play with. Put things in the pockets."

"He might try to wear them," said Mr. Jones doubtfully.

"Swear I won't, mister," Little Arthur pleaded. "I'll just creep up on them, like. It will give a guy something to do. My eyes are fair tired of human flesh."

"Will you restore the teeth to their rightful owners?"

"I'll even put 'em back in their mouths," replied the small dip eagerly.

Howls of indignation from the wronged nudes.

"I'll click my own teeth back, if you please," said the large gentleman with great dignity.

"Click," observed Mr. Jones. "My God, how descriptive!" He approached the silent Yolanda. "Come," he continued. "I promised to show you the hot houses."

As they strolled across the lawn, Yolanda made her protest.

"I undressed on the beach," she told him, "and not a man made the slightest advance. They were very rough."

"Don't let that worry you at all," said Mr. Jones smoothly. "I'll see that something is done about it if I have to do it myself."

Yolanda's wounded vanity seemed somewhat appeased.

The breeze was warm that night. A moist breeze drifting in from the sea. It trailed scarves of mist behind it and was faintly edged with the tang of salt. The water breathed quietly against the beach. It felt cool to Jo's feet as it stirred round them.

"So you still insist on making me an honest woman?" she said to Peter who was dawdling by her side.

"I wouldn't go so far as to attempt that," he told her, "but I am going to marry you good and proper the first damn chance I get."

"In spite of my depravity?"

"Because of it, Jo."

"But suppose you discover I'm not really bad?"

"By that time we'll be too old for it to make any difference, my girl."

"I really believe you're a man of low moral worth, Peter. A wicked man—not good at all."

"Maybe we're both good and don't know it."

"Wonder how one ever finds out?"

"I don't quite know, Jo. You just muddle along together. No divided loyalties. No cheap evasions. And when you're through, you quit clean and cold if and when necessary."

"But, Peter, a man and a womn never feel that way about things at the same time."

"Then one of them has to stand the rap. It's better than ducking down alleys—happier in the long run. Habit and self-interest are often mistaken for kindness, Josephine."

"Perhaps we'll last forever, Peter. It does happen, you know . . . at rare intervals."

Peter looked thoughtfully at the girl, then turned his eyes to the dark water. They were a little sad, those eyes, and touched with premature wisdom. Love did not last like that—or rarely ever. Most men were on the prowl and so many women felt the need of the prowler. It was the old army game. Quite as it should be. Of course, some couples sat at home at night and hated each other and listened to the radio and went to bed quietly but bitterly, each wanting to be wanted, yet concealing their frozen longings behind commonplace remarks. This business of romance—Peter was unable to figure it out. It was like a moth in the house, only it made holes in human emotions instead of clothes and things. He turned back to the small white figure and dropped two hands on the cool shoulders.

Then quite suddenly Jo found herself sobbing quietly all over Peter's shoulder. Perhaps he had communicated to her something of his feeling of the impermanence of things. Perhaps she felt, too, that desire itself had a longer life than passion between individuals—it was a ruggeder product, far harder to tame and forget. And somehow it made such a mess of things.

"I love you now, Peter," she murmured. "That's all I know."

"That's about all anyone can say, little chap," Peter answered as he gently shook her. "I'm very much obliged."

"You should be," she retorted. "Haven't I given you the best years of my life?"

"Those years are still to be lived, thank God," said Peter. "We'll wangle the best out of them—what say you?"

"I say you're almost pushing me out to sea," complained Jo. "Drag me back to shore or drown me and get it over with."

As they walked back across the lawn, Jo asked a disconcerting question: "What about Yolanda?"

Involuntarily Peter glanced up at her window, then stopped.

"Why, there's a man in her room," he said. "Look, Jo."

Jo looked. Outlined against the drawn shade were the figures of a man and a woman. They seemed to know each other quite well. Jo smiled cheerfully in the darkness.

"She seems to have solved your problem for you," she said.

"Think I should do anything about it?" asked Peter. "This is more of a surprise than a blow, I confess."

"What can you do about it?" asked Jo in return. "They seem to know what to do about it without your help."

"Shouldn't I at least shout?" said Peter. "Or ask them to move?"

"Forget it," replied Jo briefly. "The leader of a nudist colony has his hands full."

"Not to mention arms," said Peter. "Just the same, Jo, I'm one hell of a chaperon."

"Stupid," she replied, "if you knew women as a woman does, you'd know that each one cuddles within her the sparks of her own ruination."

Slowly they moved across the lawn.

"Is the dew upon your feet?" asked Peter presently.

"Great chunks of it," said Jo.

"Sleepy?" asked Peter.

"Not a bit," said Jo.

"Good," the man replied. "Let's turn in."

"Why, Mr. Van Dyck, you say such things."

"Yes," replied Peter, "I am quite a card."

CHAPTER NINETEEN

Sound and Fury

AT BREAKFAST THE FOLLOWING MORNING MR. JONES MADE an announcement. The nudists greeted it with cheers. Not so Peter and his party. They were considerably alarmed, especially Little Arthur and Bishop Waller.

"Ladies and gentlemen," began Mr. Jones, rising and standing with one brown, slim hand resting lightly on the table. "Fellow nudists. It is high time we interrupted our nakedness and returned to the animalism of the conventional life we have abandoned."

By this time a majority of the nudists in their spontaneous enthusiasm were stamping on the floor and tinkling their glasses with their knives. Mr. Jones waited modestly until the noise subsided.

"Spring is now well advanced," he continued, "and in this connection it is generally agreed among poets that spring is the most immoral of the four seasons. Personally I have never found any great difference between them. However, there might be something in it."

"Mr. Jones," called out the philosopher, whose name happened to be Horace Sampson, "spring is perhaps the most suggestive of seasons. It is not as immoral as summer. Summer is notoriously immoral. In the short course of a northern summer the Eskimos go mad with love, I am told."

"If I had to love an Eskimo," a slight blonde lady remarked, "I think I'd go mad myself."

"The season's so short up here," stated a lean-looking gentleman, "I shouldn't think they'd have time to get out of their furs."

"They manage, nevertheless," replied Mr. Sampson.

"Perhaps they start to undress somewhere towards the breaking up of winter," someone suggested.

"I confess," said Mr. Jones, "that I do not know the technique of the Eskimo in such matters."

"You surprise me," observed Peter. "It is difficult to believe that the women of any race or clime have quite escaped the liberating influence of your Civilized Occasions."

"I can't be everywhere at once," replied Mr. Jones.

Color was mounting to Yolanda's cheeks. She looked a little frightened.

"Well," put in Jo, "when this place is pinched, as eventually it will be, you can hurry right up to Alaska and go mad with the Eskimos."

"I shall bear that in mind," replied the leader. "Thanks for the suggestion."

"Not at all," Josephine replied. "You probably had it in mind already."

"Spring was always my most difficult season," announced a still pretty woman with large dark eyes. "I never did succeed in getting through a spring season without saying yes to someone."

"It was your generous nature, my dear," said a lady sitting opposite her. "I always found summer almost unavoidable."

"This is scarcely the time for tender confessions," remarked Mr. Jones. "If there are no further suggestions, I'll continue."

"By all means," rumbled Mr. Sampson. "Sorry I started the discussion."

"I have noticed," resumed Mr. Jones, "a growing tendency to nervousness and strain and an almost flagrant infraction of the regulations governing the conduct of our members."

"I just couldn't help it, Mr. Jones," a young lady called out. "That man kept on pestering me until——"

"No specific reference was implied, Miss Joyce," Mr. Jones interrupted hastily. "But to continue. Quarrels breaking out between the male and female members of the colony have a way of ending up altogether too amicably. Of course, there are a number of you who could still hold out for several months."

"Indefinitely, sir," said an elderly gentleman.

"Splendid," said Mr. Jones. "However, all things considered, I feel that it would be best to declare a one-week Season of Forgetfulness almost immediately. It will open tomorrow night at dinner and close, for those who have been able to stick it out, just one week later."

More cheers and thumping. The elderly gentleman who could hold out indefinitely did not join in the applause.

"For those of you who don't know," continued Mr. Jones, "everything is tolerated—nay, encouraged—during the Season of Forgetfulness—everything save murder. It is, of course, understood that husbands and wives cannot base divorce proceedings on the grounds of each other's conduct during this season. Nor can any member withdraw from the colony as a result of it. It is hoped, on the other hand, that all members will lend their willing support and do everything in their power to make this orgy a success. If each one of us does his or her bit, if each one of us gives the worst that is in him, if we all band together in a spirit of libidinous abandon, I feel that we cannot fail. Ladies and gentlemen, I thank you."

Mr. Jones, his eyes flashing with the consciousness of duty well done, sat down amid wild applause. Already men and women were beginning to size one another up.

"My dear sir," said Bishop Waller in a low voice to Peter, "I never heard anything like it. Why, one would think he was addressing a meeting of Rotarians or the members of a college football team instead of a group of eternally damned souls. Jaegers or no jaegers, accompanied or single-handed, I intend to make my escape tonight. I am determined to shake from my feet the dust of this terrible place."

The excellent Bishop was not alone in this determination. When the small band of castaways foregathered some time later in a secluded part of the lawn, they were joined by the philosopher, who frankly stated his case and asked to be admitted to their number.

"I have finished my investigations here," he said with a shrug of his fine shoulders. "All this forgetfulness stuff is an old story to me. And the way they go about it is far too collegiate for one of my temperament. Some still seem to enjoy it, but frankly I don't. I am by nature an unmoral nonconformist. I can't stand mob righteousness any more than mob depravity. I suggest we finish with them before they finish us. I say, clear out naked as we are and take a chance on finding something to drape over our bodies."

"Listen," put in Little Arthur. "I gotter pick up the lawn today, and that means sticking trash and papers in a bag. When they're all down at the beach prancing, or in eating dinner, I'll sneak some sheets inter the bag and drag 'em out to the woods. What do you say about that?"

"Merely this," replied Bishop Waller. "It strikes me that we must all be saved from Sodom through the stealth of a converted pickpocket. In the light of this I feel that it would be difficult to accuse God of being altogether lacking in a slightly ironical vein of humor."

"I trust you will use your influence," remarked Mr. Horace Sampson, "to see that the situation does not become too funny."

"If I ever get a sheet over my nakedness," said Peter, "you can laugh yourself sick for all I care."

"No doubt we will," declared Jo. "I'm going to make a hole in mine and stick my head through."

"I think I will swathe mine round the upper half of my body," said the good Bishop reflectively. "The lower half still seems able to hold its own."

"Oh, quite," replied Peter, looking sharply at the Bishop.

"If we ever get back to civilization, Bishop Waller," Aspirin Liz put in, "you should send those drawers to the Smithsonian Institution."

"I wish you would give them their proper name," Bishop Waller protested. "This garment is known as jaegers."

"Don't care whether they're jaegers, jumpers, or jiggers," the ex-model replied. "You're wearing whatever they are where most men wear their drawers."

Of all the party Yolanda alone remained silent. Why should she accompany a number of sheet-clad figures back to civilization? There would surely be a scandal.

"At nine o'clock in the woods," said Horace Sampson. "Come singly or in pairs."

The party then broke up, and for the remainder of the day its members went innocently about their separate ways. At dusk Little Arthur could have been seen, had anyone cared to look at Little Arthur, dragging an old potato sack disconsolately in the direction of the woods. But from a distance the observer would not have known that petty thief was sweating from his efforts to look as if he were not there at all.

At nine o'clock that night Yolanda was a greatly worried young lady. The spirit of the approaching festivities had entered into her blood. She felt that she deserved one Season of Forgetfulness. All her life she had been remembering herself. Now for once she would like to forget and to find out what happened. Yet she hated to admit this fact to the members of the party. She was standing deep in the woods with Peter and Josephine. The others had not yet arrived.

"Listen, Peter," she began in an agitated voice. "I can get out at any time I want. Don't you think it would be a good idea for me to return and cover your retreat in case you should be missed?"

"Do you want to go back?" he asked her.

Yolanda nodded her head in the darkness. She could not say it in so many words. When she spoke, her voice no longer carried its old imperious note.

"He comes of a fine old family, Peter," she said.

"Would you like to increase it?" asked Peter.

"Don't be common," she retorted with a small show of spirit.

Josephine put her arm round the girl.

"Do you care for the suave Mr. Jones?" asked Jo.

For a moment Yolanda was suspicious, then she capitulated to the red-haired girl.

"You know how it is," she murmured. "I—I think so now."

"Then go back and land him," said Jo, "but for the love of Mike keep your head."

Yolanda squeezed Jo's hand.

"I never knew life was so different," she offered rather timidly. "So much better and so much worse. Good-bye, Peter. Do you mind?"

For answer, Peter tilted up her chin and kissed her lightly on the lips.

"It was a nice long engagement," he said. "You deserve some compensation. Good luck, Yolanda."

The next moment his one-time fiancée was slipping among the trees on her way back to Mr. Jones and the Season of Forgetfulness.

On the outer edge of the woods a high wall confronted the escaping party, all members of which were present with the exception of Yolanda, whose absence remained tactfully unobserved. As the six sheet-draped figures stood considering this obstruction, the scolding voice of a duck churning up last year's leaves with its wings fired them into sudden action.

"My God," said Peter. "Havelock Ellis is with us."

"But not for long," said Horace Sampson, scooping the bird from the leaves. "I'm going to wring her neck."

Jo snatched the duck from the philosopher and thrust its jeering head under a wing.

"No bloodshed," she whispered. "Get me over the wall, Peter. I'll take care of Ellis."

"Are there glass or spikes?" asked the Bishop when Jo had reached the top.

"The former," replied Jo. "I am trying to sit as lightly as a feather."

Little Arthur looked at Liz and tittered behind his hand.

"What a break," he said, "for a fat lady."

"If any glass gets into me," she muttered, "you're going to pick it out."

"May my fingers wither first," Little Arthur said in an awed voice. "They've picked a lot in their day, but they'll never pick that."

Aspirin Liz's difficulty was obviated by the employment of a sheet as a buffer between herself and the glass. Soon the party was standing, a trifle torn and disheveled, on the other side of the wall.

"There is no doubt now," said the Bishop, "about there being holes in my jaegers. I can feel them quite distinctly.

"I wish you wouldn't," said Mr. Sampson.

"Pardon an old man's curiosity," replied the Bishop. "These jaegers have served me well."

A winding tree-fringed road lay in front of them. An occasional light shining through the branches marked the habitations of man. The moon was not yet risen, and the way was dark. From time to time a sleepy clucking issued from Havelock Ellis resting comfortably in Jo's left arm. She had refused to abandon the duck. In this Peter had supported her.

"I suggest," said the tall philosopher, "that we set off at a brisk trot. Mr. Jones's attendants are many, and they are strong, rough men. At any moment we might be yanked back over that wall by a dozen or more ruthless hands."

Accordingly the party set itself in motion, the philosopher setting the pace. Aspirin Liz and Bishop Waller brought up the rear, the Bishop being slightly in advance. He seemed to be experiencing considerable difficulty with his jaegers. His efforts to keep them from falling off impeded his own as well as his companion's progress. The suspense was beginning to wear on the fat lady's nerves.

"Bishop," she panted at last, "you'll have to do something about those drawers. Either take them off or keep them on. I can't stand the strain."

"After all the turmoil they've been through," retorted the Bishop, "these jaegers stay on. It is the will of God."

"He doesn't seem to have quite made up His mind," said Liz, "from the way those drawers are behaving."

"Nevertheless," replied the Bishop, giving the garment a violent tug, "at this late date you cannot expect me to abandon them."

"From several views I got," said Liz, "they seemed to be abandoning you."

"Madam," admonished the Bishop, "we're in an extremely tough spot, as the saying goes. We have no time to discuss whether I am abandoning my jaegers or they are abandoning me."

Liz heaved a vast sigh and paddled after the Bishop through the night. Suddenly the headlights of an approaching automobile threw the party into sharp relief. Without a moment's hesitation the philosopher, Sampson, turned off the road and led his followers behind a billboard.

"This is the first time," he told them, "I ever saw any good reason for a billboard. Usually I consider them the most insulting form of advertising."

"It would be pretty," observed the Bishop, "if those motorists happened to be among my parishioners. The headlights caught my jaegers at a rather daring angle."

"One moment," whispered Peter, holding up an arresting hand. "Those motorists have stopped to investigate."

Silence behind the billboard. Voices from the road.

"But if you do find a lot of naked bodies," the party heard a woman say, "what on earth are you going to do with them? Can't ask them to take a ride."

"I can ask them to go home, came the voice of the woman's companion. "Don't know what this part of the world is coming to if a man can't go driving without running into a flock of nudes."

"You're not so upset as you'd have me believe," sniffed the lady. "You're looking for that girl."

"Nonsense," retorted the man. "She was nearly wearing a sheet. All of them were, in fact."

"Sure," scoffed the lady. "Nearly but not quite."

The man disappeared behind the billboard, and in a surprisingly short time reappeared totally naked save for his shoes and socks. The philosopher was a fast worker. With the assistance of Bishop Waller they rapidly stripped the man and distributed his garments among them. To Peter's lot fell a shirt and vest. The philosopher got the trousers, which first had been unsuccessfully attempted by Aspirin Liz. Little Arthur fell heir to a pair of shorts, and Jo to the man's coat. Bishop Waller dragged a sleeveless undershirt over the upper half of his body. The frail garment came to about his fifth rib before it split up the middle. The Bishop looked disappointed.

"If we had to strip a fellow creature," he observed, "and send him back naked into the world, I wish God had seen fit to make him several sizes larger."

"He must be quite the smallest man in the world," replied Mr. Sampson. "These trousers haven't the slightest intention of meeting in the front. Just take a look at them."

"If you please," protested Bishop Waller, "my eyes have seen enough. The attempts of Liz to squeeze into them took ten years off my life."

"The seat of those pants is no bigger than a dime," Aspirin Liz put in. "Never knew they came so small. Let's take a look at the little shaver."

The assaulted motorist could not stand for this. He tore off the sheet which had been wrapped round his head by the astute Sampson, and dashed back to the car. A slight scream greeted his appearance.

"Give me the lap robe, quick!" cried the man. "They've taken all my clothes."

"You don't have to tell me that," said the lady. "If you get in this car, I get out."

"But I can't stand here naked in the middle of the road," he protested.

"Neither can I go driving on a public highway with a stark naked man," came the reasonable reply.

"But aren't we engaged?" the naked man pleaded.

"I wouldn't even do it," he was firmly assured, "if we were married by the Pope."

"Catholics," reflected the Bishop, finding comfort in the thought. "Just the same, I hope God in His wisdom will be able to find some slight justification for my ruthless conduct tonight."

It will never be known how the naked motorist and his fiancée settled their little difficulty. He may be standing there yet trying to persuade her to let him get into the car. The fugitives did not linger to listen to the discussion. Down the road they swarmed in the wake of the sprinting philosopher.

"The way that shirt flares out from your little vest," observed Jo, "is a sight to behold. You should be jumping through hoops."

"Glad you find it amusing," said Peter. "You are protruding in various spots yourself, my sweet."

"Bishop," remarked Aspirin Liz, "I'm afraid you are not improved. That shirt does no earthly good."

Little Arthur dropped back behind them.

"What do you think of the drawers, Liz?" he panted.

"Too athletic for words," said the lady. "How did you manage to get inside them?"

At that moment they caught up with the grotesque figures ahead of them. Jo, Peter, and the philosopher were peering into the back of an empty truck. Peter climbed quickly in and helped Jo to follow him. Darkness swallowed them. The philosopher sprang aboard. Rather than be left behind, the Bishop, Liz, and Little Arthur scrambled into the truck. Two men tramped from the woods and, mounting to the front seat, set the truck in motion.

"This will give us a breathing spell," Horace Sampson whispered.

"We will need it," replied the Bishop, "when those gentlemen ahead discover what they have behind."

"I have nothing behind," muttered Peter. "Forgot my sheet."

For a quarter of an hour they bumped along in silence. Suddenly and to their great consternation the truck shot through a high gate and they found themselves looking out on a brightly lighted street. The transition was so startling that even the duck awoke and began to squawk a volley of evil language.

"What's wrong with your horn, Bill?" asked the man sitting beside the driver. "Sounds sort of strange to me."

"That ain't my horn," said Bill. "Must be some guy behind us."

The squawking continued in a hoarse but muffled voice.

"Damned if that ain't the queerest horn I ever did hear," remarked Bill's companion.

"I'm going to get out and knock the block off whoever's blowing the thing at me," declared Bill with determination.

The truck drew up, and the two gentlemen descended to the street. No other car was following. Bill's friend listened intently.

"It's coming from inside," he said in a low voice.

"From inside who?" asked Bill, somewhat startled.

"From inside us," replied the other.

"Not from inside me," declared Bill. "I couldn't make sounds like them even if I did my best."

"I mean inside the truck," said the other man.

"Oh," replied Bill. "That won't be hard to find out."

They approached the back of the truck, and Bill thrust in a grasping hand.

"I've got hold of a leg," he cried in a shocked voice.

"You've got hold of mine," came the voice of Aspirin Liz. "Is that any way to act?"

"Golly," said the friend. "The whole truck is full of them —a lot of funny people."

"Get out of there," roared Bill, who at heart was not a kind man. "Get out or I'll call a cop."

"If we get out you won't have to call a cop," said Peter bitterly. "Any number of cops will come of their own accord."

"Let us depart in peace," said the Bishop in a hollow voice, "and put our trust in God."

"I'll never put my trust in a duck again," Josephine told the world as she followed the others into the light of the street from the comfortable darkness of the truck.

Bill and his friend stood speechless. This moment was one of the really few high spots in their lives, one which they realized at the time would never grow stale or lose its wonder.

"Shouldn't we call the cops anyway?" the friend at length found words to ask.

Bill shook his head.

"That guy without the pants said it," he replied. "They'll get plenty of cops without our help."

As the fugitives, now a compact mass, trotted fearfully down the street, several policemen were already following them unbelievingly. As accustomed as they were to the strange sights of Coney Island, they were nevertheless shocked by this one. Some side show had gone mad or was openly defying the law. Whistles sounded, and pedestrians stopped in their tracks. Traffic became snarled, and two automobiles collided owing to the preoccupation of their drivers.

"We are being followed," gasped the Bishop.

"I'd be amazed if we weren't," Josephine replied.

"Turn in here," commanded Mr. Horace Sampson. "And stick together. We might find some place of concealment."

But the amusement park into which the party dashed over the prostrate body of the ticket collector offered no place of concealment, although for a moment several of its members disappeared from view down the smooth, steeply slanting sides of a wooden bowl.

"I have never been able to see the fun in this sort of thing," observed Mr. Horace Sampson as he painfully collected his scattered limbs.

"What sort of thing is it?" groaned the Bishop. "And how does one ever get out of it?"

"One claws one's way up the sides," Jo remarked, "only to be hurled back by some sportive reveler, several of whom are already peering down at us and waiting for the kill. Anyone seen a duck, and where might Peter be?"

A long arm with a torn shirt sleeve reached down as the girl spoke, and pulled her up the side of the pit.

"I was just asking about you," Jo said coolly to Peter. "Where's our duck?"

"She's knocking about somewhere," Peter answered. "Do you realize we're in one of the most fiendishly playful amusement parks in the world? It's not officially open yet according to the signs."

"Well, it is now," said Jo, glancing about her. "We've opened it officially, although I am not amused. I don't want to play with this park."

The Bishop looked miserably up at them.

"I very much fear God has withdrawn His protection," he called to Peter. "Maybe you could help."

As Peter drew the Bishop up the side, the philosopher almost bounded out. He had figured out the theory of the thing, then put it to the test. Unfortunately he overshot his mark and was carried by his terrific speed onto a flat surface composed of innumerable large disks spinning in opposite directions. For a moment sheer surprise overcame his philosophical resignation as his feet went up in the air and he found himself revolving in what he felt convinced could be nothing less than five different directions at the same time. Bishop Waller, blindly following the leader, promptly found himself in similar circumstances and breathed an urgent but dizzy prayer for divine intervention.

"This one is even less diverting," shouted Mr. Sampson as he was whirled into the orbit of the Bishop.

"How does one get off?" called that good man.

"I suppose one eventually gets flung off," Mr. Sampson called back. "Either that or one keeps on spinning hither and yon until the park closes for the night or season."

Bishop Waller did not hear the end of this speech, but he heard enough to remove all doubt concerning God's indifference to his lot. He closed his eyes, and when he opened them again he saw a policeman standing at the border of the spinning plane, and this policeman, to the Bishop's horror, had his cynically amused eyes fixed on the lower half of his, the Bishop's, person. Too late he realized that he and his long-suffering jaegers had come to the parting of the ways. Other policemen collected and stood watching the twirling bodies.

"I've seen some strange sights down here," said one of them, "but this takes the cake. Naked they are, no less. What Judge Wagger won't do to them!"

As Peter and Jo stood clinging to a rustic bridge gone violently mad in every plank, they had the pleasure of seeing Little Arthur dangling in the air from the cross bar of a flying trolley. Elevated as he was from the ground, the small creature presented neither a picturesque nor modest figure to those below, especially now that he was wearing the stolen shorts upon his feet. As he sped through the night on the trolley, two large uniformed officers sped beneath him. They were waiting for him literally to drop into their hands, which inevitably he would be forced to do.

"Wouldn't like to be in his shoes," Peter chattered.

"We're not occupying a bed of roses," Josephine told him. "There is more than one policeman waiting for us at either end of this infuriated bridge."

"I suppose we're through," said Peter.

"I've been through for quite some time," came Jo's broken words. "Life goes on inside, but it is a purely mechanical arrangement."

"I wonder if I could manage a kiss on this bucking span?" said Peter.

"Come over here on my side," she told him, "and we'll swing in the same direction. I'd hate to have my teeth knocked out from too violent a contact."

Peter moved over and took the jouncing figure of Jo in his arms and in so doing succeeded in pulling her with him to the floor of the bridge.

"We're going, Jo!" he cried.

"Then go ahead and kiss me," she called out in jumping accents as she pressed her lips to his.

"Be God if they're not love-making on that dangerous contraption," said an officer in an awed voice. "And in their terrible condition and all."

Still clinging desperately together, the two bodies rolled and jostled into the arms of the law. A policeman tossed a raincoat over Jo and helped her to arise. For a moment she leaned dizzily against him, and during that moment he became a trifle dizzy himself. Peter rose more slowly and fastidiously readjusted the tails of his flaring shirt.

"Will you look at that, I ask you," breathed a policeman.

They all did.

The philosopher and the Bishop, having been tossed out

of the officers' reach by some caprice of the flying disks, were now doing their utmost to make good their escape. The philosopher was bounding up a high flight of spiral stairs, and the Bishop, clinging to his jaegers, was doing his best to bound after his friend. For a moment they stood poised on the summit of the stairs; then, with two hoarse cries of defiance, they launched themselves down the slide that snaked away from their feet. It was a short slide but an impressive one. Several policemen picked them up, then stood looking at them curiously.

"Well, you're a couple of rare birds," one of the officers said at last.

"You're wrong there, my man," replied the Bishop. "We're a couple of raw birds. Have you by chance a pin?"

"You know, my dear Bishop," said the philosopher as the policemen hustled them along, "I could almost grow to like that last thing we did."

"I very much fear," said the Bishop, "that it's the last thing we will ever do of our own free will."

On their way to the patrol wagon they were joined by the captors of Jo and Peter. At the same moment another diversion claimed the attention of the consolidated party. From the bowels of a frantically revolving barrel came the agonized voice of Aspirin Liz.

"Will one of you cops for God's sake come in here and arrest me?" the ex-model managed to get out between twirls and bounces. "I'd rather stay in jail for life than in here for another minute."

An officer reached in the barrel and dragged the lady to safety. She still had her sheet, but it was serving no practical purpose, being wrapped round her head. Another raincoat was called for and tossed over Liz.

"One solid mass of bruises," she muttered. "I wonder what black-hearted torturer ever thought out this place."

While the officers were concentrating on Aspirin Liz

familiar drowsy clucking issued from a near-by trash receptacle. Swiftly Jo reached down, seized the nodding duck, and concealed it under her coat.

"She's a very adaptable duck, isn't she, Peter?" Jo said with a smile to the man at her side.

"If she'd kept her damn mouth shut," he replied, "we wouldn't be where we are now."

"We might have been in even a worse place," she answered, "though I can't think of one at the moment."

Through two solid walls of humanity they were ushered into the patrol wagon, where Little Arthur sat huddled in the gloom. He brightened up considerably at the appearance of his friends.

"Some night," was his inclusive greeting. "What do yer say, folks? Hasn't it been some night?"

"It has indeed been some night," agreed the Bishop, "and unfortunately, Little Arthur, it is not at an end."

"We'll have to come back some time," said Jo, "and do it all over again."

"I'd rather be hung," put in Aspirin Liz, "than give that barrel another chance at me."

"One end at least we've achieved," declared Horace Sampson, a philosopher to the last. "By getting ourselves in the clutches of the law we are safe from those of the overhospitable Mr. Jones and his minions."

"It looks like a Season of Total Obscurity to me," observed Peter, pressed closely against Jo.

"We're far better off where we are," said the Bishop. "Far better off, my boy, and that is none too good."

As the patrol wagon clanged down the street between blaring and brightly lighted show places, Josephine felt around her more than the arms of the Law. With a happy sigh she settled back. She was both loved and in love. The Law did not matter.

"May I kiss my young man?" she asked one of the officers seated near the door.

"Might as well, baby," he told her. "You won't be seeing much of each other for a long, long time."

"Little Arthur," said Aspirin Liz sadly, "I think I could almost like you, I feel so sorry for myself."

CHAPTER TWENTY

Magistrate Wagger Hears a Lot

MAGISTRATE WAGGER SUFFERED FROM INSOMNIA, SO HE OCcasionally held court at night. On these occasions the delinquents brought before him did considerable suffering on their own account. Whenever the good magistrate found himself unable to sleep, he began to think of his prisoners. It galled him exceedingly to visualize them peacefully slumbering in their various cells. Why should Guilt wallow in smug repose while Justice lay haggard and stared into the darkness? Wagger could see no logical reason for this. He would give those sleep-sodden malefactors something to keep them awake for a long, long time. He would share his insomnia with them.

Of course, it may be argued that a man poisoned by the venom of Magistrate Wagger's mental outlook at these moments was in no condition to dispense justice—to hold in his hands, as it were, the fate of erring humanity. But when a judge or a magistrate has already decided to send someone to jail, the method of procedure really does not matter. Whether it is done with a cheerful smile or a dark frown makes very little difference to the prisoner. Three months are three months, regardless of how one is given them.

Withal, Magistrate Wagger's manner on the bench was not as sinister as one might expect. It was not nearly so sinister as was the man himself. Inasmuch as the night meant nothing to him, he did not care how long he sat up in court himself or others sat up with him. Here there were lights and company—conversational opportunities to bring relief to the weary mind. After he had put half a dozen offenders definitely behind the bars, Magistrate Wagger usually was able to sleep like a top.

He was a small, thin, wiry individual with a mop of gray hair that gave the impression of having been unpleasantly startled. His face was small, too, and looked like a mahogany-colored mask of enigmatic expression. If one decided that the black eyes that snapped and burned beneath the gray bars of his eyebrows were a trifle mad, one would not have been far from wrong. They were mad usually and could easily become furious.

Tonight as the six bruised and battered, not to mention almost naked, fugitives from the nudist colony were ushered into his presence, he failed to witness their demoralizing entrance, being engaged at the moment in studying some court records. When he did look up, his mind filled with other things, he did not at first appreciate the magnitude of the scene he was beholding.

"What have we here?" he began in a preoccupied voice. "What have we here?" Gradually his eyes widened and his mask of a face twisted itself into a spasm of sudden anguish. "I should have asked," he continued in a voice barely under control, "what haven't we here?" He looked about him sharply. "Who brought me all these horrible objects?" he demanded. "I want to know that."

"We did," said several policemen proudly. "There was a lot of us in it."

"Oh, there were," resumed the magistrate, insanity simmering behind his words. "Well, I see where I'll have to get me a new police force. The officers responsible for showing these obscenities to me might just as well turn in their badges and snip off their buttons." He paused; then, leaning far over his desk, addressed himself bitterly to the unhappy policemen. "Why," he exploded, "the mere sight of them has driven all thought of sleep forever from my mind. Was it your intention to kill me? Did you deliberately set out to break my health and shatter my reason? I sense a conspiracy here. You must have made them like that and then dragged them in to torture my eyes. Don't say a word. I'll find this out for myself." He scanned the group of prisoners with his mad eyes. Suddenly his hand shot out, and he pointed a finger at Peter. "You, there, in the shirt and vest. Don't lie to me now. How many degrees did these men put you through before they made you like that—or did they bribe you to do it?"

"Can't I lie?" asked Peter.

"Of course you can't lie," said the magistrate. "Did you intend to lie?"

"I had thought of lying a little," Peter admitted.

"You had?" reflected Wagger. "That's bad. But you're not going to lie now? Why not?"

"I'm too darned scared," said Peter. "My brain isn't working."

"Mine is absolutely atrophied," confided the gray-haired justice. "Come, speak up—how did you get all naked?"

"We ran away naked," Peter told him.

"What!" gasped the magistrate. "What hideous crime had you committed to make you run away in the condition you are—you and your companions?"

"They were playing all over an amusement park," an officer put in here. "Steeplechase, it was."

"That's a lie," snapped the red-headed girl in the raincoat. "We were suffering all over an amusement park, your honor. Almost dying."

The magistrate looked for a long time at Jo. She had never encountered such concentrated vindictiveness.

"When the conversation becomes general," he said in a bitterly polite voice, "we'll let you in, too. Maybe we'll all talk at once." Suddenly his jaws snapped. "Until then, hold your tongue." Once more he turned to Peter. "What were you running away from?" he demanded.

"From a lot of naked people," said Peter.

"Why should a person in your condition run away from others who, so far as I can see—and I can see much farther than I ever thought I'd be called upon to do from this bench —were no whit worse?"

"If you were naked yourself," asked Peter, "wouldn't you run away from a lot of other naked people of mixed sexes?"

The magistrate gulped, then placed a firm check on his indignation.

"I'd crawl away," he answered in a low voice, "even as I would like to crawl away from you. But I don't care for the turn this talk is taking. Ask me no more nasty questions like that last one. Why, if you were running away, as you state—why, may I ask, did you and your friends stop to play on a lot of slides and things? Have you no concentration?"

"We were looking for a place of concealment," said Peter, only too keenly aware of the utter inadequacy of his statement.

"And so you picked out one of the most popular amusement parks in the world," the magistrate observed with a sneer in his voice, "in which to hide your nakedness. Listen to me, young man. Even if I ask you questions in a moment of abstraction, don't answer them. I am trying to keep quite calm about all this, and you upset me." He paused, cast his eyes over the group, and let them finaly rest on the abashed pickpocket.

"I don't want to talk to you," the magistrate began, "but I have to talk to someone. Please refrain from being trying, and do a little something about those drawers while I am forced to look at you."

Arthur picked up a corner of the raincoat that stood between Aspirin Liz and decency, and draped it over his shorts. The result was that much of Liz became exposed—too much. The magistrate closed his eyes and looked as if he were going to faint.

"Make him put it back," he muttered. "My eyes are destroying my brain."

When the raincoat had been properly rearranged on Aspirin Liz, and the magistrate had gulped down a glass of water, he once more addressed himself to the cowering prisoner before him.

"Don't ever do that again," scolded Magistrate Wagger. "Not even if you think it amuses me. It doesn't. Now tell me who you are."

"I'm Little Arthur," faltered the small crook.

The magistrate blinked his surprise.

"Little Arthur," he repeated. "Is that a proper name for

a fully grown man? Do you hope to soften me by baby talk? Little Arthur!—just how much does that mean? Nothing! Suppose I should refer to myself as Little Wagger, or Little Alfred, which happens to be my first name—would you like it?"

"I wouldn't mind," replied Little Arthur.

"You wouldn't, perhaps," snapped the magistrate, "but think of my friends and associates. Would they like it?"

"I don't know none of yer friends, yer honor," Little Arthur stammered.

"Thank God for that, at any rate," muttered Wagger, mopping his forehead with a large white handkerchief. "Answer the question," he roared suddenly. "Little Arthur what?"

"Little Arthur Springtime," answered the crook.

"Springtime," grated the magistrate. "Why Little Arthur Springtime? Was that when you were born?"

The other members of the detained party looked upon their companion with reawakened interest. They had never stopped to consider that he might have another name, especially such a lyrical one.

"No, yer honor," replied Arthur. "I was born in the wintertime."

"Then why in God's good name did your mother call you Springtime?" demanded Wagger. "All this is a sheer waste of energy and breath."

At this point Mr. Horace Sampson felt himself called upon to clear up the confusion.

"Perhaps, Magistrate Wagger," he said in his deep voice, "perhaps the illiterate little beggar means that certain things happened in the springtime that made it possible for him to be born in the winter."

The magistrate eyed the philosopher darkly.

"How do you mean?" he demanded. "What things?"

"The usual ones," said Sampson.

"Oh, that," murmured the justice. "My brain is quite addled. That would be it."

"You see, yer honor," volunteered Little Arthur, "the fire-house moved away and Mom never could tell which, al-thought she knew it was one of 'em."

"What has a firehouse got to do with it," asked the magis-trate, "and where did it move to?"

"Don't know," replied Arthur sadly. "I wasn't born then."

"I wish you never had been," rasped the magistrate. "Do you mean to imply you're the results of an assault?"

Little Arthur dropped his eyes.

"I have been since, yer honor," he said, "but not then. The boys just used ter drop in social, like."

"Why, this is the most disgraceful story I ever heard," exclaimed Wagger. "Why are you telling it to me?"

"You kept asking me questions," the crook answered sim-ply.

"Well, I won't ask you any more," declared the magis-trate. "Decidedly not. I should think I'd go quite mad listen-ing to all this. Can't see why I'm not."

"Not what?" asked Jo.

"Not mad," said the magistrate, not thinking.

"Not mad at who?" asked Jo.

"I'm not mad at anybody," he retorted.

"Aren't you mad at Little Arthur?" she continued.

"Stop asking me questions," he suddenly roared at the girl. "I hate the very sight of Little Arthur. My God, I'm nerv-ous. Any of you boys got an aspirin?"

A clerk passed a box of aspirin tablets up to the magis-trate. He tried to open the tin container, but somehow failed to manage it.

"Can't do it," he said hopelessly. "Never can. Never have been able to. Why do they make them that way?"

"Let me try," offered Liz. "I know how."

"It's irregular," said the nervous man, "but I must have a pill."

Deftly Liz opened the small tin container, removed a tablet, and passed the open box back to the magistrate. The tablet she placed under her tongue. Magistrate Wagger was following her movements with fascinated eyes.

"Don't you take any water?" he asked her.

"I like 'em better dry," said Liz. "Under my tongue."

Wagger looked slightly shocked.

"I should think it would be uncomfortable," he ventured. "Can you talk all right? No impediment at all?"

"You get sort of used to it," she told him.

"Well, I won't try now," said the magistrate. "But I will later." He popped the tablet into his mouth, drained another glass of water, then glared hatefully at the Bishop.

"You're old enough to know better than to be going round like that," he said. "Just drawers and a split shirt, and the drawers are coming down in my face. Yank 'em up!" The Bishop complied promptly, and the magistrate continued. "That's better," he said. "And remember, if you don't care what you show, I care about what I look at. I'm very nervous now, and I want you to tell me exactly who you are. Don't try to say you're Little This or That, because I won't be able to stand it."

"My name is Waller," replied the Bishop in his most impressive voice. "Bishop Waller."

"Is the first part a name or a title?" asked the magistrate.

"It designates the office I hold in the Episcopal Church," said the Bishop calmly.

Magistrate Wagger never knew how he overcame the confused, distorted impulses that beset him at that moment. From mahogany his face turned purple. His eyes grew and grew until they ached in his head. Several times he swallowed. Finally he spoke.

"I don't believe you," he said in a cracked voice. "And

you can't say I didn't give you a fair warning." He turned to his clerk. "When I come to sentencing this mob," he said, "remind me to tack on some extra time to this ruffian's term for attempting to hide behind the skirts of the Church." He rested a pair of weary eyes on Liz. "Will you please show me what you are concealing beneath that raincoat?" he asked.

"Not on your life," said Liz. "I knew the legal mind was accurate, but I didn't know it was nasty."

"Are you calling me nasty?" Wagger asked in a voice hushed by incredulity.

"I was referring to the legal mind," hedged Liz.

"Well, my mind is legal," snapped the baited jurist.

"So is mine," replied Liz. "It's perfectly legal to have a mind, isn't it?"

"It all depends on how you use it," he told her. "How did we get on this subject?"

"I don't know," said Liz.

"Neither do I," admitted the magistrate. "I'm feeling terribly baffled by all these digressions. Will you tell what you have concealed under that raincoat if you won't let me see?"

"Everything I've got," said Liz, "is underneath this raincoat."

"And what have you got?" asked the magistrate, not to be outwitted.

"What would you expect?" the lady demanded. "Fish scales, or feathers?"

"How do you mean, feathers?" the magistrate stubbornly persisted. "Or fish scales, for instance?"

"Oh, God," breathed Liz, casting her eyes to heaven. "Take a look for yourself."

With this she threw open the raincoat, and the magistrate, after one dazed look, uttered a wild cry and collapsed on his desk. For a few moments there was confusion in the court, but Wagger did not care. At last he raised a stricken face and looked severely at Liz.

"That was a terrible thing to do," he told her. "You nearly gave me a stroke."

"You were asking for it," said Liz.

"Perhaps," he admitted fairly. "But I never thought it was possible for a woman to be so—so much, if you get what I mean."

"Without any trouble at all," she replied. "You'd be surprised to know that once I had a very lovely figure."

"May I ask," put in Horace Sampson, "is this a trial or an informal gathering?"

"You may not," retorted the magistrate. "Keep a civil tongue in your head. I've got enough on my hands."

"Enough what on your hands?" asked Jo.

"I don't know," said Wagger.

"I understood you to say you had enough tongue on your hands," persisted Jo.

"My dear young woman," the magistrate almost pleaded, "how could I possibly have enough tongue on my hands?"

"Oh, so you like tongue?"

"I didn't say so."

"But," protested the girl, "you just asked me how you could ever possibly get enough tongue on your hands."

"I meant just tongue," he explained. "Not enough tongue. As a matter of fact, I'd hate to have tongue on my hands. Don't fancy the idea at all."

"How about a dog's tongue?" she asked him.

"Whose dog?" he wanted to know. "I have no dog."

"That's too bad," said Jo. "Well, then, the tongue of any dog you name."

"Good God!" cried the magistrate, suddenly realizing the lengths to which this girl had led him. "Is this tongue discussion going to continue on indefinitely? I don't care if it's a dog's tongue or an elephant's tongue. Keep them off my hands."

"I'm not going to put tongue on your hands," Josephine replied defensively. "I was just asking."

"All right. All right," Wagger said in a weary voice. "Now let me ask you some questions. To begin with, how did you get that way?"

"Well, your honor," began Jo easily, "it was like this. You see, there was a fog and——"

"What fog?" interrupted the magistrate.

Jo looked puzzled.

"How do you mean, what fog?" she asked. "You can't name a fog or bring along a sample."

"Where and when was this fog?" he demanded.

"All over," said Jo. "I forget just when."

Magistrate Wagger looked thoroughly disheartened.

"Tell it your way," he muttered. "I won't believe you anyhow."

"And there were a lot of naked people, your honor," the girl continued.

"There still are," he said moodily.

"And these naked people," went on the girl, "took off all our clothes."

"Just where is the fog at this point?" asked Wagger, not caring whether she told him or not.

"There isn't any fog any more," she replied.

"Then I don't see why you introduced the fog in the first place," he answered. "Are you trying to interest me in a dirty story, young lady?"

"It isn't so dirty," protested Jo. "Just in spots, your honor."

Suddenly the magistrate's eyes dilated. He leaned far over his desk and fixed his wild bloodshot eyes on the middle section of Jo's raincoat.

"Why are you doing that?" he asked in a hushed voice.

"Doing what?" demanded Jo.

"You must know what you're doing," he replied.

"Occasionally I don't," she told him.

"Why does your coat go like that?" demanded the magistrate. "I insist on knowing."

Glancing down, Jo was interested to observe that from the appearance of her raincoat she had suddenly grown very fat. Jumping to conclusions, she looked reproachfully at Peter.

"Peter," she said, "we'll have to make that wedding snappy. This looks like a rush order."

"It's not that," he assured her. "Your stomach is a little upset."

"Your coat," said the judge, almost whispering. "It thrusts itself out, then suddenly collapses. Are you doing it?"

"No, sir," replied Jo. "I mean, yes."

"Then don't," pleaded the magistrate.

Jo gave Havelock Ellis a vicious squeeze, and the duck gave an equally vicious squawk. Magistrate Wagger looked startled, then peered searchingly at the prisoners before him.

"Who made that offensive noise?" he wanted to know. "It constitutes contempt of court. Come! Speak up!"

"I'll readily agree," rumbled the long silent philosopher, "that the noise was both offensive and contemptible, but I assure you, sir, I wouldn't have made it if I could, which I greatly doubt."

"How you go on!" the magistrate complained. "Who made that unusual noise? I want to know." At this moment the squawk was repeated and Josephine's stomach gave a brisk outward lunge. Wagger's eyes were popping. He had partly risen from his chair. "There it goes again," he breathed. "It went 'way out this time." He sank back in his chair and once more mopped his forehead. "Young lady," he resumed, "are you deliberately making stomachs at me?"

"Not deliberately," answered Jo, finding it increasingly difficult to restrain the aroused Ellis. "My stomach is just on its own. I have no control over it."

"I'll have no control over mine if this keeps up," he assured her. "That aspirin didn't do a bit of good. I . . ." His voice died away in his chair. "For the love of God, what's that?" he cried, pointing at Josephine's stomach.

Jo looked at her stomach, as did everyone else within peering distance. Officers and court attendants moved a little away. Under the circumstances they were not to be blamed. Braver men than they have been unnerved by lesser sights. Protruding from the raincoat at Josephine's stomach was a long, purple, snake-like head which was looking fixedly at Magistrate Wagger out of two yellow, malevolent eyes. With her free hand Jo thrust the head of the duck back beneath the coat. The air was filled with squawks. Ellis was protesting in the worst language she knew how to use.

"That," said Jo at last, feeling somewhat confused herself, "that was merely my handbag."

"Merely," wheezed the haggard Wagger. "Just a simple little handbag, eh—a mere trifle?" Then his indignation got the upper hand. "Does a handbag hurl maledictions in a foreign tongue?" he thundered. "Does a handbag peer at one out of fierce yellow eyes that look as if they had brooded on the flames of hell itself? Does a handbag have a long, death-dealing beak?"

"Yes, sir," cut in Jo. "It's a novelty handbag—a funny one. I open the beak and put things in—small change and lipstick and all sorts of things."

"Do you mean to tell me," demanded Wagger, "that you actually open that beak?"

"Why not?" Jo replied with a shrug.

"Well, I wouldn't do it if they made me a justice of the Supreme Court," he said decisively. For a moment or so he tapped nervously on his desk with his skinny fingers. "Young lady," he resumed, "I don't believe that handbag story at all. I can't believe it. There was too much life and animation in what I saw—too much noise. Are you by any chance an unfortunate freak? That head seemed almost a part of you to me."

"Not at all," replied the girl. "We are quite independent, I assure you."

It was at this point that Havelock Ellis took it into her head to prove the accuracy of Jo's words. She had been missing things too long, had the duck, Ellis. She would find out for herself what all this was about. With a vicious tug and a beating of wings, she burst Jo's coat asunder and with a wild cry of triumph fluttered to the magistrate's desk. But her cry was not nearly so wild as the one that tore itself from Wagger's throat as he abandoned the dignity of his office and sought safety behind his chair. Ellis made a vicious snap at the rear part of the departing man. Contact was established and Wagger's speed increased. After this gesture of contempt the duck settled down on the desk and remained perfectly still.

"It bit me," chattered the magistrate. "I'm poisoned perhaps! What's it going to do next?"

"Maybe she'll lay an egg," was Jo's calm reply. "She's done about everything else."

"Do you mean that duck would have the temerity to lay an egg on the desk of a city magistrate?" quavered the little man behind the chair.

"She never has yet," said Jo, "but when that duck makes up her mind to lay an egg, I feel convinced she'd produce it on the desk of the mayor himself."

"Oh!" lamented the magistrate. "Oh, dear, oh, dear! What a way for a girl to talk! What are we going to do? I won't touch that duck." Suddenly he was stung by a new and fearful consideration. "Lock all the doors," he cried. "Don't let a reporter out. If this gets into the papers I'll never hear the end of it. 'Duck Lays Egg on Magistrate Wagger's Desk' —I can see it already in headlines." He looked at the demoralized policemen. "If you boys will take that duck away, back go your badges and buttons," he promised them.

"That's my duck," said Jo, sweeping the squatting bird from the desk. "I've had a lot of trouble with that duck. If she lays an egg, that's going to be mine, too."

"Keep both the duck and her egg," screamed Wagger. "Do you think I want them? I wish I could tell you what to do with the damn duck."

"I'm afraid you'd be asking too much, your honor," Jo replied demurely.

At this moment a reporter approached the migistrate and spoke rapidly to him in an undertone. Slowly the little man's face cleared.

"You won't mention the duck?" he asked the reporter.

"Not a word," the other declared. "We'll stick to the straight story."

"And how did you get the story?" Wagger wanted to know.

"Why, if that gentleman in the drawers is Bishop Waller," the reporter said, "then naturally the people with him must be those who left the ferry in the fog."

"I wish they'd never been found," Magistrate Wagger replied. "I wish they'd been lost at sea forever and forever."

"I recognized Peter Van Dyck myself," the reporter went on, "in spite of his informal appearance."

"If you write a funny story about us," Peter spoke up promptly, "I'll call in a flock of reporters and tell about the duck and what the magistrate wanted the young lady to do with it."

"I didn't say it," shouted Wagger. "I only wished it."

"Then I'll tell the world what you wished she would do with the duck," said Peter.

"Don't do it, Mr. Van Dyck, I beg you," the magistrate pleaded. "This reporter is going to be nice. You be nice, too. That's a good chap." For a moment the courtroom was still as Wagger sat at his desk and brooded upon the many wrongs that had been done him. His indignation rose. He could contain it no longer. He spoke.

"Are you Bishop Waller?" he asked in a voice of velvet gentleness.

"I assured you I was," said the Bishop.

"A bishop of the Episcopal Church?" continued the magistrate.

"I am, sir," the Bishop replied.

"Then I have made a slight mistake," said Wagger, his voice still soft and sweet, "and I hope you won't mind if I ask you to take your naked gang and get the hell out of my courtroom."

His voice ended in a snarl, and he sank back in his chair, his eyes tightly closed.

"Have they gone?" he asked at length, pressing a hand to each temple.

"They have, sir," answered an officer.

"Thank God for that," muttered Wagger.

They had gone. They were in a taxicab with the reporter headed for the Half-Moon Hotel. As they drove away from the court, an expensive-looking car of foreign make followed them down the street. The philosopher glanced through the window and studied the imposing tower of the hotel they were approaching. It was capped by a replica of the adventurous ship from which the hotel derived its name. Many windows looked out upon the sea from the mounting structure standing out picturesquely against the blue.

"An altogether charming seaside caravansary," murmured Mr. Sampson. "I think we should do well there. It does justice to Hendrik Hudson."

"Who did he ever lick?" asked Little Arthur from his seat on the floor of the cab.

"Oh, he just knocked about the river in a boat," said Josephine.

"A ferry captain," concluded the hopeless dip. "I don't want ter hear another word."

"He was a Dutchman," put in Peter proudly.

"I'd try to keep that quiet," said Jo.

Arrived at the Half-Moon, the reporter considerately led them through the street entrance, which fortunately for the guests as well as themselves was a large secluded hall cut off from the lounge and lobby above. Here they were met by the manager, who, although warned over the telephone by the reporter, could not repress a look of astonishment when he gazed at his prospective guests.

"We need a flock of rooms," said Peter.

"You need much more than that," the manager replied with a gracious smile. "If you meet any of my guests in the hallways, I hope you won't mind if I ask you in a loud voice if you enjoyed the masquerade."

"My dear sir," replied the Bishop, "if you get us to our rooms you can ask us if we enjoyed the murder for all I care. Have you a pin, perhaps?"

The manager had no pin, but promptly obtained one from the near-by beauty salon. The Bishop accepted it gratefully and did things to his jaegers. At this moment the lift door opened and several passengers stepped out. When they gazed upon the huddled party they almost stepped back again.

"Did you enjoy the masquerade?" asked the manager in a loud false voice.

"No!" cried Little Arthur. "It was punk."

"Why, you low thief," boomed the philosopher, "you had the time of your life."

The people hurried on and the party hurried in. The dusky, good-looking girl responsible for the lift was responsible for it no longer. She uttered a frightened cry and turned her back on the worse than naked throng.

"I should have warned her," said the manager of the Half-Moon. "She probably thinks you are ghosts."

"I feel like one," declared Aspirin Liz.

"You don't look like one," said the manager.

A chauffeur in splendid livery was hurrying towards the party. When he reached the elevator, he offered a large bundle to Peter.

"Mr. Jones sends his compliments," he said in a smooth voice. "He hopes you enjoyed yourself in court as much as he did. He further hopes that you put on these clothes as speedily as possible. He himself will bring Miss Yolanda back to town shortly. He desires to meet her parents, and suggests great discretion be used on all sides."

The chauffeur paused and winked. Peter almost dropped the bundle. Quickly the uniformed man turned away.

"You can tell Mr. Jones for me," Little Arthur called after the rapidly retreating figure, "that if I ever catch him wearing pockets I'll pick 'em clean as a hound's tooth."

"You missed your chance," said Peter as the elevator shot skyward under the hand of the recovered operator. "That was Mr. Jones."

EPILOGUE

A Farewell to Drawers

BISHOP WALLER, CLAD ONLY IN A TOWEL, STOOD IN THE center of his newly acquired room at the Half-Moon. A majestic figure, the Bishop, now that at last his jaegers were off. Bishop Waller was waiting for the hotel valet. On the bed lay an orderly row of garments but recently returned to him by the considerate but reprehensible Mr. Jones. In his heart the Bishop could not thoroughly disapprove of the man. Mr. Jones had his points.

However, before the Bishop could don his rightful attire and mingle once more with his kind, he felt it essential to procure at all costs a new pair of jaegers, the extra pair having been left behind in his suitcase on the abandoned ferry. The old ones had served their purpose. They had outworn their usefulness. Yet Bishop Waller did not despise the abandoned jaegers. Far from it. He regarded them in the light of a religious relic. They deserved to be framed tastefully and hung in a church.

"Jaegers Worn by Bishop Waller in Defiance of the Nudes," or some other such terse, dignified explanation would do quite nicely, for, of course, the presence of those jaegers in a church would have to be explained.

A knock sounded on the door.

"Come in," said Bishop Waller, an invitation he would not have extended in his present condition ten days ago.

"Can I be of any service?" the valet enquired.

"Of invaluable service," replied the Bishop, tossing the jaegers over the man's extended arm. "Go out into the marts and highways of this city and see if you can match those."

The valet raised his eyebrows and considered the garment dangling from his arm a little more distastefully than the Bishop would have liked.

"It will be difficult at this hour," said the man, "to match these er——"

"Jaegers," supplied the Bishop.

"Exactly," agreed the valet. "But I think it can be done, sir. I know of one store that sells almost anything at any time of night. It's such an odd store, I'm sure they must have things like this."

"Excellent," said the Bishop, "save for the last sentence."

Half an hour later the valet returned with a neatly tied package. Eagerly the Bishop opened it and extracted the garment within. The valet produced the odd pair from another package not nearly so neatly tied. In fact, it was in an old bag that the battered jaegers had been returned. Evidently the shopkeeper regarded them even more distastefully than did the valet. Bishop Waller let this pass.

The valet held up the old pair while the Bishop held up the new. Together they compared the garments.

"To a buttonhole," cried the Bishop at last, beaming upon the valet. "Splendid work, my fine fellow. A perfect match to the last, least buttonhole. I would have said button, only there aren't any buttons on the old ones. I must have been a sight."

Aspirin Liz and Little Arthur had shifted into their respective drawers with precision and despatch. Little Arthur, as he got into his ancient pair, mutely promised the patron saint of all good pickpockets that he would never take them off again nor desire those of any other man. With Liz he had dined in regal splendor—far better than he had ever dined before—in the long, restful dining room of the hotel. Soft music together with a knowledge of his companion's alert scrutiny had so conquered his spirit that he left the silver intact. After dinner they had strolled along the boardwalk for the sheer pleasure of experiencing the sensation of being fully clad in public.

At the moment Liz was engaged in utterly demolishing Little Arthur. Seated in a tiny but apparently indestructible self-propelling vehicle, known as a Dodge-'em, she was pursuing him—likewise ensconced—round an enclosed surface presided over by a tolerantly benign Japanese. Every time she drove her midget motor into that of her light-fingered playfellow, her titanic laughter drifted far into the night. It tickled something savage and destructive in her soul to crash into Little Arthur and to shatter virtually every bone in his frail body.

"It ain't fair," screamed the small crook, purple in the face. "You're carrying too much fat."

"Oh, dear," sighed Liz weakly, tears streaming down her cheeks, "this is more fun than a kettle of fish."

She pressed her foot on the pedal and launched herself into Arthur as if she would totally destroy him. There was the sound of a mighty impact, her victim's head jerked crazily backwards, his car twirled impotently across the floor, and Liz's wild laughter drew fresh spectators from the boardwalk.

Never, decided the Japanese, had he had such a wholly satisfactory nest egg as Liz. She overflowed her car and gave the almost deserted floor the appearance of being crowded—of literally throbbing with gayety and life. The lookers-on regarded her with wonderment and respect and Little Arthur with deep commiseration.

Crashing, dodging, and steadily insulting each other, Aspirin Liz and Little Arthur spin dizzily from the page.

In the quiet, gracious lounge of the hotel filled with comfortable divans and armchairs and generously supplied with ashtrays—a stroke of sheer genius—Mr. Horace Sampson was sitting with the reporter. Sampson was in the philosophical pink. He was wondering idly what the guests of the hotel would do if suddenly deprived of their drawers—everything, in fact. He was endeavoring to imagine the reactions of the various ladies and gentlemen under his observation. That old lady with the pearls round a high stiff collar would never survive the shock, whereas there were a couple of girls over there who after a little parleying might take to it like ducks to water. It was difficult to tell at a glance. He turned to the reporter seated in a chair beside him.

"What do you think of drawers?" asked the philosopher.

"Personally," replied the reporter, "I admire them less than any garment I wear—even less than my undershirt."

"Yet," pursued the philosopher, "if you had to choose between them, the drawers would win the day."

"Naturally," retorted the reporter. "An undershirt merely keeps one warm, whereas drawers keep one decent. A man looks less ridiculous in a pair of drawers than when he is clad only in an undershirt."

"I'm not convinced," the philosopher replied thoughtfully. "Some drawers can be singularly ridiculous. For example, those worn by the good Bishop still amuse me even in retrospect."

"After your experience, Mr. Sampson," inquired the reporter, "what is your opinion of the nudist colony from which you escaped?"

"Not high," replied Sampson, "but of this I am convinced: to endeavor to conquer the flesh is a profitless undertaking. Before a man or a woman can arrive at any degree of spiritual tranquillity, he or she must give flesh the rein. Whether one is clad in bare flesh or fur makes very little difference."

"How about the health angle?" asked the philosopher's companion.

"Fiddlesticks!" he snapped. "The benefits derived from mixed nudity are far offset by the mental agitation it entails. When men and women deliberately set out to attain a state of purity and so-called innocence, they are endeavoring to capture something that never existed. And if they did succeed, they would be greatly disappointed people. Purity, my friend, is simply an escape from the obligations one owes to one's own body as well as to others much more attractively fashioned." The philosopher turned and considered the radio darkly. It was a splendid radio. A lonely little gray-haired man was clinging to it like a drowning man to a straw. "Tell me," resumed Mr. Sampson, "what is that sick sound issuing from that box?"

"That sound," replied the reporter, "is made nightly by one of the nation's most popular crooners."

For a moment the philosopher considered this in silence.

"You see," he said at last, "how difficult it is for a man of my views to live in harmony with his fellow men. To me that noise is more degrading to humanity, more destructive to the morale, more morally and spiritually enervating than strong drink and weak women—I mean by that, accommodating women." He stretched his long legs and knocked the askes from his pipe. "The chap making that noise deserves no drawers at all," he said reflectively. "He should be clad in scanties."

A full moon over the Half-Moon. Its ship-crested tower mounted high above the boardwalk and looked far out to sea. Lights on the dark ocean moving along to Europe, to the tropics and distant ports. High up in this tower Jo and Peter were standing in the moonlight. And remarkable as it may seem, both of them were dressed. Probably not for long.

"Are you going to keep this up indefinitely?" asked Peter. "You have a room of your own."

She disregarded his question, knowing he did not mean it.

"I had hoped," she said, "that Bishop Waller would marry us in his jaegers."

"And what would we be wearing?" he inquired.

"Simply ourselves," said Jo.

"All marriages should be made that way," Peter observed surprisingly. "It would save a lot of time."

"I'm afraid there'd be fewer marriages," said Jo, "if couples undressed first."

"Not at all," retorted Peter. "Many a plain face surmounts a lovely body. And you must remember, Jo, the latter is very important."

"I never forget," breathed Jo.

"Tomorrow the Bishop will marry us," he continued. "Aspirin Liz and Little Arthur will be the worst man and woman. I have decided to take them into my employment. You will be engaged in the capacity of wife."

"No longer your concubine," Jo said somewhat sadly. "I'll sort of miss that. It's been so good being bad."

She turned away from the window and went into her room. It adjoined Peter's, and the door to it had been locked when they had first arrived. Not wishing to disturb anyone, Peter had bribed Little Arthur to pick it.

"It's the most shameful thing I've ever done," the little crook had protested. "I feel like a white-slaver."

A ten-dollar bill had done much to make him forget this unpleasant feeling. Before he had left the room he had convinced his dishonest little mind that he was a public benefac-

"I guess it's better this way after all," he had admitted as he pocketed the money. "It will keep you from running up and down the halls, so people can get some sleep and you can keep yer shame to yourselves."

"Peter," Jo called from the next room, "do you like my body?"

"Sure," replied Peter. "I think it's just great."

"Then I'll tell you what let's do," she went on. "You take off your clothes and I'll take off mine and we'll play matching bruises. I got a lot in that park."

"I have so many they're merging," Peter informed her, turning from the window. "How is Ellis?"

"She's gone to sleep in the bathtub as happy as a lark."

"If Sampson were present he'd want to know how a duck can be as happy as a totally different make of bird," observed Peter.

"I'm glad he's not here," said Jo. "Wonder if Ellis is the first duck ever to have occupied a bathtub at the Half-Moon."

"I guess we will never know that," said Peter, taking off his shoes.

And in a little while Josephine and Peter were matching the various bruises they had collected during the sound and fury of their flight. They were almost like little children about it, but . . . not quite.

THE END